KENTUCKY
WEDDINGS

KENTUCKY WEDDINGS

THREE-IN-ONE COLLECTION

TERRY FOWLER

BARBOUR
PUBLISHING

Val's Prayer © 2009 by Terry Fowler
Heath's Choice © 2009 by Terry Fowler
Opie's Challenge © 2009 by Terry Fowler

ISBN 978-1-61626-126-9

Scripture quotations are taken from the King James Version of the Bible.

Scripture taken from the HOLY BIBLE, NEW INTERNATIONAL VERSION®. NIV®. Copyright © 1973, 1978, 1984, 2010 by Biblica, Inc.™ Used by permission. All rights reserved worldwide.

This book is a work of fiction. Names, characters, places, and incidents are either products of the author's imagination or used fictitiously. Any similarity to actual people, organizations, and/or events is purely coincidental.

Cover Design: Kirk DouPonce, DogEared Design

Published by Barbour Publishing, Inc., P.O. Box 719, Uhrichsville, Ohio 44683, www.barbourbooks.com

Our mission is to publish and distribute inspirational products offering exceptional value and biblical encouragement to the masses.

ecpa Member of the
Evangelical Christian
Publishers Association

Printed in the United States of America.

Dear Readers,

Thank you for choosing Kentucky Weddings. For the most part, this collection takes place on a make-believe horse farm in Paris, Kentucky. I am blessed with very good friends who live in Louisville, and when I started looking at locales, my friend urged me to choose Kentucky and promised to help me do the research. And she did. Mary and her husband Steve took me to visit all the sites you'll read about in these stories. I'm in awe of the beautiful horses and Kentucky bluegrass I've written about in this collection.

I hope you enjoy reading about my Truelove family—granted all big families aren't like this one and that's what makes them special. The stories cover the same year in the three siblings' lives. Val (*Val's Prayer*), Heath (*Heath's Choice*), and Opie (*Opie's Challenge*) are confronted with blessings they never anticipated and now they must choose the paths they will follow for their futures.

For me, there is nothing more precious than family. I'm the second oldest of five kids and thank God for my brothers and sister. My life wouldn't be the same without them. As always, the one thing I hope to share with you throughout these stories is the truth of God's love for each of us.

I love hearing from my readers and you can contact me through Barbour Publishing or visit my Web site at terryfowler.net.

Happy reading,
Terry Fowler

VAL'S PRAYER

Dedication

To My Savior—who makes all things possible.
To my friends Mary and Steve—thanks for introducing me to your Kentucky.
To my family—I love you all.

Chapter 1

"Why are you doing this?"

Val Truelove studied the man with interest. When she had spoken with Randall King of Prestige Designs earlier in the week, he'd said they would be in contact; and then yesterday Russell Hunter had called to schedule the appointment. His eagerness to work together seemed to have taken a three-sixty turn today.

For some reason known only to him, Russell Hunter had become annoyed when she outlined the job. Val considered that strange since she'd given him the same information she'd given his employer. Surely Mr. King had told him what she planned.

Handsome, confident, and well dressed, with the most piercing blue eyes and somber expression—Val wondered if he ever smiled. He looked to be around her age but acted much older. Struggling to maintain her cool even though her defense mechanism had kicked in, Val asked, "Do you always question your client's reason for a project?"

"Yours is an unusual request."

Val didn't doubt that for a moment. "The structure is part of the business I plan to run here at Sheridan Farm."

"What business?" he demanded. "This is a Kentucky horse farm. Will's Shadow put this place on the map."

He hadn't told Val anything she didn't already know. In fact, her father, Jacob Truelove, had played a major role in the breeding and training of that very same horse.

"Will's Shadow has moved on to greener pastures, and I have other plans for part of the acreage. I'm opening Your Wedding Place."

"Your Wedding Place?" he repeated. "You mean like those wedding chapels in Vegas?"

"No. Nothing like that." Placing her hands on the desk, Val pushed herself to her feet. "This isn't going to work. I don't need an architect who acts more like a prosecuting attorney."

Russ stood and straightened his suit coat. "I have a right to care about changes that affect our community. My family owns Hunter Farm."

"And yet you diversified." At his puzzled expression she said, "You chose architecture."

"My brother inherited the farm."

"And that makes you angry about my project?"

"You'd be upset if your birthright had been stolen."

She shrugged, wondering how he connected the two. "Things come and go. I consider my good name, morals, and values to be the only worthwhile birthright I have."

He grimaced and exclaimed, "Never mind. It's not something I care to discuss. We were talking about what you're doing to this community."

"I'm paying the previous owner a considerable sum that gives me the right to do whatever I want. And there aren't any provisos that I have to seek anyone's permission to do so."

"I think the zoning board might have something to say about that."

Had he just threatened her? His negative reaction stirred Val's underlying concern about her plans. Was she doing the right thing? Yes. He was wrong, she told herself. Your Wedding Place would be a success. Paris was just minutes outside Lexington. Brides would come from all over once they heard about the perfect venue for their weddings.

"There's a lot less farmland and more than one shopping center or housing development on what used to be Kentucky horse farms," Val told him. "And from what I can see, people aren't avoiding the shopping or living accommodations because you don't like change."

"I wouldn't expect you to understand. You have no idea what it's like to live on a horse farm."

Wrong again, Val thought. She had grown up right here at Sheridan Farm in the house provided for the general manager's family. When the elder Mr. Sheridan passed away and left the property to his son, they had run the farm with the absentee owner rarely stopping by to check on his inheritance.

Her respect for the farm had grown over the years, and even though she'd spent the past seven years working as an assistant to a wedding planner in Lexington, Val fully understood what it meant to her family.

She also believed God had provided her this opportunity. In the course of her work she had spent hours searching for wedding venues and believed a business offering multiple location choices would be a profit maker. But the expense involved made the project an impossible dream—until now. "Sheridan Farm is big enough to support more than one business."

"It's a horse farm."

"You obviously don't share my vision, so let's just call it quits before one of us says something we'll regret."

∾

Russ drew a deep breath. His boss had warned him about antagonizing the clients. Randall King had been very clear about the outcome last week when Russ had nearly lost a very solvent account in practically the same manner. He would learn to keep his opinions to himself or be without a job. Yet he'd just managed to irritate another potential client.

Val Truelove had a smile on her face and a welcome in her voice when she had invited him into William Sheridan's office. Now she was seconds from throwing him out. The idea of begging her forgiveness galled Russ, but he couldn't afford to lose his time investment in Prestige Designs. He was too close to completing his internship. His plan to have his own business by thirty had already been delayed when he'd wasted those years after his parents' death.

"I'm sorry, Ms. Truelove." What kind of name was that anyway? "You're right. Life moves on whether we want it to or not. Tell me more about this structure you want to build."

Russ Hunter had learned a few things about women in his twenty-seven years and was not above flirting to get his way. He flashed a smile he hoped would make a two-hundred-watt bulb look dim. "Please give me another chance. And call me Russ."

Small and petite, she'd seemed lost behind the massive desk. Her long brown hair hung straight, golden highlights gleaming in the sunlight that streamed through the bank of windows directly behind her. She'd obviously made some effort with her appearance, though the jeans and long-sleeved black top looked worn and definitely off the rack. Her features were just irregular enough to keep her from stunning beauty, but still Russ found her to be an arresting woman.

"Val," she said before sitting down. "All I want is to see the work underway. I don't care who creates the plans, but I do find it difficult to believe you can accomplish this when you obviously have problems with my converting Kentucky countryside for my schemes."

He had insulted her. "I'm one of the best architects around," Russ declared proudly. "It just happens that I have a mouth big enough to hold the hooves of more than one thoroughbred. Not to mention I'm too opinionated for my own good. I've created a number of designs for Prestige Designs. I'd be happy to provide you with my portfolio."

"That's not necessary. I don't doubt your qualifications. And if you can agree to keep an open mind I'm willing to try to make this work."

Russ nodded. "I'd like an opportunity to prove I'm capable of giving you what you want."

She eyed him for a moment longer before she said, "Okay. Here's what I have in mind."

He listened as she outlined the structure that would be used for outdoor receptions during the spring and summer months. Russ could tell she'd given the matter a great deal of thought.

"I don't know if the technical description would be colonnade or pavilion. It would be ideal if we could find a way to enclose it for fall and winter, but I suspect we'll need yet another building at a later date."

"Just how big are you planning to make this structure?" Russ asked, imagining something that put a football stadium to shame.

Val turned to reach for a stack of papers on the credenza. "I'd like to have room for three hundred people. The project goes far beyond this construction.

What I need from you is a long-range plan I can continue to develop as Your Wedding Place grows. Along with the twenty-five acres, I've included the house and gardens in this project."

"For parties?" he repeated, disbelief trickling back into his tone.

She shrugged. "I suppose we might host the occasional social event. But first and foremost, Your Wedding Place will become the premier location where every bride can hold the wedding of her dreams."

She pulled a piece of foam board onto the desktop. Shielding her plans from view, Val said, "Before I share these, you must agree to keep my ideas confidential."

"Yes," he said with a nod. "Prestige Designs guarantees complete confidentiality of all their work."

The plans she showed him, while the work of an amateur, demonstrated great promise. She'd cleverly laid out her ideas. Phase one involved the possible conversion of the main house to a bed-and-breakfast with plans to improve the existing gardens to use as individual venues. He counted four areas—English, Japanese, formal, and the informal front garden.

Her board indicated the construction of this structure as part of the second phase, but apparently she'd moved it up in priority. She had plans for more gardens, structures, even an inn, restaurant, and bakery. Russ found it mind-boggling to say the least.

"What are these?" he asked, indicating what appeared to be roadways throughout the projects.

"Carriage trails. See, Mr. Hunter. . .uh, Russ. . .I don't intend to forget the horses."

"You're going to use the finest horseflesh in the world to pull carriages?" As soon as the words slipped out, Russ winced. It would take a miracle for him to keep this client and his job.

"Don't be silly."

Russ knew the value of a good horse. Why was it silly to assume she planned to use animals that had been born and bred with the intent of making them Triple Crown winners?

"Even I know you don't use a racehorse to pull a carriage. My father will find the animals. I'm building trails, not racetracks."

"And you have the finances to make all this happen?"

"You're doing it again," she pointed out.

"I'm sorry," Russ said, indicating the board he held. "These are the plans of a major development company. I'm curious as to how it's possible one person could afford such a project."

"Let's just say my ship came in," she said with a tiny smile.

Certainly no dinghy, Russ thought. "So where do we start?"

"At the beginning," Val answered easily. "As I said, I want plans I can develop long term. We'll start small, four venues. This is the first structure I want completed. I need a place for receptions."

"Can I take this with me?" Russ asked.

Val shook her head. "That's my project board. I have a list, though, outlining what I want from you."

"Perfect. I'll take it back to the office and get back to you within the week."

"The sooner this structure is completed and earning a profit, the sooner I can move forward with my next project."

He accepted the folder she handed him. "I understand. It's been a pleasure meeting you, Ms. Truelove...Val."

"I doubt it's been the highlight of your day," she told him. "But if you're willing to design a project worthy of your portfolio, I'm sure we'll find the arrangement mutually beneficial."

Russ removed a business card from his briefcase and placed it in the center of the desk. "I accept your challenge and look forward to proving myself."

"Would you like to see the site I have in mind?"

After they completed a brief tour, Russ said he would be in touch. Outside the house, he started his car and gunned the engine, tires spinning in the marl as he drove toward the main highway. Life wasn't fair. How could she afford this?

Val Truelove didn't strike him as being solvent enough to pay for the plans she'd commissioned, much less the structure she'd asked him to design.

Her plans to destroy prime farm acreage still didn't sit right with him. Russ knew the value of good farmland. He'd expected to own a portion of the family farm one day. But when his parents died in an accident, his brother Wendell received the farm, while he'd received a cash inheritance that enabled him to complete college and live until he established himself in his chosen career.

He supposed that if he'd accepted Wendell's offer to live at the house he could have kept a portion of the funds, but he couldn't stomach the idea of living with the enemy.

Russ often wondered if his decision to become an architect had been the reason his father gave the farm to Wendell. Sure, he loved his work, but he loved Hunter Farm as well. He had seen himself as part of the farm's future, and now Wendell had everything.

He found it impossible to overcome the overwhelming anger toward his brother and parents. Why had he shared that birthright comment with Val Truelove? He never discussed his personal business with clients.

Now she expected him to play a role in destroying yet another farm. What choice did he have? His future rested on his ability to get the job done. No way did he intend to toss more than two years of on-the-job training away over his principles.

Just do the job, Russ, he told himself as he drove toward Lexington.

Chapter 2

"Val, phone!" Jules yelled down the hallway.

Drying her hands, she picked up the kitchen extension and called hello.

"Hi. Whatcha doing?"

She recognized Derrick Masters's voice immediately. His continued persistence despite her efforts to discourage him proved disheartening. "Dishes."

"That's no life for a sweet young thing like you. I called to invite you to join me for a little Louisville nightlife. There's a great band playing at this place I know."

"Sorry, Derrick. I'm not into that." She doubted he cared that the only music she truly appreciated was hymns and contemporary Christian songs.

"How do you know if you won't try?" he demanded peevishly.

"I just know."

"Ah, come on, Val. Give a dude a break. Go out with me."

"We've had this discussion before," she said. "I'm not your type."

"You could be if you'd give me a chance."

"It wouldn't work. We want different things out of life. I need to go. Have fun."

He wasn't going to give up, Val thought, a heavy sigh slipping out after she hung up the phone. Derrick had called several times since she'd left her job at Maddy's and even dropped by the farm once. And he'd sent flowers. Each time she'd thanked him and refused his offer of the day.

For years Val had managed to avoid his pursuit, and in turn Derrick had very little use for her until the changes in her financial status made her an acceptable choice. She hoped to meet Mr. Right but knew without a doubt this man was Mr. Wrong.

Walking over to the kitchen door, she looked out onto the star-sprinkled Kentucky sky. The full moon gave the illusion of pale daylight over the expanse of their backyard. She saw her dad sitting alone in the swing. She had sent her parents off to the porch to relax while she tidied the kitchen. After pouring two mugs of coffee, she pushed open the screen door. "Where's Mom?"

"Making sure everyone finished their homework." Jacob Truelove patted the seat. "Come sit with me, my Valentine."

She passed him a mug. "I could have done that."

"You know your mother. She likes to talk with the children before bed."

Val settled at her dad's side, enjoying the comfort she'd always felt in his presence. As the oldest of the children at twenty-seven, she'd sat in this very swing many a night discussing topics too numerous to recall. Jacob Truelove was a good father. He gave freely of his love and taught his children the value of working hard for the things that mattered.

"Thinking about what happened today?"

Her father's husky voice filled her ear. "Yes. Praising the Lord and seeking His guidance to keep us on the right path. We took a major step."

One she'd never dreamed of taking. When she'd handed over a check for the down payment on Sheridan Farm, the action had seemed surreal, as if she were dealing with the play money of childhood games and not the real stuff. Val still couldn't believe they owned Sheridan Farm. Sure, she'd fantasized in her youth but found the idea of owning so much now almost frightening.

Even with the down payment they owed a considerable debt. They had debated the wisdom of buying a less expensive acreage; but Sheridan Farm was home, and the people who worked there were like family. When she'd asked God to provide, she'd had no idea His provision would make them responsible for so much.

Debt had never been part of their lives. Her father's salary and other benefits had enabled their mother to be a stay-at-home mom. She'd budgeted carefully and learned to stretch their money to provide for the needs of their large family. While they might not have had all the things their friends had, they had enough.

The family weighed the pros and cons carefully, and the positives far outweighed the negatives. The well-established horse farm and her father's reputation for producing fine thoroughbreds became number one on the list. Val knew the existing beautiful gardens would save her a fortune when it came to setting up the sites. Knowing there would be an annual income over the years made the decision easier, but they knew the farm needed to cover its operation overhead to be a success. Your Wedding Place would need to do the same.

They had prayed over the situation for several days before making their decision, and as of three o'clock that afternoon her family owned 267 acres of the most beautiful Kentucky bluegrass in Bourbon County. The sale included a more than two-hundred-year-old colonial-style home surrounded by gardens; the manager's home they lived in; tenant houses, horse barns, and paddocks; a number of lakes, creeks, and ponds; a few horses, cows, and other livestock; and so much more.

They had been a quiet group on the drive home. The only celebratory dinner had been the food Opie had waiting on the table. After dinner the younger children had gone off to do their homework, just as they did every other night.

"Regrets?" she asked.

"A finer answer to a prayer has never been received, Valentine."

"But you don't like where the money came from?"

Her father's weathered face changed with his frown. "It's almost poetic justice that my dad gambled away every dime he could get his hands on, and now

15

that same means has provided his heirs with funds to improve the lives of so many."

"Maybe it is," Val agreed. "This money will provide us opportunities we've never imagined."

He took her hand in his. "That's not true, Val. You've had the vision all along. You worked hard to help Rom, Heath, and Opie get a good education. Now is your time."

"They would have taken care of the others, Daddy." She spoke of the plan for the three older siblings to help provide for the educations of their younger sister and brothers.

"Now they can use that knowledge to help with your business."

"Our business," she corrected. "Sheridan Farm and Your Wedding Place are part of Truelove Inc. It's as much yours as mine."

"No, Valentine," he said stubbornly. "The money is yours."

She looked him straight in the eye. "With the exception of the twenty-five acres I plan to use for Your Wedding Place, I'm gifting you and Mom with Sheridan Farm. I trust you to continue doing what you've always done for our family. It's time you worked for yourself. Tell me your dreams for the farm."

"There's only the one, and that's to produce the finest horseflesh Kentucky has ever seen."

Val's laughter blended with the evening sounds and squeak of the chain as it moved against the hooks. "You have plenty of competition, but you've always done the Sheridans proud. I know you'll do the same for the Trueloves."

"Do you think our lives will ever settle down again?"

"I don't know, Daddy. People are already after the money, but it's well invested and protected. I designated funds for the truly needy, but I'm not planning to fulfill any ridiculous requests. We'll be good stewards of what God has provided."

"I've heard some rich people can squeeze a nickel until the buffalo cries out."

"More likely Mr. Lincoln will sing out from my tightwad dealings with his penny."

Her dad chuckled. "God gifted you, Val. You have to make a difference for others as well."

"We will, Daddy. This money isn't going to change us."

"Already we've changed with pride of ownership of Sheridan Farm."

"We've always had pride of accomplishment, Daddy. And I fully attribute our successes to allowing the Lord to direct our paths."

Her father nodded. "Hear from your architect yet?"

Spring might have arrived, but Val could feel a nip in the night air. She rubbed her arms and snuggled closer to her father. She had shared the events of their first meeting with the family over dinner that night. "Not a word. Russell Hunter said his brother owns Hunter Farm just down the road from here."

"I've met Wendell Hunter. The parents died in an accident. Russ must have been the one who was off at college at the time."

"He mentioned his birthright being stolen. Evidently the brother inherited the farm."

"It's sad that two brothers have problems over possessions. What did you really think about him?"

"I'm not sure he's the right man for the job."

"What makes you say that?"

Val knew he'd never let her make an unjustified assumption about anyone. "You should have heard his reaction when I outlined my plans. You'd have thought I was destroying sacred ground."

"You know how some people react to change, Val."

"But it's inevitable. Nothing stays the same. You think it's a good idea, don't you?"

"I can't say I understand why people spend so much money on weddings, but if they're going to do it I see no reason why you shouldn't profit from their choices."

"I prayed about this. When Mr. Sheridan died, I asked God to keep us here if it was His will. I never expected things would turn out as they have."

"It's a major responsibility. I've never made any secret of how my father's actions hurt him and our family. He allowed his own selfish needs and addictions to take over his life. It was a miserable life, Val. I never wanted that for my children."

"We all know how blessed we are to have you as our father. We love and respect you so much, not only for the sacrifices you've made for us but for the way you prove your love. Quality time is certainly more important than any material possessions. Daddy, do you ever visit Grandfather?"

"Not for some time now. He hasn't changed, Val. He's still about the same as he was before he ended up in prison. Blames everyone but himself; claims he was framed even though there were witnesses."

She looked up at him, much as she'd done since she was a little girl. "But you've forgiven him?"

"I like to think so. Then I have times when I have to seek God's forgiveness for having bad thoughts toward him. My mother destroyed her health because of my father. I find that a very difficult pill to swallow when I read a letter he's written that generally ends in a request for money. I can only imagine what he'll ask for when he hears you've won the money."

"Would you have preferred I didn't accept it?"

He shook his head. "Part of me wanted to tell you to destroy that ticket and let life follow the same path we were on before. But, like you, I believe in the power of prayer, and knowing you earnestly sought and believed God would provide for our future makes me feel it's of God.

"As with everything else you've done in life, I'll stand behind you in this. We'll weather this storm together, and in the end we'll be stronger, better

Christians because we trusted God to provide for our needs."

"I love you, Daddy."

"I love you, too, sweetheart. It's getting late. I think I'll go in and read my Bible for a bit before bed."

"Dream bluegrass dreams, Daddy."

He kissed her forehead. "You, too, Valentine."

As she watched her father enter the house, Val thought about the family meeting where she'd made the announcement that changed their lives. Rom and Heath had been home on spring break. Opie arrived just before dinner that night. Every member of the family had been shocked when she told them how she'd come to win several million dollars.

The Hamilton wedding had made for a demanding winter at work. No one had ever been more difficult than the bride who demanded the world with sun, moon, and stars thrown in for good measure. Dealing with divas was part of the job, but Val found the spoiled young woman to be the worst she'd ever experienced in her years at Madelyn Troyer's Wedding Designs. Nothing stood in the way of the woman's plan to have the grandest wedding Lexington society had ever seen. Wendy didn't care whom she stomped on in the process. Val almost felt sorry for the man she was to marry; but then, if possible, she found him even more arrogant than his bride. In the end she decided they made a good couple. At least no one else would have to suffer the extreme boorishness.

The only positive had been that their demands had kept her mind off her own problems. The elder Mr. Sheridan had died, leaving Sheridan Farm to his son, William Sheridan III. The New York lawyer made it clear he did not intend to return to Kentucky.

Val had been almost three when the elder William Sheridan hired her father as his manager. Val, her parents, and the year-old twins, Rom and Heath, had moved into the manager's house on the farm. Before that, they had lived in another tenant house farther away. She still remembered her excitement over coming to live with the horses. With the passing of time their family had continued to grow, and all seven of the Truelove children considered Sheridan Farm home. The small town environment of Paris, Kentucky, the Thoroughbred capital of the world, fit their family perfectly.

While she knew her dad didn't want to look elsewhere for work, Val accepted it could become reality very soon. Mr. Sheridan had respected her father's beliefs and never forced him to do things that went against his religion. Val feared her father might not find the same sort of atmosphere for future employment. At forty-seven, he had years before retirement.

Val had prayed for an answer, and on Sunday morning the pastor had preached on Matthew 21:22. When he read, "And all things, whatsoever ye shall ask in prayer, believing, ye shall receive," Val had her answer. She had no doubt God would provide, and believed with every bit of her being.

On the Monday following the Hamilton wedding, Maddy had been all smiles as she passed around lottery tickets. "Thanks for all the hard work you did with the wedding," she said as she handed Val her ticket. "As much as I love my job, there were times when the Hamiltons had me thinking there had to be an easier way to earn a living."

Val fingered the ticket, thinking she would have preferred a cash bonus. She'd come to expect the impractical gifts. Expensive handmade chocolates, massages, and facials weren't bad rewards, but items like wine for a non-drinker and lottery tickets for a non-gambler were a total waste. Not wanting to seem ungrateful, she kept her opinion to herself as she thanked her employer and tucked it in her purse.

A few days later, Val overheard the staff discussing how they were looking for the winner of the biggest Powerball lottery ever. One by one they checked their numbers, groaned their disappointment, and tossed the tickets.

Later, while straightening the area, Val found the abandoned list of winning numbers on the counter. She crumpled the sheet, but curiosity forced her to take a look. She compared the numbers to the ticket from her purse, and in a moment her world changed forever.

Every number was a match. Uncertain what that meant, Val folded the paper and tucked it and the ticket away safely in her purse. After dinner that night she went on the computer and learned she had won millions of dollars.

She'd kept her secret from Thursday to Sunday, seeking guidance from God. Val asked to speak with the pastor privately and explained the situation, asking for his input. She knew her church took a strict stance against gambling and did not accept tithes from such winnings.

"You're innocent in this, but the money does come from gambling proceeds," John David Skipper told her.

"I prayed, Pastor Skipper. I asked God to provide, and I believed He would. How can this be wrong if it's His way of providing?"

"Is it, or do you want it to be?"

Val didn't know what to think. Beyond her prayers and believing God would answer them, she hadn't taken any action to make this happen. She hadn't wasted her precious dollars buying lottery tickets. She'd worked hard and been rewarded with a gift that far exceeded anything she could imagine. "I'm so confused," she admitted. "I don't believe in luck, but I do believe in God's blessings."

"How does your father feel?"

Val sighed. "I haven't told him yet. Daddy's told you about his father?"

The pastor nodded. "You can't keep it from him. You'll need to prepare for the outcome once this becomes public. This much money has a way of bringing out the bad in people."

"I know," Val said.

"But I will say that if anyone is able to handle the situation, I believe your family can. In the time I've had the pleasure of knowing you, I've come to admire the love and dedication you show one another and others. I know you'll use the money to benefit more than your family."

"Thanks, Pastor Skipper. I find it difficult to believe it myself, but I'm convinced God has answered my prayers and His intention is that the money be a blessing. I plan to be a good steward of everything He's entrusted to me."

"I know you mean that, Val, and I will pray for you and the decision."

She left feeling no clearer about what she should do than when she had entered his office. That night at the family meeting Val knew her news troubled her dad.

"All of you know how I feel about gambling," her father said. "It destroyed your grandfather."

"But Dad," Rom said, "it's an answer to Val's prayer. She believed God would provide and He has."

"Son, the Lord has provided for this family for many years," their dad said.

"All those crazy gifts from your boss, and she finally gives you something that makes you rich," Heath said with a shake of his head. "Have you told her yet?"

"I've only told the family and Pastor Skipper. I went on the computer to see what I needed to do." She explained the process.

"We'll go with you," Rom said.

"Is it okay, Dad?" she asked, looking into doe-brown eyes the same color as her own.

He appeared doubtful. "We need to pray, Val. Make sure this grace is of the Lord. It will change your life."

"Our lives," she countered. "I didn't ask for myself. I asked for all of us. If we take this money, it will be for our family."

"What are your plans?" her mother asked.

She glanced at her dad. "I'll buy Sheridan Farm."

"Are you sure?" he asked.

"Yes, sir. That was my prayer, my belief that God would provide a means for us to stay here—and He has."

Her father frowned. "But with gambling winnings. You know people will believe you bought that ticket."

Val nodded. "I've considered that. But I also know the media will provide me with the opportunity to share the truth."

"Doesn't matter," her father contended. "Those people who want to see it negatively will. Are you prepared to have your coworkers upset because you won what they feel should have been their money? To deal with the demands of complete strangers who feel entitled to share your riches? There are horror stories of people who ended up without a dime to their name after spending their millions. Not to mention those whose lives were destroyed because they did win."

"It won't last," Rom predicted. "People will say, 'Did you hear about the woman in Paris who won all that money?' They'll wish they'd won it, and that will be the end of it."

"I suspect that's wishful thinking on your part, son," her father said. "People with money continually get requests from those who feel entitled. This much money will only serve to make them feel even more so."

"Once they know where Val lives, they'll invade the farm," Heath said.

"We could change to an unlisted number and hire security," she suggested.

Fourteen-year-old Cy spoke up. "I think it's cool."

"You might not think so once your friends treat you differently because you're wealthy," Val warned.

"I'm not wealthy. You are."

"If I am, you are," Val told him.

"Will you buy me a four wheeler?"

"Val won't buy anything that goes against the rules of this family," their father told him.

She smiled at her younger brother. "I'm sure we'll all get things we've dreamed of having, within reason. But we have to bless others as God has blessed us. So Daddy, what do you think?"

"We should continue to seek the Lord's guidance."

"Mom?"

Cindy Truelove's gaze shifted from her husband back to her oldest daughter. "We trust you to do what's right, Val. God has provided you with a lot of money. It won't be easy."

Her parents' faith in her had gone a long way in reassuring Val. She agreed it wouldn't be an easy task. But as she'd always done in life, she trusted God to lead the way.

∽

Rising from the swing, she went inside and found her sister stretched out on the sofa. "What are you reading?"

Opie held up one of the free magazines she'd picked up in town. "An article on Paris's most eligible bachelors."

Val laughed. "They actually have some?"

"Yeah, they're having a bachelor auction fund-raiser. Look at this guy," Opie said, pointing to the page. "Wendell Hunter. He believes a woman's sole focus should be her family and home. That's so antediluvian."

"Hunter?" Val shut out Opie's tirade as she reached for the magazine. This was too weird. The Hunter name seemed to turn up with frightening regularity lately. "That's my architect's brother."

"Small world."

Val handed the magazine back, her thoughts on what she'd just read. "How would you like to go to a bachelor auction?"

"Are you nuts?"

Val shrugged. "No. I just thought it might be fun to check out Paris's most eligible bachelors."

"You want to check out your architect's brother."

"I do," she admitted.

"I don't think seeing Wendell Hunter strut the runway is going to give you much insight."

"I don't know. It might tell us more than you know. I'll buy you a new dress," Val offered. When Opie hesitated, she said, "Shoes, too."

"Okay, I'm in," Opie agreed. "But you have to buy something for yourself as well."

Val should have known the plan would backfire on her. She hated shopping. "Okay. Let's pick Jules up from school and take her and Mom along, too. We could all use some spring clothes."

Opie twisted the top back on the polish bottle and tossed it to her sister. "Do something with those grubby nails."

Val looked at her hands. "They're not that bad. I've been wearing garden gloves."

"If you say so," Opie said, making her examine them more closely. "Are you going into Lexington with us tomorrow?"

Val already had a full schedule for the day. "What's the plan?"

"We're meeting for lunch after Rom's interview. And Heath wants to look into something for Dad's birthday."

"Did he say what he had in mind?"

"The guys have a couple of ideas. Of course, you gave him the best gift today."

Val grinned. "I'd say I'm caught up for years to come."

"Lucky," Opie said.

"Blessed," Val countered. "I'll meet you guys for lunch. I have an appointment with the English garden first thing tomorrow."

"Want me to stick around and help?"

"Maybe later. Right now I'm hunting for treasure. I pray Rom's interview goes well. It'll be nice to have everyone home again. Have you given more thought to your plans?"

"All the time."

"You'll be around to cook Daddy's birthday supper?"

Opie nodded. "All his favorites. That's my gift."

"Talk about my gift," Val teased. "You truly know the way to his heart. Want to watch television?"

"You think there will be another Val sighting?"

She laughed. The entire family had teased her about interviews she'd given since the win. "I hope not. You think people are getting the message?"

"Definitely. You've given God the glory and talked about being a good steward. In fact, you've handled the publicity as well as any professional. I'm impressed."

"Thanks, Opie. It's pretty nerve-racking, but I believe God is giving me the words."

Her sister grinned at her. "I know. And you're so worn out from writing that big check today that you'll let me control the remote?"

"No way," Val said, settling into the recliner and hitting the ON button. "You make me dizzy with all that channel surfing."

Chapter 3

The moment he spotted Val in her old jeans and grubby UK sweatshirt, Russ knew he should have called first. "Hi. You look busy."

She nodded. "It will take a long time to undo the years of neglect."

"Why not hire someone?"

"I don't mind getting my hands dirty. Besides, the wrong person could do a lot of harm. There's priceless statuary and yard art out here. And I'm trying to restore the Celtic knot garden."

"The Celtic what?"

"It's hard to explain," Val told him. "Mainly it's a very intricate design involving well-pruned boxwood and other plants. I'll show you once it's restored."

Russ nodded and held up the portfolio he carried. "I brought the plans. I hoped you could spare a few minutes."

Stripping off her gloves, she crossed patio stones riddled with grass and weeds. "Bring them over to the table."

Russ avoided the moldy chair cushion and rusted patio table as best he could. He hadn't considered he'd end up wearing his expensive designer suit in the jungle she called a garden. Removing the plan he'd mounted on foam core just before leaving the office, Russ confidently handed it over. He felt rather proud of his work and was eager to hear what Val Truelove had to say. The lengthening silence as she studied the plans made him ask, "Is something wrong?"

"You haven't captured my vision."

Resentment flashed through him at her failure to recognize his hard work. What vision? She wanted a structure in a pasture on a horse farm. What did she think she was going to see? Greek ruins?

"Come with me," she said suddenly, pushing the board in his direction before walking away.

Russ grabbed the plans and scrambled to keep up with her long-legged stride. When Val paused by the oldest, most worn jeep he'd ever seen, he groaned silently.

She climbed inside and started the vehicle on first try. "Get in."

Frowning at the layer of dust coating the interior of the vehicle, Russ pushed the plan board into the back and did as she requested. He hoped Mr. King would find the sacrifice of his favorite suit commendable when it came to satisfying their clients.

"Hold on," Val warned as he looked around for a seat belt that had never existed or long since disappeared from the vehicle.

She drove past outbuildings and fenced areas where men worked the horses that made Sheridan Farm what it should be. She waved at an older man who waved back. "My dad," she volunteered as she stopped the vehicle. "Can you get the gate, please?"

Russ didn't even want to consider what the seat covers were doing to his clothes as he exited the vehicle.

"Make sure it's secure," she called back to him after driving through.

He closed the gate and made his way back to where she waited. A couple of minutes later, Russ grabbed hold of the dashboard when she stopped suddenly, right in the middle of the pasture.

"Can you see it?"

Russ didn't know what she expected him to see. Acres of rolling hills, green with bluegrass and bordered with black fences. A wooded area in the distance. The same place she'd shown him his first day out there. His confusion must have shown.

"What happened to the guy who knew more about Kentucky farmland than anyone else?"

Russ resented her taunting. "I thought I'd designed what you wanted."

"Is it only when horses roam here that you experience the beauty?" she challenged. "Think of it as a balcony overlooking the roaring ocean waves or the vista from a cabin porch overlooking a spectacular range of mountains. What can we do to help them see the magnificence of rolling green hills? How do we make them feel surrounded by something bigger than themselves while celebrating their love with friends and family?"

Russ understood the bigger-than-life part. He'd always felt that when viewing the majestic scenery of the places his parents had taken him when they vacationed. Maybe he had taken home for granted.

Val climbed out of the vehicle and revolved slowly. "I want this structure to be a window to my world. When someone stands here and looks out, I want them to believe there can be no more perfect spot. I want the glorious beauty to push the air from their lungs."

She didn't want much, Russ thought, struggling to determine how he could put her needs on paper.

"Do you understand?"

Her determined expression told him many things about Val Truelove. Quick-minded, sensitive, emotional at times, and temperamental when crossed, she wouldn't make this easy for him. Suddenly it became crucial that he prove he hadn't been blowing smoke when he'd made those claims. "I'll rework the plans. Bring them closer to what you want."

Val came around the vehicle and scrambled in the glove compartment until she found a small digital camera. It took her several minutes to snap the photos of the surrounding area. "Take this with you. Use the photos to give you insight into what suits the area."

He should have thought of that. "Thanks," he said, sliding the camera into the interior pocket of his suit.

On the drive back Russ asked, "Have you contacted the zoning department about your proposed changes?"

He could tell from her frown that he'd reminded her of his comment on their first meeting.

"My lawyer is looking into the requirements," Val said. "I suppose we're already zoned for business because of the horse farm."

"You're zoned for a horse farm. If you plan to convert the house to a bed-and-breakfast, there will be stipulations for parking and handicap access, and interior changes to meet code requirements. Since I don't even know how they'll categorize your business, they'll probably need a detailed business plan. Have you attended a chamber meeting yet? You should. Get word out about your intentions."

"Sounds complicated."

"It could be. Have you developed the business plan?"

"No more than I showed you when we first started talking. I can expand. Show how much money couples spend annually on weddings and venues. I'm sure Maddy has data she would share."

"I'd contact the city first," Russ suggested. "Then provide the information they request. What sort of time frame are you looking at on the structure?"

"I'd love to have it completed by my mom's birthday in early November. We're planning a combination party and family reunion."

"I doubt it'll be done by then."

"I'll have to make alternate arrangements. Opie's planning the menu while I procure the location."

"Opie?"

"My sister."

"So you have a sister?"

"Actually I have two sisters and four brothers."

He'd had no idea there were so many Truelove kids. Despite his claim of having lived on a horse farm, Russ had spent very little time at Hunter Farm. When he became old enough, his father shipped him off to boarding school and then he'd traveled abroad with his mother in the summer.

They negotiated the rest of the trip in silence, and once she parked at the house he climbed out of the vehicle, forcing back the desire to brush the dust off his suit. He didn't want to offend Val Truelove again. "I'll get back to you next week."

Russ had no idea what he'd have to offer. Right now he was drawing a complete blank.

"This isn't for me," Val said. "I want this for my clients. I already know what a treasure we have in Kentucky."

Two hours later his coworker and fellow architect, Kelly Dickerson, glanced up when Russ walked into the office. "How did it go this morning?"

He had stopped by the drugstore to print the pictures Val had taken, hoping to find something that would inspire him to the heights she expected.

"I should have made an appointment. She was working in the garden and after looking at my plans insisted we ride out to the site in what must have been one of the first jeeps ever made. I'll probably never get my suit clean."

Kelly flashed him a sympathetic smile. "She didn't like your plans?"

Fresh irritation surged through Russ. "Said I didn't see her vision. Spouted some nonsense about a window to the world." He held up the packet of photos. "I hope these help me get a visual. I'm certainly not seeing anything at present."

Kelly rolled her chair back. "Spread them out. Let's take a look."

As he laid the eight-by-ten glossies around on the drawing board, Russ noted each picture seemed to represent a different angle of the area she planned to convert. He rearranged a couple of prints and glanced at Kelly. "See anything?"

"Tell me what she said."

He attempted to recall Val Truelove's exact words.

Kelly nodded. "She's right, you know. Either you make the structure stand out, or you choose the most breathtaking vista. The perfect design would be a combination of the two. Look at how she shot the photos," she said, tapping a scene of a pasture filled with gorgeous thoroughbred horses. "Where would you stand to see this? Would there be only one lookout point from the structure? If not, what could you do to make every scene breathtaking? Would you want this as a backdrop to your event?"

Russ threw his hands up in the air. "You've got me."

"Maybe it's a woman thing," Kelly said finally. "I think I understand what she's trying to help you see."

"Then let me in on the secret," Russ requested earnestly. He'd never felt so at odds with a project.

She shrugged. "I'd only be guessing. You're the one who talked to Val. She told you what she wanted. Just remember—beauty is in the eye of the beholder. Look at these and decide what you think is beautiful. Let's hope you'll hit on the same things she's seeing."

Kelly went back to her drawing board, and Russ continued to study the pictures. "She has two sisters and four brothers," he commented idly. "What I don't understand is how they can afford this. I'm sure she paid a fortune for the farm and is now making long-range plans for a business that may or may not prove profitable. Where did she get her money?"

"Honestly, Russ, don't you ever watch the news?" his coworker asked. "Your client won one of the biggest Powerball lotteries ever."

His mouth fell open. "You're kidding. She said her ship came in."

"I'd say the fleet," Kelly said with a laugh. "She can certainly afford any vision she wants."

"But...," Russ stammered. "You should see her."

"I know Val from church," Kelly said. "The Trueloves are a nice family. They are a very driven group. Believe in helping each other. Rumor has it Val spent nearly every dime of her earnings on Rom's, Heath's, and Opie's education. Of course they're very intelligent and had scholarships as well. The twins were the first co-valedictorians at our school."

"I don't get it," Russ said. "If she's rich, why is she doing this?"

"I think you'll find the Trueloves are a unique family," Kelly told him. "I've worked with them on church projects, and they don't do anything by half."

"I can believe that," Russ agreed, his gaze moving to the pictures that represented Kentucky through Val Truelove's eyes. "Guess I'd better get to work."

"Just focus on what you saw, Russ," Kelly advised. "And what Val said. She has a vision, and it's your job to get it on paper. I doubt she will accept anything less than perfection."

The work took on a more personal aspect for Russ, and he found himself struggling to design something that would please Val. The need to prove his ability was stronger than ever after the morning's meeting.

"When does Val plan to start booking?" Kelly asked.

Russ hesitated. Val had been adamant about keeping the plans a secret. "She's working in the gardens now. Why?"

"Gabe and I are still looking for a wedding site."

"I thought you'd decided on the church."

"We go back and forth. I'd love an outdoor wedding."

"So what's wrong with your mom's garden?"

"It's not big enough. We need seating for at least two hundred. Do you think she'd book my wedding? I've heard the Sheridan Farm gardens are incredible."

Even in their overgrown state Russ had seen their potential. He dug through the papers on his desk and found the card Val had given him. "There's only one way to find out. Give her a call."

"I will. Maybe it's a woman thing, but I saw something very appealing in those pictures."

"Mr. King should have assigned the job to you."

"No, thanks. I have as much as I can handle with planning a wedding."

"How about I put the pictures on the wall and you share your thoughts?"

"I already do that, Russ."

"I'm really floundering on this one, Kel. I didn't make a good first impression."

"Oh, Russ, what did you say?"

"Mostly comments about how she didn't know what it meant to live on a horse farm and I did."

When Kelly burst out laughing, Russ demanded, "What's so funny?"

"Jacob Truelove has managed the Sheridan property since Val was a toddler. She's spent her life around horses."

It bothered him that he'd been denied an opportunity to live on the farm. Russ drew a deep breath and closed his eyes. "When will I ever learn to keep my opinion to myself?"

"Probably never."

"She must have found my ignorance entertaining."

"Don't mess this up, Russ," Kelly warned. "You've invested too much time at Prestige Designs."

"I'll see her vision or die trying."

"That's the spirit," Kelly encouraged. She glanced at her watch. "I have a lunch meeting with Mr. King and a client."

"That's right. Go enjoy yourself while I attempt to read Val Truelove's mind."

"I don't think she's looking for a psychic," Kelly said with a big grin.

"I think that's exactly what she wants. A psychic in a handsome young architect's body."

"Oh, spare me, please," Kelly said with a loud guffaw as Randall King opened the door.

"Ready, Kelly?"

They looked up guiltily.

"Yes, sir. I'll meet you out front."

Their boss didn't seem in a hurry to depart. "How's your project going, Russ?"

"I'm refining my ideas."

"Hated them, didn't she?" Mr. King asked, his knowing smirk irritating Russ even more.

"She has a vision, but I haven't given up."

"Remember, it's your job to guide her. People don't always know what they want."

Russ didn't feel that was true when it came to Val. She knew exactly what she wanted. "I'll keep you informed."

"I'll make sure you do."

Russ watched Randall King stroll out the door, reluctantly admiring the man's confident swagger. One day he would have his own office and be the one issuing orders rather than taking them. He forced himself to concentrate on the photos. Val's enthusiasm when she talked about showing the world the greater picture forced Russ to ask himself how to do that.

In his mind he saw the pastoral peacefulness of rolling hills and beautiful horses grazing on rich green grass within miles of meandering black fences. "What else?" he asked, finding it difficult to put himself on a mountaintop in the middle of a pasture. Or was it? He paused from shuffling the photos. What if the structure floor became her balcony? The acres of bluegrass her ocean?

As the idea took hold Russ hurried over to his computer, eager to capture this thought.

Chapter 4

After Russ left and she'd returned to the garden, all Val could think about was the plans he had presented. They had been substandard to say the least. Did he honestly believe he'd given her what she wanted?

Russ Hunter hadn't liked that she'd kept him in the garden either, but she'd been grimy from working outside and hadn't particularly wanted to take the dirt into the grand room Mr. Sheridan had called his office.

Why hadn't he seen her vision? Every great view was an overlook to the world. Granted, Paris, Kentucky, wasn't the world, but she considered it as beautiful as those other places. Val couldn't imagine anything more spectacular than the view the wedding guests would see from the structure.

Disappointment stabbed at her. She'd considered him rather handsome when she welcomed him into the office, but his arrogance had made a bad impression. Val thought of how he'd changed after she'd all but thrown him out. He'd shoveled on the charm. Because she wanted her project underway she'd given him another chance. He'd forced her to do the same again today. How many opportunities did Mr. Hunter think she'd give him?

The way he'd acted when she chose to drive the old jeep to the site had been almost entertaining. He'd tried unsuccessfully to disguise his dismay. She figured a dry cleaning bill would show up on her account but didn't care. If it helped him design what she wanted, she'd pay for a new suit. Val knew she shouldn't have done that, but deep down inside she believed him more competent than she'd witnessed today. She'd hired a professional, but what she'd gotten was little better than her own amateurish efforts.

"Did I do the right thing, Lord?" she asked. That same question came to mind several times daily as Val struggled with the decision she'd made. Accepting the money had enabled her to help her family in ways she'd never imagined, but at what cost? Would she come to regret what she'd done? "Guide me. Show me what You would have me do with the money and the plans You have for our family."

They already had everything they needed. Sheridan Farm had supported their family for years, and Val knew her father would do everything possible to ensure it continued to do so. But there was no role for her. She didn't want to raise horses or do farm chores.

"If this is Your will, dear Lord, help Russ create the plans that will make this work. Guide his hand in the drawing and help me find contentment in the idea."

She snipped at the vine wrapped around the statuary. Pulling the angel free, she set it over to the side. Val knew she had given God complete control and listened when He told her what to do. Everything would be okay. She believed that with every breath in her body. God's peace enveloped her there in the gardens.

Val loaded another wheelbarrow with debris. Why had Mr. Sheridan allowed everything to get so out of control? Surely he'd seen it every time he visited the gardens. Then again maybe he hadn't come out here much after his wife's death. Hadn't Daddy spoken of how heartbroken the old man had been after the loss of his wife of more than fifty years? The thought saddened Val.

Glancing at her watch, she quickly picked up her tools and headed for the house to shower and dress for the trip into Lexington. Standing beneath the spray of hot water, her conscience pricked at the way she'd treated Russ. She had been rough on him. It was possible she hadn't made herself clear. Still, anyone could have provided something that basic.

She found his boyish charm and chiseled jaw appealing and wanted to tousle his neatly styled thick brown hair. The penetrating stare of those blue eyes had a powerful effect as well.

It was nearly twelve thirty when she slipped into the booth where Opie waited. "Where's Heath?"

"He's on his way. Did you get a lot done this morning?"

"No," Val said after requesting a glass of ice water with lemon. "Russ Hunter showed up with the most pitiful set of plans I've ever seen. I drove him and his fancy suit to the site in the jeep."

Opie gasped. "You didn't."

Val nodded. "I sent him off with an earful of what I expected when he comes back."

"How did he react?"

"Surprised. I think he expected me to love what he'd done. For all his big talk I expected better. I hope he's not letting his attitude affect his work."

"You think he's trying to sabotage your idea?"

Val shrugged. "That doesn't make sense. He's paid when I'm satisfied with his work. Seems to me that jeopardizing my project would do him more harm than it would me."

"True," Opie agreed. "There's Heath." She waved at him.

Their brother slipped into the opposite side of the booth. "No word from Rom?" When Opie shook her head, he said, "His interview must have lasted longer than he thought."

"That could be a good thing," Opie said.

"Let's hope so," Val agreed.

"Did you find them?" Opie asked Heath.

"No. I found a source. I can order and have them here in plenty of time."

"What are you looking for?" Val asked curiously.

"Rom and I thought new horse blankets bearing Daddy's name would be a great birthday gift. We need someone to design a new logo."

A doodler by nature, Val had twined a T with a heart and a horse's head into the logo she used on the Truelove Inc. business cards. Pulling one from her purse, she asked, "What about this?"

"Your work?" When she nodded, Heath said, "Looks great. More creative than anything I came up with."

"What color? Royal blue?" All the kids knew that was their dad's favorite color.

Heath nodded. "With gold lettering and trim."

"He'll love them. He was just saying the other day that some of the old Sheridan blankets have seen better days."

"Val was telling me about the plans Russ Hunter brought by this morning," Opie said.

Heath glanced at his older sister. "Good?"

Val shook her head. "Pitiful."

"She took Mr. Hunter for a ride in the jeep," Opie said.

"You didn't." Heath's disbelief echoed Opie's.

Val shrugged. "It's the easiest way to get there."

"You could have used a nicer vehicle," Opie said.

"He irritated me," Val admitted. "Showed up without an appointment, wearing a suit that cost more than I made in months, acting pleased as punch with himself over a set of substandard plans."

"That's not very Christian."

"I know." Her voice rose. "He pushes my buttons and then piles on the charm. You should have heard him go on that first meeting about how he had a right to be concerned about my plans for the farm."

"Maybe you should get another architect," Heath suggested.

"I'll give him one more chance," Val said. "If this next set of plans isn't what I expect, I'm calling Randall King."

"I could deal with Russ Hunter for you," Heath offered.

Val smiled at her brother. "Thanks, but no. If I'm going to be in business, I need to learn to deal with all kinds of people."

"Especially handsome young architects that get under her skin," Opie said with a giggle. Heath laughed, and Val couldn't help but join in.

They hushed when another patron approached the small table across from their booth. Val immediately recognized the young woman. "Jane, hi," she called. "How's the job hunt going?"

Jane took a step closer to the booth. "Not so good."

Val glanced at Heath. "You remember Jane Kendrick from school?"

Heath looked startled but quickly regained his composure. "Sure do. It's good to see you."

Jane flashed him a wide grin. "You, too. Val keeps me current. Congratulations on your degree. How's Rom?"

"Thanks. He's good. We're waiting on him now. He had an interview today."

"Hope his luck is better than mine," Jane said. "I should have accepted that clerk position."

"No, you shouldn't have," Val protested. She and Jane had become friends when she used to visit the coffee shop during her workdays in Lexington. "I have a couple of ideas that might work for you in the future."

"Now is my future," Jane said unhappily. "I have to find work."

"You will. Join us for lunch."

"Yes, please do," Opie added.

"I don't want to intrude."

"You know us Trueloves. The more the merrier," Opie said.

Jane agreed and asked for a diet soda.

"Why don't you come out to the farm tomorrow? I have an idea I'd like to discuss with you."

"Can I bring Sammy? I called in the last of my favors for the interview today."

"Please do. Daddy might even take her for a ride."

"She'd love that. She's so horse crazy right now."

"Who's Sammy?" Heath asked.

"My two-year-old."

"You have a daughter?" When Jane nodded, Heath said, "I know Garrett is very happy."

Jane paled. "Garrett's dead, Heath."

"Oh, man, I'm sorry. I didn't know. What happened?"

Val and Opie shook their heads in warning, but it was too late.

"He killed himself," Jane said, her voice breaking.

Opie noted Heath's stunned expression and interceded. "Wouldn't you love to see a picture of Jane's daughter, Heath?"

He jumped, and Val knew Opie had kicked him under the table. She hid her smile.

He recovered quickly. "Sure. Is she as pretty as her mom?"

Val noticed the blush that touched the woman's cheeks.

"She's beautiful," Jane declared, digging out her photos. "But that's a very prejudiced mom talking."

As they oohed and aahed over Sammy, Val glanced up and saw Russ walking across the room.

"Don't look now," she whispered to Opie, "but that's Russell Hunter."

Opie looked up.

"I said don't look," Val hissed just as he approached their table. Recovering her poise, she said, "Russ, I didn't think I'd see you again today."

"Me either. I just wanted to let you know I've been hard at work since I left the farm this morning. I think I might be headed in the right direction this time."

"That's good news. Let me introduce you to everyone. This is my sister,

33

Ophelia," she said with a pointed look.

Opie held out her hand. "Pleased to meet you. Call me Opie. Everyone else does."

"Our friend Jane Holt. My brother Heath."

"My pleasure," Russ said.

When he reached to shake Heath's and Jane's hands, Opie leaned over to Val and whispered, "Good thing he didn't mess up the suit. He looks like a million dollars."

When Val attempted to elbow her, Opie moved out of the way and asked, "Are you here for lunch?" When Russ nodded, she invited him to join them. "Valentine," she began, throwing down the gauntlet by sharing Val's real name, "has been telling us about your plans."

"Really?" Russ asked, glancing at Val.

"She said you're reworking them."

He deflated a little. "I think I have a better understanding of what she wants."

"You have to stay," Opie insisted. "We'd love to hear what you think."

"You have a full table."

"We need to ask for a larger one anyway," Opie said. "Our brother Rom should be here any minute. I'm sure he'd love to meet you."

Russ glanced at Val. "Do you mind?"

"Not at all."

Heath signaled their waiter, and Val grabbed Opie's arm when they started to move. "I owe you one."

Opie grinned at Val's promise of payback. "Not with some of the stunts you've pulled. Come on before Heath puts his foot in it again with Jane."

Val followed, not caring for the way this luncheon was going. She hadn't planned to spend any more time in Russ Hunter's company that day.

After being seated, Russ said, "All of you have nicknames."

"We prefer them to our real names. Mom loves the classics. Daddy said she read a lot when she was expecting so I think she chose her favorite name at the time. I'm Valentine. Heath is Heathcliff. Rom is Romeo. Opie is Ophelia. There's a Juliet, Rochester and Darcy at home."

"That's Jules, Roc and Cy," Opie threw out with a grin.

"Valentine?" he asked with a raised brow. "What classic did your mom find that in?"

"I was born on February 14. A little too obvious, don't you think?"

"You could have been Cupid."

"Val works fine, thank you."

"Did you get teased about your names?"

"Some, but eventually everyone started using nicknames like we did."

"We're happy Mom didn't let Daddy name us," Opie said. "Somehow Truelove's Fancy just doesn't do it for me."

Their laughter filled the small room. Rom arrived, and there were more greetings and introductions before they got around to placing their orders.

"I hear you had an interview this morning," Russ said to Rom.

He named the prestigious Lexington company. "I hope to get into their leadership rotational program."

"How do you think it went?" Val asked.

"Pretty good. They're going to get back to me by the end of the week."

"Is it what you want?" Val asked.

"Let's discuss it later," Rom said. "So Russ, tell me about these plans for Val's business."

Russ admitted he was still trying to figure out exactly what Val wanted.

"Good luck," Rom said. "Val always knows what she wants but leaves it to the rest of us to figure out on our own."

"I do not."

"I hope to be on the same wavelength with the next set of plans," Russ said.

"Val won't settle for anything but the best," Opie warned. "This is important to her."

"I know," Russ said. "I'm trying to wrap my mind around majestic vistas."

Everyone offered their opinion of what that meant, and the conversation moved on to other topics. Russ glanced at his watch. "I'd better get back to the office. I've enjoyed meeting all of you."

"You, too," Opie said. "Feel free to visit the farm anytime."

"Lunch is on me," Russ said. "I'll be in touch soon, Val."

"Wow," Opie said after he walked away. "He's cute."

"Knock it off," Val said, not wanting her sister to find Russ Hunter attractive.

"I need to go, too," Jane said, pushing her chair back. "It's been great seeing everyone again."

"Please come to the farm tomorrow," Val said. "I really want to talk to you."

"Sure," Jane said. "Just name a time. I have a serious gaping hole in my schedule at present."

"Come around eleven and stay for lunch."

"You don't have to keep feeding me," Jane protested with a smile.

Val thought the young woman had lost too much weight in the months since her husband's death.

"I'll make one of my culinary specialties," Opie said.

"We'll be there," she said. "I warn you Sammy's a picky eater."

"She's never had an Opie Truelove meal."

"Is that like a fast-food kid's meal?" Val teased.

"Once she tastes my food, you'll have problems getting her to eat anything else."

Jane laughed. "I'll risk it. Thanks for lunch."

"Don't thank us," Val said. "Russ Hunter paid."

"Thank him for me next time you see him."

Val nodded, wondering if the meal would show up on her expense report as she made a mental note to thank him for everyone.

"How's it going?" Kelly asked Russ when she returned later that afternoon.

"I have an idea or two. How was your meeting?"

"The client approved the plans and is going to talk with Kevin Flint. Mr. King's happy about that."

Russ laid down his pencil and flexed his shoulders. "What do you suppose he meant by that comment about Val Truelove hating the plans? How did he know?"

Kelly hung her suit coat over the back of her chair and sat down. "Your body language. Usually you're more confident with your successes."

"I wondered if he'd looked at my concept before I presented it to her."

"I think it was because you didn't exude your usual cockiness."

"I'm not like that."

"Sure you are. Stop worrying. You're sounding paranoid."

He was, Russ realized. "It struck me as strange. I thought maybe she'd complained."

"Did she indicate she planned to do that?"

"No, but if he called to follow up, she might have said something."

"I doubt he did that. Maybe if they were friends or ran into each other on the street."

As far as Russ knew, Val and Randall King had never met. She had spoken to him on the phone when she called Prestige looking for an architect. "She didn't mention talking to him at lunch."

That caught Kelly's attention. "You had lunch with her?"

Russ nodded. "And her sister, two brothers, and a friend of theirs."

"Any leads come out of the conversation?"

"Her brother says she always knows what she wants and leaves it to them to figure out on their own."

"That sounds like something a brother would say."

"Or a man would think," Russ said. "I believe most women operate that way."

"Hey," Kelly said with a laugh. "For the record, men are just as confusing as women."

"I enjoyed meeting them," Russ admitted.

"I told you. The Trueloves are nice people."

"At least I have to plan a structure to please only one of them."

"I'm sure they will want a family meeting once the plan is completed," Kelly warned.

"All of them?"

"All of them," Kelly agreed with a nod.

Chapter 5

Though she hadn't intended to talk to Russ Hunter until he presented the revised plans, Val was forced to call him the following Monday. "Kelly Dickerson called. I thought we agreed my plans would remain confidential."

"We work in the same office," he explained. "She's been looking for a place for a while now. She seemed excited by the idea of getting married at Sheridan Farm."

"She's coming out to take a look at the gardens this weekend. We'll discuss the details then. Meanwhile, I suggest you make her aware this isn't something I want discussed."

"I will," Russ said quickly. "I should have called you myself. I had the photos spread over my drawing board, and she offered a future bride's point of view."

"Did it help?"

"Some. I'm making progress. Did you apply for your business license?"

"It's in the works."

"Is it safe to start booking now?" Russ asked. "What happens if things don't work out?"

"If we come to an agreement, Kelly will have her wedding regardless of the outcome. Sheridan Farm belongs to our family, and as far as I'm aware no laws prohibit an owner from having a wedding at their home."

"What about the business plan?"

"Rom and Heath are looking it over. And I downloaded the information on converting the house to a bed-and-breakfast."

"It doesn't seem right. Houses like that deserve to be loved by their owners," Russ said. "The Sheridan family loved and lived in that home for over two hundred years. Why don't you live there?"

"Alone?"

"I'm sure the family would agree if you suggested you live there."

"I think you give me far more credit than I deserve," Val said.

"Wouldn't you love to call the Sheridan mansion home?"

Though she hadn't admitted it to anyone, Val had been disappointed when her parents refused to leave the manager's house. She and Russ agreed in one regard. It was a shame to leave such a beautiful home unoccupied. "We'll see," she said. "It would have to be occupied if we turn it into a B and B."

"Why are you doing this?" Russ asked.

"I told you. It's a longtime dream."

"But you're rich. You can afford other dreams. Bigger, better ones."

He knew. Val sighed. She'd wondered how long it would be before he heard about the money. "I've always been rich, blessed with hardworking parents who loved me."

"You won the lottery. That's wild."

"The decision over whether or not to keep the money has been a struggle. Daddy's very anti-gambling. In fact, all of us are."

"But he allowed you to buy the farm with lottery winnings?"

"The ticket was a gift from my employer."

"Dress it up however you want, but it's still lottery winnings."

Why did everyone insist on making her feel she'd done something wrong? "That made the decision difficult."

"How can claiming millions of dollars be difficult?"

"It's a responsibility with a heavy price tag. If I'd gone out and purchased the ticket, it would be different."

"Sounds like you're trying to justify something you don't feel right about."

He hit the bull's-eye with that one. Val's sigh reached over the miles. "Daddy is afraid people will judge me harshly for the choice I made. The Sheridans' son wasn't interested in holding on to the farm. I couldn't bear the thought of giving up the only home most of us kids can remember and Daddy having to seek employment elsewhere. What would you have done? Would you have turned the money down?"

"No."

She knew from his quick response that Russ didn't understand her reaction. "I couldn't either. All I know is that I believed God would provide. It happened in a way I don't really understand. Maddy gave me a gift that made me wealthy."

"I don't get it. Why do you care?"

"Because it's not how we operate. Daddy's father gambled and drank away every penny he could get his hands on. He killed a man and ended up in prison when Daddy was seventeen years old. My father learned his work ethic from an overworked, underpaid mother.

"He worked two and three jobs to support his family and help his brother through college. My grandmother worked for the Sheridans for a while and got Daddy his first job on the horse farm. He learned everything he could, and when the Sheridans' old manager retired, Mr. Sheridan considered him ready to take on the job. Nothing has ever been easy for him."

"But that's changed now."

"Not really. Daddy will always work hard. He expects us to do the same. No matter what people think, life is not a free ride. We are our brother's keeper."

Russ frowned. His brother could keep himself. He didn't owe Wendell the time of day. Not after the way he had looked out for himself. Older by five years, Wendell had done everything to avoid his pesky half brother. Even at school, Wendell made it clear that Russ should keep his distance. After college, Wendall returned home to the family farm, and Russ had no doubt he'd spent the inter-vening years ingratiating himself with their father.

"I still don't get the lottery part. Why sweat what people say?"

"Dad says we have to use the money to improve other people's lives as well as our own."

"Pass it on, only on a grander scale?"

"Not grander. It's hard, Russ. We're setting up the rules as we go, but we're trying to make a difference. When I asked God to provide, I had no idea it would be this spectacular. I did believe He would answer my prayer. I figured the new owner would see Daddy's worth and allow him to work out his remaining years here at the farm while we made sure the younger kids were educated as well.

"That's a Truelove tradition. Daddy helped pay for his brother's education, and in turn Uncle Zeb helped Aunt Karen. He's a professor at Harvard. Aunt Karen is a scientist involved in cancer research. The twins just received their MBAs from Harvard, and Opie graduated from culinary school."

"So the oldest kids always lose in the Truelove tradition?"

"I derived a great deal of personal satisfaction from making a difference in their lives. Uncle Zeb and Aunt Karen helped, too."

"Your father helped them, and they helped his kids in return?"

"Rom, Heath, and Opie would have helped our younger siblings."

"But now you'll take care of them as well?"

"Some of the money has been earmarked for an education fund, and we're considering expanding beyond family needs."

"So what do your relatives think about the win?"

"They agree I was blessed. I actually considered the ticket a waste of good money when Maddy handed it to me."

"I imagine she wishes she had kept it for herself."

"She hasn't said. I owe her and feel we can work together on this venture. Please, Russ, don't discuss this project with anyone else. Ask Kelly to do the same. I don't want a lot of headaches because someone takes exception at this stage."

"It's difficult not to bounce ideas off each other when you share an office."

"I know, but there's so much to finalize before I go public."

"I'll talk to Kelly. And I'll keep your plans so under wraps you'll have to pry them out of me."

She chuckled. "You've got the right idea, but let's not go that far."

Russ Hunter was going to be trouble, Val thought as she laid the cordless phone on the desk. She'd asked him to keep the plans confidential, and yet his office mate had a very good working knowledge of what she intended here at Sheridan Farm.

Val didn't like that. If she'd wanted anyone apprised of her plans, she would be the one doing the informing. She planned to make doubly certain Kelly under-stood the need for secrecy when she saw her this weekend. Any misinformation at this point could cause major problems.

She picked up the phone again and dialed her lawyer's office. "Mr. Henderson, please. This is Val Truelove calling."

In a few moments the man who had taken on the job of counsel for Truelove Inc. asked, "What can I do for you today, Ms. Truelove?"

"I need to know how I can protect my idea for Your Wedding Place."

"It's an expensive undertaking that will prohibit a number of people from considering the idea. I suppose you could franchise. Do you feel that once the basic premise is established, others would see the merit and develop similar concepts in different locations?"

"I don't know. My plan is to focus my investment on Your Wedding Place. I have no plans to expand beyond Kentucky."

"Franchising is not cheap, but it could be a way to protect your idea. Let me do more research and get back to you."

What was it with everyone? Val thought as she agreed and said good-bye. She was ready to get started while everyone else seemed equally determined to delay the process. "Oh, well back to the garden," she said, pushing herself out of the executive chair.

"Where's Jane?" Val asked when she found Heath working alone.

"She went into Paris for those plants you wanted."

Val nodded. She had to hand it to the woman. Ever since Jane had accepted the job as her assistant, she'd taken on every task without complaint.

She picked up a pair of gardening gloves and pulled them on. "I wish I'd invited Jane to go to the bachelor auction with us. It was fun."

"What possessed you to bid on that date with Wendell Hunter for Opie?"

"She was interested," Val said, feeling guilty about the prank. She didn't know what got into her when she took Opie's paddle and bid until she won.

"Opie says she's not going."

"She'll go," Val said with surety. "She's dying to tell Wendell Hunter what she thinks of his saying a woman's place is in the home. I just provided the opportunity."

"Well leave Jane out of it," Heath warned. "She's got enough issues."

She stopped sorting through the tools and looked at Heath. "What do you mean?"

"She's angry at Garrett."

"I'd be angry, too."

"She has to forgive him if she ever hopes to move on with her life."

"That's easier said than done."

Heath sighed. "I know. I hate that she's attempting to deal with this alone. She needs God in her corner."

"I asked if we could take Sammy to church with us on Sunday, and she agreed."

"What about Jane?" he asked.

"Not yet, but I plan to keep inviting her. They're moving into the apartment this weekend. I told her we'd help if she needs us."

"I'm sure she'll try to do it on her own," Heath said.

Val nodded. Jane was having problems accepting their generosity. When she'd shared that her landlord had sold the house she rented, Val offered the two-bedroom efficiency over the garage as part of her salary package. Jane resisted at first but accepted after Val pointed out that they housed a number of the staff at the farm. "Maybe she'll accept our help. She's coming around. Said the apartment is one of the best perks she's ever had."

"Makes sense," Heath said. "With the price of gas she'll save a bundle." He reached for the hedge trimmer. "We're wasting daylight."

The heat of the day seemed to intensify as they trimmed the tall hedges. Within an hour, Val's arms ached from holding them over her head. As lunchtime approached, all she wanted to think about was a cold shower and a nap.

"Hello, stranger."

Startled, Val turned to find Derrick Masters standing nearby. She turned off the trimmer.

"I was in the neighborhood and thought I'd stop by for a visit since you're too busy for your old friends," he said, flashing a big smile.

When had they ever been friends? Derrick hadn't had the time of day for her before the win. "As you can see there's plenty to do. Feel free to jump in."

"I would, but I have plans."

"I understand completely." Val hid her grin. Derrick was allergic to real work.

"Maybe some other time," he suggested. "You still haven't taken me up on my offer to enjoy a bit of Louisville nightlife."

"I'm not the least interested in partying, Derrick. You know that."

"Dinner then. The two of us. A nice restaurant. Candles. A little wine."

Unimpressed by his attempt at romance, Val asked bluntly, "What purpose would it serve?"

"We could get to know each other better."

"You're welcome to join us for dinner here."

"I want to spend time with you," he whined. "I don't do the family thing."

"God and my family are the most important aspects of my life," Val said.

Exasperated, Derrick snapped, "I don't get you. There are lots of women who'd jump at the opportunity to go out with me."

Heath stepped around the hedge. "Then why don't you go find one of them?" His voice lacked his usual friendliness.

"Who are you?"

Heath took a step forward. Derrick took a step back. Her brothers might not be big men, but they had a presence about them when the situation warranted. "Heath Truelove. Val's brother. I'd be happy to introduce you to my twin and our father if you need further convincing."

"It's her loss," Derrick said.

41

"A decent man would have a true jewel in my sister, and I'm not talking dollars and cents," Heath said, leaving very little doubt about his opinion of the man.

"You Trueloves are crazy." Derrick flung the words at them before stomping off to his car.

"Thanks," Val said.

"Let me know if he bothers you again."

"You can't always protect me," Val said.

"Sure I can. That's what brothers are for."

"It's not your battle."

"This isn't the first time he's called since you won the money, is it?"

"No. He's determined to take me to Louisville to party."

Heath frowned. "Why isn't he getting the message?"

"Derrick's ego gets in the way of his seeing the truth. He thinks women should feel privileged to be in his presence. I saw through him from day one, but he had a reputation to uphold. When I rejected him, he tried to make me look bad. Evidently the money renewed his interest."

"Men like that give the rest of us a bad name."

"You frightened him. He wasn't expecting you to show up."

"Then maybe we've seen the last of him. Ready to get back to work?"

Val looked up at the tall wall of shrubbery and asked wearily, "Do we have to?"

Heath shrugged. "Only if you hope to finish these gardens anytime soon."

"Can we at least take a water break? I'm parched."

"Go ahead. I'll finish up here."

Val reached for the hedge trimmer. "If you work, I work."

Chapter 6

Kelly Dickerson had booked her August wedding. Val was thrilled with her first success, but she also worried things were moving too fast. Suddenly the possibility had become reality, and she wasn't sure they'd be ready.

The idea she needed to make more people aware of her plans wouldn't go away. In a way, that knowledge could be her defense. If more people knew about Your Wedding Place, it would help her defend herself against anyone trying to steal her idea. In the same vein, it could cause the problems she wanted to avoid.

After discussing it with the family over breakfast, she resolved to make an appointment with her former employer. She wanted to hear what Maddy thought about their working together. Heath and Rom had left for Boston the previous Sunday afternoon, and Jane was running errands, so Val headed to the office to make her call.

She knew something was up when her dad came in a few minutes later, his body tense with anger and a frown on his face. "Your grandfather knows about the money."

Her grandfather's calls always disturbed her dad, but today seemed worse than usual. "Did he mention it specifically?"

"He asked why none of his grandchildren ever came to visit him. Particularly his favorite, Val."

"Favorite?" she repeated, her laughter was tinged with disbelief. "I've seen him maybe twice in my life. He doesn't even know me."

"I don't want you giving him money. Karen, Zeb, and I give him sufficient to meet his needs."

"I don't mind, Daddy."

"I do," he declared angrily. "I won't have him taking advantage of you. He'll bleed you dry and step over the body without remorse. I couldn't stop my mother, but I can forbid you. I knew this would happen the moment he learned you'd won that money. Why are people so greedy? I'd rather live out my days as a poor man than be that way."

Val found the pain in his eyes heartbreaking. She'd never seen this side of her father. "Does he know you own Sheridan Farm?"

"No. Zeb, Karen, and I agreed a long time ago to keep our business private. He's a user, Val."

She touched her father's arm. "Would you like me to pray with you, Daddy?"

Tears of remorse filled his eyes. "Yes, my Valentine. Pray for your sinful father and share one of those hugs he needs so badly."

She held on tightly, wishing she could absorb his pain, and whispered, "He can't help it, Daddy. He's a sick old man. Let's pray that God works in his life in a miraculous way."

"That's a prayer I've prayed many times."

She grasped her father's hands in hers. "Blessed heavenly Father, we come to You today seeking healing for Mathias Truelove. Free him from his bondage of sin and help him understand You are all he needs in this life to be content. We ask the miracle of a changed life for our loved one. Direct his path to You. And, Lord, give my father peace in this situation. As always, thank You for the blessings You bestow on us daily and the gift You gave us with Your Son, Jesus Christ. Amen."

Her father joined in with a heartfelt amen. "Thank you, Val. I'm sorry I reacted so badly."

"Never be sorry, Daddy. You're the best father any children ever had. When I see you hurting because of Granddaddy, it breaks my heart that you didn't have what we have."

He hugged her again. "Thanks, Valentine. I'd better get to work."

"I love you, Daddy."

He touched her cheek. "I love you, too."

After he left, Val found her thoughts on her dad's pain. She knew it must run deep for him to behave so out of character. He'd never forbidden her to do anything. He had asked her not to do things, and out of respect she'd done as he requested, just as she would in this situation.

She wondered what she could do to help heal the rift between them. Val feared it would never happen as long as her father and grandfather refused to communicate.

Picking up the phone, she dialed Maddy's office. After talking to her replacement for a couple of minutes, she asked to speak to her former boss. They exchanged pleasantries, and Val said, "I wondered if you had time to discuss a plan I feel could be mutually beneficial."

"Sure. Can you come by Thursday morning? Ten thirty would be good for me. I have a lunch appointment with the Jensens, and I know it will probably run well over into the afternoon."

"See you then."

As she drove the familiar route to Lexington later that week, Val considered Maddy's reaction to her proposal. Would her former boss be willing to refer her wedding parties to Your Wedding Place?

Over the years she'd heard Maddy complain about the lack of wedding venues available to brides who didn't want a traditional church wedding or reception. Val had always been on the lookout for unique places. If she read about something in a local magazine, she'd kept a record for when there was a need. A number of brides had been very receptive to the places she found.

Val parked behind the beautifully renovated old house off Main Street and went inside.

Maddy greeted her with a hug and invited her to sit in the visitor chair. She chose the other chair, setting a casual tone for the meeting. "So what have you been up to now that you're a lady of leisure?"

Val's life had become even more hectic since leaving her job back in the spring. "Busier than ever. I wanted to talk to you because I think we can help each other." She pulled a brochure from her bag. "I'm in the process of putting together a business called Your Wedding Place."

Noting the look of concern on Maddy's face, Val quickly explained, "Not from the wedding planner aspect. I wouldn't do that to you. I promise to refer brides regardless of whether my idea interests you or not."

Maddy smiled her relief. "Thank you for that."

"You know I think you're an excellent wedding planner," Val told her.

"I enjoy the challenge."

Val handed her the pamphlet she'd picked up from the printer just that morning. "That's why I wanted to share my idea." She launched into the presentation she'd prepared. "I know how difficult it is to find adequate venues. What we hope to do at Your Wedding Place is create a variety that appeals to many couples."

As Maddy studied the pamphlet, Val pulled a business card from her pocket. She'd hired a publicist who had created the brochure, business cards, and even her Web site, which would go live once she finalized the plans.

Maddy tapped the brochure. "This is impressive, Val."

"Thank you. There are a number of expansion plans in the works. We hope to complete this structure later this year. It will be the perfect outdoor wedding or reception site for spring, summer, and milder fall weather."

"Incredible," Maddy commented.

"It's all thanks to you."

Maddy's familiar droll smile flashed as she said, "Guess that's one gift that will keep on giving."

Val nodded. In more ways than Maddy could begin to know. "That's why I'd like to continue working with you. I think we could benefit each other."

"Would I be your only wedding planner?"

"Exclusivity might not work well in this situation," Val told her. "I want to schedule enough weddings to keep the profit margin in the black, and I think that would require doing business with more than one planner."

"The premise is huge. What happens when the wedding party exceeds what you have to offer?"

"We have the house and gardens, and I'm considering adding another structure large enough to hold cold-weather or large indoor receptions. I'd also like to build a small chapel."

"Are you limiting yourself to locals who want unique sites?"

Val shook her head. "Not totally. There are hotels in Paris and Lexington that would enable us to bring in larger parties willing to accept inconvenience for originality."

"I think it's a great idea, Val. And I'll be glad to add you to my vendor list."

"I'd pay you a percentage for referrals. We'll discuss that once things are further along."

"Are you ready to book now? I have a small wedding that's looking for a place. The bride wants a garden wedding, but we haven't found exactly what she wants."

"What date? I have an August wedding booked for the English garden."

Maddy stood and moved around her desk to check her planner. She named the date.

"That's the week after the other wedding. You want to bring the couple out to see the gardens? We're working in the English and Japanese gardens."

"I'd love to see the place," Maddy said. "You deserve this, Val. I've recognized your potential for years. You're an admirable young woman." When she blushed, Maddy insisted, "It's true. I've never known anyone to make the sacrifices you made for your siblings. How is everyone?"

Another sibling might harbor bad feelings, but not Val. As the oldest of seven kids she'd decided not to burden her parents with her college expenses. Instead, she'd worked and taken night courses to obtain her associate degree in business. After graduation she'd gone to work as Maddy's assistant.

Jacob and Cindy Truelove worked hard at raising a very close-knit family. They had taught their children the importance of helping each other in whatever life brought their way. The idea of burdening Opie and the twins with student loans had prompted Val to continue to live at home, drive a secondhand car, and use the majority of her salary to support their educational endeavors. She had no doubt they in turn would help their younger siblings and their parents.

"They all have their own plans for where they might fit into the business. Rom and Heath have been helping with my business plan. Opie's considering her options."

"Your mom should open a floral design shop. She'd do an incredible job," Maddy said. They had called upon Cindy Truelove's considerable talent a few times when they had a bride in a pinch.

"She would." The grandfather clock gonged, and Val glanced up. "I've taken enough of your time." Val slid her purse up her arm as she stood. "I'd appreciate it if you kept this confidential. We're still in the planning and legal stages."

"Certainly. I'll be in touch about the garden. Is there a time that's better for you?"

"Tomorrow or Saturday would be fine. Just let me know."

"I'll call you with a time after I speak with the bride."

The meeting had gone exactly as she'd hoped. "Thanks again, Maddy."

Val was still smiling when she closed the door and stepped into the hallway she had traversed many times.

"Well, if it isn't Ms. Moneybags. What brings you down to your old stomping grounds?"

Derrick's sneer reminded Val of the numerous run-ins she'd had with the office Casanova. No doubt he'd gotten the message and reverted to his previous nasty self.

"I had an appointment with Maddy."

"Giving back some of that money?"

"It's really none of your business, Derrick."

"I worked just as hard as you did on that wedding. I deserve that money as much as you do."

Val had helped a couple of her former coworkers who had real needs, but that wasn't his concern. "I suppose that's why they call gambling chance. I prayed and believed God would provide. As answers to prayers go, it was a big one."

"Prayers," he repeated, spitting the word like one of the four-letter words he used regularly. "Winning the lottery doesn't have anything to do with prayer. It's luck."

"Call it what you will, Derrick, but I consider the money an answer to a prayer. A blessing, in fact."

"So why don't you share your blessing? I could use a million or two."

The way he said blessing bothered Val. She knew from experience that Derrick's lifestyle left no time for the Lord. "What do you need, Derrick?" If he could list one worthwhile thing, she'd happily hand over the funds.

"A new car would be a start."

She recalled how he had walked into the office bragging about his new sports car just this past January. Derrick's expensive lifestyle took every dime he made and more. Val didn't doubt he was deep in debt. "What's wrong with the car you have?"

"It's got expensive payments, honey. Ties up funds I could be spending on the ladies."

His evil leer made chill bumps appear on Val's arms. She rubbed them away, wishing he'd leave. Instead he leaned against the doorway, blocking her exit. "It was your choice, Derrick. Did it ever occur to you that I drove my old car and worked to have money to help my family?"

"Oh come on, Val. That holier-than-thou attitude of yours is wearing thin. Tell me you're not enjoying that lottery win."

"Not in situations like this," she emphasized. "Life is not a free ride, Derrick. Every decision has consequences."

"Yeah, like it took some big decision to accept that money," he mocked.

"Believe it or not, it did. I knew it would change our lives forever. And not all for the good. That's why I have no intention of wasting the money on senseless purchases."

He straightened up and leaned forward. "Doing something nice for me wouldn't be senseless."

"You're right." Val dragged her purse around and pulled out ten dollars. "Here, Derrick. Have lunch on me."

"You little—!" he shouted.

Maddy's office door swung open. "What's going on here?"

"Ah, Val and I were talking."

A flash of sympathy crossed Maddy's face. "I'm sorry, Val. Please step into my office, Derrick."

His expression spoke volumes as he maneuvered past Val, pausing long enough to snatch the money from her hand.

"See you soon, Val," Maddy said with a smile before closing the door.

∾

When the woman leaving Maddy Troyer's office charged into him on the sidewalk, Russ didn't know what to think. He grabbed her arms to keep them both standing and did a double take.

"Val?" Russ said, taken aback by her appearance. A suit and heels had replaced the scruffy jeans.

"Excuse me," she said, somewhat breathlessly. She looked up. "Oh, Russ. Hi."

He let go and stepped back. "I planned to call you later to discuss the plans. Care to join me for a working lunch?" As he watched her face transform with her smile, Russ lost his focus. "I'm sorry. What did you say?"

"I asked where you wanted to eat."

"Actually I thought we might have lunch in our conference room. I can ask our secretary to order something for us."

"Why don't we just pick up a Jack's Burger? My treat," she offered.

"Sounds good," Russ agreed.

Inside the small but popular burger joint, they studied the menu board and chose the chiliburger special.

"No doubt it will end up on the front of my clothes, but I do love this burger."

"Extra napkins," Russ told the woman at the counter.

"Lots of them," Val added with a big smile.

They stepped over to the pickup area to wait for their order.

"Nice weather we're having," Russ said as they sat on a bench and watched the other patrons come and go.

"Beautiful. I've made good progress in the gardens the past couple of days."

"What happened to the Sheridans' gardener?"

"There hasn't been one for years," Val told him. "Mr. Sheridan never cared for the gardens as much as his wife. The people he hired did an absolute minimum."

"You should hire a landscaper."

"We can have it finished by the time I explain to someone else what needs to be done," Val said. "Mrs. Sheridan taught us a lot about gardening. She really loved Heath. During the summers she'd send for him, and he got out of the chores."

"Considering the size of those gardens, I'd think the chores would have been easier."

"Heath loved helping her. He'd make suggestions, and it thrilled him when she liked his ideas."

"Must feel good to own the place now," Russ said.

"It does."

The clerk called number thirty-nine. "That's us," Russ said, jumping up to claim the bags. He carried them down the street and held the door for her to enter Prestige Designs. The office occupied the building next door to Madeline Troyer's Event Planning. Val had walked past it many times, never thinking that one day they would be working for her.

"Thanks for agreeing to this," Russ said. "Cheryl, Ms. Truelove and I will be meeting in the conference room."

Taken aback by the woman's unfriendly glare, Val smiled and responded to Russ. "No problem. I was in Lexington anyway."

"When you came storming out of Maddy's, I didn't realize it was you."

"I had a run-in with a former coworker."

Russ indicated the small conference room. "We'll meet in here. The restroom is just down the hall. I'll grab my plans and be right back."

He returned a few minutes later with a man he introduced as Randall King.

"Welcome to Prestige Designs, Ms. Truelove. It's a pleasure to meet you in person."

"You, too, Mr. King."

"I trust Russ is treating you well. He's filled me in on your plans for Sheridan Farm. I must say they are most ambitious."

"But achievable?"

The enigmatic expression on his face said little. "With good planning and sufficient funds most things are achievable."

"That's what I thought."

He nodded at the food emitting delicious scents into the room. "I see you've planned a working lunch."

"We did," Russ said.

"Then don't let me keep you. In fact, I'm inspired to dash over for a burger of my own. I look forward to our future meetings, Ms. Truelove."

Val nodded. After his boss left, Russ opened his burger wrapper and took a big bite of the sandwich. Uncharacteristic silence filled the room. "Is something wrong?"

"It's been one of those days. Something happened before I left home this morning that's weighing heavy on my mind and heart. I've given it over to God, but you know how it is."

Russ shrugged and shook his head. "Can't say that I do. There's no aspect of my life I expect God to shoulder."

"I can't imagine life without my Savior. No matter how bad things get, He's there for me."

"And yet you're troubled?"

"Not because I doubt God will handle things," Val assured him. "I hurt for Daddy."

"Your father? Why?"

"He doesn't have a good relationship with his father, and it hurts him. I hate seeing him so unhappy."

Russ shrugged. "Lots of us don't get along with family, but we get by."

"He's a Christian, Russ. The Bible speaks very strongly about being at odds with your brother."

Russ balled up the sandwich wrapper and laid it on the table. "Guess I'll never be a Christian then. I don't have any qualms about not associating with Wendell."

"It doesn't bother you at all?" Val asked. "Don't you miss having him in your life?"

"Not particularly. We were never friends."

"I can't imagine not having a relationship with my family."

"You'd think differently if one of them stabbed you in the back."

" 'And unto him that smiteth thee on one cheek offer also the other; and him that taketh away thy cloak forbid not to take thy coat also,'" Val said, quoting Luke 6:29.

He wiped his mouth. "Nice sentiment but impossible to live by. No one turns the other cheek. Nor do they give up what's rightfully theirs. Does your father see your grandfather?"

"Not often. Grandfather has spent the last thirty years in prison. Daddy's concerned because he thinks Grandfather knows I won the lottery. He's afraid he'll try to get money from me."

"Sounds like a user. Your dad's entitled to feel as he does. I know what that's like. Wendell took advantage of the situation and didn't bother to think about me. Why should I care about him?"

"Because he's your brother," Val insisted.

Russ reached for the plans and spread them across the tabletop, effectively concluding the conversation. Her gaze followed as he indicated the property layout and the code requirements for the parking area and green space.

"I want one large parking area over here." She pointed out the location on the map. "Once on the property all guests will be transported to their wedding sites."

"I wish you'd mentioned that earlier," he said, a touch of irritation in his tone.

"Perhaps you should have inquired."

Her comment reminded Russ of his responsibility to guide her through the process.

"Eat your burger before it gets cold." Val turned the pages until she reached the one showing the structure. Russ noticed she ate little as she studied the prints.

"I like the way you've placed this so the structure is here, overlooking the view."

"That's what you wanted, right?" Russ didn't care for the uncertainty that plagued him with this project. He'd never felt like this before. Determined not to disappoint her again, he'd worked and reworked his designs.

"Yes. What are we calling this?"

"I'm fairly certain the project will be classified as Assembly Group. What we call it depends on how we finish the upper floor. We could use columns and make it a colonnade, or we can use arches and canopies and call it a pavilion. Custom ironwork could be used for a top to keep it more open."

"Which do you suggest?"

"A colonnade would have a more formal feel while the ironwork would make this much more open and informal. I have a couple of plans to show you today."

She looked shocked. Russ suspected she'd been certain he'd never get what she wanted.

"I'm ready whenever you are."

Russ had exerted a great deal of extra effort on the plans. He'd even taken time to color in the scenic view in the distance on the landscaping plan.

"What are these?" she asked, pointing to the low line below the platform. "Windows?"

"Yes," Russ said, pleased she'd noticed. "I understand placement is primary, but I tried to anticipate a few other things. You can't have groups of people out there without facilities, so I thought of ways we could work those in and best benefit your business. I put all the mechanicals and bathrooms underneath, along with a large indoor area you can use for inclement weather receptions. I made the structure accessible with the ramp and an elevator here," he said, indicating them on the plan. "And I worked in a good-sized kitchen with fridges and ice machines. The facilities would enable caterers to store their food on-site. You can rent the space to those who want accessibility."

"I hadn't thought of that," Val said.

"And then there's the storage issue. I know you plan to store tables, chairs, and linens elsewhere on the property, but think of the time involved in moving the items. Having them on-site would be your best option."

"You've really thought this through," Val said.

"I think raising the structure like this and giving it a rooftop overlook not only enhances the scenery but makes the view even more incredible."

"But won't the raised height require railings?" Val asked. "Those don't fit the open concept I wanted."

"The basic premise of a colonnade is rows of columns at several intervals that support a roof," Russ explained. "I had considered balustrades in areas, but we could look into less visual options if you like the idea. What do you think about graduated steps on the end going out toward a small ornamental water feature?"

"What if we continued the steps with a patio around the structure?" Val asked. "It wouldn't need to be large. Lounge areas are popular with wedding guests. Where would the band be?"

"Here," Russ said, tapping the area along the back of the colonnade. "The dance floor is there. If you want, you could use interchangeable tiles to change designs based on your clients' requests. Wiring and lighting could be run in the posts and beams along the top of the structure."

"I like it," Val said.

Russ nearly sighed with relief.

She glanced at him. "What was your other idea?"

He pulled over another plan, not opening it. "Colonnade, one level, facilities in free-standing structure, no underground construction." He tapped the first plan. "This allows you to offer more options to the brides."

"What's the construction time frame?"

"A basement and elevator will lengthen the project time but definitely class up the structure."

"You're sure we can do a basement?"

"We'd need to do a feasibility study."

"I want to hire smaller local companies to do the work."

"I think that would be a mistake," Russ offered. "Larger contractors are better equipped to deal with some of the issues that might arise. If it's a matter of saving money—"

"No," Val interrupted. "It's a matter of helping smaller companies attain higher profit levels because they're given the opportunity. Some of these companies are as good or better than their larger counterparts."

"I still think a larger company, like Kevin Flint's, could do the job more effectively," Russ declared.

"But that's not what your client wants," Val said firmly.

"Okay, I'll hire someone to do the study. Then we'll find your contractor." He started rolling the plans for Val to take with her. "We could request the contractor subcontract smaller companies."

Val pushed their wrappings from lunch into the bag. "And watch them walk away with the profit. I want the smaller companies to benefit from the project. Truelove Inc. will adhere to this policy consistently, so if you can't work with that I'll pay for the plans and find someone else to carry them through."

"I'm just offering alternatives."

"And I appreciate that, but there are some things I will not vary from." Her eyes drifted back to the plans. "You did an excellent job with these, Russ. What helped you see the vision?"

"Your window-to-the-world comment."

"I'm definitely pleased. You've solved two problems with the basement structure. I can't wait to show the family."

"I hope they like what they see."

"Why don't you come for dinner and hear their thoughts for yourself? You could answer any questions they might have."

Kelly had been right. Val planned to involve her entire family. "When?"

"Tonight. Just a family dinner. Nothing fancy."

Russ shrugged. "I'd love to hear what they have to say."

Chapter 7

"Val, talk to your father. He won't listen to me," Cindy Truelove said, her green gaze never leaving her husband's face.

Val always found it humorous that her mother thought she could make her father do something when he wouldn't listen to his wife. She had arrived home only minutes before and gone in to tell her mother about their dinner guest.

"I won't have it," Jacob Truelove insisted. "No one comes on this farm acting like that man did."

"What man?" Val asked. "What happened?"

"Some stranger showed up earlier today, using foul language and making threats against you."

"You have no idea who he was?" Val asked.

"No. Nearly ran Clyde down with his flashy red sports car. When I shouted at him, he cursed at me."

"Can you describe him?" Val asked, almost certain she knew who the man was.

"Short guy. Blond hair. Wore a suit. Wanted to know where you were. Said it was your fault and you owed him. What did he mean?"

"Sounds like Derrick from Maddy's office." Val recounted the earlier incident. "I didn't do anything to him."

"He obviously thinks you did. I told him he's not welcome here."

"Heath told him the same thing recently."

"He's been here before?" her father demanded.

Val nodded. "He asked me out several times and wouldn't accept no for an answer. He got nervous when Heath suggested he move on. Said we were all crazy before he jumped in his car and drove off. He was his usual nasty self at the office today."

"Since when does no one tell me these things?" her father inquired irritably.

Val smiled. "Heath offered to introduce him to you and Rom. That's when Derrick opted to leave."

"Here, Jacob," her mother said when she returned with a glass of ice water. "Drink this and cool off."

"I'll check in with Maddy and see if she knows anything about what's going on."

Val pulled her cell phone from her purse, realizing she'd never turned it back on after her meeting. She saw she had a message and after listening knew why

Derrick was so angry. "Maddy fired him. She says her decision had nothing to do with me."

"Then why does he blame you?" her dad asked.

"Derrick would never blame himself. I'm sure I became the perfect scapegoat since he was arguing with me when Maddy called him into the office."

"I will not tolerate him coming onto this property and communicating threats. I'm contacting the sheriff."

While she knew it was the smart thing to do, Val dreaded involving the police. No doubt it would only fuel Derrick's anger. Resigned, she said, "I invited Russ Hunter to dinner tonight. I'll call and cancel. He can show you all the plans another time."

"No, don't," her father and mother said at the same time. Val looked from one to the other.

"Opie and I cooked a big dinner."

"And I want to see these plans," her dad added. "I know you're anxious to get started."

"Are you sure?" Val felt uncertain.

"Positive," he said.

"I'd better check the ham. Opie's been after me all afternoon to let her try something different."

After her mother left the room again, Val said, "I should have known Derrick would do something after the way he attacked me today."

"Attacked?"

"Verbal assault," she explained quickly. "He cornered me in the hallway and asked for money. Seemed to think I should subsidize his womanizing with my winnings."

"Womanizing?" Her father's expression changed to that of defender. "What did he say to you, Valentine?"

"Derrick got nasty when I explained the money was a blessing. Said that ticket could have just as easily been his and I should do something nice for him. I gave him ten dollars and suggested he treat himself to lunch."

"That doesn't sound like you, Val."

"He brings out the worst in me. And I don't think Maddy appreciated his poor-loser behavior either."

"I knew this would happen."

"I've tried to be nice to Derrick, Daddy. Some of my friends from work say he's implied things about me that weren't true."

"Why didn't you tell me this before?"

She heaved a sigh. "Because I'm a grown woman who can't come running to you every time some guy insults me."

"You can always come to me, Val. And your brothers. Any of us would have had a talk with him."

"You can't reason with Derrick. We should look into security. Make sure no one comes onto the farm without clearance at the front gate. Next time he could cause real harm."

"There won't be a next time. I plan to make sure he knows he's not welcome here."

"You don't think we need security?"

"Yes, I do. I suspect the farm is only going to become even more active, and security will make us and your brides feel protected. Even more so once those expensive building supplies start coming in. And we should hire a bodyguard for you."

He had really kicked into protective father mode. "I don't need a bodyguard," Val protested.

"You didn't before the money."

"I'll be more cautious, Daddy. Make sure everyone knows where I am when I leave the farm."

"People know you are wealthy, Val. Even if we discount this man, others are willing to do harm for money. I think we should hire a driver to accompany you when you're out on your own."

"In my old car? That would look ridiculous."

"You can afford to upgrade."

His comment surprised Val. One thing they had agreed upon was that they wouldn't flaunt their wealth. No world travels, no expensive wardrobes or costly toys, just basic needs and helping others. The only truly frivolous thing she'd done was buy that date for Opie, and even that had supported a worthwhile charity.

"And call even more attention to myself?"

"I doubt you could get more attention. Think it over. I'll check into security for the farm."

"I can do it if you like," Val said, feeling guilty to have added yet another burden to her father's load. "You already have plenty on your plate. Speaking of plates, I should help with dinner since I invited a guest."

"Seems that fellow is coming here pretty often," her father commented.

"I ran into him this morning, and he showed me the redesigned plans. They're good, Daddy. I want everyone's input before they're finalized."

"You think he can handle the Truelove gang?"

Val laughed. "He had lunch with four of us the other day and survived."

"That says something for him," he said. "Get the phone book. I'll call a few security firms while you help your mom and Opie prepare dinner for your young man."

"He's not my young man," Val objected.

"Well, he's certainly not mine," her father said, laughter booming when Val punched him playfully on the arm.

"By the way, you got a special delivery letter today. I put it on the entry hall table."

"Thanks, Daddy. I'll check it out later."

More dread than peace filled Russ as he drove to Paris that night. After Val left, Randall King had summoned him to his office. "How did it go?"

"She's pleased with the plans. She asked me to make a presentation to her family tonight after dinner."

"Good. Recommend Kevin Flint as the contractor."

"I already did. She refused."

Randall frowned. "What do you mean she refused?"

"Val plans to give her business to smaller contractors. Feels it's important that others who are less fortunate benefit from her investment."

"We always use Kevin. I expect you to convince her his is the best firm for the job."

"I've tried."

Randall King didn't look pleased. "Get the final plan approval. I'll deal with this."

Russ didn't understand why Mr. King suddenly insisted on becoming involved in this project. Val wasn't going to appreciate his interference. Not one bit. As he drove down the driveway, the setting sun formed the perfect backdrop behind the Sheridan mansion. He took the road that led to the manager's house and parked. Pulling the plans from the backseat, Russ walked to the door and knocked.

"Hi. Come on in." Val held the screen door open.

"Are you sure about this?"

"Just think of it as a dinner meeting," she suggested. "Different clientele but you don't have to pick up the tab."

"That's a first," he agreed, smiling at her joke.

"Dinner's ready," her mother called.

As they walked into the dining room, he noted the scramble for chairs. Val tapped the young man Russ assumed to be a younger brother on the shoulder and indicated he should find another chair. "Sit here, next to Daddy."

Russ looked at the boy and shrugged. His smile resembled Val's as he quickly found another seat.

"Cy likes to sit in Rom's place," she explained. "He'll have to adjust now that they're home again."

Russ noted their absence. "Where are Rom and Heath?"

"Tying up loose ends in Boston. They'll be home by the weekend."

The noise died down, and when her father reached for his hand, Russ pulled back. Jacob Truelove wasn't deterred and firmly grasped his hand.

"Grace," Val whispered, taking Russ's other hand and reaching for Opie's hand. After blessing the food, they began passing bowls. As the food moved around the table, Val quickly introduced everyone.

"Roc, leave some of those potatoes for our guest."

"Ah, Mom, you know I love your potatoes," he said, giving up the bowl.

She winked at him and scooped her serving onto his plate before serving her husband and handing the bowl over to Russ.

"Val tells me you showed her the plans today," Jacob said as he carved the ham.

He nodded. "The revised plans. She thought you might like to look them over."

"Can I see, too?" Jules asked. Val nodded. Her sister talked about becoming an architect and was very interested in her plans for the farm.

"Speaking of plans, what do you think about my converting one of the outbuildings into a restaurant?" Opie asked. "I'd need to get financing, but I think it could work."

Russ noted the way Val glanced at her parents and back at Opie before she asked, "Are you sure? I thought you wanted to expand your horizons."

"I want to cook," Opie said. "And I've pretty much decided I can be happier here with my family than off somewhere missing all of you."

"We could find a restaurant in Lexington or Paris," Val said, taking the potatoes Russ offered. "Financing won't be as difficult as you fear. I've set aside monetary gifts for all three graduates."

"No, Val," she said without hesitation. "You've done enough."

She grimaced playfully at Opie. "I have to give you something, and you can use the money to get what you want."

"It's a loan, Val. I intend to repay every dime," Opie declared.

"Not your graduation gift."

"You're so stubborn."

"Wonder where I get it from," Val countered with a grin.

"All of you get it from your father," her mother teased, smiling at her husband.

"Hey now," their father said in mock affront. "In my family it's called determination."

After the laughter died down, Opie said, "I could offer catering services to Your Wedding Place clientele."

"Won't that be too much?"

"Not if I hire sufficient staff. They should be able to work out of my restaurant kitchens."

Val smiled at her sister, and Russ paused in forking food into his mouth. He'd never witnessed such love between family members.

Their mother cleared her throat. "Heath talked to me last week, and he wants to handle the landscaping for your business."

"Landscaping? With an MBA?" Val questioned.

Her mother nodded. "You know how much he enjoys working outside. I think he let Rom convince him a degree in business would benefit the family more."

"Following his heart would have cost much less."

"Heath appreciates the sacrifices you made, Val. He fully intends to use his degree, but he wants to help you get your business off the ground. You know he took those landscape design courses at UK."

Val nodded. "He has excellent ideas. Heath always grew the biggest flowers and the best vegetables."

"Remember that year he decided to give Mom a rose garden for Mother's Day?" Opie asked.

"We begged him to let us help."

"Not that hard," Opie said. "He loved telling us what to do."

"That garden still brings tears to my eyes," Cindy Truelove said.

"It brought a few tears to my eyes, too," Opie said.

"Only because you wanted to make mud pies instead of planting flowers," Val teased.

Opie laughed. "I knew what I wanted even then. So can we work together?"

"We'll talk," Val promised. "Though I think you'll be too busy once you get involved with the restaurant."

"The kitchen area in the structure's lower floor could be used for catering," Russ said.

Opie looked interested. "There's a kitchen?"

Russ swallowed hastily. "Big sinks, prep area, industrial fridges, pantry storage, and countertops. We could add a commercial stove or two."

"It wouldn't be a restaurant," Val pointed out.

"I like the idea though," Opie told her. "Where exactly will these facilities be?"

"Right here at Sheridan Farm. In the basement of the new structure," Russ told her. "That gives Val an inclement weather area now rather than later."

"Wow. Sounds like these plans have come a long way," Opie exclaimed. When Val looked at her, she grimaced. "I mean. . .well, you said you were reworking the plan."

Russ chuckled. "I hope I've improved from those first attempts to capture Val's vision."

After they cleared the table, everyone settled in their seats for a Truelove family discussion. Russ spread the plans across the table, and the brainstorming was nonstop. Cindy poured coffee and looked over her husband's shoulder as he pointed out things he thought would improve the flow.

As planning sessions went, Russ found their input very productive. He'd notated nearly two full pages on his legal pad before realizing how late it was. When he said he needed to call it a night, Val walked him to his car.

"I'll call you tomorrow to discuss those changes."

He nodded. "Thanks for dinner. I enjoyed meeting your parents and the younger members of your family. I've never met a group that loves each other like you do."

"I don't know what I'd do without them."

"You're fortunate," Russ said. "They all want to help you succeed. Wish I could say the same."

"Would you like to talk about it?"

"It's past history. Wendell goes his way, and I go mine, and we're content with that."

"Are you really? I can't imagine any circumstance that would make me feel good about being estranged from my siblings."

"Give it time. Eventually one of them will do or say something to make you rethink that. Particularly now that money is involved. I never would have thought Wendell would stab me in the back, but he did."

"It's only land, Russ. He's your brother."

"Then why did he grab everything for himself? He knew I loved the farm."

Val shrugged. "Have you asked him?"

"There's nothing left to say."

"Being stubborn will hurt you more. Don't make that a reason not to see each other."

"I won't pretend everything is okay. Once I'm established I'll buy a place of my own. And when I have kids I won't play favorites."

"I should tell you Opie had a date with your brother Tuesday night."

"She went out with Wendell?"

Val nodded. "I bought her a date with him."

He started to say something and stopped, puzzled by Val's words. "Bought a date?"

"At a bachelor auction. Paris's most eligible bachelors. It was for a good cause."

"Why would you do that?" Russ demanded.

"You wouldn't understand."

"You think you can heal the rift between us. Well, you can't," Russ said, stomping off toward his car.

Val chased after him. "You didn't have anything to do with this."

She almost ran into him when he stopped. "What do you mean?"

"It was payback," Val admitted with embarrassment. "Remember when Opie invited you to join us for lunch?" He nodded, and Val said, "Frankly I wasn't a fan at the time. When she asked you to join us I promised retribution."

"You said it was okay."

"What else could I say?" There was a subtle challenge in her tone. "We've pulled practical jokes on each other for years. Opie showed me this man in the magazine and said his views on women were archaic. When the Hunter name started popping up around me, I admit to being curious. I suggested we attend, and after I bought the date she said she wouldn't go."

"But she did?"

Val nodded. "I think she feels challenged to divest him of his outdated views."

"Good luck. He's his father's son."

"So are you."

"I'm nothing like Wendell. I don't understand you," Russ declared curtly.

"Same here," Val returned.

Curious, he asked, "Are you still not a fan of mine?"

She shrugged and looked down at the ground. "You were such a pompous windbag that first meeting, challenging my plans and acting like owning a Kentucky farm gave you some sort of God-given right to tell me what to do."

Russ sighed heavily. "That attitude could have cost me my job. I've been warned about expressing my opinion to clients."

"You still get above your raising now and then, but I think I'm beginning to understand you better," she said matter-of-factly.

"Wendell at a bachelor auction," he said with a shake of his head. "Never thought I'd hear that."

"Perhaps you should sign up for the next fund-raiser."

"I don't live in Paris."

"You were raised here. I'm sure they'd consider you."

"No, thanks. I have no interest in being shown like a prize stallion."

"Whoa! Who has a major opinion of himself?" Val teased.

"You know what I mean," Russ said, thankful the darkness hid his embarrassment.

"I'd bid on you," she offered with a little laugh.

"You don't have to buy a date. I'll take you out anytime you like."

"I didn't mean. . . ," Val stuttered.

"I did," Russ said. "Name the date, and I'll prove I know how to show a woman a good time."

"I'm holding you up when. . .you need to get home," Val stammered. "We have the contractor coming early tomorrow to look at the renovations."

Russ nodded his head toward the Sheridan mansion. "I still say that's where you need to be. You really want to, don't you? Tell the truth."

"It's a beautiful home."

"That needs to be occupied. Spending thousands in renovations when that house is already here doesn't strike me as a wise investment."

"Mom would probably go if Daddy would agree."

"You should ask again. You never know. He might have changed his mind."

"I suppose I could. Thanks again, Russ."

"No problem. I'll be in touch tomorrow about those changes, and then we'll see what we can do to get the project underway."

"I'll look forward to your call."

And she would, Val realized as she watched his car taillights disappear into the night. She thought about Russ's feelings toward his brother. What could she do to help the situation? Only one answer came to mind, and she promised to pray for them both.

Back inside she saw the letter her dad had mentioned earlier on the entry table. The return address read KFD Corporation. She opened the envelope and scanned the contents, finding an offer to purchase Sheridan Farm at a price slightly lower than they had paid.

She found her father in his recliner, reading the newspaper. "Take a look at this," she said, passing him the letter.

He read it quickly and handed it back. "I suppose we'll see a few of those over the years."

"How did they know to address it to me? I doubt the tax records show us as the owners."

"I'm sure they did their research," her father said. "Does it bother you?"

She shrugged. "Not really. So what did you think of Russ's plans?"

"The basement is a good idea. If you drop the height on that platform you could avoid having barricades around the structure."

"What about Opie's idea? You think she can make it work?"

"I don't doubt any of my children can do anything they put their minds to. Opie's been a little flighty over the years, but cooking is the one thing she's stuck with. And she's good."

"I can see the benefit of having her here. In fact, I'd be willing to finance her restaurant."

"I don't think she wants you to do that," her dad said.

"I intend to give them money for graduation gifts."

He nodded. "Will you let Heath help you?"

"Even if I do think he's offering out of guilt, I'd be an idiot to say no. He knows those gardens so well."

"I'm sure he has his reasons. All of us want you to do well, Valentine. And if Heath gets to enjoy himself while helping you, I'd say he's the winner."

Her father had a point. For the first time in their lives they had the luxury of time to decide their futures. "I'm glad Russ got those plans worked out. I thought I would have to contact his boss."

Her dad winked at her. "Oh, I don't know. A pretty Truelove woman can generally get what she wants out of a man without threats."

"All I want from Russ is a finished set of plans," she persisted.

"I like him," her father said. "He got along well with the family and didn't seem to mind answering all those questions Jules shot his way. He made a friend for life when he invited her to his office."

"But he really harbors bad feelings toward his brother, and he's so secretive. I'm used to saying what we have to say and moving on."

"It's a rare family that can do that, Val."

Communication was a gift. "He made a good point tonight about renovations being a waste when we already have the big house. He thinks it deserves to be loved by a family again."

"Is that what you think?"

She hesitated. "I think maybe we should give it further consideration. We'll sink thousands into renovating this place when we already own the perfect house."

"We don't need the renovations, Val. This home has served us well for years."

"But the Sheridans' house has pluses, too. More room for the family. The security system. This house will be smaller with four adult children living here."

"Perhaps the adult children should consider living in the big house?" her father suggested with a raised brow.

"Not without everyone else," she protested.

He grinned. "I told you before, Val. If it's what the family wants, I'll go."

"Will you talk to Mom?"

"If you tell me why you want to move."

She must be as transparent as glass. "I love that house," Val said simply. "I have ever since I can remember. Living there would be a dream come true."

"Have you sought God's will in the matter?"

"Probably not as much as I should."

"Let's pray over it and hear what the contractor has to say tomorrow. If the Lord convicts us that it's His will, I'll talk to your mom."

Val hugged him. "Thanks, Daddy. I think I'll go talk to Opie about her plans."

She walked down the hallway to the room she shared with her sisters. Wrapped in her robe with a towel around her head, Opie sat on the bed polishing her toenails. She glanced up. "Russ get off okay?"

"Why wouldn't he?" Val asked.

"I thought maybe his head had exploded from all those questions Jules asked," Opie remarked, dodging the stuffed animal Jules threw at her. "He had a distinct deer-in-the-headlights look a few times there when all of us got started."

Jules grabbed her robe and headed for the shower, leaving them alone.

"I think it came closer to bursting when I told him you went out with Wendell." Val dropped down on her bed. "He accused me of trying to interfere in their relationship."

"What did you say to that?"

"That it had nothing to do with him."

Opie removed the towel and fluffed the damp tendrils. "Russ gets along well with the family, don't you think?"

Val refused to let her matchmaking family push her in that direction. Russ Hunter might be on her mind a lot lately, but their relationship was business. Wasn't it? "If you're so determined to play matchmaker, why don't you work on Heath and Jane?"

"Is that why you made her your assistant?"

"She needed the job, and I know she'll be an asset. She has a lot of managerial experience. Just wait. You'll see how good she is."

"Have you seen how Heath looks at her?" Opie asked.

"I think he's always had a crush on Jane but thought she was out of his league."

"And now she's going to be working here all day while he's landscaping your project."

"I don't know about that, Opie," Val said, expressing her concern. "I can't reconcile his spending years in college to come home and landscape."

"You heard what Mom said. It's Heath's choice."

"But is he doing it for the right reason?"

"You told Rom he had time when he went for the interview. Why not offer Heath the same option?"

Opie had a point. "I'll talk to him. Is this restaurant what you want to do?"

She shrugged. "Ideas are bouncing around in my head faster than I can process. Even more since Russ mentioned expanding the kitchen in the structure. I could run a catering business from there."

"You just like the idea of having a commercial kitchen at your disposal," Val teased.

"Every chef's dream," Opie agreed.

"Nothing has to be decided right away."

Opie pumped lotion into her hand and smoothed it over her arms and legs. "Russ really redeemed himself with that plan today, didn't he?"

"Yes," Val said. "I couldn't believe you said what you did."

Opie grinned. "Sorry. It slipped out. I tried to backpedal."

Val giggled. "We noticed. When I looked at the plans I knew my brides would experience my feelings when they stood on that overlook." She hesitated. "Opie, what do you think about moving into the Sheridans' house?"

Her head popped up. "Having my own bedroom? Sign me up."

"Daddy and I are praying over the situation. Will you pray, too?"

Opie nodded.

"There's something else. I feel God is directing me to visit Grandfather Truelove."

"I doubt Daddy would jump on board with that."

"Daddy has to forgive Grandfather. I think God wants us to help him find peace."

"I'll add that to my prayer list," Opie promised.

"Thanks." They heard the bathroom door open. Val grabbed her robe. "Wonder if there's any hot water left."

"Probably not. That's one thing we need to change if we stay here," Opie said.

Later that night, after the house grew silent, Val found herself unable to sleep. She had prayed, thanking God as always and seeking guidance on the family's move. She had also prayed about the situation between her father and grandfather. Thoughts of that led her back to the situation between Russ and Wendell, and she prayed for them, too. He'd really done well with the plans. She thanked God for yet another answered prayer in Russ's excellent design.

That comment about buying a date had certainly backfired on her. She'd only wanted to lighten the mood after telling him about Opie and Wendell. When he'd said that about knowing how to treat a woman she wondered what dating Russ would be like. For years she had waited for God to send the man He intended for her. Could Russ be the one?

Quietly, she slipped out of the bed and knelt to pray.

God, I don't know what You have in mind, but please guide me through this new venture. Keep my family safe and happy, and shower them with all the blessings You have in store for each of them. Give the graduates clear minds and help them make decisions that will improve their lives. Bless Daddy with the success of this farm and me with my business. And make us all better servants to You.

Chapter 8

W hat's the latest on the Truelove project?" Randall King asked the following morning when they met in the hallway.

The desire to keep walking was strong. "A few alterations, but she basically okayed the plans."

His boss smiled. "Excellent. And you recommended Kevin Flint?"

The burning sensation in his stomach increased. "We've got a problem there. I explained that a bigger company could get the job done more quickly, but she insists on giving the job to smaller contractors. She's not budging on that."

"You didn't convince her you made your recommendations based on what's best for the project. Doesn't she trust you?"

He made it sound as if Russ hadn't tried to change Val's mind. Trust had nothing to do with the situation. She viewed this as an opportunity to help the less fortunate. "She has very definite plans for her business," Russ told him. "She's already said she'll find someone else to carry forth the vision if we can't come to an agreement."

"Get her in here and let's discuss this."

"I'll see when she's available. She's very busy."

"We can go there," Randall clipped out. "I want to see what they've done."

Russ didn't like the sound of that. Still, he doubted the man could smooth talk any of the Trueloves. He'd learned the hard way that they knew what they wanted and expected of the people they hired.

"Yes, sir. Is there a time that's better for you?" Russ asked as he led the way into his office. The man pulled out his PDA and listed several appointment times. Russ carefully noted them and promised to get back to him.

Val wouldn't like this, Russ thought. He figured she'd construe it as his effort to coerce her into doing what he'd recommended. That definitely wasn't the case.

As he settled at his desk, Russ wondered why Mr. King insisted Kevin Flint be brought in. He knew the two men were great friends, but Flint Construction had plenty of business already.

Aware Val wouldn't be in the house at this time of day, he dialed her cell number. As the phone rang, he considered the previous evening. He'd actually enjoyed himself. And while he wouldn't admit it to anyone else, Russ envied the devotion of the Truelove family. In the years since the death of his parents he had felt alone, particularly when he found himself in family settings.

When Val spoke of the monetary gifts she planned for the graduates, he couldn't help but think she'd already given up so much for them. He found it difficult to believe she was willing to give more.

"Hi, it's Russ," he said quickly. "Hope I'm not interrupting."

"I'm due a break."

"Thanks again for dinner. I really enjoyed myself."

"Consider yourself welcome any time."

Taking a deep breath, Russ jumped into the reason for his call. "Mr. King asked me to contact you and set up a time to visit the site."

"Is that the next step once the client approves the plans?"

Russ swallowed, feeling deceitful as he said, "I think he just wants to get an idea of what you have in the works."

"When did you have in mind? Morning is best for me."

"Ten o'clock okay?" Russ asked after double-checking the list.

"Nine would be better," Val said.

"I don't think he has an opening then."

"Ten is fine. Come to the English garden."

"Uh, Val, where is that?"

"Behind the house. Where I was working when you came by with the first set of plans."

"Oh, okay. How did the contractor visit go?"

"Like you thought. We don't have the final figures yet, but he said it would cost a lot to do all we want to do. I talked with Daddy, and we're praying over moving into the big house."

"Hope it works out for you."

"Thanks, Russ. What did you think of Daddy's suggestion that we lower the structure?"

The conversation turned to the pros and cons of changing the plans.

"I'll make those revisions this afternoon and bring the plans out tomorrow. Please thank your parents again for their hospitality."

"I will. See you soon."

Early the following morning Russ found himself in the passenger seat of his employer's expensive sports car. While he enjoyed the luxury of the fine automobile, he dreaded the upcoming meeting.

"You know Ms. Truelove best," Randall King said. "How should we approach her?"

Russ had learned what he knew the hard way, and deep down inside he suspected this visit was a mistake. "Advising fast action is vital for her business, I suppose," he said, hoping that didn't sound too stupid.

Randall glanced at him. "You'd think that would be important. Time and money are key factors in getting any new operation off the ground. Does she strike you as hesitant about this project? Maybe she's in no hurry to see the structure completed?"

"No, sir. She's one hundred percent ready to start. From what she's told me, this has been a longtime dream she had no hope of achieving until she won the money."

"That's incredible luck."

"Luck isn't a word the Trueloves use," Russ told him. "They attribute it to God answering Val's prayers."

Randall glanced at him. "Really?"

"Yes, sir. I wish He'd answer some of mine like that."

"You a praying man, Russ?"

"No, sir," he admitted.

"There are some good connections to be made in church. Lots of networking gets done on Sunday mornings."

He might not be a Christian, but Russ had attended church enough to know that using God's house for anything other than worship wasn't the act of a wise man.

"I spoke with Kevin just this past Sunday about pending projects. He's very interested in this job."

Probably thinks he can gouge Val outrageously, Russ thought.

Randall King slowed and hit the signal as he approached the entrance to Sheridan Farm. Like other farms in the area, a stack stone fence stood there with a plaque indicating the property name. "I haven't been here since Mrs. Sheridan died. The old man didn't entertain after that."

"It's a definite showplace," Russ agreed.

They were surprised when a guard came forward at the closed gate. Russ wondered what had precipitated the need for protection. After giving their names, the man checked his list and directed them through.

"Why do they have security?" Randall asked.

"I don't know. There wasn't anyone here the other night." Russ indicated the area to their right. "Park here. Val said she'd be in the garden behind the house."

As they approached, Russ noted how they had worked to restore the beautiful garden to its former glory. The difference between that first visit and now was incredible.

"Watch your step," Val called when they approached the area where the stones were missing.

"Hello, Ms. Truelove. Good to see you," Randall King said, extending his hand as he moved forward.

Val pulled off her garden gloves and shook his hand. "You, too, Mr. King. Russ."

"You've been busy," Russ commented.

Val nodded and looked back at the expansive area. "I have a wedding and reception scheduled in this garden for August."

"You're already scheduling?"

His boss sounded surprised. "Kelly is having her wedding here," Russ offered, avoiding Val's gaze when he realized she wouldn't like his sharing that information. He looked at her and mouthed, "Sorry."

Val gave him a hopeless shake of her head and turned her attention to Randall King.

"Certainly a beautiful place. I was just telling Russ I attended many parties here before Mrs. Sheridan died."

"She did love to entertain," Val said, remembering the elderly woman fondly. "Would you like a tour? We're concentrating our efforts on the English and Japanese gardens."

They strolled along the paths, discussing the various plants that had begun to bloom. "I adore spring," Val said. "It's so wonderful to see the flowers after the long cold winter."

"The cycle of life," Randall King commented.

Val glanced at Russ. "I asked the contractor to give me quotes on smoke alarms, doors, and emergency lighting for the B and B."

"You found a contractor?" Russ asked.

"Not for the structure."

He almost groaned when she gave Randall King the perfect lead-in. He grabbed the opportunity. "Russ tells me he recommended Kevin Flint's company."

"He did," Val agreed. "And I explained I want to provide the opportunity to a smaller company. I'm sure Mr. Flint does excellent work, but I feel this is a chance to give back to the community."

"But surely you understand we only have your best interests at heart," Randall said. "As a businesswoman, you need the job completed in a timely, efficient manner by someone who knows the ins and outs of construction."

"I do know that," she agreed. "And my plan is to find the contractor who can complete the plan as well as Mr. Flint's company."

As Russ watched the interplay between them, he realized it pleased him she didn't allow the man to intimidate her.

"You realize we cannot recommend these other contractors?"

Appearing somewhat surprised, Val asked, "Does Prestige only do business with one contractor? I would have thought a company your size would have many contacts for their various projects. Giving preferential treatment to one company doesn't strike me as timely or efficient. What happens when Mr. Flint's company has more projects than it can handle at any given time?"

"He hires more crews."

"How can he be aware of what's going on at the different sites?"

"Kevin is the owner," Randall said. "He has site foremen who report back to him."

"I suppose that's an okay way to do business, but I want to be more involved in the process. I plan to know exactly what's going on with my business at any given time."

Randall looked skeptical. "While I appreciate the motivation behind that at startup, you will find that as the business grows you'll be forced to depend on others to keep you apprised of day-to-day operations."

"I don't think you believe that," Val told him. "You gave this assignment to Russ, and yet your presence here indicates a personal involvement on your part."

Good one, Russ thought, glancing over to find his boss's expression growing tighter by the minute.

"I'm sure Russ told you we approved the plans night before last," Val said. "I'm eager to get started. Would you like to see the site?"

"Certainly."

Russ groaned inwardly at the thought of the jeep and his boss's expensive suit. Relief filled him when today's vehicle of choice was a golf cart. He wondered why she'd stuck him in that old jeep as he settled in the back, leaving the front passenger seat for his employer.

"Will you get the gate?" she asked Randall King a couple of minutes later.

"I've got it." Russ jumped out and ran to release the latch, reversing the process after Val drove through.

"Good view," Randall commented when she pulled up before the vista.

"God truly had a red-letter day when He created the Kentucky bluegrass region."

"Spoken like a true Kentuckian."

"Imagine this venue with all the accoutrements of romance—a beautiful structure, happy guests, moonlight, stars, and abiding love."

"You evoke many possibilities in my mind," Randall said.

Russ doubted the man had any romantic thoughts beyond the dollars and cents of business.

"I hope to evoke more than a few memories over the years," Val agreed. "Our intent is that Your Wedding Place becomes the premier venue for weddings within Kentucky and maybe an even broader appeal to the bridal community. Before we're finished I'd love to hear Your Wedding Place become a name on every bride's lips."

Randall King nodded. "Given your funds, you can do whatever you want. Why weddings?"

"The money is a blessing," Val agreed. "We've been able to make decisions that will affect the future of every member of the family. But none of us believes God provided the money to be wasted. I'm hoping this business will secure my future. In turn, each of my siblings will do the same with their plans."

"And if this fails?"

"We put our faith in God and trust Him for our success," Val said confidently.

Randall nodded as he glanced at his watch. "Regretfully, I must get back to the office for a lunch meeting. I hope to see more as things develop."

Val flashed him a brilliant smile. "Who knows? Perhaps you'll even avail yourself of our services one day."

"Perhaps I will."

Russ felt a surge of jealousy as he watched Randall King flirt with Val. The man had already left one wife behind, and if the rumors were true, he dabbled with the affections of a great number of other women. He should warn Val to steer clear.

She parked the cart near the sports car, and after Randall King climbed out she looked at Russ and whispered, "We need to talk."

He'd known this was coming and could tell from her tone she wasn't pleased. "I'll call you later."

"Do that."

"Ready, Russ?"

"Yes, sir."

"It's been a pleasure, Ms. Truelove."

"Please call me Val."

"Only if you call me Randall. I hope you will reconsider allowing Kevin Flint to build your structure. You'll find him very reliable."

"I'm sorry, but no. I know I can find a suitable contractor who deserves a chance."

"Full of herself, isn't she?" Randall King said minutes later as they drove off the property.

"She knows what she wants."

"Does she?" he inquired blandly. "She's a little girl playing grownup in the real world. I don't think she truly has a clue about what lies ahead for her."

"What do you mean?"

"Let's just say she's not chosen an easy path. That type of business comes and goes. There's no security. But I suppose with her funds she can keep trying until she gets it right."

"I think she has a good idea," Russ said.

"You're here to do a job. And I suggest you complete it as quickly as possible," Randall suggested. "Prestige has other clients we need to focus on."

The man's attitude seemed to sour more with each word. She'd really upset the big boss, Russ thought. "I told you she has very definite ideas about what she wants."

Randall's piercing gaze focused on him, his words accusatory when he spoke. "But you allowed me to waste my time?"

Russ resented Randall King's attempt to turn the situation on him. "I'm sorry, sir, but I did warn you."

"You did nothing to support me in convincing her to change her mind."

Russ closed his eyes, holding back the sigh that threatened to escape. "I've tried. I hoped that hearing it from you would make her rethink the situation."

"I don't expect you to give up. I want Kevin Flint on that job."

Russ didn't understand his insistence.

"When you hire Prestige Designs, you receive the benefit of my years of experience. Can you believe she actually thinks she's going to be hands-on with every aspect of her business? She's a lamb in a world of wolves."

After watching the two of them earlier, Russ thought Val could hold her own with any wolf. He listened to Randall King vent throughout the remainder of the drive and was glad when his boss pulled into his parking space at the office. "Wrap up the plans for the Truelove project and move on," he ordered as they entered the building.

Russ wanted to argue there was considerable work to be completed but decided it best to keep quiet for now.

Randall King stomped off, and Russ felt overwhelming dread. He told Cheryl he was going to lunch and checked to make sure he had his cell so he could stop along the way and call Val. Gut instinct warned him not to call from the office. Once in his car, he dialed and waited for an answer.

"What was that visit about this morning?" she demanded without greeting. "Your boss may be big on Kevin Flint, but I've heard things about him and his company and don't care to become involved. I'm beginning to wonder if I made a mistake by choosing Prestige Designs."

"I'm sorry we blindsided you." Russ meant that. In the past he'd probably have shrugged and gone on with his business; but he liked Val, and now that they had sorted out the plans he looked forward to working with her. If Mr. King allowed him to continue, Russ thought. "I should have warned you when I called, but please understand I'm in a precarious position. I'm close to completing my internship at Prestige. Once I pass my exam it will be different. I can't jeopardize all my hard work."

"Common courtesy would have been a heads-up that he was gunning for me to hire his contractor," Val said, sounding none too happy.

Between these two he couldn't win. "I get the point. He's not very happy right now, either."

"Do I need to take my plans and move on?"

"I wish you wouldn't," Russ said. "As I told you before this is a first in my career, and I'd like to see it completed."

She remained silent for a few seconds longer. "I don't like being played."

"I tried to tell him, but he felt we could talk you into changing your mind."

"And you agreed he should try?"

"What choice did I have, Val?" Russ asked, his ire rising. "The man is my boss."

"You already pointed that out, but I'd like to believe you feel some loyalty toward your clients as well."

"What would you have done? You worked for Maddy. I'm sure there were times when she wanted you to do things you didn't necessarily agree with. Did you tell her no?"

"I understand what you're up against, but I don't like being challenged either. It's important I carry through on my plans with or without Prestige. Why does he want Kevin Flint involved anyway? I'd think the two of them would have bigger projects to pursue."

Russ agreed with her. "I don't know."

"I'll give you the benefit of the doubt, but please don't allow this to happen again. Company loyalty aside, you need to understand I won't tolerate deception."

"When did you get the security guard?" Russ asked, hoping to change the subject.

"Today." She told him about Derrick's visit. "Daddy wants me to hire a driver."

"Other farms have their own police forces to protect the horses. Don't you consider yourself as important as any horse?"

"I'm not interested in being followed around."

"But you realize it's a practical consideration."

"I suppose so," Val said. "For all of us. Anyone who wanted to get to me could easily do it through any member of my family. They're going to be upset."

"But safe, and that's all that matters. Hey, the garden looks great. You'll be ready for the wedding soon."

"That brings me to another subject."

"I know. Kelly's wedding. It just slipped out."

"What if she doesn't plan to invite him?"

"She already has. He won't come though. He'll offer his regrets and send a gift. He doesn't socialize with the lower ranks of his staff."

"I don't care for your involvement in my business. Having access to information involving Your Wedding Place does not give you the right to apprise others of my plans."

Russ couldn't help himself. "Well, truthfully I didn't get the information from you. Kelly told me. So basically, I shared what she told me."

Val's heavy sigh reached across the miles. "Just finish the plans, Russ. I have a few contractors lined up to come and look over the job. I want to get this in the works quickly."

They had left the farm barely an hour ago. "Where did you find contractors?" he asked curiously.

"I figured I'd better find someone if I didn't want Kevin Flint shoved down my throat. A couple of companies in Lexington showed an interest."

"When are you meeting with them? I need to be in on the discussions."

Val gave him the appointment times and wrapped up the conversation with a warning reminder that she didn't expect any more surprises.

Chapter 9

Maddy brought her bride out on Saturday morning, and the woman fell in love with the Japanese garden.

"It will be even better by your wedding day," Val promised.

"I can't imagine that," Leah Bainbridge said, looking around at the perfect arrangement of water, stones, and greenery. "Do you live in the house?"

Val shook her head. "My family lives elsewhere on the property."

When the woman looked surprised, Val fought back the temptation to explain the recent acquisition. She'd learned the less said, the better.

"And this garden is available on the fourth Saturday in August?"

"It is. We've only recently begun booking weddings. You're our second bride."

"Second? I don't—"

Maddy interceded quickly. "Val worked as my assistant for years. She knows the business inside and out. In fact, I depended on her to procure the best venues. She does a masterful job. I'm so thankful she's started this business."

"Your Wedding Place will do everything possible to fulfill your needs," Val assured her.

Leah nodded. "Is it possible to have the reception here as well?"

"We could set up tables and chairs around the area after the ceremony. Or, we plan to bring in a large tent for a wedding the weekend before yours. We could make that available for your use."

The woman looked at Maddy.

"The tent sounds like a perfect solution. We'll discuss it further and get back to you."

"I'll e-mail you the cost sheets," Val said.

After the women left, Val felt a huge sense of accomplishment. She hadn't even opened for business and already had two bookings. That certainly boded well for the future. The desire to share the news with someone was strong. Opie had left for New York that morning, and her mother had gone with Heath and Jane to run errands after driving her to the airport. Without thinking, she dialed Russ's number.

"Hi. I just booked my second wedding. It's the week after Kelly's, but we'll be able to use the tent set up for both weddings. I'm so happy."

"I can tell," Russ said. "Hang on."

She listened to the music for a couple of minutes before he returned. "Sorry. I had a client on the other line."

"I caught you at a bad time. I'll let you—"

"It's okay," Russ said. "I have to get some information together and call back. Would you like to go out tonight and celebrate?"

"Yes," she said without hesitation.

An unfamiliar feeling of anticipation filled Val that night as she walked into the living room to await Russ's arrival. She'd found herself going back and forth ever since she'd said yes, wondering if she'd made the right decision.

She wore one of the sundresses she'd bought on the recent shopping trip along with a pair of sandals. Her freshly washed hair hung down her back.

When Russ rang the bell she greeted him and accepted the bouquet of spring flowers he offered. "I should have done this when Kelly booked."

"Before or after I bit your head off for telling her my business plans?" Val asked with a grin.

"Maybe before if I'd been faster on the draw," Russ countered with an easy smile.

He drove to the French restaurant Kelly had recommended in downtown Paris. The warm atmosphere of the old commercial building was evidently popular with the locals. After noting the way people stared and whispered, he said, "I'm sorry. It didn't occur to me people would act this way. I suppose it has to do with your recent celebrity status. Becoming rich overnight is a major accomplishment."

"I certainly don't want a lottery win to become my biggest achievement in life," Val said. "And I wouldn't mind people treating me like they did before the money."

Russ seated her in the chair that put her back to the group. "Would you give the money back if you had to decide again?"

"Maybe. At least on some days. I was so unprepared for instant wealth. People believe they can handle it, but I can list two negatives for every positive." She sighed. "I always said I wanted to get to the point where a hundred dollars wasn't a lot of money."

Russ grinned. "You're definitely past that."

Val shook her head. "No. It's still a lot of money. I've made a couple of spur-of-the-moment decisions I don't regret, but managing this much money isn't as easy as people think. Every decision involves a great deal of prayer. Daddy's managed Sheridan Farm for years, but even he agrees there's an unexpected level of responsibility that comes with ownership. Basically, we handed the controls over to God and listen when He tells us what to do."

"I'm sure it'll get easier with time." After Russ ordered an appetizer of calamari, he lifted his water glass in a toast.

"I'm so happy. I can't help but hope this is a hint of what's to come."

"You say Maddy referred this bride?"

"She's agreed to recommend Your Wedding Place. I need to contact other planners and get the interest going there as well."

"You should have a launch party. Allow the planners to stroll the gardens."

Val liked the idea. "We could do tours and pass out literature. Opie could handle the refreshments."

"What happened to keeping a low profile?"

"It occurred to me that publicizing Your Wedding Place gives it a stronger foundation than secrecy. If someone steals the idea in my head, I can't argue the point. If people are aware it's my business, I stand a better chance. I considered franchising."

Russ let out a low whistle. "That's expensive."

"And it might make sense if the venue idea caught on, but given the cost I decided to invest the money back into my business."

"Give them what they want so they'll come?"

"I hope so."

After they placed their orders for the house special chicken, Russ suggested, "Let's talk about something other than work."

"Like what?" Val asked.

"Tell me about you," Russ invited.

"Not much you don't already know. I was born in Kentucky and basically grew up here in Paris as the oldest of seven."

"What's that like?"

"You're never alone," Val offered with a tongue-in-cheek grin. "You've witnessed it for yourself a couple of times."

"You never wanted to break away from the family?"

"No. I like having them around. I'm glad Opie and the twins are back. I missed them."

"Do you want a large family?" Russ asked.

"I'll take what God gives me. I've always thought three kids would be good."

"Why three?"

"I feel sorry for that half kid in the averages," she said, grinning at Russ's surprised expression. "I figure if I take my half kid and someone else's, we can get a whole kid into the world." She broke into laughter. "Just kidding, Russ." The irony struck her, and Val laughed harder. "Kidding," she repeated. "I'm sorry. Guess you have to be there," she said, wiping her eyes carefully so she didn't smear her eyeliner.

Russ laughed at her fit of giggles. "It's a good number. I know what you mean about the age gaps. There are five years between Wendell and me."

"Your mom must have been surprised when you came along."

"Wendell's mom died when he was three. Our dad married my mother a year later. Then he went away to school not long after I was born. We never had much of a relationship."

"You didn't attend school here?"

"Dad sent us to boarding school. I spent very little time in Kentucky after that."

Russ's life struck Val as sad. He'd spent his formative years under the guidance of others. When he could have forged a deeper relationship with his family, his parents had died. Their loss had resulted in the estrangement over the farm that destroyed any hope of Russ's forming a relationship with his brother.

"It's not as if you can't afford your own place," Russ said, taking the conversation back to her.

"I could." Val's shoulders lifted in a tiny shrug. "If I decided that's what I want. I need to remain close to the farm since my business is there."

"Yet another reason to live in the Sheridans' house. It's more than large enough to hold all of you."

"We're looking at options. If I convert to a B and B, I'd have to live there when guests are in the house. If I rent to overnight parties, they wouldn't want me around."

"That house is much too valuable to rent out like a hotel room," Russ objected. "People are too careless of other people's things."

"Things could happen even if I lived there. We're back to business," Val pointed out. "Your turn. Where do you live?"

"I have a two-bedroom, two-and-a-half-bath condo in Lexington. I considered renting, but the condo was the better investment."

"And it's yours, and you can make changes if you want," Val said.

Russ's smile told her he got her point. "And if I respond to that we're back to discussing business."

"Yes," Val agreed, "but then business is key to our relationship, don't you think? You invited me to dinner to celebrate my latest success."

"The most recent of many," Russ pronounced.

"I pray that's the case. I do like your idea of a launch party. In fact, I can hardly wait to start planning."

"You really want this, don't you?"

Val felt self-conscious as she noted the way he studied her. "More than you can imagine. Did you ever dream of something you knew you'd never get to do?"

Russ nodded. "My dream seemed more achievable in my youth when I thought I'd inherit a portion of the farm. I honestly believed I could have it all."

"You could still own a farm," Val said. "Perhaps not as grand as Hunter Farm, but there are other acreages available."

"And you could have had your business," Russ said. "Not as a site provider but a procurer."

"So we've limited our visions?" Val asked. "I suppose I could have found a way, but it always seemed impossible. Now that everything is unfolding, I feel God has worked the most incredible miracle in my life."

Russ took a sip of his water. "You talk about God a lot."

"He's important to me. I'm nothing without Him," Val said simply.

Russ's puzzlement forced her to explain.

"I can't take full credit for my accomplishments," Val said. "It isn't anything I do. God knows the plans He has for me. Yet He gave me freedom to make choices and even knows the choices I'll make."

Russ frowned and shook his head. "I doubt God has time to worry about me."

"Why do you doubt Him? He cares about His lambs."

Her words reminded Russ of Randall King's comment about Val being a lamb in a world of wolves. "I've never been referred to as a lamb before."

"Come to church with me," Val invited impulsively. "You're an educated, informed man. Don't you think it's fair to give God a chance before making the decision not to follow Him?"

The way Russ concentrated on the food, placing his knife and fork just so, folding his napkin and doing everything but look at her, provided her answer. Seeing his discomfort, Val retreated. "This meal is really delicious."

"Not as good as your mother's," Russ said.

"Mom's adapting to Opie wanting to try different techniques with her basic meat-and-potatoes foods."

"They're excellent cooks."

Val smiled. "If I tell them that, you'll have a standing invitation for dinner."

"I wouldn't mind that."

"There's always room for one more around the Truelove dining table."

They finished their meal and opted for coffee instead of dessert. "I really appreciate your celebrating with me," she said as she stirred sugar into her cup.

"I'm happy for you, Val. I don't think I realized how much all this meant to you until tonight. I look forward to playing my part in seeing your dreams fulfilled."

"Thanks, Russ. I need all the help I can get."

"Oh, I'm beginning to see you as a mover and shaker in this world."

"That might not be a good thing."

"Whatever it is, I'm happy to be part of your successes."

Chapter 10

With August drawing near, the pace picked up around the Truelove home. From the time the younger kids wrapped up their school year in early June, they jumped in to help wherever they could. The days of summer rolled forward as they all worked toward a shared goal, and together they had made great strides with the gardens.

She and Heath had talked, and she agreed he should do what he wanted. She even paid him a salary, insisting she'd do the same if she hired someone for the job. Opie had done some stints as a private chef and helped when she had free time. She continued to review her options and assisted their mother in preparing family meals and taking care of the house.

Rom accepted the Lexington job. When he asked for apartment leads, Russ offered his guest room for as long as Rom needed. Russ and the twins shared many common interests and often did things together.

Jane added joy to every activity with her laughter and teasing. Val couldn't help but smile as she considered the conversation they'd had earlier when she asked how Jane felt about antiques.

"I suppose they're the distant cousins to my decorating style. Early castoffs."

Val explained her plan. Antique shops filled downtown Paris, and she hoped to replace the pieces the Sheridans' son had taken from the house.

"I'll try anything once," Jane said. "You should know I know nothing about antiques."

"Me either. I think it might be fun to see what we can find. I particularly want to retain the authenticity in the first floor rooms."

Jane had agreed, and Val planned to set a time for their antique hunting.

Jane and Sammy were a good fit to their family. From the moment she'd laid eyes on Sammy, their mom had fallen in love with her, and the toddler spent most of her days playing with Cindy Truelove nearby. When Jane asked if it was too much, Val's mom told her she'd missed having small children around the house.

Val knew her mother wanted grandchildren; and while being married and having a family had always seemed to be one of her more achievable dreams, here she was single with her business capturing first place. Life certainly had taken a full turn.

Her prayers that the Lord would guide her to the right man remained unanswered. Nevertheless, when she found Russ playing around in her thoughts more often, Val didn't know what to think. She liked him a lot, but the fact that he didn't have a relationship with Jesus Christ made her think twice about getting involved with him.

They had interviewed a number of contractors and found one that could handle the project. Todd Bigelow's company might not be the largest in Lexington, but after talking with him Val knew he was the best man for the job. A believer like her, he felt led of God to do the best possible job for every client. She knew he would have said no if he didn't feel he could handle the work.

Russ called late one afternoon and suggested they get together to discuss the project. Tired after a busy day, she had refused but then relented when he insisted it was important they talk. That evening, he visited with her family while he waited for her.

"You look nice," he said, rising to his feet when she entered the room.

"Thanks."

He took her hand, calling good night to the others before they walked out to his newer model sports car.

Russ drove to his favorite Lexington restaurant, an out-of-the-way place he said would give them anonymity. They followed their waitress through the cozy old building to a table near the window facing the street. After studying the menu Val ordered grilled pork chops, and he opted for fried chicken, both with a variety of vegetables. The scents from the pie store next door nearly drove them crazy.

"I'm not leaving here without dessert," Russ said.

"Maybe we should just skip dinner and go straight for the pies."

"What would your mother think?" he teased. "Okay, so what's your choice? Colonnade or pavilion? You need to decide so I can order the trim."

"The house is colonial, and I love the columns; but I'm not sure I want a big Greek-style structure out there," Val said. "I saw something the other day with a wrought-iron top I really liked. Still, I don't want the brides thinking we've created a folly and saying no thanks to that either."

When reviewing the various structures, she'd learned a folly was a building considered strictly as a decoration. She had no place in her project for something like that.

"If you make the other structure an enclosed fabric-covered building, you don't really want canopies here, do you?" Russ asked.

"Yes and no. I like the idea of being open to the sky, but some brides will want protection for their guests. Could we do the wrought iron with rods underneath so we can connect shade fabric if requested?"

He found an envelope in his pocket and quickly sketched swirls and twirls into a design for the iron. "What about this? Panels domed over the top of the structure."

"How would they be supported?"

"We could bring the wrought iron down support posts. Or use arches."

"The arches could be placed to mimic windows," Val said thoughtfully.

"So it's going to be a pavilion?"

Val felt torn. The right look was crucial. "I don't know. What do you think?"

"Black wrought iron would probably suit the area best."

"Then let's make it a pavilion."

"Mr. King is pushing me to wrap up your project."

Val appreciated his candor. "You think it's because I wouldn't choose his contractor?"

"I have no idea, but I plan to keep working with you until the job is completed."

"Aren't you afraid you'll get into trouble with your boss?"

"I understand why that might be a concern for you, but I promise not to compromise the project for fear of losing my job."

"We'll work it out," Val said.

&

She had believed they could—until Todd called to say the plans had not been approved because of missing documents. Val wanted to scream. With the demands of two weddings and the launch party, she didn't need this. After taking a few minutes to pray over the situation, she dialed Russ's cell phone.

"Hi. What's up?"

"Nothing, thanks to you," she ground out angrily.

"What do you mean?"

Val knew she needed to calm down. "Todd checked online to see if the plans were approved, and evidently they were rejected because they were incomplete. When did you plan to let me know?"

"Why didn't he call me?"

No doubt that's what Kevin Flint would have done, Val thought. "Because he wants to start work for *me*," she stressed, "and can't seem to get a permit. You need to sort this out. I don't want to lose this contractor, and we don't need any more holdups."

Thus far they had dealt with problem after problem. The initial plan creation had taken longer than expected, and then Prestige had delivered the package to the wrong review board. Now there was no permit. Val couldn't help but wonder what was going on.

Russ called back an hour later to say everything was under control. "I know those documents were in the plans I gave Mr. King."

"Why would you give them to him?"

"Because that's the way he does business," Russ told her. "He delivers them personally to the planning office."

"The wrong planning office," Val emphasized. "I hope this gets resolved quickly. Todd's eager to start construction, but he can't wait forever for permits."

"I'm on it."

"Times like these make even the pitiful offers like that one from KFD Corporation look good."

"Who?" Russ asked.

"I have no idea who they are. I received a special delivery letter with a post office box in Lexington. I had Mr. Henderson reject the offer."

"Why haven't you mentioned this before?"

"Because selling the farm isn't a consideration," Val admitted, suddenly shamed by her fit of pique. When would she learn to stop reacting?

"I don't understand. Why would they make an offer when you've just bought the place?"

"I have no idea. Sheridan Farm isn't for sale at any price."

After they hung up, Val still felt ill at ease about the situation. What had happened? Had Russ intentionally delayed the project? He seemed to have corrected the problem easily enough.

She didn't want to doubt Russ, and yet she couldn't help but feel something wasn't right. He knew how important this was to her. Even his guarantees didn't make Val feel reassured. She wondered exactly what had happened. Russ had been so confident the information was there, but it was possible he had made a mistake.

Val bowed her head in prayer, beseeching the Lord to bless her project. Pulling her work gloves on, she found Heath placing koi fish in the pond in the Japanese garden. She shared the news with him. "I don't understand these delays."

"I'm sure this type of thing happens all the time, Val."

"Maybe, but Russ said Randall King delivered the information. Wouldn't he check to be sure everything was there?"

Heath reached for another container. "Not if he assumed Russ had done his job. Do you honestly believe Russ would harm your project?"

The thought made her feel sick to her stomach. "I don't want to, Heath, but I can't help but remember that first meeting. He got so upset that he allowed his personal feelings to overwhelm his professional opinion. What if deep down inside he still feels that way?"

"I don't think that's the case. He created an acceptable set of plans and has stuck it out despite his boss's orders to move on."

"More than acceptable," Val agreed. "As I said, I don't know why it bothers me."

"Maybe because you like Russ and don't want to have doubts about him."

She did, and yet Val accepted they were different on too many levels. She suspected involving herself with Russ would be relationship suicide. "He is a nice guy. I like working with him."

"I suspect it's more than that," Heath said.

"No matter how good a friend Russ is, there can't be more," Val said.

"Because he's not a Christian," Heath said. "It's too bad. He has a solid future ahead of him, and I don't think you'd have to be concerned he's after your money."

The Truelove children had the best role models in two Christian parents.

They had witnessed firsthand what it took to have a harmonious life and to live in one accord with God.

"Only one thing is certain, Val. God is in control."

"He is, and I'm so very thankful for that."

∽

Russ couldn't get the Truelove project off his mind. How had that document gone missing? He was positive it had been there when he double-checked the plans before handing them over. Val probably thought he'd done this on purpose. Luckily enough it had been resolved, but he would pay closer attention and make sure nothing else happened.

He glanced down at the notes he'd doodled while talking with Val. Who was this KFD Corporation that had made the offer for the farm? Something about the situation bugged him, and he made a mental note to follow up.

He needed to talk with Val. Make her understand. It seemed strange to think he'd been working with her for so long now. They'd come a long way from their first meeting.

At first he'd wondered why her every conversation seemed to come back to the same subject—God. He'd attended church as a kid, but now something better always seemed to crop up on Sundays, whether he was hung over from a late night or wanted to golf or sleep in.

He thought about Val's carefully crafted question and wondered why she equated intelligence to serving God. The bad things that had happened to him weren't exactly what he'd expect from a loving God. Still, Russ had learned to respect Val and her family and their desire to do the right things in life. They'd opened his eyes to why certain things mattered to people who followed God.

He hadn't taken Val up on her invitation to attend church, but he'd awakened early on a couple of Sunday mornings and found himself wondering if he'd get anything out of the experience. Maybe he'd attend after Kelly got back from her honeymoon. That way he'd know someone other than the Trueloves.

∽

The week preceding Kelly Dickerson's wedding had them all working overtime. Val verified the delivery of the tables and chairs and the tent setup, and later worked with Heath replacing the flowers in the planters as requested by the bride.

"We probably should consider using containers that can be lifted in and out easily," Heath said. "I think a greenhouse might be a good addition to the plan. We could grow some things ourselves."

"And break the heart of many a businessman in Paris. We've invested heavily in their profit margins thus far."

On Thursday and Friday Val worked with Kelly, her family, and the wedding planner, making the site everything the young woman wanted. Saturday dawned bright and clear. Val made herself accessible to Kelly and offered rooms in the house for the bride and for her attendants to dress for the event.

She glanced at Heath. "You'd better get dressed if you plan to attend the wedding. Is Rom coming?"

Heath, Rom, and Jane had been part of Kelly's graduating class, and she had invited them to her wedding.

"I don't think so, but Jane and I will be there."

After he'd gone, Val wandered into the garden for one last look around. She found herself looking at the area as a bride would. Yes, she could appreciate this venue for her wedding, though she preferred the view from the new structure. She followed the path to the huge white tent the rental company had erected.

"How's it going?" Russ asked, catching her by surprise.

"You're early." He looked very handsome in his formal wear.

"Thought I'd check in and see if you needed help."

They remained outside the tent. "We're good. Kelly's dressing. The garden is beautiful. I'd give you a peek, but that wouldn't be fair to her."

"I'm sure everyone will be impressed." He looked around. "I never realized how big these things were."

She frowned. "I need my structure completed. Tents are expensive. I should probably invest in one."

"You'd have to hire people to put it up," he said.

"True. But even so I hope there will be more than a few tent rentals before the pavilion is completed."

"Are we okay over the permit problem?"

Val noticed he watched her closely. "I suppose. Todd started work."

"They're excavating the area?"

She nodded. "Daddy and Heath took some of the guys and went in to restructure the fence to make the work area more accessible. They brought in some big equipment."

"Any regrets over seeing your beautiful area dismantled?"

"Not when I know what's going to be there in the end."

"I'm eager to see the end result myself. Though I will say I'm impressed with what I'm seeing already."

"Thanks. Kelly is pleased. It's an honor to know I've played a part in her happy day."

"It's just beginning, Val."

"I pray Your Wedding Place is a success."

"Sheridan Farm will be here no matter what."

"So you do think the business won't survive," she challenged.

"Stop putting words into my mouth. I knew you were still angry."

"I don't understand, Russ," she admitted. "I paid good money to ensure everything moved forward without delay, and we've had nothing but problems."

"I can't explain what happened. I'd swear on my life the information was there when I turned the papers over to Randall King."

"Don't do that," Val chided.

"I didn't do anything to hold up your project," he insisted.

"I want to believe you're with me in this."

He stepped closer, taking her hands in his. Their gazes locked. "I am fully committed to your success. Please believe that." He squeezed her hands gently. "I promise I'm going to see this through to the end. I'll be right here with you all the way."

Electricity charged the air as neither of them moved. Finally Val said, "I'm glad. I need to finish up a couple of things before I turn it over to Kelly."

"She's talked about getting married here ever since she booked."

"She told me. I gave her a special discount for being my first bride. And she's agreed to allow my photographer to take a few photos for publicity purposes."

"You're on your way," Russ said, leaning to kiss her gently before he released her hands. "No more problems," he promised.

∾

He'd surprised her with the kiss, but his own inner turmoil surprised Russ. He'd never felt this way when he'd kissed other women.

Russ hoped he could keep his promises. He recalled the conversation he'd overheard when leaving the office last night. He'd slowed his step when he heard Randall King's comment. Russ knew he shouldn't have eavesdropped but couldn't help himself.

"I know you wanted that property, but she's determined to turn it into something to serve a few brides."

Russ wondered who was on the other end of the line.

"Yes, we could have offered more for the acreage, but we wouldn't have had to if Sheridan hadn't dumped the property so fast." More silence and then Randall King's laughter. "Yeah, I heard that rumor. Even if the old man did hold him in high esteem, it's not likely he'd have instructed his son to give the farm away if he decided to sell."

More silence. "Give her time. It'll get old, and then we can buy the farm for a song. I need to get moving. Dinah promised me a romantic dinner tonight." The man's almost evil laugh gave Russ the creeps.

He knew he should tell Val, but fear silenced his tongue. He'd come too far with Prestige Designs to jeopardize himself at this stage in the process. He had delayed his career for a few years after college while he rebelled out of hurt. When he'd found no peace in his actions, he'd vowed to show them all. Becoming a successful architect in his own right would prove he needed no one but himself.

Still, Russ promised to keep his eyes and ears open. He'd meant it when he said he was with her all the way. No one was going to hurt Val. He'd do everything humanly possible to protect Val and her family.

Chapter 11

Val felt a great deal of satisfaction as she glanced around the area. With Jane's help, she had contacted every wedding planner within miles of Paris and invited him or her to the launch party.

The roses were in full bloom, and she looked forward to welcoming everyone to see their beauty. The theme was a Summer Rose Tea Party, and they had invited the attendees to wear the pastels of a summer bouquet, including hats or parasols. Pastel cloths draped the tables, and real English bone china teacups and silver teapots added the perfect final touch. She had even found a rose paperweight for each guest and had them engraved with Your Wedding Place's name, phone number, and Web site.

Euphoria from the success of Kelly's wedding had carried Val through the last four days. Having the two weddings on connecting weeks along with her event enabled her to split the tent rental three ways. She scheduled her event for Thursday afternoon and opted to serve refreshments there rather than in the house. Opie had prepared a true English tea with scones, savories, and a multitude of other items.

The ad agency had used some of Val's photographs to create the banners that hung from the walls of the tent. Large prints of the structure and the plans stood on easels behind a small replica of the pavilion Russ had created for her. They had made the right decision with the wrought-iron top. He'd incorporated ribbons in part of the design to show the option of shade fabric.

"It's fantastic," Jane declared as she set the vase of pastel roses on the table. "I'd book my wedding today," she declared. "Well, if I were getting married."

Val smiled. "I know God has a Mr. Right who will love you and Sammy as you deserve to be loved."

She noted the way Jane's gaze moved across the room to where Heath worked.

"I hope so. I'd like for Sammy to have a man in her life."

"What about Jane?" Val asked.

Her friend grinned. "She could use one in her life, too."

Val picked up rose petals and pushed a rose further into the container. "I've been thinking." Jane groaned playfully. "No seriously," she said. "We could host an annual event for brides and couples. Show them what we have to offer."

"You could rent space to planners and other service providers to help offset the cost."

"Maybe even give a wedding venue as a door prize."

"We haven't even gotten through our second event, and you're already planning for more."

"Advertising has resulted in a number of calls from brides. I had a couple inquire about spending their wedding night in the house last week."

"What have you decided?"

"We'll be moving into the Sheridan house. Only the grand staircase and drawing room will be available for weddings."

"I'm glad. It's such a beautiful house."

Val agreed. She'd always loved the Sheridan home, and knowing her family would live there made her feel blessed beyond compare. The decision had not been easy. They had prayed about it and had a few family discussions over whether it was the best move. Understandably, her parents had the most ties to the old house where they had raised their family, but they'd agreed the extra space would be nice. They even understood why she wanted to share the home with them. "I know we'll be happy there."

∾

The event had been a big success. The planners loved the theme. Many of them wore hats Val felt certain they'd purchased for Derby parties. Val blushed when Maddy told them she'd lost her star assistant but gained a wonderful new vendor. The one negative had been Derrick's arrival with his new boss.

"You can't keep a good man down," he sniped when Val welcomed them to the event. She managed a smile, all the while praying Derrick didn't cause a scene.

"Val and I worked together in our former lives," she overheard him telling one of the other planners. "She really lucked out when Maddy gave her that winning lottery ticket."

"I see Derrick's already hard at work, doing what he does best," Maddy commented when she walked over to where Val stood.

"Making me miserable?" Val guessed. "I wish he'd never found out about the money."

Maddy grinned. "Hard to keep something like that a secret."

"I know, but this event has to do with my business."

Maddy shrugged. "So tell them the money's an answer to a prayer and launch into the Your Wedding Place spiel. Then have your wait staff inundate Derrick with refreshments. Maybe that will shut his mouth."

"Hmm, that's an idea. Where's Opie?" Val asked, glancing around for her sister. "She can talk food ad nauseum. With any luck she'd drive him out of here in a few minutes."

Maddy laughed. "You can do this, Val. Remember the time you talked that bride into having her wedding at the Cane Ridge Meeting House?"

"She wanted an old church."

The Cane Ridge Meeting House was just east of Paris and built in 1791. The church had hosted one of the largest camp meetings on the frontier in 1801.

Between twenty thousand and thirty thousand people had brought their live-stock and spent six days worshiping the Lord. Today a superstructure housed the old restored church which could be used for special occasions.

"And you pleased her with the suggestion. It's a great party, Val. The setup is perfect. People are raving over everything. I'm sure you'll have plenty of interested planners. Now get out there and network." Her former employer gave her a little nudge.

"Thanks, Maddy."

Val noted that Derrick kept his distance, but his in-your-face attitude bothered her a great deal. She asked God's protection and felt happy when he left the party early.

Russ showed up a few minutes later.

Val looped her arm through his. "I'm glad you could come."

He glanced around. "Good turnout."

"The planners are very receptive," Val told him.

"Looks like we'll have to go out and celebrate again."

"This one's on me." A group beckoned her over, and she said, "Visit the refreshment table. Opie outdid herself."

&

He watched as Val greeted her guests and talked exuberantly about her new business venture. Russ couldn't help but be impressed by what he'd seen. No doubt a number of brides would enjoy their weddings all the more because of Val's business. She had a good idea. He'd done a bit of research and been surprised by the amount of money being spent on weddings.

Russ spotted Opie when he neared the food table. "Your sister has been bragging about you."

Opie smiled. "She's doing incredibly, don't you think?"

"Val always impresses me."

"Really?"

"Don't get that look in your eye," he warned. "We're friends."

"Lots of couples have started with much less."

Russ considered Opie's comment as he filled his plate and found an out-of-the-way place to sit. He did admire Val and found her attractive. He also knew Val would expect things of the man in her life that he wasn't certain he was prepared to give.

How would a man deal with all that money? Not that he had minded helping spend a bit of it with the project, but Russ didn't care for the idea of being kept by his wife. Their dad had taught his sons that a man's role in the family was provider. Russ didn't plan to settle for less. When it came to his wife and kids, he would be the breadwinner. Still, he couldn't help but consider the possibility of having Val in his life.

"Hi. Val tells us you can answer any questions we might have."

Russ glanced up at the two women standing there and swallowed hastily.

He wiped his mouth and spent the next few minutes talking with the planners.

"And when do you project it will be ready?"

"Definitely before spring."

"Val certainly has a good idea," one of the women declared.

"I know Maddy hates that she gave her that ticket," the other one said.

Feeling protective, Russ said, "I'm sure Val will be happy to help you ladies with bookings if you're interested."

"And what did you say this—?"

"The pavilion will be the ultimate reception site. The upper floor has a breathtaking view of the pastoral rolling hills of Kentucky. We're keeping the structure low to the ground with steps that lead to terraces with seating, fountains, and beautiful landscaping. The underground room is well lit and not the least confining. The upper structure will be open-air. Val tells me brides will fall in love all over again while they share their day with their guests. You should come back once we get closer to completion. The view goes on for miles."

"Did Russ answer your questions, ladies?" Val asked as she joined the group.

"He did. We can't wait to see the area. It sounds spectacular. You should have another party to show it off," the planner suggested.

"We probably will," Val said.

"I can't wait," the woman enthused. "I can't tell you how many brides want something other than a big tent. This sounds perfect."

"Be sure to read the literature in your goodie bag. And let us know if you need more information or a site tour."

After the women left, Russ looked at her. "You did that on purpose."

"They saw you hiding out over here and asked who you were. They thought you were a new wedding planner." Val grinned at his look of disbelief. "They perked right up when they heard you were an architect. I knew they wanted to meet you. Are you staying for Daddy's party?"

Russ considered the gift he'd picked up for Jacob Truelove last night. He'd enjoyed finding something the man would like. "If you're sure it's okay."

"Daddy likes you, Russ."

"I like him, too. And I'd love to stay if you think it won't be a problem."

"By now you surely know the Truelove motto."

"The more the merrier," Russ said, laughing with Val as they spoke the words together.

Later that afternoon they cleared the area in preparation for Saturday's wedding. Maddy had said they would be out on Friday to set up the tent for the reception. Russ stayed to help Val finish up after she sent Jane to the house to pick up Sammy. Afterward they walked up to the house together.

"Val, tell your father he has to go to the hospital," her mother said the moment they entered the living room.

She glanced from one to the other, wondering what was going on. Her dad sat in his recliner with his leg propped up, an ice bag against his head.

"Tell her," her mother insisted.

Her dad rolled his eyes. "Your mother is upset because Fancy nearly broke my leg today."

"And his head. You were unconscious, Jacob."

Val gasped and demanded, "Are you okay?"

"He doesn't know," her mother said, her voice rising almost hysterically. "He refuses to get himself checked out."

"Woman, it's my birthday," he growled. "My daughter has cooked all my favorite foods, and my family and friends will be here soon. I don't plan to sit around the emergency room and miss my own celebration."

"We could wait until you get back," Val suggested.

"Or we can celebrate now, and I could go to the hospital later if necessary. I wish I knew why Fancy went crazy like that."

"Is she okay?"

He shrugged. "Bill says she's calmed down. He put her in the stall and called the vet. We'll know more after Doc checks her out."

Cy rushed into the room and to his dad's side. "Mr. Bill said you were knocked unconscious."

"Bill has a big mouth," her father muttered.

"He was," her mother told their son.

"It takes more than a thump against the fence to break this hard head, Cindy."

"Let's hope so. One of these children should become a doctor."

"I plan to be a veterinarian," Cy volunteered.

"That should work for your father," she said with a stern look at her husband.

Val's father roared with laughter. "Woman, I love you even when you nag me unmercifully."

She squeezed his hand, her eyes conveying that same love to her husband.

After a dinner of his favorites, her dad sat in his recliner with his leg propped up as he held court. Sammy had abandoned their mom in his favor. Val suspected it had to do with the presents that surrounded him. Little Sammy had all the Truelove men wrapped around her tiny fingers. All she had to do was flash that baby smile at them and they'd do anything for her.

"She's worried about his owie," her mom said as they watched them together.

"I know Dad loves that. Did she kiss him to make it better?"

Sammy was an energetic child, and they frequently had opportunities to kiss her owies away.

"At least twice on the cheek."

"Then I'm sure he's much better," Val assured her. "I'm so thankful he didn't get hurt worse."

"I still think he should be checked out."

"Maybe later," Val suggested.

"You know your dad. He'll pretend he's fine."

Val hugged her mom and sent up a quick prayer. "We're all keeping watch. Let him enjoy himself."

"I'm trying," her mother said before going over to sit in a chair next to her husband.

While the others visited, Val slipped out to the horse barn to check on Fancy. She pushed the metal stall door open, and when the horse pushed her head out the opening Val paused briefly to be certain Fancy had calmed down.

When the horse had first come to Sheridan Farm, her dad had expressed his belief that she was a winner. Because of his faith in her, Mr. Sheridan had named her Jacob's Fancy, and upon his death he'd left the horse to her father with permission to stable her on the farm for as long as he remained there.

Over the years their dad had taught them to exercise a great deal of care around the horses, and tonight more than ever before that training came to mind as Val assessed Fancy's current state. After determining the horse had returned to normal, she found a peppermint and held out her hand, palm up. Fancy took it and crunched the candy in her powerful teeth while Val rubbed the horse's forehead. "What happened today, girl?" she whispered. "Why did you act like that?"

"Everything okay?" Russ asked when he located her in the horse barn.

Fancy's nicker of response gave her no answer.

"I hope so. She's in a delicate condition." She didn't share that the expected foal would be the result of a deal between his brother and her father. "What happened, Russ? Fancy has never acted like that before. Daddy could have been killed."

Russ slid his arm about her shoulder. "He's okay, Val. I don't imagine it's the first time he's been injured."

"No," she admitted, petting the horse when she butted her head against Val's shoulder, demanding attention. "He asked the vet to run tests."

"Good idea."

"I'm glad you stayed for the party. Daddy's enjoying himself."

"It's been fun. I was surprised to see Wendell."

"Opie invited him. I should have warned you he'd be here. Did you talk?" she asked almost hopefully.

"We exchanged pleasantries. I would have come anyway. I like your dad."

"He likes you."

"What about his daughter?"

"You're a great friend, Russ."

He looked disappointed. "Why do you always qualify our relationship as friends?"

"Aren't we friends?" Val said.

"I think you know by now the pavilion is only an excuse to get out here and see you."

Val had seen the signs pointing in that direction and avoided the discussion until now. Sadness filled her as she considered how he would react to what she had to say. "We need to talk."

"Want to show me that Celtic knot garden in the moonlight?"

"Please, Russ, this is serious." Val knew Russ didn't have a clue as to what she needed to tell him. "Let's go to the Japanese garden," she said, hoping the beautiful area would provide the peace she was far from feeling. "I need to check to see that everything is in order for tomorrow."

Not sure where to start, she said, "When you consider the woman you will marry, I'm sure things you share in common are high on the list."

He took her hand, playing with her fingers for a moment before wrapping her hand securely in his. "It helps, but it's not a total necessity."

"Some things are important," Val said. "Couples have to be tolerant of their differences, willing to give and take, but there's one thing I'd never give on."

"What?" he prompted when she paused.

"My faith."

"I wouldn't expect that of you."

"But you could affect it in ways you can't begin to imagine. I could try to play God and hope I'd change your mind over time, but we know that doesn't happen. People don't change because that's what other people want. Marriage—"

"Whoa," Russ said. "Who said anything about marriage?"

"I did. For me the next logical step beyond friendship is love and marriage. I can like you as a friend or love you as a husband. There's no in-between ground."

"What happened to dating?"

"When I date I do so with marriage in mind," Val told him. "The man has to be as committed to me as I am to him. We'll come to know each other and our families well. We will have common goals and hopes for the future. Most important we will share a very spiritual relationship with our heavenly Father."

"And you don't see me as that man?"

"I'm sorry, Russ. If I allow our relationship to progress, we'll both end up getting hurt."

"No problem." He dropped her hand and left the bench, moving over into the shadowy edge of the garden.

She knew that wasn't true from the way his voice roughened. "Why are you angry?"

"I didn't think you were the manipulative type."

"I'm not."

"You're basically saying that unless I choose to follow your God you want nothing more to do with me."

"I never said that," Val cried out. "You're my friend. I'll always treat you as a friend."

"So I'm good enough to be a friend but no more in your life?"

"What do you expect, Russ? God comes first. He always has and always will. Every member of my family believes just as I do."

"Then you should warn your sister to steer clear of Wendell. He has less use for religion than I do."

"That's sad," Val said softly. "Jesus loves you. Why can't you love Him in return?"

Her question went unanswered. "I think I'll call it a night. Thank your parents for me."

"Russ?"

"Don't let it worry you, Val. It wouldn't work anyway. We want different things."

∾

Later that night when Rom returned to the apartment, Russ sat on the sofa watching a sports program. "How's your dad?" he asked when Rom settled into the leather armchair.

Rom had remained at the house for a while to determine if his father needed to go to the emergency room. "Still insisting he's okay. I don't think they'll get him to the doctor. It was a great party. Opie outdid herself. That girl can cook."

"She can, and it was," Russ agreed, adding, "at least until the end."

"Why? What happened?" Rom asked.

"Your sister."

Rom leaned back. "What did Val do now?"

"Gave me the old we-can-be-friends spiel."

"You are friends. What's the problem?"

"I don't like being manipulated by women," Russ said. "I asked about dating, and she goes straight to marriage and how important it is that I share her faith."

"It's called being equally yoked."

Russ frowned. "You mean like a horse and wagon?"

"Actually that's a good simile. Think about what would happen if you stuck a racehorse in front of a freight wagon."

"It would be a bumpy ride."

"Exactly. Our parents taught us the importance of sharing relationships with believers. Friendship is nice, but love is better, and knowing that person is going to be around for the long haul makes all the difference."

"That's not always the case," Russ said. "Christians divorce."

"They do," Rom agreed. "Generally because they don't make God the head of their marriage."

"Why is God so important?" Russ muted the television and stuck a pillow under his head as he stretched out on the sofa. The brown leather squeaked with his movement.

"God is so much bigger than we can imagine. Haven't you ever wondered?"

"Not really. I attended church because it was mandatory. Not because I wanted to be there."

"Val's trying to tell you how she feels."

"That I'm not good enough for her because I don't love her God?" Russ demanded.

"Or you're good enough that she cares that you don't know God," Rom suggested. "She's only trying to keep you both from getting hurt in the long run."

"By rejecting me?"

"By being realistic. Val is not a manipulator. She's a good person who honestly cares about others. A rare jewel in today's world."

Russ knew Rom was right. Still, it pricked at him that she wouldn't consider furthering their relationship because of his lack of religion. "So what do you suggest I do?"

"Don't look at Val as a challenge because she says no," Rom said. "I like you, Russ, but don't fool around with my sister's heart."

Friend or not, Russ had no doubt the Truelove men would come after him if he tried. "She invited me to church a while back. Said an intelligent man ought to give God a chance before deciding not to follow him."

"Sounds like good advice to me," Rom agreed. "But it's doing what your heart leads you to do. Inviting people to church is like leading a horse to water. You can't make them drink living water either."

"Living water? What's that?"

"Jesus Christ is living water. Eternal life. In John 4:10 he spoke to the woman at the well and said, 'If thou knewest the gift of God, and who it is that saith to thee, Give me to drink; thou wouldest have asked of him, and he would have given thee living water.'"

Russ looked puzzled. "Why do you love God so much?"

"The relationship between God and man is special. As corny as it may sound, I love Him because He first loved me. I try to act responsibly, but I sin. I'm human, and God knew I would. That's why He sent His Son to die on the cross for me. When I repent He forgives me, and I strive to do better."

"You do a lot of praying, too?"

"And Bible study. I plan to be active in my church, and those studies will help me with whatever role I'm asked to perform."

"You work in church, too?"

"Definitely. Faith without works is dead."

"Do you date?"

Rom smiled. "There's a woman who figures prominently in my future. She joined the Peace Corps after we graduated from UK. I plan to ask her to marry me when she comes home."

"Why didn't you go with her?"

"Not in the plans. I had a mission here at home. Before Val won the money, my role was to help provide for the kids who will soon graduate."

"What keeps you here now that Val set aside funds for their education?"

"I need to be here to support Val and my family. And I'm working toward my future with Stephanie. I can get started in my career and save for our future. Meanwhile, I plan to support Stephanie's work in Africa. I want to visit her and make her life easier while she's there."

"You know, Rom, you Trueloves are too good to be true," Russ said.

"Mom always says the cream rises to the top."

He slung a sofa pillow in his friend's direction.

Rom caught it and laughed. "Don't get me wrong, Russ. We make mistakes and do stupid things, but we're a family with God at our center. And that does make a difference."

Chapter 12

Their lives continued to change over the next weeks. One noticeable difference was the lack of Russ's presence in her life. Val knew he checked the job site and saw other members of her family but did everything possible to avoid her. Even when they talked on the phone he kept the conversation all business.

She missed him, but she knew the reason for the absence. Val still believed she'd made the right decision. She prayed, giving the situation over to God. Only He could open Russ's eyes to the fact that she cared enough for him to want his salvation.

Rom had shared some of his conversation with Russ and agreed Val had done the right thing. Russ's comment about Wendell had forced her to talk with Opie only to learn she and her sister were in the same situation. Both agreed the struggle to do right was even more difficult when the heart was involved.

The move to the Sheridan mansion was complete. They had all been teary-eyed when they closed the door on the empty house they had called home for so many years. Val had no doubt it would have been much worse if they had been required to leave the farm.

Living in a new place would be different, but from the first time she'd walked through the front door, Val had felt at home. Once the family agreed to make the move, she wanted them to feel the same way. She struggled to convince her parents to take the Sheridans' suite until they finally agreed. She, Opie, and Jules shared a guest wing and for the first time in their lives had rooms of their own with private baths. Roc and Cy opted to room together.

Heath would have his own room, but Rom would bunk with him during his frequent visits home.

But for now Heath slept in a downstairs bedroom. During the move he had tripped over Sammy on the stairs and sported a cast on his leg while the two-year-old wore one on her arm. Thankful their injuries hadn't been worse, Val insisted Heath follow the doctor's instructions. She missed him in their daily activities but knew he would have difficulty getting around on crutches.

Jane blamed herself, saying she should have taken Sammy home when Mrs. Cindy couldn't babysit. They had all reassured her, but she refused to be comforted. The situation worsened with the arrival of Jane's in-laws and Clarice Holt's demands to spend time with Sammy back at their hotel. When the child wanted nothing to do with the woman, Cindy Truelove suggested that the Holts along with Sammy and Jane stay in a couple of the guest rooms at the house so

Sammy would be more comfortable. Clarice had gone out of her way to make everyone miserable, and the entire family had been happy to see her depart.

Despite her unhappiness, Val threw herself into making Your Wedding Place a success. Even though she had more than enough funds, she forced herself to be cautious with her expenditures. Your Wedding Place would operate in the black much sooner if she built the business slowly. Advertising drew a number of brides. Their frequent indrawn breaths of amazement assured her their efforts had been successful.

They hosted three receptions in September, and when the calls for corporate parties, bridal showers, engagement parties, and birthday events increased, they decided to try a few events. Despite their limitations, they had booked events into October.

Nearly a week of heavy rains had thrown the project schedule off even more. The sun had broken through over the weekend, and the construction crews had returned to work on Monday. The excavation work was nearly completed, and Todd Bigelow said they would be pouring concrete soon.

The gorgeous late summer days made her anxious to offer the pavilion as a venue. Several brides had booked for the coming year based on the drawings alone. Though some planned church weddings, they chose the pavilion for their reception site.

The need to talk to her dad had grown stronger with the passing of time, and Val awakened that morning with a plan to seek him out. She started across the yard and stopped to speak to Bill as he led a stallion across the yard. "He's a real beauty," she said, admiring the handsome animal from a distance.

Bill nodded. "I told Jacob he should think about buying him."

"Maybe he will," Val said before continuing her mission to find her dad. The scent of horses and leather filled her nostrils as she stepped into the farm office room. Opening his office door, she asked, "Got a minute?"

"Sure."

Val walked around the old metal desk and propped herself against the edge. "I don't want to upset you." That comment gained his attention. "But this has weighed on my heart for some time now. Daddy, will you go with me to visit Grandfather Truelove?"

His immediate withdrawal spoke volumes. "Why? What purpose would it serve?"

"I don't know," she answered honestly. "But I've prayed over the situation, and the only answer I can give you is it's time. When Jesus commissioned us to witness, don't you think He knew our family and friends would come first? How can we witness to Grandfather if we never visit him?" He remained silent. "I think maybe it's time I have an adult relationship with my grandfather."

Her dad pushed his chair back from the desk and stood. He walked over to the window and looked out. "He's been in prison longer than you've been alive. I tried to be a good son. When you and the twins were little, I took you to see him, thinking he might want to make a good impression on his grandchildren. He hardly spoke to you children. He only wanted to hear about the horses I worked with here at the farm. Wanted me to place a bet for him.

"Every visit was pretty much the same. The last time I went, he asked why Mom never contacted him. I told him we'd nearly lost her to a heart attack, and all he said was too bad. After that, I refused to go back. Those collect calls are the only contact we've had for years."

"Doesn't Grammy talk to him?"

"No. They're divorced. His creditors came after her when they couldn't get to him. She lived on disability, and we encouraged her to make their separation legal. She had done everything humanly possible to be a good wife and didn't need the added stress."

Val nodded. "How would you feel if he weren't your father?"

"I suppose I could summon more sympathy for a complete stranger dealing with the same demons."

"You've given up hope, haven't you?"

"Yes. I can't reach him."

"We'll respect your wishes," Val told her father, "but I think it's time we visited him. If you'd rather not go, I'll ask the others."

"Do you need an answer now?"

"No. I'm only asking that you pray over the situation."

∽

Later that afternoon Val was working in the office when the doorbell rang. She was surprised when Russ walked into the room. Val thought he looked good in his worn jeans, golf shirt, and work boots. "What brings you out this way?"

"I needed to check the progress of the concrete pour and thought I'd say hello first. How's Heath?"

Val had wondered what made today's visit different. It hurt that he could remain friends with her family and not her. "Jane took him in for his doctor's appointment. He's hoping to get the cast off soon."

"Tell him I asked after him," he said. "I'd better get to the site."

Val refused to allow him to ignore her. "Mind if I ride out with you?"

As they walked out to the golf cart, Russ commented, "Looks like you've settled into the house well."

"It's been a process. We wanted to get moved before the kids went back to school."

"Where did the summer go?" Russ asked with a shake of his head.

"It's been a fast one. Jules is a senior this year."

"Still thinking about becoming an architect?"

"It's all she talks about. Thanks for inviting her to your office. You inspired her more than you know."

"At least I inspire one Truelove woman."

Val parked the cart at the job site. "Can't we get beyond this, Russ?"

Ignoring her question, he jumped out of the vehicle and walked over to look at the concrete pour for the lower structure walls that had occurred that day. He glanced back. "This isn't right."

"What do you mean?"

He pointed out the areas that were off. "What's going on here?" Russ demanded when Todd Bigelow joined them. "That concrete isn't poured according to the plans."

"You should know," the man said with a disapproving frown. "You sent that e-mail this morning an hour before the pour. We had a time making this many changes before the trucks came."

"I haven't sent any e-mails," Russ said, glancing at Val. "I met with a client all morning."

Todd pulled out his phone and pulled up the message. "Says it's from you."

"I didn't send that e-mail," Russ repeated. "I haven't done anything since you called yesterday and left a message that the pour was scheduled for today."

Seeing Russ's shocked expression, Val took the phone and studied the screen closely. "It has your e-mail address."

"I can see that," Russ said, his voice rising with his frustration as he looked over her shoulder. "But I didn't send it."

"It's not my mistake. I shouldn't be expected to absorb the cost," Todd declared.

Val looked at Russ, and when he didn't speak she said, "Fix the problem. Mr. Hunter and I will work out the specifics."

"And don't act on any more e-mails until we get to the bottom of this," Russ warned.

"That's going to throw the schedule off even further," Val said after the man walked away, mumbling about modern technology.

"I didn't send it, Val."

She wanted to believe him, but all the evidence pointed directly to Russ. "Who else has access?"

"No one. I need a copy of that e-mail."

"What are we going to do about the cost?"

"I don't know that either," Russ said. "Mr. King will be upset when he learns about this mistake. It'll be costly to correct."

Anger shot through Val when Russ showed concern for his boss instead of her project. "And it's fair that I bear the cost?"

He cradled his head in his hands, burying his fingers in his hair. "I'm trying to figure this out. Don't do anything yet. Let me see if I can restructure the plans."

"And wait to have everything re-permitted? It would be quicker to break up the concrete and start over. I'll cover the costs, but I expect you to find out what happened."

"I want to know who did this, too."

Val called out to Todd. "Can you forward a copy of that e-mail to me? We need to look into this further."

"Yes, ma'am. There's something else. I got a call from the ironwork company demanding to know why we cancelled the order. They weren't happy when I told them I didn't know anything about a cancellation."

She looked at Russ again.

He looked stunned. "I haven't cancelled anything. That trim was special order. We need it on-site ready for installation."

"Something else you need to check into?" she asked with a frown.

Russ rubbed his face wearily. "Can we discuss this privately?"

At the house Val pulled up the e-mail and printed off a copy.

He read it again, the paper wrinkling with the pressure of his closed fist. "Todd left a message at the office yesterday saying the pour was today. That's why I came out this afternoon."

"You can send e-mail from anywhere with your PDA."

He looked disappointed by her conclusion.

"But I didn't. I was in a meeting and didn't take it with me because the client hates interruptions and I didn't want to risk upsetting him."

"Well, somebody did, and I want to know who."

"So do I. You know I've been behind you and this project ever since I started the plans."

He relented at her look of disbelief. "Okay. Once I understood how important it was to you. And even if I didn't agree with you personally, I would not disrupt your project. My reputation is on the line."

"Well, someone did. How do you suggest we handle this?"

"I have a friend who knows computers. I'll see if he can help. I wouldn't do this, Val. I care too much for you to hurt you like that. I know what you said," Russ told her. "I can't turn my feelings on and off at will. I'm not trying to charm my way out of this mess. I'm being honest. I don't know who sent that e-mail or made the call, but I intend to find out."

"We should call Randall King."

"I'd like to talk with Jason first. See if he can help me get a lead on where the e-mail originated."

Val tilted her head and looked at him curiously. "What aren't you telling me, Russ?"

"I'm asking you to trust me, but I can't say I'd blame you if you didn't."

"I might if you give me reason."

Russ sighed. "I don't know, Val. I don't want to go off half-cocked and make accusations that will destroy my career."

"What do you know?"

"Promise you'll keep this between us until we know for sure?" When she nodded, he said, "I overheard a phone conversation that I think had to do with you and Sheridan Farm. I think Randall King is part of this KFD Corporation that wants your farm."

"Is he behind the delays?"

"If he is he's covered his tracks well," Russ said.

"You don't trust him?"

"I never had a problem before."

"What's making a difference this time?" she asked curiously.

"You. I won't let him hurt you or your family."

She had her reason. "Okay, Russ, I'll give you a couple of days."

∾

Back at the office, Russ contacted his friend immediately. They had met in boarding school, and Jason had subsequently gone into the military and worked for the FBI.

"You've got to help me out, buddy," Russ said. "She thinks I did this."

"You have no idea who did?"

"No. I was in a meeting when it was sent. It's my e-mail address."

"Who has your password?"

"It's on file in the office. Randall King insists on that."

"Do you think King sent the e-mail?"

"Doesn't make sense he'd do something that would result in a major liability to his firm."

"Anybody there have a grievance against you?"

"Not that I'm aware of."

"It does seem more directed toward the Truelove woman," Jason commented. "She got problems with anyone in your office?"

"She's only worked with me."

"Can you have her send me the e-mail?"

"I have a copy I can fax right now."

"Do that but send me the real thing. Some people can hide their trail, but others don't realize it's there."

"Thanks, Jace. My integrity is at stake here."

"That something new you've picked up since we used to hang out together?" his old friend joked.

"Yeah, since I grew up and got involved in the real world. This is important. I care what this woman thinks of me."

"It always involves a woman."

"The woman," Russ told him. "She's important to me, and we've already got enough issues. I don't want total lack of trust to become another."

"I'll get back to you as soon as I know something."

Chapter 13

Every passing hour increased Russ's angst. He wanted to prove his innocence but didn't know how. He made several trips out to the site. He was thankful they had poured only a portion of the concrete. When he heard about the tear-out, Heath suggested using the concrete they removed for their landscaping projects. The new pour had taken place the day before, and the construction was back on track.

When he finally heard back from Jason, he took the evidence straight to Randall King. He was still reeling after learning the e-mail had come from their office using his e-mail address.

"Does Mr. King have any time open this morning?" Russ asked Cheryl.

She pulled up Mr. King's calendar on her computer. "He's free now."

"Please ask if he can see me."

While Russ worried about Randall King's reaction, he also knew he had to do this for Val. No matter what the cost to his career, he owed her that much.

His boss looked up from his seat behind the massive desk when Russ entered. "What can I do for you this fine morning?"

"There's a problem with the Truelove project."

"With that contractor she chose," Randall said confidently.

"No, sir. Val made an excellent choice. I'm impressed by Todd Bigelow."

When there was no invitation to sit, Russ slid his hand into his pocket and fought the urge to jiggle coins.

"Then what's the problem?" Randall demanded, his gaze narrowing.

Russ slid the folder containing the information he'd gathered onto the desktop. "Someone sent this to her contractor using my e-mail."

"How is that possible?"

"I wondered the same thing. I was meeting with Harry Marshburn at the time. There's a statement in there attesting to the fact that I didn't send any e-mails while I was in his office.

"In fact I left my PDA in the car. Mr. Marshburn has a very strong dislike of interruptions, and I didn't want to take any chances. There's also a copy of the report where I logged the hours."

"And you have no idea where it was sent from?"

"I had my friend help determine the source, and it appears to have been generated from this office using my e-mail account."

"Are you accusing someone here of doing this?" Randall demanded.

"I'm telling you I was out of the office when it was sent and had no means of sending an e-mail so it had to be someone else. Val expects someone to cover her loss. A substantial loss. They had poured the concrete by the time I arrived that afternoon."

"This wouldn't have happened if she'd used Kevin."

"We don't know that to be the case. As I said, Todd Bigelow is proving to be a very competent contractor. I could see him handling future projects."

Randall flashed him a strange look. "How do you think we should proceed with this?"

"It's my understanding e-mail is forever."

"Who told you this?"

"My friend Jason. He's a computer expert with the FBI." Russ thought his boss looked surprised. "He says we can have the document retrieved. Meanwhile, I plan to change my passwords, and I won't be sharing them with anyone. I've also directed Todd not to make any future changes unless he hears them directly from my lips."

"Has Ms. Truelove spoken about suing the firm?"

"She's very upset," Russ confirmed. "I wouldn't be surprised if she's consulted her attorney regarding the matter."

"Can the floor plan be reworked to accommodate the error?"

"I suggested that, but Val was more concerned about the time involved in re-permitting. She ordered it ripped out. I understand her concern. We've already had another delay with a document missing from the initial plan submission."

"Why wasn't I informed about that?"

"She called me after her contractor checked online and saw the plans had been rejected. I was able to resolve the matter and get the permit issued without further delay."

"I don't care for my firm looking bad to the clients."

"I don't care for being made to look bad either," Russ said. "I didn't send that e-mail, and until we figure out who did we have a problem."

"I'll handle it."

"There's something else," Russ said. "A woman called the ironworks company and cancelled the order. She used Val's name. Luckily they contacted Todd, and we got the job order reinstated. I don't know what's going on, but I don't like it one bit. What do I tell Val Truelove?"

"That I'm looking into the situation," Randall King said brusquely.

Back in his office, Russ called to tell Val exactly what his boss had said to tell her. The desire to share Jason's information was strong, but company loyalty forced him to keep silent. Still, that didn't mean he wouldn't continue investigating things on his own. Someone was after Val, and he wanted to know why.

Chapter 14

When Russ told her his boss was looking into the situation, Val recognized the message for what it was—a delay tactic. Still, she'd witnessed Russ's shock and believed he intended to protect them. That's why she'd promised to trust him—why she'd prayed he could prove his innocence.

A more important family matter took precedence in the Truelove household. Her father had agreed to visit Mathias Truelove, and Val didn't plan to give him time to change his mind. After much discussion, Val, Opie, Rom, and Heath decided to go with him to visit their grandfather Truelove at Kentucky State Penitentiary. Her father insisted Jules, Roc, and Cy stay at home with their mother. Val respected his need to protect the younger children.

They left after lunch to drive up to Eddyville and spend the night in a hotel to be there for the 7:30 a.m. visiting hour the following day.

As they approached the prison, Val remembered the imposing structure from her childhood. "I can see why they call it the castle," she told the others.

"Has a definite European flair," Opie agreed.

"Are you sure you want to do this?" their father asked. "We can still turn back."

"We need to do this, Daddy."

Resigned to his fate, Jacob Truelove nodded. A few minutes later they entered the room where the older version of their father waited. Prison had aged him far beyond his sixty-seven years, and the standard issue clothing seemed a bit loose on his sparse frame. His back stooped slightly when he stood.

"I was surprised when your dad said you were coming to visit. You're all grown up." He glanced at his son. "So Jake, tell me who's who."

"This is my eldest, Valentine," he said, laying his hand on first Val and then Opie's shoulders. "Our second daughter, Ophelia. And our twins, Romeo and Heathcliff."

"Never did understand why you let that woman of yours hang those names on your kids."

"Our children," Val's father told him. "Cindy had as much of a right to choose their names as I did."

"Still cranky as ever, aren't you, boy?"

As the two of them glared at each other, Val realized how alike and yet how different they were. Their appearance might be similar, but their personalities were worlds apart. "Please don't argue."

Her grandfather looked at her, started to say something, and stopped. "So what have you children been doing?"

"Rom and I just completed our MBAs at Harvard, sir," Heath said.

The old man looked unimpressed. "What happened to your leg?"

Though he no longer used crutches, Heath wore a brace.

"Fell down the stairs."

"Too bad."

Val glanced at her father, aware he remembered a time his father had used those same words many years before.

"And I graduated from culinary school," Opie said, picking up where Heath left off.

"A cook, huh? We could use a good one around this place."

"Actually a chef," Opie told him.

"Ain't that a fancy name for a cook?" he demanded, not waiting for an answer. "And you, Valentine—Jake tells me you had a bit of luck with the lottery."

"I didn't tell you anything," her father said.

"Please, Daddy," Val said.

Her grandfather shrugged. "Must have heard it somewhere else. You take after your old grandfather and enjoy playing games of chance?"

Val shook her head. "No, sir. Daddy doesn't allow us to gamble." He looked confused. "I prayed, and God provided."

The older man looked at his son. "You filled their heads with that nonsense?"

"Believing in God isn't nonsense," Heath told him. "In fact, it's pretty smart."

"God never did anything for me."

"You never did anything for Him either," their father said.

"Save your talk, boy. I already have enough people preaching to me."

"We won't apologize for loving the Lord," Val told him.

"So how did you win the lottery?"

"The ticket was a gift from my boss."

The old man laughed and slapped his hand against his leg. "Talk about luck. Wouldn't be here today if I'd had a bit of that myself."

"We consider it a blessing," their father told him.

Ignoring his son's words, he asked Val, "What are you doing with your money?"

"Investing in our future and helping others by meeting their needs. We've donated food and clothing to the homeless shelter, supported mission work in Africa, funded scholarships, and paid for church camp for needy kids. We've helped families with financial problems caused by major illness and were blessed to be able to help another family who lost their home to fire—"

"Doesn't sound like fun to me," he interrupted.

Her father grunted, and Val squeezed his arm in a gesture of comfort. "We never needed money to enjoy ourselves," she assured her grandfather.

"You still run that farm?" Mathias Truelove asked his son.

"Yeah," he answered, his tone surly and unfriendly.

"What are you kids gonna do with your lives?"

All throughout the trip their father had cautioned them not to share their private business with their grandfather. He'd even made them promise not to trust too quickly. "I'm working with a wedding venue business," Val said.

"Landscape work," Heath said when his grandfather looked at him.

"Not much of a job with that fancy education of yours."

"It's good for now," Heath said.

"And you?" he said, looking at Rom.

"I took a consulting job."

His grandfather nodded approval. "And what about you, missy?" he asked, directing his question at Opie.

"I'm helping out around home, but I've done some catering and worked as a personal chef."

"Goofing off, huh?"

"She just got out of school," Val said.

Her grandfather looked at her. "Lots of restaurants out there. Shouldn't take long to find work if she's good."

"I'm very good," Opie said.

He allowed his gaze to move from face to face. "I have some good-looking grandkids. Ain't there more of your kids?"

"Jules, Roc, and Cy are at home with Mom," Val said.

"Why didn't they come?"

"I didn't feel it was a good idea," her father told him.

"Did you bring pictures?" he asked. When his son shook his head, the older man asked, "How's Lena doing?"

Her father's voice tightened as he spoke about his mother. "She has her ups and downs. Karen called last week and said they're running more tests."

"Takes after her mother with that heart disease," their grandfather said with a shake of his head. "She's a good woman. Too good for the likes of me. It's great seeing all of you. I don't usually have visitors."

The thought saddened Val. For thirty years her grandfather had sat in prison, alone, believing no one cared anything about him. Wasn't that punishment enough for his mistakes?

He asked questions and rambled on until they ended visiting hours. "It's been mighty fine seeing all of you today. I hope you'll come back and bring the other kids."

"That was really heartbreaking," Val said as they climbed into the SUV for the drive home.

"He doesn't deserve better."

"Do you really believe that, Daddy?"

"Yes, Val. I have asked God to help me forgive him, but I can't. Every time they put Mom into the hospital I get angry all over again."

"But you heard what he said. Grammy's mom had heart problems, too. You've never sent him pictures of us?"

"No. And I don't plan to start now."

"What harm would it do?"

"Think about it, Val. He's in prison for life, knows you have money, and knows people who would do anything to get a bit of that money."

His succinct answer hit home. Mathias Truelove had failed his son in every way possible. "Uncle Zeb and Aunt Karen don't visit either, do they?"

"He got to you, didn't he?"

"I feel for him. He sits in prison day in and day out with no family who loves him, and he makes the occasional collect call to children who couldn't care less if they hear from him. What encourages or motivates him to be a better man?"

"That's the point, Val," her dad said, his voice rough and unfeeling. "Nothing motivates him. You heard him today."

"I did. I do feel sad for him. In fact, I feel sad for every man in that prison."

"Well, I don't. Every one of them is getting exactly what he deserves."

"There but for the grace of God," Val said softly. "Would you love us any less if we had made wrong decisions and ended up there?"

"You know I wouldn't."

Silence stretched as they drove toward home. Val dealt with today's visit in the only way she knew how. Prayer. Only God could heal the rift between father and son.

Chapter 15

The pavilion project was well underway by the time she received a call from Randall King asking her to come to his office. Val wondered why Russ hadn't contacted her but assumed Mr. King had taken control because of his firm's liability. She'd asked her lawyer to accompany her, and they waited in the Prestige Designs conference room.

Randall King and Russ entered together, and his boss chose the seat at the head of the table while Russ sat on the opposite side facing her. Randall King began with an apology. "I'm sorry this happened, and I assure you Prestige Designs will accept responsibility for the incident."

"I don't know how it happened, but there are questions I'd like answered," Russ said. The situation became even more tense when Russ confronted his boss with his concerns. "I overheard you telling someone Val would probably lose interest soon enough and sell the property."

"I never said any such thing," Randall denied.

"You might not have called her by name, but it was very clear who you were talking about," Russ said. "And I've learned you're a partner in this KFD Corporation that made an offer for Sheridan Farm."

"What's your point, Russ?" he demanded. "Are you accusing me of sabotaging a client's project? If so, I hope you're prepared to prove that's the case."

"I'm not accusing you of anything," Russ said. "I'm stating facts. I overheard you talking about Val's business. You made an offer to buy the farm after Prestige had taken on the project."

"Yes, we wanted the land," Randall admitted. "It's an excellent location, and we had plans to build several multimillion dollar homes. But when Sheridan sold it to the Trueloves, we accepted that wouldn't happen."

"Then why make the offer? That's why you were so insistent I use Kevin Flint," Val guessed. "You knew he'd take his time and thought it would discourage me enough to sell, didn't you?"

"You hired your own contractor," Randall said in answer to her accusation.

"You were angry Val rejected Flint," Russ said. "So much so that you kept insisting I wrap up her project and move on. We've never done that to another client."

"Look. I'm not the bad guy here," Randall told Val, ignoring Russ's comment. "I didn't do anything to affect your project. In fact, I had my IT staff continue what Russ started with the e-mail research and learned where it generated. That's why I brought you in today."

"I'm glad you didn't just let it drop," Val said.

"As I told Russ, I don't like looking bad to my clients. Now that I know who sent the e-mail, I accept full responsibility. I'll give you a check for your losses before you leave here today."

Val glanced at Russ. His left eyebrow shot up a fraction, and he shrugged when Mr. King asked Cheryl to join them in the conference room.

When the door opened, everyone's gaze focused on the new arrival. Val recognized the secretary and wondered what she had to do with the situation. Randall directed her to have a seat.

Val felt almost sorry for the woman as she scurried to a chair next to Russ. Her nervous demeanor was that of a person with something to hide. After seating herself, she carefully arranged her pad and pen on the tabletop and looked expectantly at her boss.

"Cheryl, we have an incident regarding an e-mail that was sent from this office using Russ's e-mail address. It's been traced back to your computer."

"Everyone uses my computer," she said, immediately going on the defensive. "I've asked them not to, but they won't listen."

"Russ has an alibi in this instance," Randall told her. "He has a client who recalls their meeting and stated he did not send any e-mails during the time they were together."

Cheryl glanced at the pad of paper. "Why would anyone use his e-mail address? We all have our own."

"Because this person obviously wanted to cause trouble," Randall told her. "In this case, the incident cost Ms. Truelove several thousand dollars which Prestige will have to absorb."

Cheryl's pale skin went even whiter.

Randall King didn't let up on his attack. "Russ requested help from the FBI, and it has been determined the e-mail was sent from your computer. Do you have something to share with us regarding the situation?"

Silence stretched in the room as no one spoke. Finally she looked up, tears trailing down her face. She swiped at them ineffectually and admitted, "I did it."

"Why?"

"Because Derrick asked me to."

"Derrick?" Randall King repeated.

"Derrick Masters?" Val demanded.

Cheryl sniffed back tears and nodded, her voice almost inaudible when she continued speaking. "I thought he loved me. He talked about getting married, and then he ran off with that woman he met at one of his weddings."

Everyone around the table shared looks but kept quiet as she continued.

"Derrick and I met when I came to work for Prestige two years ago. He saw me in the parking lot and came over to introduce himself. He asked me out, and we've dated ever since."

Val wondered if Cheryl knew about all the other women Derrick had dated.

"He worked hard for Maddy. We only saw each other for lunch some days and then the occasional weekend. He said he was doing it for us," she added, her voice changing with emotion.

Val felt sorry for the woman. Derrick had lied to her. His work schedule was nothing like he'd led her to believe.

The not-so-young woman looked at Val. "I know what I did was wrong, but I loved him."

"So you admit to sending the e-mail," Randall said, his face expressionless. "What else?"

"I called and cancelled the iron work order. Derrick said we had to pay her back. Said the money should have been his." Her accusatory gaze fixed on Val. "Derrick said Maddy started to hand him the lottery ticket, and then you walked up, and she handed it to you instead."

The depths of Derrick Masters's deception astonished Val. "That's ridiculous. He hadn't even come to work when Maddy arrived that morning."

Cheryl's mouth dropped open.

"Anything else?" Randall asked.

"I took information from the plans before I delivered them," she confessed. "I never believed he'd take advantage of me like this. He knew I'd do anything for him."

Val didn't doubt Derrick would take advantage of his mother if he had one. Feeling sorry for the misguided woman, she made a decision to forgive. "I won't file charges."

"Oh, thank you," Cheryl cried.

"I can't speak for Mr. King," she warned.

Cheryl glanced at her boss and back at Val. "Derrick is a rat," she pronounced vehemently. "There was something else. He thought it was so funny. He left your launch party at Sheridan Farm early and managed to feed one of your horses drugged sugar cubes."

"Are you sure?" Val demanded.

Cheryl nodded. "I remember how happy he was to have rubbed his presence in your face. He tried to stir up the planners to ask questions about your money instead of your new venture. Said you didn't like talking about winning the lottery. When that didn't work he left early.

"He was furious that you'd done so well with your business. I wouldn't be surprised if he's picking the new wife's pockets to come up with funding to start a similar business. He thought it was the ultimate payback. Said you'd never figure out it was him."

"My father was injured because of that incident," Val told her. "The horse reacted very badly and threw him against a fence. He was knocked unconscious and hurt his leg on his birthday."

"Oh!" Cheryl cried, covering her mouth with her hand. "I'm so sorry."

"Derrick is fortunate Daddy didn't suffer any long-term consequences," Val said, anger rising up in her throat at the thought of anyone doing something so evil. "Though I'm not sure what decision my father will make regarding Derrick's actions when he learns the truth. That horse and the foal she's carrying are very important to him and worth a considerable sum."

"I hope he makes him pay," Cheryl said, emotion fueling her fury.

A few moments of silence and uncomfortable stirring followed her words.

"You can go back to your desk, Cheryl," Randall told her. "Don't leave the building. We're not finished with this discussion."

"Yes, sir."

Val looked at Russ. "I'm sorry. I shouldn't have doubted you."

"I understand," he told her, his eyes communicating his sincerity. "You couldn't know Derrick and Cheryl were involved. I didn't either. I suspected Mr. King, and I should have shared the truth with you sooner. I let cowardice stand in the way of protecting you."

"I didn't do anything," Randall objected.

"Only because God protected Val's family from your efforts," Russ told him.

"None of these incidents had anything to do with me," Randall King declared.

"Why did Cheryl deliver the plans?" Val asked. "Russ told me you always do that."

"I was tied up and asked Cheryl to leave work early and take them."

"I knew that package was complete when I handed it over," Russ said.

"Here's your money," Randall said, pushing a company check across the table. "I can only apologize and assure you nothing like this will happen again."

Val pushed the check back. "I meant what I said. I'll absorb my loss. I won't file charges either." Rolling her chair back, she stood. "You have to make your decision, but she's more victim than criminal. Thank you for resolving this matter.

"I do have another request," she said, glancing over at Russ and then back at Randall King. "Russ is a good friend, and the stance he's taken today has been in my defense. I'm asking that you do the honorable thing and not seek retribution. He battled company loyalty against our friendship, but he's also been dedicated to his work here at Prestige. I haven't made it easy for him. I've put him in tough situations, but he's done a commendable job. He will make a fine architect, and I don't want his internship to suffer because of this incident."

"I'll take your request under advisement," Randall agreed.

Val tapped the check and reminded him, "Do unto others, Mr. King."

Respect filled the man's expression as he nodded.

The attorney paused to speak to Randall King, and Russ followed Val from the conference room. He waited while she walked over to the front desk and spoke to Cheryl. The gratitude on the woman's teary-eyed face spoke volumes.

"What did you say to her?" Russ asked.

"That I was sorry Derrick misled her. I can't believe he took advantage of her like that. I'm furious he caused that accident. Daddy could have been killed."

"Anyone know where he is?"

"No."

"The police would find him if you filed charges."

"I plan to tell Daddy and leave the decision to him."

"Good idea," Russ agreed. "Thanks for what you said in there."

"Thanks for doing what you did," Val said. "I know it was difficult to risk your standing in the firm."

"Not really," Russ admitted. "Lately I've learned doing the right thing might not be easy, but it makes you feel better about yourself."

Val wished she felt better. Blaming Russ had been easy. She called herself his friend, but she hadn't trusted him. "I'm so sorry I doubted you."

"I'm ready to put this behind us. I want to finish your project."

"I don't think anyone else could do it justice," she said.

Their gazes met and held. "Thanks. Can I come over tonight to talk? Just hear me out. That's all I'm asking."

She owed him that much. "You want to come for dinner?"

"Not tonight. I'll be there around eight if that's okay."

"I'll see you then."

Val barely touched her meal as she considered what Russ wanted to discuss. Anxiety filled her as she wondered if he thought they could pick up where they had left off. Val wished they could. Why couldn't things be different? She'd been so relieved today to learn he hadn't been involved.

When he arrived Russ spent a few minutes discussing their meeting with Val and her family before he asked if she'd like to visit the site with him. She drove the golf cart and parked near the structure.

"I know you wonder what's on my mind."

Val nodded.

"I care about you, and while I consider you a friend my feelings go much deeper."

"Why are you telling me this, Russ? Nothing has changed."

"It has. I have." His earnest declaration reached out to her in the darkness. "I need to understand what you expect from me."

Puzzled, Val said, "I can't expect anything of you. The decision is yours."

"What if I said I'd like to take you up on your offer to visit your church?"

"There's nothing I'd love more, but I'd ask why."

"That's fair," Russ said. "I really want to put this behind us, but you need to hear this. I haven't felt this alone since my parents died. I didn't know how to prove my innocence. I didn't even know what would happen when we walked into that conference room today. Once Randall King took over the investigation, he shut me out. I think he had his doubts about where my loyalties lay.

"But God has been busy in my life. Rom picked up where you left off. I couldn't understand why a loving God could let my parents die in that horrible accident or have Wendell betray me. Anger has controlled my life for years, and

I haven't wanted to let go. One night we sat down to dinner, and Rom prayed that God would protect me from all harm.

"It threw me back to a time in school when I pulled another crazy stunt and the doctor said God must be working overtime to protect me. I wondered how that could be. God never had any reason to care about me. I found myself needing Him to care. I dug out my Bible and tried to go it alone, but I needed spiritual feeding. I went to church and enjoyed the experience."

Surprised by his revelation, Val asked, "What have you decided?"

"That I'm committed to developing a relationship with my Savior. I know I have a long road ahead of me. I'm taking baby steps. Trying to understand where I fit in." Russ smiled. "I took a wise woman's advice and did what she said a smart man would do. I'm finding my answers."

Joy blossomed within her like a glorious rose on a sunny day. "I can't tell you how happy that makes me."

"Because we're friends?"

"Yes," Val said. "Definitely that, but I wanted you to know the peace that only God can give you."

"I want to know it."

She grinned. "Can I hug my dear friend?"

Russ opened his arms, and Val leaned forward, into the arms of the man she loved with all her heart.

Chapter 16

I'm sorry the pavilion isn't ready for the party," Russ said the morning of her mother's birthday. He had arrived with Rom the previous evening and stayed to help them set up for the events.

They planned a day of parties for her mother's celebration. The day event included family, friends, and the entire church. There were games and activities, and Opie had planned an extensive barbecue luncheon. That night they would celebrate with family and close friends with a dinner at the house.

"Just gives us a good reason to plan another reunion for the spring," Val assured him with a smile. "Aren't the gardens beautiful?"

Not as beautiful as the woman who stood before him, Russ thought. "We'd better get busy. The guests will be arriving soon."

He remained by her side as they completed the million-and-one tasks. Her mother was very surprised, and it was a wonderful day; but by that afternoon, Val was exhausted. She found her paternal grandmother inside the tent and hugged her. "It's so good to see you, Grammy."

"You should visit me more often."

Val dropped into the chair next to her. "The business keeps me occupied."

Her grandmother Truelove nodded. "Your dad keeps me updated on what you've been doing. I'm proud of the way you've handled this situation."

Val smiled her thanks. "You could come and spend time with us now. There's a guest room."

After her last heart attack, Lena Truelove hadn't been able to travel much. She lived in an assisted living apartment in Florida, and her daughter, Karen, who lived nearby, checked on her daily. "Has Jacob adapted to living in the big house yet?"

"He's trying."

The two women shared a familiar smile. "I'd love to see that for myself. Probably want to wait until it's warmer though. These old bones have adapted to Florida weather. And who is this young man I've seen you with today?" she asked, indicating Russ who stood nearby talking with her uncle Zeb.

Val motioned him over. "This is Russell Hunter. Russ, this is my grandmother, Lena Truelove."

"My pleasure, ma'am," he told her with a big smile.

"I've wanted to meet Val's young man ever since her daddy told me about him."

Val felt the blush warming her skin in the cool November air. "Oh, he's not... what did Daddy say?"

"He mentioned Russ about the time he started coming to the farm. Jacob says there's something about the two of you together. He had a feeling."

Val glanced at Russ and said, "We certainly argued enough in the beginning."

"But you like me now," Russ said confidently.

Her grandmother chuckled. "Your dad told me about visiting his father. Thank you for that."

While Val believed God had directed her in the situation, she could only hope she'd handled it in the right way. When she shared her concerns with Russ, he suggested she give it time. He'd reminded her the situation hadn't developed overnight.

"You think it was a good idea?"

Lena nodded. "Your dad has been angry with his father for a very long time. Jacob is a good man, but he's letting this stand in the way of his complete fulfillment with God. It's time he let it go."

"He was furious when Grandfather Truelove learned about the money."

Her grandmother's soft smile told Val she understood her son. "Jacob's afraid for you, honey. Mathias won't help himself. I knew he had problems when we met, but I allowed myself to hope."

"He asked about you," Val said.

Her grandmother's smile was bittersweet. "I loved him. In some ways I still do, but I'm a much wiser woman since I started thinking with my head instead of my heart."

Val glanced at Russ. She knew he'd read her mind.

"Jacob blamed his father for so much, but the decisions were mine. I could have said no."

"Why didn't you?" Russ asked.

"The others wised up to him pretty quickly, but I gave Mathias chance after chance. I hoped he'd prove everyone wrong."

"You loved him that much?"

"He was my husband. After I committed to your grandfather and the children came along, I did what I had to do to keep my family intact. He might not have been much of a husband or father, but he was all we had. I have my regrets. Between us we forced Jacob to grow up too fast. He was determined none of them would follow their father's example. No child should have to shoulder that kind of burden at such a young age."

"I don't know if we'll ever reach Grandfather Truelove, but I know we have to try."

"Keep at it, Val. You'll make a difference. And I might just go with you one of these days and see Mathias myself."

The comment surprised her. Val knew her grandmother's health had deteriorated after her grandfather's incarceration. The first heart attack had nearly killed her, but her children had rallied around to protect and care for her. More scary times had come up in the intervening years, but God had answered their prayers and kept her with them. "I doubt you could talk Daddy into that."

"You forget I'm his mother," she said, her brown eyes so much like those of her son and granddaughter. "If I say I want to go he won't like it, but he'll take me."

"Pray for him, Grammy."

"I do, honey. Every day of my life I pray for each one of you. Now you two run on and spend time with your mother. It's her day."

Later that evening, after they had dressed for dinner, Val and Russ took a walk out to the pavilion. They stood atop the structure looking out into the distance. The beauty of fall surrounded them in the glorious russet reds, oranges, and golds of the trees and the glow of a beautiful sunset.

"Can you imagine how this will look come spring?"

"I'm told by a very reliable source it will be spectacular," Russ teased.

"Just wait and see," Val said.

"I plan to be right here. I've enjoyed hearing myself referred to as Val's young man today."

"I'm so embarrassed. My family gets carried away at times."

"I like that about them," Russ said. "It's good to be around people who say and do what they feel without hesitation."

"Oh, that's always a definite in this group."

Silence stretched for a couple of minutes as they both looked out over the vista.

Russ turned to face her and reached for her hand. "Val, I'm very glad to have you as my friend."

She squeezed his hand. "I learned a valuable lesson on friendship and trust from you."

"From me?"

She nodded. "You can't have one without the other. I said you were my friend; but when things got bad I didn't trust you, and that was wrong."

"But I understood why."

"Not at first. You were hurt and angry and wanted nothing to do with me, but you didn't let it stand in the way of looking out for me when things got bad."

"Because I care for you."

"I know. And I care for you."

"Enough to consider me as a potential future mate?"

The breath rushed from her chest. "Do you understand where this is headed if I say yes?"

"Just so you're clear on my intentions, I want to spend time getting to know you and your family better with the intention of holy matrimony in our future."

"What about your family? Did you see Wendell today?" Val asked, hopeful Russ had taken a step toward healing their relationship. He nodded, and she knew without asking that they hadn't spoken to each other. "At least talk to him, Russ. He's your brother."

"Why do you insist when you know how I feel?"

"Didn't you hear anything Grammy said today about forgiveness? Do you really want to waste years of your life hating your brother? Just listen to what he has to tell you."

Russ frowned and asked suspiciously, "What do you know, Val?"

"Wendell told Opie his mother left Hunter Farm to him."

"His mother?"

Val nodded. "It was part of her inheritance. The will stipulated that the farm go to her firstborn son."

"But it has Dad's name."

"I don't know the specifics, but I'm sure Wendell will tell you if you asked."

"Why hasn't he said something before now?"

"Would you have listened?"

"No," he admitted guiltily. "My determination to play judge and jury didn't provide much opportunity for him to share the truth."

"He's your brother, Russ. That didn't change because you were angry with him."

"I've shut him out for too long, Val. He's not going to talk to me."

"Your job is to seek forgiveness. His is to forgive. If you're truly committed to changing your life, you have to do this."

"You never stop asking the impossible of me."

"It isn't as impossible as you believe. You can live out your days on earth without your family, or you can enrich your life and Wendell's by being his brother. One day you'll be an uncle to his children. Do you want to miss out on that because of something so silly?"

"Not if what you say is true."

"Opie got it straight from Wendell's lips."

Russ shook his head sadly. "Dad always made such a big deal about a man being the breadwinner for his family. Now I'm thinking maybe he said that to cover his shame because Wendell's mom provided his livelihood."

"I'm sure your father did his part to make the farm successful," Val said. "Neither you nor Wendell has ever lacked for anything."

"That's true."

"I don't want money or possessions to come between us."

"We won't let them."

"They came between you and Wendell."

"Because I was young and foolish and thought I knew everything," Russ said. "I've changed, and I promise you now that we'll take all the time we need to come to an agreement over our future. I know you have the money, and I will support you in the decision-making process."

"Finances could play a major role in our relationship."

"Not if we give control over to God. If we seek Him in our decision making, we will always make the right choice."

"We will," she said, smiling. "And, yes, I'd love to get to know you better with the intention of becoming your wife."

Russ hugged her, swinging Val about in his joy. Their laughter floated in the evening air.

"Sorry to interrupt, but Opie says it's time for dinner." They turned in the direction of her dad's voice as he walked toward them.

"Good. I'm starved," Val said.

"Russ, can I have a couple of minutes with my daughter?"

"Yes, sir. I'll tell everyone you're on the way."

After Russ disappeared down the stairs, Val asked, "What's wrong, Daddy?"

"I didn't mean to eavesdrop, but what you said to Russ about his brother. . . that applies to me and my father, too." His voice choked up, and tears spilled from his eyes. "For years I've blamed him for the things he did, certain he could have been different if he'd loved us enough. I call myself a Christian, but I forgot one major thing. Forgiveness. I need to forgive my father. I don't want to hate him anymore."

Val wrapped her arms about his waist. "Then forgive him, Daddy. Tell him and know you're a better person because you no longer harbor that anger. Pray that God will open his eyes to the life he's living and turn him around so we'll see him in heaven one day."

"I'm with Russ on this one. It seems impossible."

"Haven't you always told us nothing is impossible when God is in it? Pray for the right words and the strength to do what you need to do. I'll pray, too. And if you want, I'll be right by your side when you go to tell him."

"I love you, Valentine. You know, I never considered just how much parents learn from their children. You're one wise young lady."

"Who has been blessed with very wise parents," she told him. "Daddy, will you help me help Russ through this situation with Wendell? He needs to seek his brother's forgiveness, too."

"We'll all help each other. You made a very strong point for Christianity today, Valentine. We both got the message loud and clear."

❧

Russ nearly did a jig as he ran down the steps and toward the house. She'd agreed to consider a future with him. The utter hopelessness that had filled him for so long had lessened with his growing relationship with God. The hope Val had given him for their future and the love he had for her made him happier than he'd thought possible.

The last few weeks had definitely been a season of growth in his personal life. The pastor's sermon on that first Sunday he'd attended church had been on persecution. Russ identified with his subject. While Russ understood his experience was nothing like that of Jesus Christ, he couldn't help but wonder why things happened as they did. That morning's scripture had been Hebrews 13:6, "So that we may boldly say, The Lord is my helper, and I will not fear what man shall do unto me.'"

Russ remembered sitting in the pew after the sermon ended, his head filled with all he had heard and read. He reread the scripture. Was this how Val handled the situations that confronted her?

When Pastor Henry came to stand by the pew and asked if everything was okay, Russ glanced up. "Yes, sir. I was thinking about your sermon."

They discussed the message for a few minutes before the pastor asked, "What brought you to our church, Russ?"

The truth poured from him like water from a pitcher. "Something happened, and all fingers pointed to me. I'm innocent, and the one person I wanted to trust me most had doubts. I understood why. . ."

"But they hurt?"

"Yes, sir, they did."

"Why do you suppose that happened?"

"I acted in a way that led her to have those doubts."

"But if she's a friend. . ."

"She is. She worries about my salvation."

"Ah," Pastor Henry said with a nod of his head. "A very good friend indeed."

"I'm beginning to see that more clearly every day. When I asked her out she refused. I thought she had played me along, but then I realized she's standing up for her beliefs."

"Sounds like she's more than a friend."

"I'd like for her to be. That's one of the reasons I'm here." When Russ saw his words displeased the man, he said, "I know the most important reason is to get to know Jesus as my Savior."

Pastor Henry nodded. "And have you?"

"I'm working on it. God was never part of my life so I didn't feel any connection. It's only since I met this wonderful family that has God at their center that I've begun to wonder."

"Are you open to the possibilities?"

"I think so. Her brother has helped me understand so much. He attends with me when he can, but he's very active in his own church."

"Why didn't you go there?"

"I didn't want to raise their hopes. If this doesn't work out. . ."

"Do you doubt it will?"

"No, sir. In fact, my mind is clearer than it's been in a very long time."

Pastor Henry smiled. "Would you care to join us for lunch?"

Russ stood quickly, gathering his papers together and stuffing them into his Bible. "I'm sorry. I'm holding you up."

The man patted his shoulder kindly. "They know not to wait on me. My wife has kept many a plate warm while I minister to my flock. Feel free to talk to me anytime you feel the need."

Russ thanked the pastor for his time and left. He'd taken the man up on his offer in the passing weeks. Pastor Henry had helped him a great deal.

Too bad he wasn't around now to help him talk to Wendell. Russ dreaded the conversation. He'd misjudged Wendell, and now he had to make it right. No time like the present, he thought as he let himself into the house.

Chapter 17

Will these do for where you're taking me tonight?" Val asked as she entered Opie's room carrying a pair of boots. She wore the long-sleeved, jewel-toned wool dress Opie said would look nice and help ward off the winter chill.

"They're fine," Opie said. "You might as well give up, birthday girl. It's a surprise, and you're not going to get it out of me. And would you please stop moping around like you've lost your best friend?"

Val looked meaningfully at the vase of roses sitting on Opie's nightstand. "At least the man in your life remembered Valentine's Day. You should have gone out with him. You would have had more fun."

Opie walked closer and rubbed two fingers together in Val's face. "Know what this is? The world's smallest violin player. The poor-little-me act isn't working."

Val laughed. "Okay. I'll try to have fun."

"That's all I'm asking." Opie walked away and paused at the window. "Looks like someone left the pavilion lights on again."

Dropping onto the side of the bed, Val tugged on her boots. "I'll run out and turn them off while you finish dressing."

"I'll be ready by the time you get back," Opie promised before she disappeared into the bathroom.

Val wondered where everyone was as she walked through the house, pausing in the mudroom to pull on her coat. In the garage, she opted for the jeep, thinking it would have better traction in the lingering snow. She couldn't wait for spring.

Her thoughts returned to how Russ had called early that morning to cancel their date. Not only was it Valentine's Day, but it was also her birthday. It hurt that he considered anything more important than that.

In the past months they had grown so much closer, and she had hopes their relationship would soon advance to the next step. When Heath proposed to Jane at Christmas, Val had been happy for them but wished it were her and Russ. She longed to be his wife and in time the mother of his children. She'd been at his side when he committed his life to Christ. Her entire family had celebrated his baptism with him. That night over dinner he'd explained that the baptism was his outward expression of the man in Christ he planned to become.

Russ's determination to do things right meant growing in his relationship with God as well as with her. Val knew his relationship with God would strengthen theirs as well.

God was definitely hard at work in their lives. She was thankful Randall King had not taken any action against Russ. He'd been able to use his time with the firm when he applied to take his exam. Val had been so happy when he told her he'd passed. They had discussed his opening a business in Paris but made no final decision.

Russ and Wendell had talked and Val was happy his brother hadn't turned him away. Val felt confident they would eventually heal their relationship. She wasn't as sure about the relationship between Opie and Wendell. Her sister admitted to caring deeply for Wendell and Val wished she'd never taken her to the bachelor auction.

Glad they had restructured the entrance to the colonnade so it no longer required gates, Val drove up as close as possible and climbed out.

She noted that the lighting wasn't typical. It looked more like a canopy of twinkling lights over the ironwork. Had Jane forgotten to tell her the area was booked for the evening? Probably by a romantic out to impress his girl.

Val patted her pockets and realized she'd left her cell phone at the house. She couldn't even call and ask. She decided to check out the situation before putting someone in the dark.

At the top of the steps, she paused, puzzled by the sight of a single table and chair, a long red rose, and Russ wearing a tuxedo. "What's going on?" she asked, looking around.

"I see you drove out in our chariot," Russ said, indicating the jeep. They had laughed together when Val admitted she had intentionally used the jeep that day. He held out his hand. "Please join me."

"I can't," she whispered. "Opie's waiting at the house."

If his smile hadn't given away that Opie was in on this, his words told Val. "Oh, I don't think she'll have a problem if you don't come back right away."

"What's going on, Russ?"

He took her hand and led her over to the chair draped with a faux fur lap blanket. After seating her, Russ pulled her coat closed and tucked another blanket about her legs. He reached for the rose. "For you, my sweet."

He had been busy. Not only had he strung hundreds of lights, he'd also cleared the pavilion floor of snow and ice. He must have spent the day out here setting up his surprise. Now she understood why Opie had kept her away from home. A gust of wind hit them, and Val shivered. "It's freezing out here."

"I know. We'll go inside soon. Happy Valentine's Day, my Valentine. Forgive me?"

"I thought you forgot."

"Never," he said with a big smile. "Because of you, Valentine's Day will always be a favorite celebration in my life."

"It is hard to forget Valentine's Day when you love someone," she told Russ. "You hurt my feelings when you cancelled our date."

"I know, and I'm truly sorry, but I had to do it to carry out my special plans."

Taking her hands in his, Russ said, "When we first met last spring, I had no idea how much I would come to love you."

Tears filled her eyes with his declaration of love. It thrilled her to hear him say the words.

"You've been a true blessing in my life, Val. Before we met I was content with my life of sin; but now I know what it is to be loved by Jesus, and I'll never accept anything less again."

He knelt on a tiny footstool at her feet. "I owe you for leading me along the right path. If you hadn't shared your faith I might never have realized how lost I truly was."

Val wrapped her arms about his neck and hugged him tightly.

He maintained that hold. "I know you're wondering why I brought you out into the cold tonight."

She nodded and hiccupped slightly. "We thought someone left the lights on accidentally."

"No accident. Only the best of intentions," he promised.

"Russ?" His name came out as a mere whisper.

He pulled back and focused on her. "I chose the place that has been significant in our relationship to ask you something very important. The pavilion drew us together in a way no other place ever could. We overcame great obstacles here.

"I came to appreciate the beauty you wanted me to see from day one. But I found something far more beautiful here at Sheridan Farm, Val. Far more incredible than Kentucky farmland, thoroughbreds, and rolling hills. I found you."

"Oh Russ."

He touched his finger to her lips when she started to say more. "I know I haven't been easy to work with. Probably even frustrating at times; but after I understood, I only became more determined to make you happy.

"When all those crazy things started happening, I became afraid for you and for the family I'd come to love. I never want anything bad to happen to any of you.

"You irritated me when you refused to side with me about Wendell, but once the truth came out I knew I'd been wrong. I'm thankful to have my brother back in my life. I owe that to you, Val.

"You've helped me understand how money can be both a blessing and a burden. I'll never look at worldly possessions in the same way now that I have heaven as my ultimate destination."

She shivered, and he pulled her closer. "I know, talk faster," he teased.

Russ pulled a blue velvet jeweler's box from his pocket. "I love you with all my heart, Valentine Truelove. Will you do me the honor of becoming my wife?"

"Oh Russ." She sounded like a broken record.

"I don't hear a yes in there."

She took his face in her hands and said yes each of the three times she kissed him.

He slipped the ring on her finger, and Val admired the heart-shaped diamond with two hearts of smaller diamonds curved along the sides.

"I hope you don't plan to make me wait too long."

"Is June soon enough?" she asked. "After all, we already have the perfect venue, and I know the ideal wedding planner and caterer. And there just happens to be one weekend open in Your Wedding Place's schedule."

"I always wanted a June bride," he declared before kissing her soundly. "Come with me. I have another surprise."

He summoned the lift, and they went to the lower floor where she found the room filled with their family and friends. She looked at him and smiled. "You were awfully confident. What if I'd said no?"

"I wasn't confident at all," Russ admitted. "If you refused, you had a Valentine-themed birthday party. If you said yes, it became a Valentine-themed birthday/engagement party. Opie even made two cakes just in case."

"Oh, there was no way I was going to let you get away once you popped the question," Val said with a laugh.

Russ pulled her into his arms and kissed her.

Opie pushed her way through the crowd, Wendell in her wake. "Did you say yes?"

Val held up her hand. "You know I did."

"You did good," Opie commented, clapping her future brother-in-law on the back.

"Thanks for sending her out," Russ said.

"We weren't sure how to get you out here," Opie explained. "The lights did the trick."

"Congratulations," Wendell said, hugging Val and then his brother.

Their closeness brought tears to her eyes. "Where are Mom and Dad?" Val asked, looking around. Her gaze followed Opie's pointing finger as she indicated the far side of the room. "Do they know?"

Opie nodded. "They're pleased with your choice."

"Me, too," Russ declared with a grin.

She grasped his hand in hers and pulled him over to where her parents stood.

"She said yes."

"I thought she might," Jacob Truelove said. "Russ asked my permission a while back. I said it was up to you, but both your mother and I approve of your choice. Russ is a fine young man."

Val looked at him through tear-filled eyes. "He's the answer to a prayer."

Chapter 18

R eady?"

Unable to push any words past the emotion that blocked her throat, Val nodded.

When she'd talked with her mother about both parents escorting her down the aisle, Cindy Truelove refused.

"Your dad has always looked forward to walking his girls to their future husbands. Let's not take that away from him."

Val understood. She felt that same love for Russ.

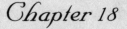

Nervous excitement filled him as Russ glanced over at Wendell at the baby grand piano and grinned. Over the past months he'd developed a definite appreciation for his future wife's love of weddings. The planning sessions had gone on forever, and today things had fallen into place with the precision of a well-orchestrated production.

When Val stepped forward, Russ felt as though his heart would leap from his chest. Cinderella couldn't have been more beautiful. The sun sparkled off the crystals in her tiara and the gold overlay of the white wedding dress.

Her father's proud bearing showed his enjoyment of the day, and more than ever Russ felt honored to become part of this family. Jacob placed Val's hand in his, and they walked to where the minister waited beneath the pavilion.

They shared a smile of joy when the man bowed his head and said, "Let us pray."

Author's Note

Typically, in fiction, when the author wants a character to have lots of money, they write their character into someone's will. When I started my "what if?" for something unique, I thought about someone telling me they had given lottery tickets as gifts, and asked myself how most Christians would deal with innocently winning the lottery.

As Christians, we often have a more conservative outlook toward the temptations of life. I personally have concerns with the lottery on many levels; so you might ask why I wrote this story.

Because I realized it could happen. Even though some of us choose not to expend funds on games of chance, millions of people do. What if someone gifted you with a winning lottery ticket? Would you be prepared for the outcome? Do you think it possible God could answer your prayers for financial help in such a way?

Val prayed and believed God would answer her prayers. She worked hard, and her boss rewarded her with a gift that made her a wealthy woman. What should she have done? Do we judge her harshly because she chose to be a good steward of the funds she felt God provided? What if it happened to someone you know?

In the story, Val worries about people judging her for the choice she made, and yet when she's confronted with the doubts about Russ, she judges him wrongly. Later, when she realizes what she's done, she seeks his forgiveness and grows in her service to God.

I truly felt the guiding hand of God in the creation of this story. It made me think, and I've had conversations with people about gambling that I would never have had otherwise.

My prayer is that if anyone is struggling with this addictive lifestyle and reads this book, they will understand that God loves them just as they are, and He can change their lives if they will only trust Him.

Terry Fowler

HEATH'S CHOICE

Dedication

To my brothers Billy, Steve, and Tim. Love you guys.

And to those forced to live with the choices made by loved ones.
May they feel God's healing love.

Chapter 1

"You remember Jane Kendrick from high school?"

His older sister's voice faded into the distance as Heath Truelove stared into the beautiful green gaze he'd found so mesmerizing in his youth. If possible, Jane Kendrick Holt looked more beautiful today than she had in high school.

She flashed the appealing smile that had first attracted him to her. *She hasn't changed,* Heath thought. "Sure do," he said as he moved to stand. "It's good to see you."

"You, too." Jane waved him back into the booth and when he slid over, sat down next to him. "Val keeps me current on you guys. Congratulations on your degree. How's Rom?"

Heath swallowed hard and said, "Thanks. He's good. We're waiting for him now. He had an interview today."

A frown touched her beautiful face. "Hope his luck is better than mine. I should have accepted that clerk position."

"No, you shouldn't have," Val said. "I have a couple of ideas that will work for you in the future. You deserve better than a minimum wage job."

"Now is my future," Jane said unhappily. "I have to find work."

"You will. Join us for lunch."

"Yes, please do," his younger sister, Opie, said.

"I don't want to intrude."

"You know us Trueloves. The more the merrier," Opie said with a big grin.

Jane accepted and ordered diet soda. Heath sat back and watched the interplay between her and his sisters. Obviously she and Val had formed a close friendship. Heath wondered when that had happened.

"Why don't you come out to the farm tomorrow? I have an idea I'd like to discuss with you," Val said.

"Can I bring Sammy? I called in the last of my favors for the interview today."

"Please do. Daddy might even take her for a ride."

"She'd love that. She's so horse crazy right now."

"Who's Sammy?" he asked.

"My two-year-old."

"You have a daughter?" Jane's nod reminded him she was off-limits— another man's wife. "I know Garrett is very happy."

Jane's ivory skin paled even more before she said, "Garrett's dead, Heath."

His heart took a nosedive into his stomach. "Oh man, I'm sorry. I didn't know. What happened?"

The words were out before he caught his sisters' warning headshakes.

"He killed himself," Jane said, her voice breaking.

The revelation stunned Heath. Why hadn't anyone told him? He talked to his family regularly, and no one had said a word. It couldn't have been that long ago. Last time he saw them, they were living and working in Lexington after Garrett dropped out of the University of Kentucky. He had visited the coffee shop now and then while he waited for Rom. He'd enjoyed watching Jane with the customers. Her friendly personality made her popular with the patrons.

"Wouldn't you love to see a picture of Jane's daughter, Heath?" Under the table, Opie's foot connected painfully with his leg.

He jumped and said, "Sure. Is she as pretty as her mom?"

Heath noticed the way Jane's cheeks flushed with the question. He appreciated his sister's attempt to salvage the situation. He'd blundered big-time. He should have just waited and let it come out naturally.

"She's beautiful." She dug around in her huge purse and pulled out a brag book. "But that's a very prejudiced mom talking."

As he viewed the photos, Heath had the feeling that little Sammy looked very much as her mother had as a child. "You're entitled. She's gorgeous," he said, handing the photo book back to Jane.

"She makes my life worth living."

"I can see why."

"I've spoiled her terribly," Jane admitted. "She can be quite a handful."

Their group continued to grow as they waited for Rom. Russ Hunter, the architect who Val had hired to design a structure for Your Wedding Place, showed up at the restaurant, and when he stopped to speak to Val, Opie invited him to join them. They asked for a larger table, and Rom joined them a few minutes later.

Just as Heath expected, Jane fit right into the group. She caught up with Rom, who somehow managed to avoid the topic of Garrett's death. When Russ brought up the subject of the seven Truelove kids' nicknames, she chuckled and said, "I still remember the first time I heard them called by their real names. We had a substitute, and she was checking attendance. When she said Heathcliff and Romeo Truelove, I couldn't believe they were really named that."

"Jane is a name from the classics, too," Heath said.

She made a face. "Jane is a grandmother's name. Not romantic or fancy. Just plain Jane."

The conversation moved on to Val's project and other topics, and Heath found himself following Jane's responses. She laughed, joked, and stayed right in the middle of everything, just as she'd done all those years ago. All too soon lunch was over, and the group started to break up. Russ made his excuses and returned to work.

"I need to pick up Sammy," Jane said. "It's been great seeing everyone again."

"You, too," Heath said, standing when she pushed her chair back. "I'm really sorry about Garrett."

Jane smiled sadly. "Thanks."

"Please come to the farm tomorrow," Val said. "I really want to talk to you."

"Sure," Jane said. "Just name a time. I have a serious gaping hole in my schedule at present."

"Come around eleven and stay for lunch."

"You don't have to keep feeding me," Jane protested with a smile.

"I'll make one of my culinary specialties," Opie offered.

Jane nodded. "We'll be there, though I warn you Sammy's a picky eater."

"Ah, but she's never had an Opie Truelove meal."

"Is that like a fast-food kid's meal?" Val teased.

Opie grimaced at her sister and then said, "Once she tastes my food, you'll have problems getting her to eat anything else."

Jane laughed and said, "I'll risk it. Thanks for lunch."

"Don't thank us," Val said. "Russ Hunter paid."

"Thank him for me when you see him again."

She waved bye as she walked toward the door. Heath's gaze never left her.

❧

Jane unlocked her truck and climbed inside. She had needed this. Limited conversation with a two-year-old made those times she was in the presence of adults even more special. She had enjoyed the lively interaction of the five adults and the challenge of keeping up with the discussion.

Yet another reason she missed her job at the coffee shop. She'd enjoyed catching up with the people who came in for their daily coffee runs.

As she drove out of the parking lot, Jane wondered what Val wanted to talk to her about. The need to find work had become a necessity, but Jane couldn't imagine what Val thought she could do to help. Then again, Val had the money to do whatever she wanted. Maybe she planned to open a coffee shop. Jane still couldn't get over the fact that her best friend had won millions with a lottery ticket gifted to her by her boss.

Val had shared a number of her plans, including the purchase of Sheridan Farm where her father had worked as a manager for the previous owner, and then her plans for Your Wedding Place had struck Jane as a total fantasy with a healthy dose of financial reality. Her friend planned to utilize twenty-five acres of the farm, including the spectacular existing gardens and the house to create venues for brides who wanted unusual wedding locations.

Jane had no doubt the Trueloves would utilize their money to help others as well. She'd witnessed Val's huge heart many times since they had struck up a friendship. And she remembered Heath and Rom from high school. Everyone in their class knew the two kindhearted, intelligent young men would go far.

She had enjoyed seeing Heath and Rom. Like everyone else, the twins fascinated her, but today as she looked at them, each so alike and so different, she saw men who stood on their own. Jane didn't know why she'd never realized how attractive Heath was. His strong, clean-shaven facial features and neatly trimmed dark hair said a lot about his need for a clean-cut personal appearance. He'd worn well-pressed khakis and a long-sleeved baby blue oxford shirt that lay open at the neck.

Jane found his personality to be his best feature. He could laugh at himself, didn't mock people, and obviously loved his family. She had always considered him serious-minded and more mature than his years, and yet today he'd been right in his element with his sisters and brother teasing him. If anyone fit the family man image, it would be Heath. The way he laughed with easy abandon fascinated her. It had never been something she associated with his more serious nature.

The Trueloves had an interesting family dynamic. She wondered if the others had noticed the change in Val when Opie invited Russ Hunter to join them. The two sisters had lingered behind when they had changed tables, and Jane didn't think Val had been too happy about the situation. His references to making progress on her project seemed to strike a dissonant chord as well. Perhaps they were at odds over the work.

She signaled and turned into her friend's driveway. She'd visit for a while and then take Sammy home. At least she had something to look forward to tomorrow. Maybe even plans for the future, and she couldn't think of anything she'd like more.

Chapter 2

Early the next morning Heath lay in bed, thoughts of the reunion with Jane filling his head. Awakened by the younger boys' school preparations, he hadn't been able to go back to sleep. His mind reeled with the news of Garrett's death. "Hey Rom, you awake?"

His twin grunted from the lower bunk of the beds on the opposite side of the room and pulled the covers over his head. The four of them had shared the room with two sets of bunk beds since the two younger boys had moved out of cribs.

He crossed his arms behind his head and said, "Jane looked good, don't you think?"

Rom grunted again.

"She's coming out this morning to talk to Val about a job."

Rom thrust the covers aside, pushed his legs over the side of the bed, and sat up as much as the lower bunk would allow. "Yeah, I heard."

"She looks good."

"Yeah. I heard you the first time." Rom rubbed his face. "You always said she was out of your league."

Heath exhaled noisily and said, "I know, but I felt like I'd been poleaxed yesterday when she looked at me and smiled."

"She's still a looker," Rom agreed.

Heath knew what Rom was thinking. His twin had seen through his efforts to hide his attraction back when he was a boy of fourteen and Jane had entered their freshman class in Paris, Kentucky. He still remembered the first day she showed up at school.

She gained everyone's attention when she walked into the classroom, her waist-length blond hair swaying as she flashed the liveliest smile and whitest teeth he'd ever seen. She sat one row over from him and always seemed to have something going on.

Jane wore her hair short now, but though it was as blond as it had been then, he didn't think the color came from a bottle. Petite and thin, she didn't look like she had a two-year-old child.

For years he had admired her from afar. The cheerleader and most popular girl in their class had been nice to him, but he had known he didn't stand a chance of getting a date with her. Particularly after she'd become involved with the football quarterback, Garrett Holt. Then in their senior year she and Garrett had married hastily. That summer, rumor had it their baby had been stillborn. That fall, Jane and Garrett had moved into married student housing at the University

133

of Kentucky. Occasionally he saw them on campus, but he and Rom had driven from Paris to Lexington and lived at home, so he hadn't seen them often after graduation.

"Always has been. You know how I felt."

"I know you said you didn't stand a chance," Rom said. "What makes you think differently now?"

"I'm not thinking differently," Heath said somewhat defensively. "I'm just saying it was good to see her."

"Oh, you're thinking," Rom said without doubt.

"I'm praying that God will send the right woman, but so far that's not happened either."

"You think she's the one? Did you hope that Jane would become available again?"

Heath shot up out of the bed. "No way. I was shocked when she said Garrett was dead. How did you manage to avoid the subject?"

Rom stopped rummaging through the dresser drawer and looked at him. "You didn't know?"

"No. I can't believe no one said anything. I felt like a blundering idiot."

"I thought I told you," Rom said thoughtfully.

Heath shook his head. "No one in the family said a word. Not even Val and she attended the funeral."

"They probably thought you'd seen it in those local papers they sent us in Boston."

"I definitely missed the obit. What if seeing her again is a sign?"

Rom pulled on a T-shirt and asked, "Do you want it to be?"

Heath considered the question.

"You know how she was in school," Rom said when Heath didn't say anything. "Do you believe she's changed?"

"I know what was said, but I never believed Jane's reputation was as bad as gossip made it sound."

Rom's skeptical expression showed he lacked his twin's opinion of Jane. "I don't know, Heath."

Determined to put her in a better light, he said, "Think about it, Rom. She only dated Garrett. Then she married and stayed with him. Don't you think he would have dumped her if the rumors were true?"

"Who are you trying to convince?"

He shrugged. "I doubt it matters anymore now than it did then. I'm not Jane's type. She likes the more athletic type."

"Don't sell yourself short. You have a lot to offer a woman."

"Yeah, a couple of college degrees really go a long way when it comes to attracting a woman."

"Don't put yourself down like that. You'll be a much better provider because of those degrees."

Heath pushed down the guilt that spiraled through him at the dread of taking an office job. These last few days had been a reprieve from the responsibility he knew he had to shoulder. "Guess I'd better get started if I plan to finish those trees today."

"I'd help, but I promised Dad I'd give him a hand."

"I've got it under control." Heath grabbed his robe and headed for the shower.

"Heath," Rom called as he neared the door. "I'm praying, too. You'll find the right woman."

∽

Jane awakened early that morning, her head filled with the myriad of worries that weighed her down lately. She sat at the table, enjoying the diversion of the two squirrels that chased each other in the small yard as she drank her coffee.

Her eyes dropped to the bank statement on the tabletop. The minute savings account she'd managed to hold onto was dwindling fast. The rent on the little house she'd lived in for the past three years was paid until the end of June. After that, she had no idea where she and her child would lay their heads. That frightened her most of all. She didn't want Val Truelove doing anything out of charity, but if it was a legitimate job offer, she had no choice but to accept.

The mother in her instinctively recognized the sounds of stirring that came from Sammy's bedroom. Pushing open the door, she took a moment's pleasure in the room she'd decorated so lovingly when she learned her child was on the way. Once she became pregnant, Jane had insisted that they find a house. Apartments with no lawns weren't what she wanted for her child.

" 'Morning, sweetheart," she cooed as she lifted Samantha and gave her a hug. "We're going to see the horsies today."

"Horsies?"

Jane carried Sammy over to the changing table and quickly changed her and dressed her. Sammy wasn't as cooperative when it came to the socks and sneakers and curled her toes.

Jane drew a finger along the sole of her foot, and Sammy giggled. Her daughter was very ticklish. "We're going to see Mommy's friends who have horsies."

"Fends? Me see horsies."

Taking advantage of Sammy's distraction, Jane worked the tiny foot into the shoe and pulled the Velcro tab into place. She lifted and swung her around, enjoying her laughter. "Yes, sweetness. Let's get you fed and go meet Mommy's friends."

∽

When Heath saw Jane's truck drive up, he put the chain saw aside and walked over to greet them.

"Hi," Jane said, smiling at him before she opened the back door and leaned in to unhook Sammy. The child all but bounced out of the car seat.

"Well, hello there, cutie," he said to the little girl. "I'm Heath. Can you say Heath?"

Sammy rewarded him with a smile and stretched out her arms to him. "Want Hef hold me."

"May I?" he asked.

Jane let go when Sammy bounced impatiently, all but diving into his arms. "What is it?" he asked when he noticed Jane's widened eyes and wrinkled forehead.

"She never goes to strange men like that."

"I'm not strange," Heath protested with a grin. "Am I, Sammy?"

The little girl patted his cheeks with her tiny hands. "Hef have horsies? See horsies?"

"No, you're not," Jane said, embarrassed by her words. "I just meant…Garrett would get upset because she cried when he would take her."

"Me see horsies?"

He chuckled. "Somebody has a one-track mind. Think she'll stay with me while you go in and see Val?"

Jane hesitated. It would help her discussion with Val go more smoothly. She'd wondered how she would keep Sammy quiet long enough for them to talk. Leaving her with Heath seemed like the perfect solution, but Sammy had no idea who this strange man was. "I don't know, Heath. She can be a handful."

"What if I promise to bring her to you if she starts to cry? Otherwise we'll stay right here in the garden and play. You'll be able to see us from Val's office. All right, Sammy?"

The child clapped her hands together. "Sammy see horsies."

Jane relented. "Thank you."

He flashed a smile and said, "Val's waiting in the office. Go in the front door. First room on your left."

Jane watched as he stood the toddler on her feet in the grass. Sammy immediately took off, and Heath easily captured her. Jane laughed at his "Whoa there, little miss" when he pulled her back by the tail of her shirt. His soft tone as he talked to the little girl filled her heart with longing. Jane had dreamed of Sammy having this type of relationship with her father, but Garrett had destroyed any hope of that happening.

Pain spiraled through her. She couldn't think about that now. Jane hurried inside. It wouldn't be good for her to take advantage of Heath for too long. Inside the mansion, she stared in awe of the beautiful surroundings. What would it be like to own such a home?

"I thought I heard the door," Val said as she stepped into the hallway. "Quite a place, isn't it?"

"Incredible." Jane allowed her gaze to shift about the room. "I had no idea."

"I lived on Sheridan Farm all my life, but the big house was off-limits. Now that it's ours, we're all adjusting to the changes. Where's Sammy?" she asked.

"In the garden with Heath."

Val nodded. "Come into the office."

Jane listened while Val outlined the position duties. She couldn't help but feel as if it was too good to be true.

"It's not anything you're used to," Val said. "Daddy might send you into town to pick up a part. Mom could send you to the grocery store. You'll be helping in the gardens. Later, you'll assist with bookings and site preparation for the weddings."

"And you really intend to hire an assistant?" Jane asked. "I mean. . .well, I don't want you feeling like you have to help me."

"If it's not you, it will be someone else," Val said. "I've seen you in action at the coffee shop and think your experience would be a bonus for us both. It's not going to be easy. I'd expect you to work as hard as we do, but I'd pay you a fair wage. Later, as the plans develop, you would be considered for any managerial position that comes open if you're interested."

"When would I start?"

"Whenever you want. Tomorrow is good."

Why couldn't she just put aside her doubts and accept the opportunity she was being handed? "Can I think about it and get back to you later?"

Val flashed a sympathetic smile. "Don't think too long, Jane. You said you need to work, and I'm offering you a job. I have great plans for my business, and I'd like to have you with me. If you're concerned about it being a new business, let me assure you I have sufficient funds set aside to accomplish my goals. I'm not planning to change my mind and leave you unemployed again."

Jane couldn't dispute that she needed to work. Now wasn't the time to be stupid. "You're right. I do need to work. I accept your offer. I'll have to get Sammy enrolled in day care before I can start work."

"That's fine. We're working in the gardens right now, readying them to serve as venues. You met Russ Hunter yesterday. Hopefully he can wrap his mind around the idea and design the structure I plan to use for receptions."

Her words confirmed Jane's suspicions that things were not what they seemed between the two of them. "I got the impression he was having difficulties."

Val nodded. "One more thing. I'm keeping everything under wraps at present. So I'd appreciate it if you do the same."

"No problem. In fact, I consider confidentiality part of the job," she said.

Val grinned and said, "I'm going to like having you around."

It was close to lunchtime when they concluded the interview, and Val insisted she and Sammy join them.

"There's my Sammy girl," Val declared, taking the child from Heath's arms. "Come up to the house."

As Heath and Jane followed along behind, he asked, "How did it go?"

"She offered me a job as her assistant."

"So what do you think?"

Jane swept her hand through her bangs, pushing them out of her face. She needed a haircut. "I don't know, Heath. I've never done anything but manage a coffee shop. That's different from what Val has in mind."

"You don't feel like you can handle the job?"

"I guess I want to believe Val truly needs me," Jane admitted. "She's a good-hearted person who responds to people's needs."

"Oh, I suspect Val knows she'll be the winner in the deal. She's told us how good you were at your job."

His comment surprised Jane. "I should be. I worked there from the time we went off to UK." She'd started out as a clerk and worked her way up. Then the business had sold, and the new owners had no need for a manager.

"Yeah, but there's still work ethics. Not everyone cares about the quality of their work."

"That's true," Jane agreed.

"What does the job entail?"

"Why? You thinking of applying?" she teased at his curious question.

He laughed. "Maybe. I do need a job."

"Val said part of my duties would be helping out in the gardens. Then there's the scheduling for the venues, setting up for weddings, and running errands."

"A Jane of all trades?"

"And master of none," she said with a little frown.

"Don't be so hard on yourself. You think Val knows what she's doing with this new business venture?"

"At least she knows the business from the wedding planning perspective."

Heath shrugged and said, "I remember how nervous she was when she went to work with the wedding planner. She was certain she'd never get through the first day."

Jane felt uncomfortable with his revelation. "I don't think she'd care for you sharing that with me."

"Val would tell you herself if you voiced your concern," he said confidently. "She's not offering the job out of pity, Jane. She needs people she can depend on, and evidently you're at the top of her list."

His words gave her pause. "Thanks, Heath. Truthfully I can't refuse any valid job offer, but you've calmed my fears. I told Val I'd give it a try, and you make me believe I can do this."

"Sure you can," Heath said. "Now let's go see what Opie's prepared to tempt Sammy's appetite."

In the kitchen, Cindy Truelove held Sammy, and the child was all smiles.

"I can't get over how she's responding to all of you. I generally have to peel her off me around strangers."

"Maybe she feels safe," Heath said.

Jane understood how that could be a possibility. She had the same feeling in their presence. Over lunch around the crowded table, Jane sat on one side of Sammy with Heath on the other side. She bowed her head as Jacob Truelove blessed the food and then accepted a serving bowl from Cindy.

"Val tells me she's hired you as her assistant," Jacob Truelove said.

"I've agreed to try the job."

He nodded. "I'm sure you'll do fine. When do you start?"

"As soon as I get Sammy settled in day care."

"Why don't you bring her to work with you?"

Surprised, she looked at Val's mother and then at Val. Thoughts of how little she'd accomplish with her daughter around all day filled her head. "I couldn't," Jane said.

Cindy Truelove's gaze rested on Sammy. "I'd be happy to watch her. I miss having little ones around."

Jane looked at Val again, uncertain what she should say. "I'm sure your schedule is much too busy."

"Not at all. The other children will be out of school soon, and they could help, too."

She would love having Sammy nearby but didn't want to impose on the Trueloves anymore. Jane doubted Val's teenage sister and two younger brothers would appreciate babysitting a two-year-old all summer.

At her mother's hopeful look, Val said, "You might as well bring her along. Mom's not going to be happy until you agree."

A new job and a family of babysitters. Jane didn't know what to expect next. "Well, okay, but if it gets to be too much. . ."

Jacob roared with laughter. "You think one itty-bitty little girl will be too much for a woman who raised seven children of her own?"

"Yeah, Mom will have her doing chores in no time," Heath said, smiling when his mother tsked at him.

He leaned over and pretended to gobble up the bite of food Sammy held. She giggled and stuffed it in her own mouth. Opie had done well, providing a plate of bite-size foods that Sammy ate eagerly.

"Behave," Cindy told him before she spoke to Jane. "This way you'll be close by when she needs you, and she can see you throughout the day. No separation anxiety."

Sammy had gone to day care almost from birth. Even when he was out of work, Garrett wouldn't care for her, so she spent long hours with other people while Jane worked. She'd only taken her out of day care after she became unemployed and couldn't afford it.

"Jane's schedule will be flexible," Val said. "I'm thinking maybe nine to five thirty or so. Does that sound okay?"

She was used to much longer hours. "I can come earlier if you need me."

Val shook her head. "That's plenty early. Gives you time to drive from Lexington to Paris."

After lunch was finished and the kitchen cleaned, they all went to the horse barn with Sammy to visit the horses.

Evidently Heath had made a major impression, since she returned to him when she wanted something. The sight of Sammy reaching up her tiny hand to him so trustingly made Jane teary eyed.

He swung her up into his arms when Jacob brought out the horse. After his father climbed into the saddle, Heath passed Sammy up to him. Her smile reached from ear to ear when he settled her comfortably and set the horse off into a slow walk. While the Trueloves called out encouragement, Sammy clapped her hands in pure little girl joy and chattered to Jacob.

Heath walked over to stand by Jane's side. "I think we have a budding equestrian on our hands."

Jane nodded. "It's a good thing I took the job. It's Sammy's only hope of coming near a horse."

Chapter 3

Jane found that a routine developed quickly. She arrived around eight thirty, and they discussed plans for the day over a cup of coffee in the Truelove kitchen. Her confidence level increased daily as she mastered her assignments and realized Val hadn't created the position as a kindness to her friend. It felt good to know she could help Val while helping herself.

That afternoon Val went into Lexington and asked Jane to work with Heath in the English garden. She loved being outdoors, so the thought of spending any part of the beautiful day gardening suited her perfectly. The warmth of the sun against her skin made Jane feel like singing as she all but skipped out to the gardens. Heath worked at trimming the hedge wall, and she picked up a couple of handfuls of long clippings and offered an impromptu cheer.

"Come on, let's go! Let's go!" she shouted, gaining his attention. Smiling broadly, she moved her arms with the snappy motions she'd learned in cheerleading camps. "Trim that hedge! Trim it neat!" She tossed the trimmings into the garbage can with a flourish and added with a clap of her hands, "Truelove gardening can't be beat!"

"Go team!" Heath shouted, pumping the hedge trimmer into the air with one hand. "Jane, you're something else."

"Isn't it a glorious day?"

"I see Val kept you inside too long."

"She said I should work with you."

Heath flashed Jane a welcoming smile. "Where is Val?"

"She went into Lexington to sign papers. I asked why she didn't have them brought out here. She said she can't hide for the rest of her life."

Heath carefully tucked the trimmings from the rosebush into a trash bin. "We've teased her unmercifully about the Val sightings, but she's done a really great job of giving God full credit for the win."

Jane nodded in agreement, rubbing her hands together while she asked, "So what's the plan for today?"

"We can't get more of the material Mrs. Sheridan had laid for the patio in the formal garden, so Val and I agreed it's best to replace the stone. I thought we might get a start on pulling it out."

Jane reached for a pair of gloves. "How much are we removing? Would it work in that little sitting area off the water garden?"

"Hmm." Heath's eyebrows arched. "Great idea. Recycling could save some serious bucks."

"What if we hook up a hose and wash it off as we go?" Jane suggested. "If we had a cart, we could load it, too."

"You're full of good ideas. You hook up the hose, and I'll get the cart."

They worked steadily, prying the reluctant stones from the ground where they had lain for at least three decades. Heath propped and held the stone up while she aimed the hose. She missed, and the pressure of the flow shot dirt and water into the air.

"Hey, watch it," he said, stepping out of the way when her next effort splashed mud on his bare legs.

"Oh, I got you dirty," she said with teasing laughter. "Let me help."

The spray saturated his white sneakers and socks and splattered the cargo shorts he wore.

"Stop it."

"Don't be such a stick-in-the-mud." Jane laughed when he dropped the piece of stone, splashing even more mud on himself.

"Give me that hose," Heath said, chasing after her.

She aimed protective bursts of water in his direction as she agilely dodged him. Jane turned away when he came closer, and he wrapped his arms around her from behind and wrestled the hose away. After a few seconds, awareness made them both uncomfortable, and they moved apart.

"I'm sorry. I shouldn't have done that."

"No, you shouldn't have," he agreed, rejecting her attempt at remorse by aiming the spray at her legs and laughing when she darted across the yard. Moving target that she was, he still managed to hit her several times with his well-aimed jets.

"Okay, enough," Jane said, brushing her wet hair from her eyes. "We've got work to do."

"Spoilsport," he said with a laugh.

They returned to their task, Heath keeping his distance as he placed the stones against the cart for Jane to rinse. It wasn't long before she felt the results of the strenuous labor in her arms and back.

"Take a breather. You don't have to do it all," Heath said.

"That's what I'm used to," Jane told him. "Even when I worked all day, Garrett flopped in a chair and stayed there until I had dinner on the table."

"He didn't help with the chores?"

"Wasn't a man's place," Jane said, sarcasm filling her voice as she walked over to a bench and sat down. "His mother told him that. Clarice Holt waited on her husband and son hand and foot. According to Garrett, his parents wanted him to concentrate on football. I was so blind."

Heath paused in loading the stone onto the cart. "What do you mean?"

"I came to Paris from an even smaller town. Guess you could say I started to come into my own about the time I turned thirteen. I filled out, the braces came off, Mom took me to the dermatologist, and I got contacts." Jane couldn't believe she'd told him that. "You should know, very few women are natural beauties."

"I have three sisters. I know how much time you girls spend in the bathroom."

The changed appearance gave her the confidence to try new things. Becoming a cheerleader provided the opportunity to move in a different social group. "Because of Garrett, I became part of the popular crowd. My parents were happy that I was involved in activities at school, but they had no idea what I was doing. To them, I was good little Jane, but peer pressure had me doing things behind their backs."

Heath walked over and sat down next to her. He smiled warmly, touched her hand, and said, "We all do things we aren't proud of, Jane."

Unconvinced, she said, "I made some pretty bad choices in my teen years, but I accepted the outcome. Garrett's life wasn't the only one that changed. I took our vows seriously. I thought maybe we'd become a team. After the baby died, things went downhill from there.

"We went off to UK and got a place in married student housing. He had his football scholarship, and I took a few classes. Then we needed more money, and I took a job at the coffee shop. Then in Garrett's junior year, he hurt his knee, and his football career was over. No more scholarship. I went to work full-time, thinking once he got his degree and a good job that I'd go back and get mine."

Once she opened up, Jane couldn't stop. The words poured out, and she could only wonder what he must think of her.

"It wasn't wonderful, but it was my life. His glory days were over. Garrett started hanging out at the frat house. He never let a day go by that he didn't blame me for ruining his life." She shrugged and said, "I never understood how he came to that conclusion, but maybe I did. At least I played as big a role in ruining our lives as he did."

"I'm sorry, Jane."

His soft apology nearly undid her. No one had ever known what she'd gone through. "It was my choice. I got everything I deserved."

"What happened?"

In an effort to regain her composure, Jane concentrated on brushing the mud from the legs of her jeans. "Garrett flunked a lot of courses and finally dropped out. He took a job selling cars. I think he hoped people would remember him from his football days, but he was never a good salesman. The coffee shop owners saw my potential and promoted me to manager. It wasn't as if we couldn't use the money, but Garrett couldn't deal with my success.

"I nearly gave up on us, but then I got pregnant with Sammy. He seemed happier after she was born. I hoped she'd make a difference for us. But all too soon, he hated her crying and resented her demands on my time.

"I think her real value to him was his parents' love for their grandchild. He took advantage of them every time he could. He'd say she needed things but never spent their money on Sammy." She pushed up from the bench and took a couple of steps away. "I'm sorry. You don't want to hear this."

"I don't mind listening. You need to talk. Sounds like you're pretty angry at Garrett."

Agonized, she turned back and asked, "How could anyone be so selfish, Heath? He never once thought about Sammy and me or what his action would do to us. If he'd been sick or something, I could understand. But he just gave up on life. Being the 'G man' was all that was ever important to him." Jane remembered the day he'd been dubbed with that stupid nickname. She'd come to detest all it stood for. "Evidently fulfilling that role for your wife and daughter isn't the same as a stadium of adoring fans. I should never have allowed our parents to force us into marriage."

"Then you wouldn't have Sammy now," Heath reminded her.

A sad smile touched Jane's face. "And that would truly be depressing. She's my reason for existing."

"You need more, Jane. What happens when Sammy grows up? You don't want to become one of those women who guilts her child into coming for visits."

"If I'm smart, I'll raise my child like your parents raised you. They will never have to guilt you into anything. You love them too much."

"Love your daughter, and she will love and respect you," Heath said. "But give her wings."

"That's a long way down the road. She's only two."

"Time flies. It's been more than ten years ago that you walked into that classroom. Look at everything that's happened since."

"You've accomplished a lot since then."

Heath shook his head. "I have a couple of pieces of paper with my name on them. You've accomplished more. You're the one making a difference in someone's life."

Jane's mouth dropped open in surprise. She had never looked at her life that way. "I can only hope to be a good mother."

"From what I've seen so far, you're doing a great job with Sammy. She's a blessed little girl."

∽

After Jane left for the day, Heath thought about what she had shared with him. She needed to deal with more than grief. Her anger would destroy her if she didn't forgive Garrett and move on with her life.

Heath understood internal turmoil. His own feelings of guilt over allowing his family to help him get the expensive education he hadn't really wanted grew stronger by the day. Sure, he'd convinced himself it was for his own good, and he'd worked hard to achieve his goals.

He had put aside his youth and assumed the responsibility of helping his family prepare for the future. Heath loved his twin, but his competitive nature would never allow him to be bested by Rom. That same nature, combined with his father's insistence that no child of his would waste his life, had pushed him to the level of overachiever.

His parents wouldn't have cared what career field he chose so long as he gave it his all. When Rom suggested they get their MBAs, Heath felt that an ability to earn a good salary would enable him to achieve his personal goals even more quickly. An executive job would help him put aside funds for the younger kids' education, allow him to marry and have a family sooner, and not feel he was cheating anyone.

In high school Heath focused on a grade point average that would help him get the scholarships that paid for most of his undergraduate education. Those same grades had helped him get into Harvard.

Up until a few weeks before, their plan had been that he, Rom, and their sister Opie would do their part and use their degrees to help the three younger siblings get their education. There had been no doubt in his mind about what he had to do.

The self-imposed burden that made his high school and college years stressful also made him become an adult at an early age. Failure meant disappointing his family, and he cared too much to allow that to happen. He had no time for fun and games. He'd thought maybe one day he could develop a few of his interests, but there had never been time until now.

Then Val won the money, bought the farm for their parents, funded the younger kids' education, and threw him in a total confusion. For the first time in his life, Heath had no plan for his future.

His nature never allowed him to take things lightly. He'd pushed for years to be able to fulfill his established role for his family. Heath intended to polish his résumé and find the perfect job.

Then he'd come home to Sheridan Farm and the welcome companionship of his family and friends. The peaceful, settled environment always made him feel secure, and now he didn't want to leave. He started helping out in the gardens and enjoyed the work so much that he didn't want to stop.

He hadn't broached the subject with Val. Heath just reported every morning and helped with whatever task she had in mind for the day. He found working in the gardens with his hands comforting. Avoiding the inevitable while enjoying himself as he hadn't done since he was a boy made each day a vacation from his feelings of personal responsibility.

Val had suggested they all consider what they wanted from their futures, and Heath knew he wanted to help Val.

Every time she'd sent him more of her hard-earned dollars, he'd vowed to pay her back. He wanted to work with her on this project. Help her achieve the success she dreamed of having in Your Wedding Place. But he didn't know how to ask her to let him help. He had the feeling she would consider it too much of a sacrifice.

These last few days in the gardens had made him more content than anything he had done in a very long time. Maybe he'd talk with his mother and see what she suggested. Surely he could convince Val that she needed him as much as he needed her. He had a million ideas on how to make the gardens even more spectacular, and as far as he was concerned, all Val needed to do was say yes.

Chapter 4

May slipped into June, and Jane found herself growing more comfortable with her job and the Truelove family. Val never assigned a task she wouldn't take on herself, and they often worked together. Jane understood Val's frustrations over the holdups with the plans for the new structure and hoped they would soon be resolved.

Heath had so many great ideas for the gardens and impressed Jane with his knowledge of plants and design. She found herself looking forward to the days she worked with him. She did wonder why he wasn't pursuing another job as Rom had done but figured he had his reasons. He certainly was a hard worker, and Jane considered Val fortunate to have his expertise.

It had been a particularly tiring day, and when the phone rang that night, Jane wasn't happy to hear her mother-in-law's voice. At the woman's insistence, she put Sammy on the phone. The toddler lasted a couple of minutes before she dropped the phone and climbed off the sofa. Jane retrieved the cordless and announced her daughter's abandonment.

"Who is this man Samantha's calling *Daddy*?" Clarice Holt demanded. "Who are you seeing?"

"No one," Jane said. "Sammy hears the Truelove children call their father *Daddy* and does the same."

A few moments of silence stretched over the miles before Clarice said, "It's not right."

"She's only two. Mr. Truelove doesn't mind."

"Well, I want it stopped. Garrett is her father. He's the only man she calls *Daddy*."

Jane found the woman's domineering attitude difficult to take. There had never been any love lost between them. Like her son, Clarice frequently expressed her opinion that Jane had ruined Garrett's life. Jane could do nothing right. Jane had trapped him by getting pregnant. Then after the stillbirth, she'd mocked Jane for being incapable of giving her son children.

Sammy's birth had disproved that, but then she'd been a daughter instead of a son. Then Clarice criticized her skills as a mother. Jane had long since decided that the only way to coexist with her mother-in-law was to ignore her.

"Perhaps you shouldn't take her there. Those places are dirty, and she could get hurt."

Jane nearly laughed at Clarice. A multimillion-dollar farm didn't fit that image at all. "Sammy is well cared for. I don't put my daughter at risk."

"I won't stand for her calling another man *Daddy*."

"I see nothing wrong with my daughter loving someone who loves her in return." Something fell in the other room, and her child cried out. "I need to go. It's Sammy's bedtime."

Jane knew the conversation wasn't over, and when the phone rang later that night, she wondered if Clarice was calling back to continue her tirade.

"Clarice called me about Sammy calling someone *Daddy*. What's going on, Jane?"

Hello to you, too, Mother, Jane thought. Their long distance interference was a bit much. If they were here, they could see for themselves that the situation was innocent. For that matter, if they were here, Sammy could be spending her days with them. "Clarice is trying to cause trouble. Sammy hears the Truelove kids calling their father *Daddy* and does the same. What's wrong with that?"

"Nothing, I suppose."

"That's what I told Clarice. They're good people, and I'm fortunate to have them helping care for Sammy. She's very happy with Cindy Truelove, and I love seeing her throughout the day. We eat lunch together, and I get to spend time with her when she plays in the gardens."

"Weren't some of their children in your class?"

"Heath and Rom. They were the class co-valedictorians."

"I remember them. Handsome young men. What are they doing now?"

"They graduated from Harvard in May. Rom has a job in Lexington, and Heath is helping his sister with her new business."

"So you're working with the sister and Heath?"

"Her name's Val, Mom."

"Don't be so testy, Jane. I'm just curious about these new people in your life."

"They're very nice. Why don't you and Daddy come for a visit and meet them?"

"Your father is busy at work. And church, of course."

Jane was used to her mother's excuses. Her parents had been too busy to do anything with her since the truth had come out about her and Garrett. After the wedding, they had taken advantage of a job transfer to leave her and Paris, Kentucky, far behind. The loss of her relationship with her parents was one more thing Jane regretted.

"How is my granddaughter?"

"Sammy's doing great. You should see her with the Trueloves. She's not shy at all with them."

"Be careful, Jane. You don't want her upset if this job doesn't work out."

"This job is working just great, Mom. Val assures me she's pleased with my work."

"That's good, but you know your tendency to make unwise decisions."

"One unwise decision," Jane said softly. "Will you ever forget it?"

"I don't mean to hurt you."

"Then why do you do it? I know you and Daddy were disappointed and embarrassed, but I'm your daughter. I made a mistake. Is that sufficient reason to have nothing to do with me?"

"We stood by you."

Jane could almost see her mother's tight-lipped expression. She'd witnessed it enough in those last days before they left. When her parents suggested she give her child up for adoption, Jane asked for time to consider her options. Her mother said there was no time to waste. "No, you married me off to Garrett and left town. Didn't you ever make a mistake, Mom?"

"I'm not having this conversation with you again."

"That's right. Nip it in the bud so you don't feel guilty for not knowing what your wayward child was doing behind your back."

"Good night, Jane. Your father and I are praying for you."

Jane hit the OFF button and tossed the cordless phone against the opposite end of the sofa. "Praying." She spat it out like a bad word. She didn't want their prayers. She wanted their love. Why was that so difficult for them to understand?

∾

Thanks to the phone arguments, Jane didn't rest well and then overslept the following morning. When she called Val to explain, her boss told her to take all the time she needed.

Nearly an hour later, Jane set Sammy on her feet in the Truelove kitchen and watched as she ran to Cindy. The woman hurriedly dried her hands and greeted the little girl. Sammy chuckled and held up her tiny arms. Cindy swung her up and squeezed her close.

Sadness washed over Jane as last night's conversation with her mother came to mind. Her parents would never know their granddaughter like this.

"Something wrong?"

She'd noted Cindy's frequent glances in her direction. "Family problems. Garrett's mom started in on me last night, and it went downhill from there. She demanded to know who Sammy is calling *Daddy*, and when I explained that she'd picked it up from your kids, she went off on me."

"Oh honey, I'm sorry," Cindy said, settling Sammy at the table with crayons and paper before coming over to give Jane a hug.

Cindy's gesture of comfort brought tears to her eyes. "I try not to let it bother me, but she says I'm a bad mother."

"Don't you believe it for one second. You're doing a great job raising your daughter."

Jane smiled her thanks. "Sammy is a baby. She doesn't understand the difference."

"Jacob doesn't mind."

She used the tissue Cindy gave her to dry her eyes. "I know. I appreciate the positive male influence in her life. She hasn't had much of a role model."

"You just keep doing what you're doing."

"She says it's my fault Garrett did what he did," Jane said.

"She's hurting. Lashing out because you've moved on with your life and she can't. Let's not discuss this in front of Sammy. I can ask Jules to watch her if you need to talk."

What was it about these Trueloves? First she'd opened up to Heath about her feelings regarding Garrett, and now she'd done the same with his mother.

Jane stood up straighter and shook her head. "I need to get to work."

Cindy patted Jane's shoulder. "Just remember I love you girls like my own. I'm here for you anytime."

"Thanks," Jane said, somehow managing to get the word past the knot in her throat.

∾

Heath could see Jane wasn't her usual self when she joined him in the garden.

"Everything okay?"

She explained the situation. "I'm so over them trying to run my life but not wanting to help. I'm doing the best I can."

"You're doing a great job. Sammy is happy and healthy. That's what counts. Not whom she calls *Daddy*, though personally I think she's got good taste."

Jane smiled. "She does. Jacob is the best. Now what do you need me to do today? Or at least what's left of the day."

"It's warm today. I thought maybe we'd work on the fountains."

"You want to get wet again?"

Heath shook his head. "I don't plan to put a hose in your hand if that's what you're asking, but I figure we can drain them and clean them up."

Jane eyed the massive fountain in the back of the garden. "Do we disassemble that? It's pretty big."

"We'll start small and work our way up to the big ones. We don't want them looking new. They need to retain that aged look the years have provided."

"So basically we're scrubbing the interior and getting the gunk out of the works so they can keep flowing."

Heath nodded.

"There's a lot to be done now that Kelly Dickerson booked her wedding," Jane said. "I'm so happy for Val. That first booking is a big deal."

"It's definitely a beginning," Heath agreed. "We'll get it done. Do you remember Kelly from school?"

"Vaguely."

"She's nice. Val's not happy about the way she got the referral, but a booking is all that matters."

Jane's head tilted to one side in question.

"Val wanted to keep things quiet," he explained. "She said Kelly knew a lot about her plans, but she and Russ Hunter share an office."

"I never realized just how much there was to starting a business. It seems like a lot of work."

"Start-up can be a challenge. Particularly with something like Val has and

149

going from the ground up. Imagine what it would be like if she didn't have the established gardens."

"Success would definitely be much further away."

"School wasn't easy, but there was a routine about it," Heath said. "I like the newness of this project, but I'm glad I don't have to make the final decisions."

"I know what you mean. I worked at the coffee shop for a long time. I went from waiting tables to being in charge. It's the gradual learning over jumping in feet first. But this is like a new beginning for you all. The future is calling your name, and you can go anywhere you like."

"You, too."

"Not with a child to provide for. When Val first suggested this job, I doubted she needed someone. Boy, was I wrong. It's been exciting and fun. Ordinarily I'd never have considered something like this, but I'm glad I did."

"I've enjoyed being in the gardens again. It's been years since I helped Mrs. Sheridan." He'd spent some of his happiest summers right here in these gardens and feeling particularly pleased when Mrs. Sheridan liked his ideas.

"I'm sure Val appreciates your help, and you do seem to enjoy this type of work. Is it something you'll pursue?"

"Probably only as a hobby," Heath said. "Once I get a job, I won't have much time to work outside."

"Is that why you haven't gone job hunting yet?"

No doubt the rest of the family is wondering the same thing, Heath thought. "I've enjoyed helping Val. I wouldn't mind doing it for a while longer."

"You should talk to her."

Heath didn't know how to make Val understand. She would think he wanted to help out of guilt, and while he felt he should do everything possible to aid in her success, he wanted to do something he enjoyed. At least for a while before he joined the suit-and-briefcase brigade. "Maybe I will."

"What do you want to do?"

Heath wanted to be selfish. He wanted to spend his days sharing the beauty of God's garden with those he loved. But Jane's question was more than curiosity. "It's more about what I'm expected to do. You don't obtain an expensive education and not use it."

"Do you wish you hadn't?"

He shrugged. "I suppose it's like other things in life. Sometimes we want what we can't have."

"I don't understand."

"I'd love to do this full-time, but gardening doesn't pay the bills."

"It could. But aren't you excited? With your degree you can write your own ticket for the future."

The options didn't thrill him, but he'd do what God directed. "I suppose."

"But you've got a college education. It will take you wherever you want to go."

Heath could hear the wistfulness in her words. "You should talk to Val.

We've been trying to convince her to go back to college. You should consider doing the same."

Jane shook her head. "I'm sure she's much too busy. As for me, it's not feasible with a small child and a full-time job."

"It's not as impossible as you think. Given this family's philosophy on education, I think there's a good possibility Val would help if you asked."

Horrified, Jane said, "I can't take any more from her. She's all but claiming me as a dependent as it is. She gave me a job. Your mom cares for my child, and I eat at your place more than at home. I'm a definite liability."

Heath could relate. Beyond the work in the gardens, he wasn't contributing anything to the family coffers. "You're not. You pull your weight around here."

And she did. Heath didn't think Val could have found a better assistant.

"Maybe I'll go back one day," Jane said.

"One day what?" Val asked when she walked up on their conversation.

Jane glanced at Heath and back at her employer. "We were talking about the future."

"What about it?"

Poor Jane, Heath thought. There was no way she could avoid this.

"Heath and I were discussing education."

Val glanced at him.

"I suggested she consider going back to UK for her degree."

"They suggested the same thing to me," Val told Jane. "I'm too busy right now."

"It's difficult for me with Sammy and work."

"Would you like to go?"

"Maybe after Sammy starts school."

"You shouldn't put it off," Heath said. "You'll only have more responsibilities then. Like driving Sammy to activities. She'll probably be a cheerleader like her mom."

"I hope not. I'd rather she be like you and concentrate on her education more than her social life."

"A good balance doesn't hurt."

"The wrong focus isn't good. You're all on track with your futures."

Maybe the others, Heath thought. Definitely not him.

"You know where you're headed because you planned and carried that plan through. You'll get there faster."

"So could you," Val said. "We would help care for Sammy if you wanted to enroll in classes. You could probably go a couple of days a week and finish in no time."

"I only had three semesters at UK."

"There's no time like the present," Val said.

Jane looked uncomfortable, and Heath stepped forward. "Speaking of which, we'd better get those supplies if we plan to get anything done today."

Chapter 5

The days flew past, each so filled with change that Jane had little time to think about anything other than her daughter and work. Now that the venue had been booked, the push was on to get the gardens looking nothing less than spectacular. Since the end of the school year, they had made great progress with the help of the younger Trueloves.

When she'd finally thought things might be improving, her landlord sold the house she rented and told her the new owners planned to occupy the residence. Jane knew she didn't want to live in an apartment complex. Moving to Paris seemed the most logical choice. She mentioned it to Val, and the next thing she knew, Val offered her the efficiency apartment above the garage behind the mansion.

Jane wanted to refuse, but then Val pointed out that a number of the farm staff received housing as part of their employment and that she didn't see any reason why Jane shouldn't as well. She argued that having them living closer to the farm would make things easier for everyone. Jane knew it would make things easier for her. Though it wasn't a long drive, she wouldn't mind not having to travel to and from Lexington on a daily basis.

"I think you'd move us into the house with the family if you had room," Jane said when Val continued her efforts to convince her.

She grinned and said, "Well, once Rom finds a place in Lexington, his bunk might be available."

Jane laughed and shook her head. "No thanks. I'll stick with my queen-size bed."

After much thought, Jane accepted the offer. The men moved her and Sammy into the apartment before Heath and Rom left for Boston on Sunday afternoon. Heath had said they needed to tie up loose ends. Jane had no idea what that meant.

The Trueloves quickly absorbed them into their family. She and Sammy ate lunch and dinner at their house on most days. Cindy and Opie insisted there was plenty. Their lively conversation made the meals even more enjoyable.

With Heath gone, Jane worked alone. After Val left to go to Lexington to talk to Madelyn Troyer, Jane carried trays of nursery plants over to the bed Heath had marked on his landscape plan. As she dug in the newly enriched soil, Jane realized she missed him. When she tried to define the role he played in her life, *friend* came to mind. Only a friend would stick around after someone dumped her pathetic past on him.

But there was more. When she looked at Heath, she found it easy to admire the handsome man he had become. When he smiled that sweet, gentle smile of his, she couldn't help but smile back. It was more than his smile. It was his presence. Being with Heath was comfortable. He treated women with respect. She could talk about anything without fear of him belittling her. And when she talked, Jane felt as if he listened and cared about what she said.

While she might consider him as cuddly as one of Sammy's stuffed animals, Jane noticed his muscles when they worked. She'd observed a lot about Heath Truelove and liked what she saw. She couldn't help but wonder why she'd missed it before. Sure, she'd seen the sweet, shy, sensitive Heath, but he hadn't fit into her life then. Was it possible that he could fit now?

∾

Val returned late that afternoon, excited that her former boss had agreed to use the services of Your Wedding Place and would be bringing another potential bride out to look at the gardens. She was even happier that Russ Hunter had created a workable plan and had invited him to dinner that night.

Jane didn't object to being sent home early with orders to join them for dinner and stick around for the unveiling of the plans. Jane arrived to find Jacob angry because one of Val's former coworkers had shown up at the farm cursing, throwing out accusations, and nearly injuring one of the workers with his car. From what Opie told her, the man blamed Val for losing his job.

The incident convinced Jacob and Val of the need to hire security. Jane thought it was a good idea. The security measures would make the farm safer for everyone. She knew she'd rest better.

The evening proved very interesting. Apparently Russ Hunter had redeemed himself with the new plans. Val seated Russ next to her father, and Jane sensed something more in the interaction between the couple. A definite change from that first lunch they shared. When Opie threw out her idea about starting a restaurant in one of the farm outbuildings, there was discussion over whether it was a good idea. That led Cindy to bring up Heath's desire to work with Val on her Your Wedding Place project.

Val's mention of Heath's expensive education made Jane wonder if she would be agreeable to what Heath wanted. She supposed she'd find out when he got back from Boston and they talked. Jane definitely wanted to keep working with Heath. He had such a gentle, peaceful way about him and plenty of good ideas for the gardens.

When the plans came out, a major brainstorming session ensued. Sammy's bedtime came and went. Jane appreciated the way the family took turns entertaining the little girl. After a while Sammy fell asleep in her mother's lap.

"What do you think, Jane?" Val asked.

"It's a perfect addition to Your Wedding Place."

"You believe the structure will interest the brides?"

"Most definitely. Once word gets out that it's here, I'm sure you'll find more than one bride who can't resist the allure of the location."

"Allure, huh? I like that. Remind me to use it in the advertising," Val said.

The resulting laughter caused Sammy to shift restlessly and whine. Jane soothed her as she maneuvered her chair about and stood. "We're going to call it a night."

"You need help getting her home?" Val asked.

"We're fine," Jane said softly.

"I'll walk you home," another family member volunteered.

She smiled her thanks and left the family discussing the plans.

∾

Clarice's early morning call on Monday was the last thing Jane wanted to start her day. "Did you remember what today is?"

She could tell the woman had been crying. Jane had battled a few emotions of her own. Grief mixed with a great deal of anger toward Garrett for what he'd done. "Yes, Clarice. I know."

"Do you plan to take Sammy to put flowers on her father's grave?"

Jane didn't want the child remembering her father that way. "I put an arrangement on his grave for Father's Day."

"Did you take Samantha? Do you ever take her to see his grave?" Clarice demanded, her voice rising to a near screech.

"No, I don't. Sammy has a photo of Garrett in her room, but I don't drag her to the cemetery to pay homage to a grave marker. She's too little to understand what happened."

"No, she isn't. You have to keep his memory alive for her. She has to remember her father."

"What do you want her to remember? That her father was too selfish to be there for her?"

"He was a good man."

She'd heard that one too many times over the past year. "Garrett didn't love any of us enough to stick around to fulfill the roles he chose in life, Clarice."

"He didn't choose. You forced him into the role of husband and father."

The sucker punch hit home as the woman intended, but Jane wasn't down for the count. "And he forced me into the role of wife and mother. We both made bad choices. You don't see me taking the easy way out. You seem to think your son would have been better off without me in his life. Well, maybe we both would've been better off if we'd never met. He played as big a part in what happened as I did. I won't accept the blame for his decision."

"You did this to him. Garrett was a good son." Clarice had obviously worked herself into a fine rage on the anniversary of her son's death.

"He was spoiled and never thought of anyone but himself. Garrett's dead. You'd be better off if you accepted that and moved on. I have no plans to elevate him to sainthood in Sammy's eyes. If she has questions when she's older, I'll answer them."

"If you have your way, she won't know who her father is."

"No doubt you'll fill her in on what a wonderful man Garrett was," Jane said, the words drenched in sarcasm. "You may share the fantasy, but I'll make sure she knows the truth. Sammy is the only wonderful thing that came out of our marriage. Personally, I intend to be around to see my daughter and grandchildren grow up."

Her words hit home, and Clarice responded in kind. "We'll see about that. I have letters Garrett wrote telling what a bad mother you were. I'll take you to court."

"Do what you have to. If you want the real truth about Garrett coming out in a courtroom, we'll go there."

"Don't think you can blackmail me, missy. I will not allow you to destroy my granddaughter's life like you did her father's."

Trembling with rage, Jane shut the phone off. How dare she make such accusations? Jane had done everything humanly possible to make their marriage work. Garrett hadn't cared about any of them. It wasn't her fault.

Sammy came into the room carrying the horse Heath had given her under her arm and dragging her well-worn blankie. "Mommy cry?"

Jane regretted the angry words as she swung the little girl into her arms and enfolded the child in a hug. More tears came to her eyes as she buried her face in Sammy's baby-sweet fragrance. "Yes, sweetness. But Mommy loves her Sammy so much."

" 'Kay. I get down."

The child squirmed for release, and Jane didn't want to let go but knew she had to. Standing Sammy on her feet, Jane managed a smile as she adjusted the hair barrette in the baby-fine curls. "Are you taking Horsie to Mrs. Cindy's today?"

Sammy nodded and babbled about her horse. Heath had made a big hit with the stuffed animal he bought in Boston. She hadn't put it down since he'd given it to her the night before. Jane held out her hand. "Let's get you ready to see Mrs. Cindy."

Sammy looked up at her and asked, "Me see Hef?"

Jane smiled. Her daughter enjoyed seeing Heath as much as she did. They had missed him while he'd been away. "Sure. We'll stop by and see Heath, too."

Later they visited in the gardens, Sammy hiding her face in her mother's neck as Heath played peekaboo with her.

"Let me take her to your mom, and I'll be back to help."

They spent the first hour working in silence before Heath asked, "What's wrong?"

Jane supposed her missing nonstop chatter had been a dead giveaway. "Today's the first anniversary of Garrett's death."

His expression of sympathy warmed her heart. "I'm sorry. Do you need to take the day off?"

"Thanks but no. I don't intend to waste another minute of my life trying to understand why he did what he did. His mom called this morning and made a big production over my refusing to take Sammy to visit his grave. She got her jabs in. Blamed me and threatened to use letters he'd written claiming I'm a bad mother to take Sammy from me."

Heath's appalled expression spoke volumes. "That's not going to happen, Jane."

"No, it's not," she said. "It's not the first time she's threatened me. I don't want to crucify a dead man, but if she forces me to, I will. Garrett may have fooled his parents, but I knew exactly what was going on. He'd call them up and claim Sammy needed something but never spent a dime they sent on her. He'd take their money and buy beer for his buddies. Good old 'G man.' Life was just one big party for him. My parents helped, too. I spent every dime of their money on Sammy. My salary went for the basics—rent, food, and debts. I'm still paying off Garrett's school and credit card loans."

"Didn't he have a scholarship?"

"It wasn't enough. He breezed through every dime he could get his hands on. I tried to tell him there were bills to pay, but he turned a deaf ear. The phone would get cut off, or we'd eat macaroni and cheese or ramen noodles until we got money."

"Why did you live like that?"

"My parents were already embarrassed and disappointed by their wayward daughter. A divorce would have killed them. After Sammy was born, I was determined she would have a roof over her head and food to eat."

"How did they react to what Garrett did?"

"We never discussed it. I suppose it's just one more major embarrassment in the mess I call my life. My mom is always quick to point out my bad choices. Then Clarice throws her two cents in. I try to be the bigger person and not get into arguments, but they won't let me."

"Mrs. Holt is hurting, Jane."

She understood his defense of the other woman but felt disappointed when he didn't side with her. "So am I, but you don't see me calling her up and attacking her. I try to respect the fact that she's Garrett's mother and Sammy's grandmother, but obviously she doesn't respect me in return."

"Why not?"

Jane shrugged. "I wish I knew. I tried to be a good daughter-in-law. We lived with them after we got married. It wasn't what I wanted, but my parents moved away, and there were no funds to pay for an apartment. Garrett was too busy with football, and I had a difficult pregnancy and couldn't work, but I helped around the house. I went to my doctor appointments alone because Clarice was too angry and my mother was too embarrassed to stand by me. I still remember the day the doctor told me my child had died."

"You were alone?"

Emotion clogged her throat. "I've never been more alone in my life."

Heath stepped forward and enfolded her in a hug. "I'm sorry, Jane. I wish it could have been different for you."

Tears trickled down her cheeks as she stood there, the memories almost more than she could bear. Garrett insisted they not name the baby after him since he planned on a living son carrying his name. They placed tiny James Edward Holt in a small casket and buried him. His service consisted of her former pastor speaking a few words by the grave site. Her parents hadn't even come for the funeral. Her mother said God always allowed things to happen for the best. The issue of the unwanted baby had been resolved for everyone but Jane. Her lost child would always hold a special place in her heart.

She still wondered why Garrett hadn't asked for a divorce after the baby died. Maybe because he had hopes of them becoming the same carefree pair they had been before the pregnancy. Jane knew they could never be that couple again. Her roles of wife and almost mother for a short time made it impossible for her ever to see things in the same way again. While she grieved the loss of their son, he talked about them going off to college and being free of his parents. He behaved as if their son had never existed, and it broke her heart.

Jane pulled herself together and stepped away. "I'm sorry, Heath."

"You know you weren't truly alone, don't you?"

Puzzled, she looked at him.

"God was there. Waiting, hoping you'd turn to Him in your time of need."

She shook her head. "God wanted no part of me."

"He knew, Jane. Every choice you made, He knew you'd make. That doesn't mean He wouldn't forgive you for making them. All you had to do was ask."

She sniffed and said, "I know. I accepted Jesus as my Savior when I was ten years old." She could see that surprised him. Jane knew her behavior at school showed no indication she loved God.

"What happened?"

She shared the sad story that had become her witness. "When I was older and had the opportunity to make the right choices, I didn't choose Him. I got involved with the wrong crowd, and peer pressure caused me to live a less-than-pleasing life. I'd go and listen to the sermons and know I was sinning, but I didn't stop. We were in church for every service. It got uncomfortable, but I'd zone out and think about my plans with my friends after church. When I got into trouble, I thought about how I'd sinned and convinced myself I destroyed God's love for me just like I'd done with my parents. After they married me off and moved away, I didn't attend church anymore. Garrett and his parents weren't Christians. Later I worked most Sundays at the coffee shop."

"It starts off by missing one Sunday, and then it becomes easier to miss the next, and before you realize it, you've shifted God out of your life entirely."

"I justified my actions and told myself I wanted to be different, but I wasn't."

"Have you ever thought about going back?"

"I always thought I would. One day."

"Why not now? Sammy needs to attend church with her mother, just like you attended with your parents."

"Let's hope I can be less judgmental if she falls short of my expectations."

"We all fall short, Jane. God doesn't judge us as harshly as we judge ourselves. You should come back to church."

"I'll think about it. I could use a shoulder to lean on, particularly now that I'm responsible for Sammy's future. I want to help her make the right decisions. But it's not really something I can control. She can be president, or she can marry young and be a stay-at-home mom."

"And it doesn't matter as long as she's happy. Don't regret the choices you made, Jane. You learned something from every one of them."

Val joined them. "Are we transplanting the lilies today?"

As Heath and Val discussed the merits of moving the bed, Jane thought about what he had said. She had chosen to love Garrett. Their relationship had changed her plans, but it had been her decision.

What if she'd opted for someone like Heath? Her life would have been very different. For one thing, she'd be educated. The coffee shop had been fun. She liked being around people, but she'd wanted to obtain her business degree and find a job where she could make a difference. She felt like she'd put her dreams on hold permanently after marrying Garrett.

❧

Their discussion stayed on her mind over the rest of the day. Heath's statement about God being there kept coming back to Jane. Knowing He was there watching hadn't kept her from making mistakes. What had seemed thrilling and exciting had taken a turn down a path she didn't want to follow. There was no turning back. No changing the inevitable.

Jane often wondered why she'd been seduced by popularity. Choosing to be one of the in crowd threw her life into a downward spiral until she finally took back control. Learning she was pregnant with Sammy provided Jane strengths she'd never realized existed. She insisted Garrett find work and located a home for them like the one where she'd lived with her parents.

Heath's comfort today reminded her that some men could be kind and loving. If she hadn't fallen for the lies, she could have been with a man who loved and respected her as his wife. A man whose focus went beyond the next sports event.

In her youth, she confused the real gold for the dross. It wasn't too late. She could find a man who would love and treasure her and Sammy. A man who would not feel inconvenienced by their existence. She could have happy ever after.

After lunch Jane returned to weeding and deadheading. The hot days and rain showers provided for a bountiful crop of weeds and grass, and the blooms on some of the flowers didn't seem to last very long. Jules had gone into town with Heath, and the two younger boys were helping their father. Val said she needed to return phone calls, and Jane worked alone.

"So how was the date?" Jane asked when Val came outside. Russ Hunter had invited Val out to celebrate her second booking.

"I enjoy spending time with Russ."

"I'm sure you do. When's the second wedding?"

"The Saturday after Kelly's. Russ suggested we have a launch party. I thought maybe Thursday of that week since we'd already have the tent up. What do you think? Too much?"

Jane let out a low whistle. "That's going to be a challenge, but we might as well get used to turning the areas over quickly."

"I really do appreciate your help, Jane."

They worked companionably for the next hour before they took a water break. They enjoyed the coolness beneath the huge trees as they sipped ice water from the bottles they kept in a nearby cooler. "Okay if we take Sammy to church?"

Right after she moved into the apartment, they had asked if she could go. Jane couldn't think of a reason why her daughter shouldn't attend church with the Trueloves and said yes. Sammy enjoyed her weekly excursions.

"I thought I might go, too," Jane said.

"Can I ask what made you reconsider?"

"I've been feeling left behind," Jane said. "Sammy is so happy when she comes home. All of you are reenergized, and I want to experience that for myself."

Val nodded. "We leave around nine fifteen."

"I can drive Sammy and myself."

"If you want but there's room for you both."

"I'll let you know."

On Sunday Jane and Sammy rode in the big SUV with Val, her parents, Opie, and Jules. Heath and the younger boys rode in Heath's truck.

"I should have driven," she said.

"Heath always drives separately," Opie said from behind them. "He says it's good to have a second vehicle in case someone gets sick or there's an emergency."

Jane hadn't thought of that.

They dropped Sammy off in the nursery, and Val, Opie, and Heath took her to the young adult Sunday school class. Jane enjoyed meeting a number of women and men her own age. Offers to join in other church activities and invitations to come back abounded.

"I can see why you enjoy attending church here," Jane said as they moved to the sanctuary for the morning service. The Trueloves filled the pew but made room for her. "Everyone is so friendly."

"They are wonderful people," Val said. "We leave Sammy in the nursery. She got restless out here. They called us the first couple of weeks, but she stays the entire time now."

Embarrassed, Jane said, "Why didn't you tell me? I should have come with her."

"She's a smart kid. She didn't like sitting on laps and being shushed."

"She's not quiet."

"The structure is good for her, and so is being around other kids her age."

"I probably should get her into more activities."

The music began, and they turned their attention to the worship service. It had been a long time since she'd last attended church, but the familiarity of the experience—the music, the scripture, even the format of the service came to her quickly. The hymns were the same, and she even knew some of the praise songs from hearing them on the radio.

After the service Heath pointed out the various areas of the church when he took Jane to the nursery to pick up Sammy. The child came running, screaming their names.

"We do not yell like that, Samantha Mary," Jane said without hesitation.

Heath swung the child up into his arms, making her giggle before he said, "I didn't know her middle name was Mary. Did you name her after someone?"

"It's my first name." She waited for a comment on the old-fashioned name, but he said nothing.

"I hope she's not too much trouble," Jane said when Heath introduced her to the nursery director and staff.

"Not at all. We love having her with us."

"Mommy. Oah," Sammy called, holding up her picture.

The multihued page was so marked up Jane couldn't make out what it had been. She looked to the other women for an explanation.

The director smiled and said, "It's a rainbow. We studied Noah and the ark today."

She nodded. "I see that now. Good job, Sammy," Jane said with a proud smile. "I'll should find some Bible storybooks. Sammy loves being read to."

"Check our library here," Heath suggested. "They have lots of children's books."

"But I'm not a member."

"No problem. In fact let's go now. You can choose what you want, and I'll check them out for you. Mom would probably appreciate some extras. They have videos, too."

The variety of books in the library surprised Jane. Sammy pulled books from the shelves until Jane told her to stop. After picking out several she thought Sammy would enjoy, Jane said, "I'm sure everyone's waiting on us."

A few minutes later Heath checked out the books, and they were on their way.

"I've been looking for you," Val called when she spotted them leaving the library.

Heath hefted the pile of books into his arms and said, "Jane wanted Bible stories."

"Good idea." She glanced at Jane and asked, "Did you find anything for yourself? They have some great Christian fiction."

"Maybe next time. I do like to read."

"We have time if you want to look."

Jane wouldn't think of holding them up any longer. "I'll check next time."

"There are plenty of books at the house already," Heath said. "I'm sure you can find something you haven't read."

"I could start with my Bible," Jane said. "I haven't read that in a while."

"Sounds like a plan."

Chapter 6

Heath stuck his head around the office door and asked, "Got a minute?"

Val glanced up and said, "Sure, what's on your mind?"

He made himself comfortable in the visitor chair. "I wanted to talk about helping with Your Wedding Place."

Val smiled, stood, and came around to prop against the desk. "I wondered when you were going to ask. Mom dropped that news on me the night Russ showed them the plans."

"What do you think?" he asked eagerly.

"I'm not sure it's in your best interest."

Heath sighed. Opie had already told him about Val's reaction. He understood why she felt as she did, but that didn't ease his disappointment. He'd prayed she'd be receptive to accepting his help. After spending hours planning the direction she could take in the gardens, he wanted to be around to see how they worked.

"But Daddy says we'll both be winners if I agree."

Her words gave him the little bit of hope he needed to continue his quest. He leaned forward in the chair. "I know I need to think about getting a job, but I'm enjoying working in the gardens. Of course I realize I need to add to the family budget, so what if I give back the money you gave me for graduation?"

Val laughed. "Are you trying to pay me to work in the gardens?"

Feeling sheepish, Heath said, "I suppose I am."

Val shook her head. "The money is yours. I've set aside the same amount for Jules, Roc, and Cy. Theirs will be bigger, though, since it's invested, but the initial amount is the same."

"It's not fair to you," Heath said. "Not after the sacrifices you made to help us. You put your life on hold to get the three of us through school."

"Not really. I had to work anyway. I became a better steward of God's money by helping you, and look at how He rewarded me."

"But what about a home and family?"

She shrugged. "God hasn't sent the husband."

"You could have used the money for yourself. Gotten your degree. Improved your life."

"I did it my way, Heath. And I'd do it again."

"I should do like Rom and get a job."

"Rom has future plans. He'll marry Stephanie when she comes home from Africa. He's using his money to help her now and saving for their future."

Heath wanted to feel relieved but didn't. Rom had dated Stephanie throughout college and planned to marry her, but he knew that if things hadn't happened as they had, his twin would have set aside those plans to help provide for the kids' education.

"It's your choice," Val said. "What do you want from the future?"

Heath might be confused about a number of other things, but he was clear on one point. "I'd like to marry the woman of my dreams and have a family."

Val shrugged. "That shouldn't be difficult."

"You'd be surprised," Heath said. Ever since Jane had come back into his life, the idea that they could be a couple lingered in his mind. But his doubts kept him from pursuing her. Her anger at Garrett made him believe she still loved her husband. The fear of fighting a dead man for her affections seemed to be a greater obstacle than he could overcome.

"You can't rush God," Val said. "Let me tell you what I have in mind. You work with me setting up the gardens. I pay you a weekly salary. . . ."

"No way," Heath said. He didn't want to take more of her money. He wanted to pay back a little of what she'd given him.

"I'd pay anyone else I hired, so why not you?"

"I want to help you. You don't have to pay me."

"I pay you, or we don't work together," Val said with conviction. "You need money to cover your expenses."

"I have the graduation money."

"It's invested, and there would be penalties for early withdrawal."

He knew she was right, and while it seemed like a lot of money, it wouldn't take long to spend a big chunk of it on living expenses. "Okay, but you have to let me work."

"Have I held you back thus far?"

"No, I mean more like a job," he said earnestly. "You tell me what you want, and I get it done."

Val laughed and joked, "It's more you telling me what I want done, but we'll work together to get the job done. Even more now that we've got two weddings and the launch party booked." Val stood and stretched out her hand. "Welcome to the Truelove Inc. family."

He stood and hugged her. "You're a nut, but I love you."

As he left the office, Heath could hardly wait to share his news with Jane. He found her pulling weeds in the front garden. She grabbed hold of a particularly large specimen and put all her weight behind her effort, only to end up flat on the ground.

He laughed when she waved the offending weed in victory and scrambled to her feet, yelling, "Go, weed!" Heath moved closer and brushed at the dirt on her cheek. "You trying to plant yourself?"

"I could think of worse places to live. Where have you been?"

"Talking to Val. You have a cheer in your repertoire for her agreeing to give me a job helping with the gardens?"

"Yes!" she screamed, doing a little dance before she hugged him. "Congratulations."

Jane's exuberance knocked him back a step, and Heath wrapped his arms around her to keep them standing. When she made no effort to separate, he held her a little longer. "Thanks. I wasn't sure she'd agree at first, but I'm glad she did. I wasn't looking forward to an office job after working out here."

"I can understand that. I've enjoyed communing with nature myself."

"Let me help with those weeds."

"I need muscle. Knock yourself out. I suspect the roots go all the way to China."

∿

The day of Kelly Dickerson's wedding dawned bright and beautiful. Heath had been out since early morning, making certain the last-minute details were finished.

"Happy?" he asked Val when she came out of the house after showing Kelly where her bridal party could dress.

"Oh yes. Kelly is happy, too."

"Then we've done our job," Heath said.

"And done it well. We've come a long way since we started working on these gardens. Mrs. Sheridan would be proud."

After having seen the gardens in their glory, they knew Mrs. Sheridan would have been heartbroken by their deplorable condition. They concluded that Mr. Sheridan's caretakers only performed minimal work after his wife's death. Mowing and weed eating didn't begin to account for the continual grooming and maintenance the vast gardens required.

"I think so. She loved them so much. We should get a sign. What do you think about 'Esther's Garden' for the English garden?"

"Great idea. Let's order little hand-carved signs and tuck them into out-of-the-way places so people just happen upon them."

He nodded. "Any potential brides in this group?"

Val grinned at him. "Maybe one or two."

"Where's Jane?"

"She had an appointment. I told her we'd finish up without her."

Heath wondered what was up but didn't ask.

"You should get dressed if you're going to attend the wedding."

Kelly had invited him, Rom, and Jane to the wedding, assuring them their former classmates would love seeing them. Rom had other plans, but Heath couldn't very well escape when he lived and worked right there at the farm. When Jane said she planned to go, he asked if she'd like to go together. She agreed, and the idea of spending time with her made putting on a suit and tie and frittering away hours with people he hadn't seen in years a little more appealing.

∿

"Wow," Heath exclaimed when she walked toward him. "You clean up nice."

Jane grinned. "So do you."

"That's some dress." *And what you do for that dress is fantastic,* he thought. He'd always thought her beautiful, but today she looked stunning. She would turn more than one head.

She held out the little bolero jacket and twirled around on the high heels she wore. "I couldn't very well wear my gardening clothes to Kelly's big event."

Heath offered his arm. "Shall we do Your Wedding Place proud?"

"Why of course."

In the garden entrance, an usher stepped forward and escorted Jane to the bride's side. Heath followed. He noted the way Jane checked out her surroundings. "See anyone you know?"

"Some people from school. One or two I used to see at the coffee shop. Russ Hunter is over there." She indicated his location with a tilt of her head. "I saw him talking to Val earlier. She didn't look happy."

"She's not. There's been a hang-up with the permits." He didn't share that Val suspected Russ of deliberately delaying her project.

Jane leaned closer, and the light scent of her perfume filled his senses. Her voice dropped lower when she said, "I'm so excited for Val. This is a major first for her business. I want to take it all in. Find the areas we can improve on. Maybe even things we could offer that would expand her profit margin."

"Val doesn't expect you to work."

She nudged him playfully. "I know. But I need facts for when we talk weddings tomorrow."

Women and their weddings. He'd never understand the fascination. Men tolerated them for the women they loved, but most of them would rather be stuck in the eye with a hot poker than stand around in a tuxedo for hours on end. "Anything outstanding about this one?"

"Fairly traditional for the most part," Jane said. "But I haven't seen the dress yet."

The attendants came down the aisle in their lavender dresses, lining up to the left of the flowered arch. Most of the greenery was live, and he and Val had added the cut flowers and ribbons earlier that morning.

The bridal march began, and they stood. Jane's gasp when Kelly entered made him lean down and ask, "How's the dress?"

"Fabulous. She's a beautiful bride."

The couple had opted for a traditional religious service with a few extra elements. Afterward Jane and Heath exited the garden with the other guests. She held on to his arm as they walked toward the tent, trying to keep her heels from sinking deep into the thick grass.

"I'm glad we don't have to set up for a reception," he said.

"I'm sure it's just a matter of time before someone asks," she said.

Alex Casey, another one of the high school jocks from their class, made a beeline for them. "Jane, good to see you. You're looking great."

"Thanks, Alex. You remember Heath Truelove."

"Yeah. Good to see you," he said, swinging his hand with one of those cool handshakes Heath detested. "It's been awhile. What are you up to these days?"

"Not much. What's up with you?"

"Took a job in Denver. My girlfriend is one of Kelly's bridesmaids. How's your brother? Can't recall his name."

"Rom is great. He's working in Lexington."

"Excuse me," Jane said. "I need to see what Opie wants."

The two men watched her walk over to where Opie stood.

Alex released a low whistle. "That's one hot woman. Hey man, can you believe old Garrett killed himself? I always thought he was too egotistical to do something like that. With a wife like Jane, he must have really been nuts. You two dating now? What's she like? Were the rumors true?"

Heath found the man's steady flow of questions offensive. "No, we're not dating. The rumors were all lies. Jane is a decent, loving mother whose focus is on her child. She didn't deserve all that junk that was laid on her then, and she certainly doesn't deserve it now."

Alex's eyes widened. "Hey dude, lighten up. I didn't mean anything."

"Good luck with that job." Heath walked away, confused by his reaction to the man's words. He hadn't expected to feel the need to defend Jane after all these years. Sure, Jane was a beautiful, vibrant woman and men would always wonder if they had a chance with her, but Heath didn't have to like it. Why hadn't he told Alex they were dating? Because in his heart Heath wanted nothing more.

"Everything okay?" he asked when she returned to his side.

"Sammy couldn't find her horsie. Where's Alex?"

"Far away, I hope." Heath had few dealings with the guy in high school and hoped to have even fewer in the future.

"What happened?"

He might as well tell her. No doubt it would be the gossip of the wedding. "Walk with me."

They went into the garden and sat on a bench, watching as the photographer posed the wedding party.

"Tell me."

"He asked if the rumors about you were true."

She didn't look surprised. "Why?"

"He thought we were dating."

Realization dawned in Jane's eyes. "Alex isn't the first to ask that question. They know me. They know my past. I can't get around that."

Her earlier sparkle disappeared, exchanged for a mask of sadness, and that angered him. Heath served the God of forgiveness. If He could put Jane's past behind her, other people could, too. "It's none of his business."

"Small town, Heath. Everyone makes everything their business."

"It's the past," he insisted. "Alex Casey should leave it there."

"But he won't. They never do. My reputation will follow me the rest of my life. I accept that."

"Why should you have to, Jane? Was what you did so bad that you feel you have to pay for your mistakes forever?"

"Think what you want, but I defend my choices, too. Maybe they weren't good, but I exercised the freedom God gives us all. I loved Garrett, but I never did any of those things people said I did."

"So why didn't you tell them?"

"Garrett said no one would believe me. The guys winked and nudged, and he played up to them. The girls seemed even more determined to fling themselves at him."

"Did he ever. . . ?"

She shook her head slightly. "I don't know. I didn't want to know."

Heath hadn't cared for Garrett Holt. He flaunted his popularity at every opportunity, making everything about him. When Jane chose to date him, Heath worried that she'd fallen victim to that public persona. "Did you let it happen, Jane?"

She shook her head. "No. I had dreams, too. I thought we'd go to college and then have a magnificent wedding. Garrett would work, and I'd be a stay-at-home mom until my kids went to school, and then I'd have my career. Pretty fantasy, huh?"

Heath didn't say anything. Not for him. Heath planned to provide for his family so his wife could be there for their children.

"Learning I was pregnant was a major shock. Everyone had suggestions about what we should do. Garrett suggested abortion, but there was no way I'd do that to my child. Clarice just wanted me to disappear. My parents thought adoption was best. When I wouldn't agree, marriage became the only option. They hustled us off to the magistrate's office and got it done quickly. Our parents made the decisions for us.

"We kept going to school, but things were different. All my friends avoided me. We were living with Garrett's parents, and they weren't very friendly. Mom and Dad moved to Colorado. I didn't have anyone but Garrett and my unborn child."

"Do they know what happened to the baby?"

"The doctor said it happens. Knowing my baby would be stillborn was the worst thing that ever happened to me. I had such high hopes for the future."

"You can't survive without hope," Heath said. "It's the only thing that motivates us to get out of bed every morning."

"You're right. I still hope to one day prove myself to all these people who saw the bad Jane."

Somehow he had to convince her that she wasn't that person. "Bad Jane is a figment of your imagination," Heath said. He stood and held out his hand. "Come on. They've finished the pictures. Let's get seated before they introduce the wedding party and serve dinner."

Chapter 7

Jane watched Sammy pat Jacob's hand to get his attention. It was his birthday, and his family and friends congregated to celebrate. That afternoon he'd injured his leg and been knocked unconscious by a horse. Every family member believed a hospital visit was in order, but Jacob stubbornly insisted on sticking around to enjoy his party.

His smile widened, and he swung the child up onto his lap. Jane smiled when Sammy kissed Jacob's cheek. Sammy wanted to comfort Mr. Jacob's "owie," just as the entire family often did for her.

These were the kind of grandparents her child deserved. Loving, good-hearted people who didn't pass judgment on those they cherished.

"Enjoying yourself?"

Jane glanced at Heath, her heart picking up speed at the sound of his voice. *I'm in trouble,* she realized. Her awareness of him increased with each passing day. Now that her eyes were open to the good qualities a man should possess, she recognized many of them in Heath. Jane particularly loved the way he treated his family.

Earlier in the day, while working with Val to set up the business launch party for Your Wedding Place, her friend had suggested God would send the right person for her and Sammy. As she looked deep into Heath's gaze, she couldn't help but think He already had. That overwhelmed Jane. If only Heath felt the same, but Jane sensed he held back from her and wondered why.

"I'm so thankful your dad is okay. I was afraid when I heard he'd been injured."

"I wish he'd go get checked out," Heath said.

Jane smiled in understanding. "I was here when they brought him in. Val sent me up early to get Sammy. She thought your mom might need to finish a few things." She shook her head. "Cindy was beside herself."

"I'm glad you were here for her."

"Me, too. She does so much for us. Did they figure out what happened?"

"Not really. Evidently Fancy went crazy, and Dad got in the way."

"Why would she act that way? She's the most docile horse you have."

"We don't know. Bill called the vet to check out Fancy and her baby."

Jane's hand went to her mouth. She hadn't thought about the horse being pregnant. "I pray they're all okay."

"Me, too. Are you ready to eat? Let's check out the food."

Her mouth dropped open. "You can't still be hungry after all that food at the launch party."

"That was snack food. This is meat and potatoes."

Jane laughed and followed him across to the dining room where the Truelove women had set up quite a feast. Opie's gift had been to prepare all of her father's favorite foods. No wonder Jacob objected to leaving his guests and his birthday dinner.

Heath filled a plate, and Jane picked a few things to taste. After taking a bite of the melt-in-your-mouth pot roast, she understood Jacob's objections. "This is wonderful. The tea party refreshments were fantastic, but this is even better."

Heath barely stopped eating long enough to agree. "Food is definitely that girl's calling."

∾

The evening passed quickly, and soon it was time to say good night. Jane looked down at her daughter sleeping peacefully in Jacob's arms. "Time to take her home."

"You're welcome to leave her here tonight," Cindy said.

"She sleeps better in her own bed. She'll wake the entire house with her cries if we upset her routine."

"I'll carry her to the apartment for you," Heath volunteered.

He scooped up the child and adjusted her against his shoulder. Sammy's eyes flickered open for a moment and then closed. "She's out for the count," he said with a grin.

Jane repeated her birthday wishes to Jacob and told everyone good night before holding the door open for him. "She's not used to so much excitement. You saw how she was in the thick of things."

"Has her mom's personality," Heath commented.

"Let's just hope she makes better decisions than I did."

"Every parent wants that for their child," Heath said. "They want us to make better decisions than they did, and she'll want her children to make better decisions than she does. That's human nature."

Jane wondered if that were true. Her parents had never admitted regretting their decisions, but she wondered if they did.

They moved along the pathway to the apartment, enjoying the beautiful summer night as they walked. Heath followed her up the stairs and stepped aside on the landing while she unlocked the door.

Longing filled her as she wished they were a family returning home for the evening. As she watched him lower Sammy into her toddler bed and kiss her cheek ever so gently, Jane couldn't remove her gaze from him. She could love this man with every bit of her being. In him, she saw everything she needed.

She pulled a light blanket over the sleeping child and turned on the night-light before pulling the door closed behind them. "Would you like something to drink?"

Heath rubbed his stomach and shook his head. "I don't have an empty spot left."

Jane sat on the sofa and pointed at the seat next to her. "I don't think any of you will be hungry again for weeks."

Heath joined her, leaving a space between them. "We'll be ready for the leftovers tomorrow. I hope Dad shares." He leaned back, yawning as he said, "I'm tired. It's been a busy day."

"It's been a busy week. Val's launch party went well. I spoke with a number of interested planners. It's so exciting," Jane enthused. "People asked about booking other events, too. Val deserves this. I'm so happy we've become friends." A thought flashed into her head. "You know, now that I think about it, I didn't really have a girlfriend after Garrett and I got together."

"How did you and Val meet?"

"She used to come into the shop to pick up lattes for Maddy Troyer. She introduced herself, and I asked if she knew you and Rom. We clicked. She's become a good friend. My best friend. She came to Garrett's funeral and brought food to the house. I couldn't believe how supportive she was. She kept coming back."

"That's our Val."

"You're each special in your own way," Jane said, placing her hand on his and squeezing gently. "I'm so thankful to have you back in my life."

They stared into each other's eyes for several moments before she shortened the distance between them and kissed him. Heath looked as surprised as she felt. The kiss left her feeling shell-shocked.

"I'd better go. It's getting late."

She didn't want him to leave. "Stay."

"I'm sorry, Jane. I can't."

Disappointment filled her. "You don't want to?"

"It's not that," Heath said without hesitation. "But out of respect to you and myself, I can't."

"We're consenting adults."

"Accepting what you offer goes against everything I believe."

"You sound almost like a. . ."

"I am," Heath said before she could finish the sentence. "I'm saving myself for the woman who will become my wife. Purity is a gift. Not to be taken lightly."

"But you're a man," Jane said. "Surely you have. . ."

"I'm normal. I have biological urges, but I control myself. I learned many years ago that life is not about making conquests with women."

"I see," she said, feeling ashamed that she'd thrown herself at him like that.

He took her hand in his and squeezed. "I'm not judging you. I never believed your reputation was as bad as the gossip made it sound."

"Garrett was the only man in my life."

"I thought that was the case."

Their gazes met and held. "Why did you care?"

"I liked you. I didn't want to believe the rumors."

Jane didn't understand. Why would he care what people said about her? She'd heard the rumors, and when she wanted to defend herself, Garrett had said no one would believe the truth. In hindsight, Jane realized the rumors that ruined her reputation enhanced his. "Sometimes I cried," she admitted, her voice so low she wasn't sure Heath could hear her. "I was so hurt that my love for Garrett had been reduced to a bunch of lies."

"Didn't he defend you?"

Heath had defended her. Though she hadn't heard what he'd said, she knew he'd spoken up in her defense. Unlike Garrett, he never worried about their former classmates taking offense. He hadn't worried about what others would think or say. He just spoke his piece and dealt with the consequences.

Jane shrugged. "When I'd get upset or angry, he'd appease me by saying we knew the truth and the others didn't matter. I accepted I couldn't change their minds."

She realized now that the people who mattered respected Heath because he was trustworthy and decent.

"Heath, about this woman you're saving yourself for. . . Do you expect the same purity from her?"

"It's in God's hands. The only thing I can say for sure is that she will be pure in His eyes. Pure in heart."

How could that be? "I don't understand."

"When Jesus forgives us, He washes us clean with His blood."

The reminder of how Jesus had died for her made Jane feel even more unworthy of His love. Her impulsive action didn't reinforce the beliefs she'd been taught to honor. "I'm sorry, Heath. I shouldn't have acted like that."

He looked her in the eye and said, "Sometimes we can't accept the gifts we'd be honored to receive. I can't deny I've always been very attracted to you. You impacted my life that first day you walked into the classroom, but it wasn't meant to be then."

And it still isn't, Jane concluded forlornly. Why had she allowed herself to think she'd ever be good enough for Heath? She was spoiled goods. A sinner in God's eyes. Her life had been in turmoil ever since she'd started making her own decisions.

"I'd better head back," Heath said. "Tomorrow will be another busy day with the prep for Saturday's wedding."

Jane nodded. "Val said Maddy will be here first thing tomorrow to start setting up."

"I'm sure Val is looking forward to seeing her. She and Maddy worked well together."

She followed him to the door and wished him good night. When he stepped out on the porch, Jane called, "Forgive me?"

He pulled her into a hug, and she went into his arms willingly. "Nothing to forgive. I care for you and Sammy. I always will."

After he left, Jane turned the lamp off and sat in the darkness. When the tears started, she couldn't stop them. Though she understood, his rejection hurt. She'd tried to show him how she felt in the only way she knew how, and he'd rejected her.

Hadn't she done the same to him? In her girl's heart, she'd known the shy smiles and boyish behavior had been more than friendliness. But he wasn't a popular kid. Not even a wealthy one. Just smart, hardworking, cute, and kind. Not someone her immature self would have considered a soul mate.

That had been then. Now Jane knew she'd feel honored to be Heath Truelove's woman.

"Help me, God," she whispered into the darkness. "I've made so many mistakes in the past. Change my future. Direct my path. Make me a good enough person to be Heath's friend."

&

Heath paused when the lamp went off in the apartment. He loved Jane. He always had, and walking away from her just now had truly been among the most difficult decisions he'd ever made. He had no other option. He could unite himself with Jane, but without God's presence in their lives, nothing would ever be right.

"Help her, Lord," he prayed. "She needs Your magnanimous love more than she realizes. Only You can reassure her fears and doubts and help her see she's always been loved by You."

He turned and walked toward the house.

"Everything okay?" his father asked when he came into the sitting room.

"Not really." Heath dropped down on the sofa next to his mother. It was getting late, and the others had already gone to their rooms.

"Want to talk about it?"

"I'm in love with Jane. I think I've loved her since the first moment I saw her."

His dad nodded. "I can see how you feel."

Heath started. He hadn't thought he wore his heart on his sleeve.

"It's not that obvious," Jacob reassured him.

"She's grieving still. I admire Jane. She's accepted full responsibility for the choices she made when she could easily blame Garrett."

"Jane is a good person," Cindy said. "But is she a Christian?"

"She believes," Heath said. "Jane attended church with her parents as a young girl. She told me she accepted Jesus as a child. It was only after she became a teen that she fell away from Him. She thinks all is lost because she fell in with the wrong crowd and made wrong decisions."

"Life is about choices, Heath. We can't help but reflect on how different life is when we choose the right path or even when your heart pulls you along the wrong path. I know you want a wife and family, but don't let your desire to find the right woman push you to make a wrong decision."

Heath shrugged and said, "I think I've found her, but I can't be sure. I wasn't the man she wanted when we were in our teens. What if that's still the case?"

"God can change anyone, son. This family is living proof of that."

"We are. My commitment to God is not something I take lightly. He's always first in my life. Even when I'd like to follow my heart."

"Never allow your heart to rule your head," Jacob cautioned.

~

Jane went to bed, but when sleep wouldn't come, she felt the need to do something. Packing boxes from their house sat in the corner of her bedroom. After his death, she'd donated Garrett's clothing with the exception of his letter jacket and football jersey. She'd saved those and some of the trophies for Sammy. She had put off sorting through his personal effects and papers for over a year now. She'd used her work schedule and time spent with the Trueloves as excuses, but truthfully she didn't want to mess with the stuff. Jane didn't want to be alone with her memories of Garrett.

The realization that she'd probably have more alone time now that she'd all but attacked Heath hit her hard. His family would be disappointed when they heard what she'd done.

She should have known better. Blame it on the night. A wonderful evening, filled with good friends, people who didn't hesitate to show their love. When she'd witnessed his tenderness with Sammy, it had been all she could do not to throw her arms around him and never let go.

Was Val right? Would God send someone to love them? Maybe she should give Him a chance to provide. She hadn't done well on her own.

Even though they had been infrequent, she missed the good times with Garrett. They had enjoyed each other's company, and in his own way, Jane believed he had loved her. He just loved himself more.

She sat down on the floor and dug into the first box. If she was going to dwell on the past, this was the job for it, she thought as she lifted out a number of pictures. She studied the framed shots of Garrett in his uniform, reminded of a time when they had decorated their first apartment. Most newlywed couples had beautiful wedding photos but not them. They had Garrett's glory shots with a couple of small photos of them as a couple. Thinking Sammy might enjoy them one day, Jane slipped them from their frames with the intention of placing them in a scrapbook for their daughter.

She emptied the box quickly and put the frames back inside. Dragging over another box, she found his personal papers. A small bankbook inside a brown envelope gave her pause. She opened it to find that Garrett had started a savings account for Sammy on the day she was born. Though there wasn't a lot of money in the account and at times the withdrawals had exceeded the deposits, it pleased her to know he had cared about their daughter's future.

Oh Garrett, why didn't we ever really talk? So much of their lives had focused on Garrett and his needs and her anger because he wasn't the man she expected him to be. She laid the passbook on the nightstand.

As she continued to dig, Jane found herself pulled deep into memories of the past. She removed tax files from the records and laid aside old check stubs and medical bills for the shredder. One bill caught her eye, and she picked it up. Why had Garrett visited an oncologist? What else hadn't he told her?

The long day began to catch up with her, and Jane yawned widely. Rubbing her face wearily, she laid the paper on the nightstand with the passbook. She'd call the office and ask some questions. Probably a follow-up for something that he'd considered too insignificant to mention.

She returned the boxes to their corner and turned out the light. The tears came many times in the cover of darkness. Jane went back to another time when her insecurities had held her hostage. Garrett cajoled and threatened, and the anxiety over his true feelings for her never left Jane. Did he love her, or had her refusal to give him what he wanted become a personal challenge for him? He certainly had told her often enough that there were other girls who didn't have her hang-ups.

Those insecurities had precipitated the action that made her a woman before her time. She had cried that night, too. The overwhelming feeling behind her error in judgment had eaten at her. She'd tried to justify it, but knowing how much her action displeased God made it even worse. The purity she'd been taught to cherish had been lost. She couldn't undo what happened, and mistake or not, her only option was to go forward with life.

Based on her experience, she'd advise any young woman to wait. She had considered herself old enough to make her own decisions, and because of that, she'd been forced to deem herself mature enough to live with the outcome of those decisions.

She learned the hard way that planning to wait meant keeping yourself from temptation. No one should pressure others into making choices.

Jacob and Cindy Truelove had been able to impart this knowledge to their children. Val told her the rule was they couldn't date until they were sixteen. The rule was the same for boys and girls. Even then they were told to choose carefully.

Their parents had to be introduced to every person they were involved with, and people who couldn't deal with family couldn't be involved with the Trueloves.

She'd asked how that affected them about dating someone their parents didn't approve of, and Val had said it was a nonissue out of respect to them.

Today's kids might look down on that arrangement, but given the mistakes she'd made, Jane could see the merit. She cuddled under the blanket, watching night transition into dawn. Only time would indicate whether she'd made a mistake with Heath last night.

Jane woke with puffy eyes, and no amount of makeup disguised the fact that she had cried into the night.

Sammy wandered around the bedroom while Jane dressed, finding her way into the keepsake box Jane had set off to the side. The child pulled out her pompoms and cried when Jane took them away. One look at her sad face made Jane give in.

At the Trueloves', the women and Heath cheered with Sammy as she dragged the pom-poms around the kitchen.

"Why so glum?" Val asked when she set the cup of coffee before Jane.

She smiled her thanks and took a sip before she said, "I know it's silly for a grown woman to hold on to mementos like that, but I didn't want her to have them," Jane said.

"That's not silly. We'll tell Mom and Opie to hide them when Sammy gets sidetracked. You can pick up a little girl set in Paris."

"Thanks, Val." She finished the coffee and took her cup over to the sink. After rinsing and placing it in the dishwasher, she kissed Sammy and headed out to work. Heath followed.

She glanced at him. "I suppose you think I'm being silly about the pom-poms."

"No. We all have our keepsakes."

She stopped walking and turned to face him. "Maybe I should let them go. Cut myself free of the past."

"Not until you're ready. I'm sorry about last night," he said.

Jane felt deep shame and looked away. "I apologize for making you feel uncomfortable."

Heath caught her chin and pulled her face up to look into her eyes. "Don't. It wasn't my intention to hurt you, Jane. I just need you to know what's important to me."

"You have to find the woman who shares your beliefs."

He nodded. "Yes, she has to believe."

She believed in God. Her relationship wasn't much to speak of, but she did believe Jesus Christ was God's Son and died for her sins.

Heath cleared his throat and said, "I hope you don't take this the wrong way, but I care about you, and I don't want to hurt you or see you hurt by someone else. You are grieving your loss and reaching out to others for comfort. Not all men are going to say no."

Before she could speak, he raised his hand. "Let me finish. Think before you take that step. Make sure the man you choose can be everything you need. I'd say the same to my sisters."

"I'm not your sister."

Jane wanted to be insulted that Heath would think that of her, but what else could he think? She'd thrown herself at him. He couldn't know she wasn't looking for other men. Only him.

∾

Heath watched her leave. Things would be so much simpler if she were his sister. When he offered his advice, they knew it was out of love. He wouldn't have to deal with the mixed-up crazy emotions that had him running outside to corner Jane early this morning. Or fear he might have done more harm than good with his comments. He loved her, but until he had his answers from God, he couldn't show that love as anything more than a friend.

"Oh, Heath, there you are."

He turned as Val walked around the corner of the house.

"What's up?"

"I need someone to run into Lexington and pick up the chair covers Maddy rented. She's nearly here and realized she forgot them."

"Sure. Do you want me or Jane to go?"

She considered his question for a moment and said, "Jane. We'll need your help unloading Maddy's van."

"I'll find her."

"That's okay," Val said, pulling her cell phone from her pocket. "I can call."

Probably best, he thought. No doubt he was the last person Jane wanted to see right now.

"I took the displays down in the tent," he said. They had moved out the food and serving trays but left the other stuff with the intention of returning later. Their father's injury had thrown everything off kilter, and they had hung around the party until it was too late to get it done. "Where do you want to store them?"

She held up a finger while she gave Jane her instructions. Pushing the phone into her jeans pocket, she said, "Somewhere they'll stay dry. I hope to use them at other events. Maybe I can get Maddy to put one of the smaller signs in her office."

"I'll put them in the office until you decide."

"Thanks, Heath."

They spent a hectic day helping Maddy, but by the end everyone was satisfied with what they had accomplished.

"I'm so thankful I could set up today," Maddy said. "There's no way I'd get all this done if I had to wait until tomorrow."

"Looks like the bride's got a lot of stuff," Heath said as they removed another load from the van.

"There's more on the way," Maddy said. "I'm not even sure they'll be able to see the garden for everything she wants to add."

He stopped unloading and asked, "She's not thinking of altering the garden, is she?"

"No. The garden is fine. She wants to hang lanterns in the tent and has these elaborate table arrangements. There's special china, stemware, and silverware. She even wants the table and chairs changed out. I told her the chairs would be under the covers, but she insisted." Maddy shrugged. "It's her money. As long as she can pay the tab, we'll give her whatever she wants. I hope the rental truck gets here soon. I need to make sure all that stuff is on-site."

"I'll let you know as soon as it arrives."

Jane returned with a truckload of boxes.

"Are all those chair covers?"

"I don't know. They kept loading boxes into the truck. I didn't know what to expect."

Heath turned and called to Maddy. "Where do you want all this?"

"Along the walls of the tent for now."

"From all Maddy says, I think we might be in for a wild ride with this one," he said to Jane.

"I'm sure every wedding will be different. At least Kelly was pleasant to work with."

Heath wheeled a cart into place and began shifting boxes. He looked up at Jane on the back of the truck as she pushed the boxes toward the tailgate. "Still upset with me?"

"Let's not talk about it anymore. I made a mistake last night."

He caught her hand. "You didn't understand."

"Well, I do now. You can relax. I won't be throwing myself at any other men. I let myself get caught up in the celebration last night and had a lot of mixed emotions when you walked me home."

"I have mixed emotions, too, Jane. Lots of them."

She stared at him for a moment. "Just don't hold my misguided act against me. I'll get myself sorted out eventually."

"Friends?"

She nodded in agreement and offered her hand to shake on it.

Chapter 8

So what's the plan for today?" Jane asked Heath when she saw him crossing the yard. She'd attended church with them on Sunday, and he'd treated her as usual. None of the family had commented on her wayward behavior, so just maybe it wasn't going to be as bad as she feared.

"I'm taking the day off. Want to come along?"

She didn't know what to think. Spending the day with Heath appealed to her even though she knew it was senseless. "I'm sure Val has all sorts of things that need doing."

"You've worked two weekends in a row. You're due a day off. Ask Val. She'll tell you."

"Sammy. . ."

"Baking cookies with Mom. Last I saw, she looked like a ghost under all the flour."

A wry smile touched Jane's face. "I can't compete with cookies. What's the plan?"

"I want to visit Wallis House and the Bernheim Arboretum and have lunch in Paris."

After their discussion, Jane went off to clear her schedule and make sure Cindy Truelove didn't mind babysitting Sammy. A half hour later she waited by the truck for Heath.

"Sorry about that," he said when he finally appeared, pulling the keys from the pocket of his cargo shorts. "Dad asked me to give him a hand getting into the living room."

"How's he doing today?"

"His leg's swollen, and his head hurts."

Jacob Truelove had seen the doctor on Friday and learned he had a concussion and a severe contusion. He'd joked about all the C words the doctor used.

"He's chafing at the bit to get out and do things."

"Maybe I should stay here. Your mom needs to take care of him."

Heath shrugged. "He won't let her coddle him. I figure Dad will read to Sammy or they'll watch her favorite movie, and he'll feel like he's helping Mom instead of being useless."

Jane hesitated.

"You'll help Mom more by going than by staying."

He opened the passenger door and stepped aside for her to climb in.

"The forecast says rain today. I hope they're wrong."

Heath laughed and said, "It wouldn't dare rain on my day off."

Jane laid a brown envelope on the seat. "Val asked if we could take these papers by the courthouse. She said Mr. Henderson should be there."

"I don't see why not."

"You were right. Val said I should take a couple of days off."

"I knew she would. Although I'm not sure my plans are what you had in mind."

"Tell me about this place."

"Wallis House is the 1851 home that serves as headquarters for the Garden Club of Kentucky and has an arboretum with lots of native and flowering trees and plants."

"This sounds work related."

Heath shrugged. "You never know where you'll find ideas."

"You need to learn how to have fun," Jane said.

He talked about what they would see, and before she realized it, he had parked in the courthouse square. "You should come inside and take a look. I did a paper on Paris's historical sites, and this was one of them."

They walked up the high steps and into the building, their footsteps resounding on the marble floors as they walked toward the courtroom in their search for Val's attorney.

"Very *To Kill a Mockingbird*-ish," Jane said in a low voice as she studied the old wooden chairs and balcony area.

"I think they filmed a remake or something here," Heath said once they were back in the hall.

"All this marble must have cost a fortune."

"This is the fourth courthouse. The others burned. They just finished a million dollar renovation to preserve the building. Let's go up so you can get a better look at the paintings."

They walked up the stairs and over to the rotunda to view the artwork illustrating the four seasons of farming in Kentucky. "What's that?" Jane asked, pointing to one of the scenes.

"Hemp. Back when it was used for rope instead of the more well-known illegal use today."

Jane turned slowly, looking at the paintings and then the interior of the building. "Incredible."

"A friend says today's buildings aren't meant to be around in a hundred years," Heath said.

"Definitely not the same quality construction," Jane said.

"Ready for Wallis House? It's another example of a fine house with staying power."

"It's looking gloomy out here," Jane said when they exited the building. They were almost to the truck when the rain started. She took off running and jumped inside the vehicle, shivering when the rivulet ran down her back as she brushed the water from her hair. She said, "Guess the weatherman knew what he was talking about."

"You want to go home?" Heath sounded disappointed.

"No. I won't melt. You have alternate plans?"

"We could visit Hopewell Museum. I researched it when I did my paper."

"Lead the way."

The rain didn't let up as Heath drove over to the museum and parked. They made a dash for the building, and Heath held the door for her, impressing Jane with his gentlemanly behavior. He performed the tasks automatically but managed to make her feel very special. He guided her to the left and said, "It was the old post office. See that window?" Her gaze followed his pointing finger. She nodded.

"That's where the auditors viewed the workers. They would climb ladders from outside to sit up there and watch. Later they installed a spiral staircase. It's in a closet at the back of the building. The workers didn't know when they were in the building."

Jane followed Heath through the area, finding him both interesting and entertaining as they discussed the various displays. "You know a lot about the museum."

"I spent a lot of time here." He pointed to the floor. "They have marble, too. Just in the public sections of the building. The workers got wood floors."

They wandered through the rooms and enjoyed the artists' paintings on display.

"There's the gift shop, and this is the computer room," Heath said. "Too bad they didn't have this when I used to come here. The old safe is in those closets," he said, pointing to the back of the room.

"I'm impressed. You could be a tour guide for Paris."

"I love history. We'll have to come back for Wallis House, Duncan Tavern, and Claiborne Farm another time. Ready for lunch?" He glanced out the window. "I think the rain has slacked off." On the way out, Heath tucked a donation in the box. "I thought we might eat at the emporium and look at antiques after lunch."

The ambience of the place made it a good choice. Dr. Varden had built the drugstore in 1891. The interior of the store was lined with South African mahogany and Tiffany & Co. stained glass. Over their lunch of chicken salad and fresh lemonade, the conversation turned to the future.

"I want so much for Sammy," Jane admitted. "I hope she doesn't follow in my footsteps. Your family is a good role model for her."

"You're a better role model, Jane. Why are you so down on yourself?"

"I lived two lives, Heath. At home I was good little Jane. Model student, cheerleader, polite, well behaved, and in church with my parents. But at school I became popular Jane. Some areas overlapped, but that life was about Garrett. I loved him. You know what I don't get," she said with a wave of her hand. "Why didn't you get caught up in the peer pressure?"

Heath shrugged. "I suppose my sole focus on getting good grades kept me too busy to care about popularity."

"Too bad I didn't have that problem," Jane said with a self-deprecating laugh.

"You said you turned into a swan," Heath offered. "Maybe you were flattered by Garrett's attention."

Jane felt her skin turn warm. "Not a swan. But you're right. I did enjoy the attention. Of course that changed fast. Ever since they found out, my parents have questioned every choice I've made. They actually suggested I have my baby and put it up for adoption. Their grandchild! Would your parents do that?"

Heath didn't need to answer. She knew they wouldn't. Jacob and Cindy would welcome the child into their home. They would care for their grandchildren. Not label them as mistakes. Jane laughed and said, "My dad said a jock couldn't support a family, but they forced me to marry Garrett. The entire ordeal was very stressful." She sighed and said, "See what you get? Make one simple comment, and I turn it into my life story."

"I don't mind."

"I know you don't. You're a good man, Heath Truelove. The best. I promise to be a better friend than I was in high school."

"The past is behind us, Jane."

"Is it really? I don't think the past ever truly lets go."

"God forgives us. Our sins can be as far away as the east is from the west."

"I suppose I can't forgive myself. Knowing how much God loves me and how I let Him down is a load to bear. I appreciate the fact that you and your family are Christians. You're good people. That's why I agreed to let Sammy go to church with you. But I'm not sure there's a place for me there anymore."

"Jesus didn't insist you carry your own cross," Heath told her. "He carried it for you."

"I know. I'm praying about it. For now, it's really important to me that Sammy's in church."

"God's house has a place for everyone. Sammy likes church. She enjoys her class and the other kids."

Jane nodded in agreement. "I love your mom, and I know Sammy loves her, but I wonder about that connection with other children."

"Maybe you should find other activities for her. What about ballet? She'd be a cutie in a tutu. I see her dancing around to Mom's radio at the house."

The idea had merit. "Or gymnastics. I suppose I could afford classes since Val has been so generous."

"I wouldn't mind helping out."

"No. I have to draw the line somewhere. You and your family are far too generous."

"We've been blessed," Heath said. "And Dad says we need to pass that blessing on."

"To the less fortunate?" Jane asked.

"I wouldn't even suggest that. I think Sammy's very blessed to have a mom like you."

After lunch Heath picked up the tab, and they checked out the gift shop before they headed for the truck.

"Do we have time to run by the superstore to pick up something for Sammy?"

"She's already got tons of toys," Heath said.

"I wanted a set of pom-poms for her. I suppose I could drive back tonight."

Heath shook his head. "We'll go. What else are you going to get?"

"I have to see what speaks to me."

"You mean something that talks?" he asked, confused by her words.

Jane laughed. "No, silly. You have to think like a two-year-old. See what toy you think she'd love the most."

Heath shook his head. "The only certainty is nothing you buy is going to entertain her longer than two or three minutes."

"Yeah, but your mom has her putting one thing back before she takes out another. That's a gigantic step forward."

He laughed. "You learn to do that with so many kids, or the house would be unlivable. Of course, Sammy tries to pull one over on the rest of us. She dumps everything out, and when we tell her to pick it up, she says, 'You do it.'"

"Sounds like my Sammy. She cried when I made her help."

They spent the next hour examining every toy in the aisles.

"It's like the three bears," Heath said. "Too old, too young, and just right. What about this?" he asked, holding up a huge boxing glove.

Jane looked appalled. "Not unless you want her beating up on you."

"We didn't have lots of toys," Heath said as they walked through the aisles. "Mostly we played outside."

The need to show him how to have fun overwhelmed Jane. "You have to pick something out, too. I'm buying you a present."

Heath frowned and shook his head. "Don't waste your money."

Jane refused to listen. "I know exactly the thing." She dragged him over to the remote control cars. "We'll buy two and race."

Heath looked embarrassed.

"Come on," she said. "It's fun." She hit a button, and raucous carnival music played while a voice spoke.

"We'll buy them for Roc and Cy."

"They can play with them, but I'm buying them for us," Jane insisted.

"Okay. Okay," Heath agreed. "It's your money."

"You'll play with me, won't you?"

"Sure. Looks like fun."

Jane punched him in the side with her elbow. "You know you wanted to all along. You work hard. You need to learn how to play. Which one should I get?" she asked, juggling the cars as she pointed to two of the books.

"You could put the cars back and buy both."

She grinned and reached for a book. "Or I can buy her this one."

"And I'll buy the other one," Heath said, taking it from the shelf. "We'll keep it at the house."

"Where are we going to hold our race?"

"Depends on what kind of terrain that little car you bought can handle. Flat open, we can use the pathways to the barn. Or more rugged, we can head for the hills."

"Oh, I think my car can beat yours on the hills," Jane returned confidently. "I'll even give you a learning curve."

"I'll take it."

∾

Later that afternoon the rain moved on and the sun shone brightly when they met for their race. When Cy and Roc got word of the competition, they told the others, and soon Val, Opie, Jules, Sammy, and their mom gathered to see what was going on.

"You should have seen his face when I said I was buying him a toy," Jane told the women. "Heath needs to learn to be a kid again."

Val took her mother's handkerchief and said she'd be the starter. When she gave the go-ahead, Jane's car shot forward. The group meandered along behind them as they raced their cars along the pathway. Jane's laughter was a constant as she managed to obtain the lead while Heath's car raced every way but straight ahead.

"I don't know what to do with this thing," he grumbled.

Jane stopped long enough to show him a few of the basics and then frowned when he managed to get his car several yards ahead of hers. "No fair."

"Learning curve, remember?"

"You just look out, Mr. Truelove. I can be a speed demon when the situation warrants."

Chapter 9

"Is the move still on for tomorrow?" Heath asked Val as they walked back to the house.

"Opie and I have been moving boxes a few at a time. We need to pick up the pace. Summer is winding down, and the kids return to school soon."

When the family came to the agreement to move into the Sheridan mansion, Heath found himself torn over living in such a fine home. Granted, their lives hadn't been the same since Val's win and he wouldn't mind having a larger bedroom, but he missed having Rom around during the week. His brother was living in Russ Hunter's spare room and coming home on weekends. Some nights he showed up for dinner, but it was different.

As twins they had been inseparable for twenty-four years. They shared the same room with their younger brothers. They drove back and forth to UK together, and Uncle Zeb had offered them a finished room over his garage when they lived in Boston.

They hadn't experienced a traditional college lifestyle, but they had been together. In a way, Heath figured this separation was good preparation for the future when Rom married Stephanie and they became permanently separated. He missed his twin and wondered if Rom felt the same way. "Want me to help with the move or work in the garden?"

"The next bride requested the English garden. Other than a few requested changes, it's ready, so let's get moved and settled. Once that's out of the way, we can get back to work on the business."

❧

Early the following morning they loaded boxes into the truck and drove over to the mansion. Cindy had taken the younger kids into town for school supplies and doctor appointments. She'd offered to take Sammy, but Jane knew the little girl would tire too soon and give them a hard time.

She settled Sammy in the office with her books and toys but had her doubts about her daughter's staying power. Jane carried her box upstairs and checked in on the trip down. Sammy had abandoned the items in favor of a video someone had turned on for her.

"Why don't you take her home until Mom gets back?" Val asked when she walked up on Jane peeking into the office.

"Let's give this a try. If she refuses to listen, I'll take her."

Jane and Val got into a routine, taking the boxes from where Heath stacked them to the various rooms. They had just placed their last boxes in the bedroom when they heard Heath cry out Sammy's name.

The crashing sound along with some other indistinguishable cries had them running to find Sammy, Heath, and the box lying at the foot of the curved staircase.

"What happened?" Jane knelt by Sammy's side. Her daughter's pained cries were interspersed with two words: "Mommy. Hurt."

Heath tried to shift his leg, and Jane saw him writhe with discomfort. "I had that tall box and didn't see her. Is she okay?"

She tried to check her daughter for injuries, but the child cried harder when she touched her right forearm. "I think her arm might be broken."

"Oh, Sammy baby, I'm sorry," he said, anguished over what had happened.

"It's not your fault," Jane said. "I should have taken her home. What about you?"

"My leg."

"I called 911," Val said, tossing Jane a throw as she knelt by Heath's side and spread the second blanket over him. "How bad is it?"

He sucked in a deep breath and said, "Bad."

"What happened?" Opie demanded when she came into the house. "Daddy said there had been an accident."

"I tripped over Sammy on the stairs, and we fell. I tried to grab her, but I was afraid the box would hit her. She could have been killed." Heath shuddered at the thought.

"I left her in the office with her toys," Jane said. "I thought she'd play for a while."

"I know," Heath said. "Last time I looked, she was watching the video. I should have checked again before climbing the stairs."

The paramedics arrived and splinted Sammy's arm and Heath's leg.

"Take her and Jane in the ambulance," Heath told them. "I'll go in the truck."

Jane climbed inside the vehicle and tried to comfort her child while Val summoned their driver to help Heath out to the vehicle. Opie promised to come as soon as she finished her job at Wendell Hunter's.

∾

Everyone but Heath returned home much later. Sammy had fallen asleep, and Jane waited while Val unlocked the apartment door.

"I'm so sorry Heath got hurt."

"Jane, stop," Val ordered. "It couldn't be helped."

"I could have taken her home."

"I could have insisted," Val agreed. "But it never occurred to me that this would happen. The most important thing now is to get through it. Why don't you put her to bed? I'll bring you something to eat."

"I can fix something later."

"I'm sure there's food at the house. It will only take a few minutes."

Jane agreed, not certain she could stomach anything right now. After Val left, she dialed Heath's hospital room. Steve, the physician's assistant, had convinced

Heath to stay. He sounded very fuzzy when he answered the phone.

"It's Jane. I just wanted to see if you're okay. Do you need anything?"

He murmured something that sounded very much like "love me." She must be losing her hearing. "I'll let you sleep. And say a prayer for your healing."

After another mumbled response, Jane hung up the phone.

Oh, why hadn't she taken Sammy home? Didn't she have enough to make her look bad to Heath already? As her mother would say, another bad choice that hurt someone else. One she'd have to live with for weeks.

Val returned with food and instructions for her to take a few days off to be with Sammy. "But you have to get moved, and there's that wedding next weekend."

"I can hire a mover or even get some of the guys to help out. Don't worry. We'll get it finished."

"I want to do my job."

Val shook her head and said, "You're officially on sick leave until Sammy is feeling better. Don't argue with your boss."

Later Jane did what she'd put off for hours. Drawing a deep breath, she prepared for censure as she called Sammy's grandparents to tell them about the incident. Her parents weren't home, so she left a message for them to return her call. Clarice answered the phone on the first ring.

"He could have killed Sammy."

Clarice's reaction to the incident didn't surprise Jane, and she defended Heath. "It was an accident."

"Why are you standing up for that man? He broke your daughter's arm."

"Because it's not his fault." If anyone was to blame, it was she. If she'd made the right decision, the incident would never have happened. Heath wouldn't be in the hospital, and Sammy wouldn't have a cast on her arm. "Sammy had no business on the stairs."

"What happened to that woman who keeps her while you work?"

"Cindy wasn't available."

"You should have watched her better."

Jane couldn't deny the fact. "Accidents happen, Clarice. I agree, but this sort of thing happens to every mother at one time or another. Garrett showed me the scar on his hand where he cut himself making a sandwich when he was little. I'm sure that was an accident."

"His father was watching him."

Of course he was. Perfect mother Clarice would never have allowed her child to make his own sandwich.

"Sammy's fine. She doesn't mind all the attention she's getting. Heath will have to have surgery."

"You care more about those people than your own child."

"*Those people* have been very good to me and my daughter, and yes, we do care about them."

"We're coming to see Sammy for ourselves. I want to be sure she's okay."

Jane resented the implication that she'd lied about the situation. "You'll have to stay in a hotel."

"We want to spend time with Sammy."

"You're welcome to see her."

"I'll let you know when to expect us."

Just what she needed. Clarice would focus on making her life miserable for the duration of the stay. Not to mention she had no idea how Sammy would respond to the grandparents she hadn't seen in a year. Well, she'd worry about that when she knew for sure that they were coming.

∾

"I'm going to work harder and do everything Heath planned," Jane vowed when Val came by the following morning with breakfast.

"Don't be silly."

She wilted. Now Val thought she was being ridiculous.

"Jane, I mean this in the most loving of ways. Give it a rest. You're blaming yourself, and you need to stop. It's not anything you can change."

"I could have."

"Could you really? What if you'd taken Sammy home and Heath stumbled over his own feet?"

"He wouldn't have been hurt as badly."

"Do you know that for sure? Trying to keep the box from hitting her could have kept him from falling on something sharp. He could have broken his neck. They were halfway up the stairs."

"I made a bad choice."

"Well, get in line. We all did."

"He's not going to be able to get around. Do you realize how that's going to make him feel?"

"Heath will be okay. Our family will take care of him. Just as we'll help you take care of Sammy."

"I don't deserve you as a friend."

"Sure you do." Val tilted her head toward the cries coming from Sammy's room. "Your most important responsibility needs attention. Call if you need help today."

"I will. Will you let me know how Heath's doing?"

"Not if you're going to obsess over the situation." Val stopped at the door and smiled at her. "He was awake when Mom called this morning and said the pain meds have everything under control. He wants pajamas. He's not in love with those hospital gowns."

"Few people are," Jane said with a big smile. She didn't know why she'd been blessed with people like the Trueloves in her life, but she thanked God for putting them there.

Chapter 10

Heath came home from the hospital on the same day the Holts called to say they were on their way. That news didn't thrill Jane, but she'd done everything possible to prepare herself for the onslaught of criticism she knew Clarice would provide.

She returned to work after a couple of days off. Sammy started figuring out how to play around the cast. While Jane helped Val prepare the wedding venue for a wedding on Saturday, Sammy stayed with the Truelove family.

Despite Jane's concerns that it was too much on her, Cindy welcomed the child back, insisting the two patients could comfort each other. Sammy took her books and toys to Heath, who was pretty much off his feet until the doctor put a walking cast on his leg. He could get around with the crutches but said it wasn't the easiest thing he'd ever done.

When they came to the house for lunch, Jane found Sammy banging her storybook against Heath's arm in an effort to wake him. "Sammy, no. Heath's resting," she said, swinging the child up into her arms.

He woke and offered her a sleepy smile. "It's okay. I told her to get her storybook and fell asleep before she got back. Let her stay. She's good company."

Jane lifted the child onto the arm of his chair. "I'm so sorry about this, Heath."

"It can't be helped."

"It could. Now both of you are in pain, and it's my fault."

"I'm not in pain," Heath said, pulling a bottle of pills from his shirt pocket and shaking them at her.

Horror filled Jane.

"What's wrong?"

"You can get addicted to those things."

"I only take them when the pain is really bad."

Jane reached for the bottle and read the label. "Garrett took those for his knee injury. He said he could stop anytime, but he couldn't."

Heath frowned. "I was only trying to lighten the mood. I'm not a pill taker. Never have been. I rarely take aspirin. I might be a little uncomfortable, but I'll survive. Sammy will, too."

Jane fingered her daughter's blond curls. "Please watch her around those pills."

He slipped them into the back of the table drawer under some papers. "When do you expect the Holts?"

"This afternoon." She found the idea depressing.

"It will be okay, Jane."

"I hope so."

∾

Her in-laws hadn't been there an hour when Clarice started. "We want to take Sammy back to the hotel and spend time with her there."

Her grandmother held out her arms, but Sammy turned her head into Cindy Truelove's neck. When she refused to let go, Clarice pulled her from Cindy's hold. Sammy sobbed.

"Is it necessary to upset her like this?" Cindy asked, dismayed by Sammy's distress.

"She's my granddaughter. I think I know what's best for her. She'll calm down once she's in the car."

Sammy's cries turned into screams as she reached out to the people she knew and loved. Jane stepped in and took her child from Clarice. "No. I'm not putting her through this. You can visit here, and if she becomes comfortable and wants to go with you later, we'll decide then."

"You can use the living room," Cindy volunteered.

"No," Clarice said. "I have gifts for her back at the hotel."

Jane rocked the child, smoothing her hair and whispering that it would be okay. "The gifts can wait. Thanks for the use of the room, Cindy."

The Trueloves left them to visit, all on alert for Sammy's cries.

"I can't believe you're treating us like this," Clarice told Jane.

"Can't you see she's scared? She hasn't seen you in a year and has no idea who you are. Give her time to adapt."

"She's certainly adapted to this family," Clarice sniped.

"Do you want to visit your granddaughter?" Jane asked, one breath away from ordering them to leave.

Edward Holt stepped forward. "She's right, Clarice. We need to give Sammy time to know us."

"It's a sad day when a grandmother can't hold her own grandchild," she mumbled angrily.

Garrett's dad sat by them on the sofa, talking softly to Sammy. Soon he caught the child's attention, and she lifted her tearstained face to stare at him.

∾

"What's wrong with Sammy?" Heath demanded when Val and his mom entered the family room.

"The Holts want to take her back to their hotel, and she's not having anything to do with them. Her grandmother tried to force the issue."

"Poor kid," he said. "This must be why Jane dreaded their visit."

Cindy glanced at Val and asked, "What do you think about offering the Holts a guest room? Sammy and Jane could stay, too. That might make things easier for Sammy."

"Good idea," Heath said enthusiastically. "Why don't you run it by Jane now and see what she thinks?"

"I'll ask after a while," Val said. "Let them have some time alone first."

After they left the room, Heath found himself listening for Sammy's cries. He didn't want her upset. Particularly since he knew her arm probably hurt as bad as his leg.

∞

Much to Jane's dismay, the Holts accepted the invitation and arrived with luggage the next day.

"I appreciate your family suggesting we all stay here," Jane told Heath. "Sammy's more comfortable with me nearby."

"And you're more comfortable here, too?" Heath asked.

For the first time since she had become a Holt, Jane felt as if someone was on her side. She appreciated the Trueloves' sacrifice. Maybe things would have been different if her own parents had been there for her. Jane nodded. "There was no way I'd allow them to take Sammy off alone after yesterday. And going anywhere with Clarice would be like going to war. I can do no right as far as she's concerned. Having the family as a buffer helps."

"People can be like that," Heath said. "Particularly when they're angry or grieving."

"I didn't make Garrett's choice."

"Think about how you've blamed yourself for the accident. Don't you think Clarice wonders if she should have done something differently?"

Jane knew Heath tried to be the voice of reason but didn't believe Clarice would ever feel that she could have played a part in what happened to Garrett. It had been bad enough when Garrett was alive, but since his death, it had become intolerable. "No. She's placed the blame solely on me. It's my fault. I drove her precious son to do what he did."

"I pray it stops."

"It had better. I'd hate to cut them off from Sammy, but I won't continue to tolerate Clarice's attacks either. I can't. It's very demoralizing to have someone tell you you're lousy at everything you do."

∞

As the week passed, Heath could definitely understand Jane's frustrations. No matter what Jane said or did, Clarice belittled her. At times it got so bad that his mother sent Jane off to take a break while they babysat Sammy.

The child warmed up a little to her grandfather but kept her grandmother at arm's length. Instead of backing off and giving Sammy an opportunity to adapt, Clarice pushed even harder.

Sammy often played in the family room with Heath nearby in the recliner. That afternoon Clarice used his lack of mobility to move Sammy out of sight. He'd tried not to interfere, but when Sammy's screams reached him, Heath called Jane.

"I can hear," Jane said the moment she answered.

Sammy's shrieks became even louder. A few seconds later she ran into the room and over to Heath. He dropped the phone and lifted her into his arms, holding her close and whispering soothing words. "Calm down, Sammy. It's okay." After she grew quieter, he picked up the receiver and said, "She's with me."

"I'm coming up there to talk to Clarice. This is ridiculous."

"I'll talk to her if you'd like." Heath had no idea what he could say to the woman, but he'd do what he could to help.

"Oh, I'd love to push that off on you, but I can't."

Deciding a confrontation was the last thing they needed, he said, "Finish your work, Jane. Sammy's okay. You can talk to Clarice later."

"Thanks, Heath."

Clarice entered the room. "Sammy, there you are. Why did you run away from Grandmother?" The way the child hid her face in Heath's chest made the woman even angrier. "Why do you keep interfering with my efforts to spend time with Sammy?"

"For the same reason you insist on forcing her to do something she doesn't want to do," Heath said, not bothering to temper the truth. "She's a child. Give her a chance to get to know you on her terms. All this chasing and dragging her off against her will only makes things worse."

Her sniff of disapproval spoke volumes. "What do you know about children?"

"I was one. I wouldn't have liked it either."

That gave Clarice pause. "So what do you suggest?"

"Sit down and have a conversation." Heath indicated the chair next to his. "Sit there. Maybe read us a story."

"Us?"

Heath grinned and raised his leg. "Sure. I'll listen. It's not like I'm going anywhere."

The next half hour proved to be interesting. Clarice actually did an excellent job of reading the story. "What do you think, Sammy?" Heath asked. "Pretty good, huh?"

Sammy's curls bobbed when she nodded. Her grandmother beamed.

"I used to volunteer for library story hours."

"You don't do it anymore?"

"Not since Garrett's. . ." She trailed off.

"You should. You're really good," Heath complimented. "You do great sound effects."

"I used to make up stories for Garrett. Every night before bed there was one. The ongoing story of Maxie Cat. . ."

"Why don't you tell us?"

She held up her hands. "Oh, I couldn't. Too many memories."

"I'm sure Sammy would like to hear the stories you told her dad."

Clarice began telling the story of Maxie, the fat white cat that liked to hang out in the trees with the birds. Sammy settled back against Heath's chest and soon drifted off.

"You think she's bored?"

He looked down at the little girl. "Jane said she's not sleeping well."

"Why didn't she tell me that?"

Heath shrugged. "Maybe because she knows how you'll react."

Clarice puffed up. "I have a right to know."

"I'm not trying to offend you, Mrs. Holt." He searched for a way to change the subject. "Have you ever considered writing a children's book? That's a very entertaining story. I really liked the part where he tried to fly when he scared the birds away."

"Garrett laughed so hard when I told that one," she said, her eyes filling with tears. "I don't have the heart for it anymore. Since Garrett's death, I haven't felt like doing anything."

"You have to find reasons to keep going," he said gently. "I'd say this one right here is mighty precious."

Clarice's gaze focused on Sammy. "She is. Would you like me to take her?"

"She's okay. She gets grouchy if we wake her before her nap is over."

"I'm so thankful she wasn't hurt worse."

Her tiny cast rested on his arm, reminding Heath of their tumble. "Me, too. I did everything possible to keep from falling on her."

"How bad is your leg?"

"They put me back together with a plate and screws. Doctor says I'm young, and he expects a full recovery."

"This wouldn't have happened if Jane had—"

"Please don't finish that," Heath interrupted. "It wouldn't have happened if I'd looked before starting up the stairs with a big box blocking my view. I knew Sammy could be anywhere, and I didn't check."

"But Jane—"

"Is a good mother, Mrs. Holt. Accidents happen. There are too many kids out there with parents who don't care to criticize those who do."

Heath doubted she was ready to accept anything less than an error in judgment on Jane's part. He knew they were all at fault and each of them carried their own guilt.

"I think I'll go up and lie down for a while. Something I ate isn't agreeing with me."

Heath hoped she didn't insult his mother and sister with that comment. Lunch had been delicious.

∾

As Heath feared, the mood in the house didn't improve with the passing of time. That night at dinner, Sammy was whiny.

"Stop it, Samantha, or you'll go to bed now."

"Don't talk to her like that. She's tired," Clarice said from her seat across the table.

Jane looked at her and said, "I realize that. But I will not allow her to behave this way."

When Sammy flung her spoon with her good hand, Jane removed her from the high chair.

"No, Mommy!" she screamed when Jane asked everyone to excuse them.

"She's too hard on her," Clarice said to her husband.

Ed Holt continued to eat his dinner.

"The child needed discipline," Jacob said. "She's eaten at our table many times, and I've never known her to behave this way."

"She's overexcited. And in pain. Jane should know that."

"Why do you do that?" Heath demanded.

Clarice looked surprised. "Do what?"

He noted the way Clarice hid behind her innocent facade. He'd held his tongue for too long. Someone had to say something, or it would never stop. "You constantly criticize Jane."

"You're in love with her," Clarice accused, glaring at him.

"I consider her a good friend."

Clarice looked at her husband. "See. He knows better than to get tied up with her. He knows the kind of person she is. They went to school together."

Heath shook his head. "No. You don't understand. Jane doesn't deserve the way you treat her. No one does."

"She drove Garrett to do what he did."

Frustrated by her failure to understand, Heath hit his hands on the tabletop, raising his voice as he declared, "No, she didn't. We make our own decisions in life. When are you going to accept that she's still grieving, too? Maybe you should try putting the blame where it belongs. On your son."

"Garrett had a good future ahead of him before he got involved with her." Clarice's eyes became glassy and her voice more emotional. "And now that he's gone, he'll never know his daughter."

"Jane is carrying her own load of guilt, and you're only making things worse. As long as you blame her, you don't have to open your eyes and see your son had the real problem."

"Heath," his mother said.

He flashed her a repentant look as he said, "I'm sorry, but it needs to be said. They can help each other heal or destroy each other. Don't you want a relationship with your granddaughter?"

"Of course I want only the best for Sammy."

"Sammy is the most important person in Jane's life. She loves her a great deal and takes excellent care of her." The rest of his family nodded in agreement.

"She's got you all fooled. Just like she fooled Garrett."

"Jane is honest and sincere," Val defended. "She's genuine. Not at all deceptive."

❧

Jane had carried Sammy into the family room to calm her down. She could hear their raised voices as the argument continued. This situation wasn't fair to the Trueloves who had done far too much for them already. She needed to take Sammy home, and the Holts could go back to a hotel.

The dinner soon broke up, and as the others left the dining room, Jane considered what she should do.

"Where's Horsie, Mommy?" Sammy asked sleepily.

Jules came into the room, and Jane asked her to watch Sammy while she retrieved the toy.

Heath still sat in his chair, staring idly out the window, when she walked in. "Sammy forgot Horsie," she said, picking up the stuffed animal from the buffet.

"Is she okay?"

"Tired and cranky, but she'll be fine. I heard what you told Clarice. Thanks for defending me, but you're wrong. I deceived my parents in my quest for popularity."

"I'm not judging you, Jane."

"I feel guilty, Heath. I let so many people down."

"You were blinded by love and needs far bigger than you realized at the time."

"What made you different? Why didn't you do the things Garrett did?"

"I knew God."

"I knew Him, too, but He wasn't my focus."

"That's what happens when we lose sight of God and the plans He has for us. He gave you free will, allowed you to make your own choices. And He's stood by you throughout it all, Jane."

"Why didn't He stop me?"

"Would you respect God more if He controlled you like a puppet?"

Jane shook her head.

"It's not a pick and choose kind of relationship. You can't live as you want and expect Him to keep you from making mistakes."

"I know. It's like Sammy getting hurt when I've warned her not to do something."

Heath nodded. "All you can do is comfort her and say you're sorry."

"God's like that, isn't He? When we're in the right relationship with Him, He sends comfort and soothes the pain."

"He is. So why did you separate yourself from His love?"

Jane shrugged. "I'm not known for making the best decisions."

"You could be. None of us knows what's best. You don't think I've had doubts? Part of me feels I should be out there earning a living with the education my family sacrificed to help me achieve."

"But another part wants the landscape job," Jane said slowly. Heath struggled with his choices as well. "Didn't you want the MBA?"

"Yes and no. If I get a good paying job and make the right decisions, I can do what I really want to do—support my wife and family."

"You think maybe God redirected your path when He blessed Val with the funds?"

"I considered that. He certainly opened doors. I'd like to repay Val for what she's done for me. I want Your Wedding Place to become wildly successful."

"I know what you mean. I feel like she's gifted me time after time. Her generosity can be overwhelming."

Heath laughed. "She'd give you the clothes off her back if she thought you needed them. But in your case, you're helping each other. Val knows she can depend on you to get the job done. She's being a good employer when she provides you with benefits."

"All of you have been there for me lately. I can't even say that about my own parents."

"I believe God gives us what we need."

Jane nodded. She knew she should go home but couldn't bring herself to walk away from their support. "I pray He gives me the strength to get through this visit without doing harm to Clarice."

"He will," Heath promised.

"I'd better get back to Sammy. I asked Jules to keep an eye on her for a minute. She'll wonder what happened to me."

"Pray and believe, Jane. God will truly bless you. Just ask Val."

Chapter 11

Jane found when she did as Heath suggested that her prayers strengthened her throughout the Holts' stay. At times she thought she saw sympathy in Ed's eyes, but he never said anything about his wife's behavior. She couldn't say who was more relieved when Ed announced they would be leaving the next day.

After waving them off early Saturday morning, she packed their things, apologized to the Trueloves yet again, and moved back home. The Truelove home was wonderful, but the few days with Clarice made Jane long for the privacy of her own home.

They had a wedding on Saturday, and when Val gave her Monday off, Jane used the time to give her home a good cleaning. The papers on her nightstand reminded Jane to call the doctor's office. She dialed the number and said, "This is Jane Holt. I was sorting through my late husband's papers and came across a statement. Can you tell me why Garrett Holt was seeing Dr. Arnold?"

The woman paused. "I'm sorry, ma'am, but we're not allowed to give out information on patients without permission."

"But I'm his wife," Jane objected. "And he's deceased."

"Hold please, ma'am."

A couple of minutes later another woman came on the line. "Mrs. Holt, this is Geraldine Green. I will need to check your husband's file to see if he authorized us to share that information with you. We also need to verify you are his wife."

"Garrett is dead. He's been dead for more than a year now. He never mentioned seeing Dr. Arnold."

"Ma'am, if you'll give me a number where you can be reached. . ."

Jane gave her the number. She understood they had a job to do, but she couldn't let confidentiality laws keep her from getting the answers she needed.

After finding her marriage license and Garrett's death certificate, Jane put Sammy in her car seat and drove to Lexington. The doctor was out of town, but the staff verified her identity, copied the papers, and promised to have the doctor contact her when he returned. Accepting she'd done all she could for now, Jane took Sammy grocery shopping and drove home.

It took a few days for the doctor's office to get back to her. She was shopping for antiques in Paris when her phone rang.

"Mrs. Holt, this is Dr. Arnold. My staff tells me you're inquiring about your husband's visits to my office."

"I'd like to know why he saw an oncologist. Garrett never indicated that he'd seen anyone other than his orthopedic specialist."

"According to our records, he came in for a second opinion. The diagnosis was stage-four pancreatic cancer. We concurred with the initial physician that his cancer was too far advanced to take any further actions."

Startled, Jane grabbed the back of a Chippendale chair she'd been admiring and held on. "Cancer?" Her eyes drifted closed as she drew several deep breaths.

"Yes. It's difficult when a man as young as your husband learns he has terminal cancer."

Why hadn't he told her? The idea that they had lived as man and wife and he'd kept this kind of information from her broke Jane's heart. "He committed suicide, Dr. Arnold."

"I'm sorry, Mrs. Holt. If he had come to see us earlier. . ."

The drinking. The drugs. Had depression over the news pushed him to this?

"Do you recall his state of mind regarding the diagnosis, Dr. Arnold?"

"I do remember your husband. I saw him play at UK. It really was a shame when he injured his knee. While I can't speak as to his frame of mind, I will say I've dealt with lots of cancer patients and most are shocked when they learn they only have a short time to live."

"How short?" she demanded.

Papers rustled, and he said, "I estimated Mr. Holt had three months."

Garrett must have been devastated. And so afraid. He hadn't been very brave when it came to the bad things in life. How could he keep that kind of secret and not turn to anyone for help? "Why wouldn't he tell me? His parents?"

She heard papers rustling again. "I'm afraid I can't say. I only saw him a few days before he died. May I ask why his death was ruled suicide?"

The images of that day were vivid. When she arrived home and couldn't wake Garrett, she'd called 911. Their efforts to revive him were futile. "When we found him, there was an empty pill bottle and liquor."

"If there was no weapon involved, I would wonder if his pain-management techniques caused problems. He was on a strong medication that doesn't respond well to alcohol."

"Are you saying it could have been an accidental overdose?"

"He would have been in a great deal of pain, and he could have confused his medication times and overmedicated himself."

"I thought the pain medication was for his knee injury." She paused, mulling over an idea that had just occurred to her. "Dr. Arnold, is it possible to amend a death certificate? I'm sure his parents would like to know, and I know I would, particularly for our daughter's sake. I don't look forward to telling her what happened to her father when she's older."

"You can appeal through the county coroner or state medical examiner. Have your attorney contact me, and we'll discuss the matter further."

She couldn't afford an attorney. She had a little saved since working with Val, but that was for their future. "My husband's death left me with expenses that pretty much take every dime of my income."

"I understand, Mrs. Holt. Talk with your family. If I can be of assistance to you in the future, feel free to contact me."

"Thank you."

Another wrong assumption, Jane thought. Granted, experts had agreed, but maybe if she'd been a better wife, more open to the truth rather than frustrated and angry with Garrett because he wasn't accepting his responsibility, he might have told her. She wept. Huge tears flowed for the loved one cancer had claimed.

Randi Cole, an acquaintance from high school who now owned the antique store, came to where she stood. "Jane, are you okay?"

"I'm sorry. I need to go."

∾

Lost in a maelstrom of guilt and grief, Jane sat in the truck. She had no idea how much time had passed when Heath tapped on the passenger side window. She couldn't look at him as she released the lock, and he swung himself inside.

"Randi called the house. She's worried about you. What happened?"

"I'm sorry." The words came out in a croak. "The doctor called." The tears returned.

"Jane? Talk to me. Are you sick?"

His obvious anxiety forced her to respond. "No. Garrett had cancer. He never told me."

Heath slipped his arm around her shoulders. "How did you find out?"

"I discovered a bill from an oncologist while sorting his personal papers. He had stage-four pancreatic cancer."

When Heath wrapped her in his arms, she went willingly. "It hurts so much that he didn't tell me. The doctor said he only saw him days before he died."

"Maybe he thought it best not to fight the disease and was afraid you wouldn't agree."

What if Heath was right? Did that mean Garrett hadn't considered being there for her and Sammy sufficient reason to fight the illness? "The doctor said he would have been in a great deal of pain. I was working so much, and now that I look back, there were nights when Garrett was already in bed when I got home from work with Sammy. It drove me crazy that he couldn't be bothered to spend time with his family. Now I realize he was sick."

"Don't blame yourself, Jane. You couldn't know."

"I should have known," she said.

"Let's get you home."

"I should apologize to Randi."

"You can call her tomorrow. I want you to ride with me and Jim."

"But the truck—"

"We brought Glenn." Heath named two of the security staff who now worked at the farm. "He'll drive the truck home."

Jane didn't argue. She was in no shape to drive anywhere. A few minutes later she sat in the backseat of the SUV, Heath's arm about her shoulders. "Thanks for coming."

"You can always count on me, Jane."

∽

At the farm Heath suggested that she take some time for herself. He promised to bring Sammy home after dinner. Afraid her state of confusion would upset her daughter, Jane agreed, and Heath took time to pray with her before she left the vehicle.

A couple of hours later Jane had cried herself dry and forced herself to look at the situation objectively. What could she do to turn this around for Sammy? If she pursued the matter, would they find it had been an accident? Money held her back. She couldn't afford to invest her savings in what could be a futile venture.

Heath and Val brought Sammy home around 8:00 p.m. "She's bathed and changed into her pj's," Val said as the child reached for her mother. "Everyone says to tell you that you're in their prayers."

Jane hugged Sammy close and smiled at them. "Thank you," she mouthed.

Heath rested his hand on her arm. "Are you okay?"

She nodded. "Let me put her down, and we'll talk."

Jane read Sammy a story, and she drifted off to sleep. Jane doubted sleep would come as easily for her that night.

When she walked into the living room, Heath hit the remote and turned off the TV. "Val said to tell you she'd check in with you later."

Jane nodded. "Thanks for all you've done. I wasn't in any shape to keep her earlier."

"I can take her back to the house if you need more time."

"No. We'll be okay. I was so upset that I didn't tell you everything. The doctor thinks it's possible Garrett's death wasn't suicide." She told him what the man had said. "I'd like to clear his name for his parents and Sammy."

"What about you?" Heath asked as he took her hand in his.

"I'm at peace with what I've learned." The moment the words left her lips, Jane realized that she did feel relieved. She attributed it to the prayers offered up in her time of need. "Thinking it could have been a mistake makes the situation more tolerable. The doctor said there's an appeal process with new evidence. He said he would talk to my lawyer, but I told him I couldn't afford legal assistance."

"Would you like me to help?"

She smiled and shook her head. She refused to take advantage of him in yet another way. "I'll tell Garrett's parents. If they want to pursue the matter, they certainly have funds to do so."

"Do you think it will change Clarice's outlook toward you?"

"I doubt it. She'll only wonder what I did to Garrett to make him not tell me."

"He must not have told her either."

Jane flashed him a wry smile. "Maybe that will make a difference."

Heath woke early the following morning, determined to do something productive with his day. He convinced Roc to bring a shovel and a tray of asters out to the front yard before leaving for school. After several failed attempts at working around his disability, he became frustrated.

"You're going to hurt yourself worse," Jane said when she found him trying to balance on crutches and work a shovel. "Tell me what you're trying to do."

"I want to plant those bulbs over here."

"What else?"

She listened as he outlined the things he wanted done. Jane found him a chair and placed it in the shade before she started work.

"There," she said, patting the soil about the transplanted bulbs. "Is that what you wanted?"

He stood and swung himself over to take a look. The crutch pushed into the soft ground, and he nearly toppled. Jane jumped up and grabbed his arm.

Disgusted with himself, Heath jumped back on more solid ground. "Yeah, that's good. If you get me a pair of clippers, I can sit down and work on these low shrubs."

They worked in silence until Heath needed to move on to the next shrub. Each time, she repositioned his seat and made certain he had everything he needed before returning to her task. By lunchtime Heath accepted that he was more of a hindrance than a help. "I'm sorry, Jane. I've been so preoccupied with myself that I didn't even ask how you were feeling this morning."

Jane stopped to pull a weed from the bed next to the house. "I'm okay. Still working through a few issues in my mind, but at least yesterday's news gave me hope where there was none."

"Hope?"

"For Sammy. One day she'll ask about her dad. It would be better to say his death was accidental rather than intentional."

Heath understood why she'd want that for her daughter.

"You want to go to the antique store with me this afternoon?" Jane asked as they entered the house. "I called Randi earlier, and she said they received some things they think Val would like."

"Might as well. I'm useless on the landscaping until this comes off. We could take Sammy along."

"To an antique store?"

He grinned. "I see your point."

Heath soon realized things weren't going to be any better for him at the store. Navigating the antique-filled room on crutches would be impossible. "Why don't I sit here while you take a look at the items?"

"What if we bring them to you?"

"That would work."

Randi Cole helped Jane with a mantel clock she thought the Trueloves might like. Heath agreed, and they bought the clock, a silver sugar and creamer set, and a pair of candlesticks.

While Randi wrote up the order, Jane looked down into the display case and gasped. "Can I please see that garnet ring?"

Randi slid the door open and pulled out the tray. "We just got these in last week."

"It's my birthstone."

"When is your birthday?" Heath asked.

"January 31st."

The ring fit perfectly. He noted the way she twisted her hand from side to side, enjoying the play of light on the beautiful stone. "You should buy it."

Her gaze shifted to the ring and back to him before she sighed and slipped it off, laying it back on the tray.

"Another time, maybe." She picked up the few items Randi had wrapped for her and said, "I'll put these in the truck and come back for the clock."

Randi called out to her husband then said to Jane, "David can take that out for you."

The chimes over the door rang as they went out.

Heath did a one-legged dance as he got to his feet and shoved the crutches under his arms. He moved over to the counter. "I want to buy that ring."

Randi smiled. "She'll love your gift."

Heath pulled his wallet from his pocket and handed the woman a bill, pushing his change and the receipt back inside the wallet before he pocketed the ring.

Randi came around the counter and held the door open for him. "How long before you get that off?"

"Soon, I hope." He winked down at her. "Thanks for your help. Have a good day."

Heath moved down to where the sidewalk dipped for wheelchair access and into the parking lot. Jane had the extended cab door open as she placed the items in the back. She opened Heath's door for him. "I think Val will like those candlesticks. She wanted a set for the fireplace mantel."

"It's great that they know what we're looking for," Heath said.

"I appreciate all the help I can get. Ready to go home?"

He leaned up against the truck and pulled the bag from his pocket. "I bought you something."

Jane frowned.

Heath pushed the bag in her direction. "Here, take it."

"You can't buy that," she protested when she removed the ring.

"Why not? You bought me a gift."

"Yeah, but. . ."

"No buts. Do unto others."

She slipped it on her finger and held out her hand, admiring the gorgeous ring. Jane turned and threw her arms around his neck, almost unbalancing them both with her exuberance. "Thank you!"

~

"Hey, Jane, we're going to a UK football game," Opie said over the phone. "Want to come?"

Memories washed over Jane. She'd spent hours too numerous to count in Commonwealth Stadium, cheering Garrett on, play after play. Seeing happiness in his expression that she never saw when they were alone together.

"Jane?"

"I'm here. I don't know if I can."

"You already have plans?" she asked.

"No. Too many memories."

"Oh. I hadn't considered that."

Maybe it would be good for her to go back again. Make new memories with new friends. "Who's going?"

"Heath, Val, me, and you if you want. A client gave Russ the tickets. We're meeting him and Rom."

"I need to find a babysitter."

"Mom said you can bring Sammy over."

"What time?"

"We're leaving in an hour."

"I'll be there."

Opie paused. "Jane, you don't have to do this."

"I want to. See you soon."

Later, as they followed crowds of students, fans, staff, and alumni into Commonwealth Stadium, Jane couldn't help but wonder why she'd agreed to this. The idea of enjoying herself with new friends warred with the fear that she could be a wet blanket and ruin the outing.

They picked up Russ and Rom at the apartment, and Jim dropped them off at the entrance. Jane smiled when Val and Opie jostled each other like playful puppies. They would root for UK, but win or lose it was all about fun. Once they arrived at their seats, Jane ended up next to Heath. That was more than okay with her.

Things weren't as bad as she had feared. From the kickoff, Jane quickly got into the game.

"Go, Cats!" Jane shouted, pumping her arm in the air when they scored their first touchdown. Fireworks shot from atop the scoreboard.

"Having fun?" Heath asked, grinning at her enthusiastic high fives to the others.

The Wildcats were ahead at halftime when the championship cheerleading team came on the field. She watched their routine with interest.

"Did you try out for the squad?" Heath asked.

Jane's heart had been so burdened by grief that she'd never considered trying out. She shook her head.

The game resumed with the home team managing to maintain their lead. In the fourth quarter, the quarterback raced down the field, the ball clutched in his arms. How many times had she watched Garrett run exactly like this kid, confident, taunting them as he nimbly dodged their grabbing hands and charging bodies? Just when she thought he might make it, the kid went down under the pile of players. When they rolled away, he writhed in agony, clutching his knee.

Jane shot to her feet. "Do something," she called as if they could hear. "He's hurt."

Heath stood, his arm going around her waist. "Shh. It's okay. See, they're helping him."

She couldn't look. Jane knew she had to escape. She looked at Heath and implored, "Let's get out of here. Please."

"Want to take a walk?" Heath asked.

Jane nodded.

"We'll meet you guys out front."

As Jane fled the stadium, Heath followed at a much slower pace. "Hey, slow down," he called.

Seeing that young man down took Jane back to the incident she considered the downfall of her marriage. It still hurt that football made Garrett happier than being married to her. "I'm sorry." She spotted a bench over to the side. "We can sit over there."

"Are you okay?"

Embarrassed by her reaction, Jane looked down. "Better. You probably recall I'm a wimp when it comes to someone getting hurt."

"You were enjoying the game."

She nodded. "I always enjoyed football. In high school, people saw the perky cheerleader on the sidelines, but I understood the plays. When I asked Garrett why they didn't try a new play, he listened. I think he made the coaches think they were his ideas. I should have joined a sport, but I stayed with cheerleading. My mom thought that was more feminine. She didn't want her daughter to become a female jock."

"You're no jock," Heath said. "Why didn't you join the cheerleading squad at UK?"

She shrugged. "I didn't have the heart for it anymore."

As their conversation veered toward the campus that had been a part of their lives, Jane said, "Seems like a million years ago."

"I didn't get to a lot of games. Rom and I lived at home and drove to classes."

"Not your usual college experience. Did you miss living on campus?"

"The education was more important. That degree opens the door to opportunities."

Jane realized he hadn't seen college as a means of escape from his parents and family. He'd set his priorities and gone after what he considered to be important, all the while considering the people he loved most. "What about your résumé? How will helping Val affect that?"

"Working for the family business," Heath said. "Write enough technical jargon, and it fits."

"Particularly when your sister is a multimillionaire," Jane agreed. "So you don't plan to landscape forever?"

"I probably will in some way, but it won't be my job. When we finish up Val's plans, I'll find a position like Rom's."

Jane knew Heath would set another priority and sacrifice his happiness because he thought it was the right thing to do. "You could make a living designing and installing landscapes."

"I've thought about it," Heath admitted. "More than a time or two."

Jane smiled at him. "You'll make the right decision."

Chapter 12

Heath lay on the sofa flipping through the television channels. In the weeks since the accident he'd been unable to help in the gardens.

"You're looking glum," Val said as she walked into the family room.

"I'm over doing nothing."

"There's not much you can do at this point," she reminded him.

"I know. I was thinking about visiting My Old Kentucky Home."

"Are you up to walking that much?"

Heath shrugged. "You mentioned a country garden recently, and that struck me as a place that would offer some good ideas. I figured I could find places to rest when I need to."

"Jim could drive you."

Heath shook his head. They had hired the driver/bodyguard to transport the women in the family to wherever they needed to go. He wasn't about to leave them stranded while he went sightseeing. "He needs to stick around here."

"What about Jane? I can spare her if you think she'd like to go."

Things hadn't been the same between them since his dad's birthday. Maybe spending some time together would help them overcome the situation. "I suppose we could ask."

A couple of minutes later, Val laughed as she slid her phone back into her pocket. "Given how quickly she said yes, Jane must really want to go."

"Probably thinks it's the least that she can do. She keeps apologizing."

"I've heard you apologize to Sammy more than once," Val said.

He nodded. "It's a vicious circle. Guilt is a terrible thing."

"I know. I told Jane you'd meet her at the truck."

"Thanks. I'd better tell Opie we won't be around for lunch."

"I'll do that."

"Thanks, Val." Heath grabbed his crutches and started out the door. He paused. "You want to come with us?"

"Not today. Have fun but don't overdo."

Jane echoed Val's sentiments a few minutes later when he approached the vehicle. "Are you sure you're up to this?"

"I'm going crazy sitting in the house."

She opened his door and gestured him in. Once inside she took his crutches and placed them in the backseat. Jane went around and climbed into the driver's seat. "What's the plan?"

"My Old Kentucky Home."

She looked baffled. "I thought you'd lived here at Sheridan Farm all your life."

"Not mine. Federal Hill in Bardstown. It's where Stephen Foster wrote the song when he visited his family."

"Oh, *that* Old Kentucky Home," Jane said. "Never been there."

"I'll put the address in the GPS," Heath told her. "Val says after you get past being freaked out because this box knows your every move, you love it."

"Must have been created by a man who hated asking for directions."

"It's a woman giving the directions," Heath said, grinning when he added, "I figure some poor wife couldn't stand the arguments and created the thing for her poor misguided husband."

Jane started the vehicle and put it into DRIVE. She laughed when the woman's voice directed her to turn right. "So why did you choose My Old Kentucky Home?"

"I wanted to check out the grounds."

"Sounds like a lot of walking."

Jane's dubious expression made him wonder if he'd made the right decision. "I'll have to take breaks, but it beats sitting around home all day."

"I'm..."

"Don't say it. In fact, don't even think it," he ordered.

"But you're frustrated, and I'm sorry."

"It's not your fault," Heath said.

"I should have taken Sammy upstairs with me."

"Life isn't in our control, Jane. We both learned valuable lessons. I learned it's not smart to carry boxes that block your view up the stairs. At least not before making certain the path is clear. Sammy learned not to play on the stairs."

"And to watch out for big men carrying boxes," Jane said.

He nodded. "We're not used to having little people around. We'll have to pay closer attention to keep her protected."

"I'm used to doing it alone."

"Now you have a village. Why not use it?"

"I trust Sammy with your family, Heath. I'm thankful for all you've done for us both. Val paid the hospital bill. She said she couldn't believe she hadn't thought about health insurance benefits for us." She was silent for a few minutes. "What kind of garden is Val considering now?"

"She mentioned a country garden. We'll look at what they have, and then I thought we'd check out Bernheim Arboretum and have lunch at the tavern in Bardstown."

"Okay, but promise to tell me when it gets to be too much?"

Heath nodded. The trip went quickly as they discussed the gardens at Sheridan Farm. She parked and went around the truck to help. "They might have a wheelchair."

Shaking his head, Heath placed his crutches underneath his arms. No way would he force her to push him around in a wheelchair. "I've got it under control."

Inside, Heath gave her money for the tour tickets. They walked past the family cemetery and down pathways leading toward Federal Hill.

"Stephen Foster wrote the state song, 'My Old Kentucky Home,' while visiting his cousins back in 1852. I'm going to give the house tour a miss." When Jane looked longingly at the house, he said, "You go ahead. I'll meet you out back in the gardens."

While he waited, Heath found a bench and enjoyed the music playing over a speaker. He watched as people decorated the pergola for a wedding and realized Val's structure would be pretty much the same, only on a grander scale. When Jane exited the back door of the house, he came over to where she viewed what had been the house's kitchen.

"Has Opie seen this?"

He nodded. A fireplace was the room's focus along with a couple of tables. "Can't imagine her cooking in a place like this. Her idea of roughing it is using an electric hand mixer and can opener."

"Then she'd really hate this kitchen. No modern conveniences."

"I wonder if she'd find cooking as interesting without those things."

"Oh, I think so," Jane said. "Opie loves to cook." As they moved on, Jane said, "Life was much simpler then. The size of the house surprises me. The guide talked about the guests they had. Where did they put them? There are only three bedrooms."

"I read the house originally had thirteen rooms. Supposedly thirteen is repeated throughout the house to honor the thirteen colonies. Thirteen windows on the front, thirteen steps to each floor. Plus I think the families shared beds back then," Heath said.

"You should be a tour guide."

As they moved through the gardens, Heath asked, "Think we could re-create this at home?"

"Why would we want to?" Jane asked. "I mean they're nice, but the gardens we already have are exquisite."

"Val thought we might have brides who wanted something simpler."

"I doubt that bride would come to Sheridan Farm. She'd get married in someone's home garden and save her money."

Heath listened as Jane shared her thoughts.

"People expect spectacular for the money Your Wedding Place charges. You could set up chairs in the front yard and have what you have here. If you want to grow Your Wedding Place, add an atrium. A butterfly garden. A secret garden, even."

"You should suggest those to Val."

Jane turned away. "She knows what she wants."

Heath wondered at Jane's reluctance to share her opinion. Her outspokenness on so many levels made it seem strange. "I'm sure she'd appreciate your opinion."

"I'm no expert."

"You're a woman. A potential bride. You know what you'd choose."

"I'd never be able to afford one of Val's venues."

Heath laughed at that. "Me either, but knowing Val, she'd do it gratis or at least give us the employee rate."

"Do we have an employee rate?" Jane shrugged. "And since I'm not getting married, it's a moot point anyway."

"Would you like to be married again?"

"Are you asking?"

He knew her question embarrassed her when she quickly added, "Just kidding." The color rose in her cheeks. "Actually, when marriage is good, there's nothing better. Having someone who loves and cares for you is wonderful."

"I hope to find my soul mate and settle down. I feel like my life is on hold until I do."

"Don't rush things. If you manage to get the cart in front of the horse as I did, you give yourself unnecessary grief. My hope for the future is to find a man who loves Sammy and me as we deserve to be loved. Next time I'll find a man who knows where he's headed in life."

Her words hit Heath. Did she see what he was doing now as playing around with the future?

Sure, he enjoyed his work, but what did he have beyond the money Val had given him for graduation and the weekly paychecks? Maybe more than some men but definitely no career plans.

"Not that I don't believe everyone has the right to make the decisions that affect their future," Jane added. "But he needs to have a plan in mind. Even if he's not established, he should know what he wants to do with his life."

"Do you have a plan?"

Jane shrugged. "I've thought about having a business to support Sammy and me. I'm putting away a little money every pay period. Val pays me well, and not having housing expenses helps."

"What kind of business?"

"The coffee shop is all I know. I suppose I could do that."

"You can do whatever you put your mind to, Jane. You're a dedicated worker. People recognize that about you."

"I hope so. I'm tired of making bad impressions."

"You never did that."

"Ask my parents or my in-laws. They'll tell you differently."

"There's only one judge who counts, Jane."

"Then I'm really in trouble."

He shook his head. "Sometimes when you get so far from God, you think you can't find your way back. He's right where He's always been."

"Your God, maybe."

"Yours. Mine. There's no difference. He's waiting for your return."

"And I'm trying to find my way back. I suppose the main thing I'm looking for in a future husband is not a plan but a desire to accomplish something worthwhile with his life."

Responsibility. Heath knew the feeling well. His brother's keeper. People had to help one another.

"A small gazebo like this one would be nice for brides with small parties," Jane said.

"You should tell Val. The secret garden is good, too. A private walled area could be a good addition."

∾

Heath was glad to get back to the truck. "Let's just drive through Bernheim. I'm having muscle spasms from walking so much."

"Do we need to go home?"

"No. I just need to get off my leg."

He set the GPS for Bernheim and leaned back in the passenger seat.

"How's the leg?" Jane asked a few minutes later.

"Better. My bones are protesting because I'm making them work today instead of lying around the house."

Jane chuckled. "Let's hope they don't go on strike. Tell me where we're headed."

Since his injury, Heath had done a lot of reading and research. He remembered the area from a previous visit. "We're going to see nature as God intended. Isaac W. Bernheim established the Bernheim Arboretum and Research Forest back in 1929 to be used as a park. Fourteen thousand acres. It's been years in the development. There are hiking trails, lakes, wildlife, the arboretum, art. So much we're not going to see in a drive through."

"Maybe we can come back and spend more time after your cast comes off."

"Let's plan on that." He'd love to spend time hiking and connecting with Jane. She enjoyed the outdoors as much as he did, and Heath suspected she'd enjoy spending time in the beautiful natural setting.

After paying their admission fee, she drove the circular route through the park. Several times they stopped to study the sculpture collection along the way.

"People use the area for business and educational meetings. Val could increase her profit margin by doing retreats," Heath said.

"The wedding venues are her focus for now, but as she becomes more comfortable, I think she'll branch out into other events."

"Baby steps," Heath said with a nod. "Makes sense."

They drove back into Bardstown for lunch at The Old Talbott Tavern. Choosing Kentucky Hot Brown from the menu, they enjoyed the open-face turkey sandwiches with bacon, parmesan cheese, and Mornay sauce. Heath shared about the historic old tavern and how it was said to be the oldest western stagecoach stop in America when the westward expansion brought explorers from the east into Kentucky.

"It's a bed-and-breakfast, too. We gave Mom and Dad a couple of nights in the Lincoln Suite for their anniversary last year. Mom loved it. Dad liked the My Old Kentucky Dinner Train." Heath's phone rang. "Excuse me."

A couple of minutes later, he slid the phone back into his pocket and said, "That was Val. Wanted to know when we'd be home."

"Why? Is Sammy okay?"

"She said everyone's fine. Maybe she's just checking up on me." Something told him there was more to it than that.

"Let's go," Jane said, sounding frightened.

Silence stretched on the trip home as they tried to understand what could have happened.

∽

"Hef. Mommy," Sammy cried, jumping to her feet and racing across the room when Jane entered the Trueloves' kitchen. Jane allowed herself the luxury of a lengthy hug.

"What happened?" Heath asked.

"A process server came by to see Jane," Val said. "He left his card with security. I figured the sooner she knew, the better. Do you have any idea what's going on?"

Jane shook her head. She didn't have a clue. Taking the card, she swung Sammy up into her arms. "I intend to find out."

But no one answered when she called. She left a message on voice mail and then spent the evening wondering what was going on. Nothing came to mind. It couldn't be debt collection. Jane knew she wasn't behind on any of her bills. She'd committed no illegal acts. She hadn't done anything to be sued over.

Still full from her late lunch with Heath, Jane called the Trueloves to tell them she and Sammy wouldn't be coming over for dinner. She prepared Sammy's meal and played with her before putting her to bed.

Frustration over the situation and thoughts of the day she'd spent with Heath made Jane more miserable. Every minute spent in his company only made her want what she couldn't have. Finally, in desperation she picked up her Bible and started to read. She soon read Matthew 6:34: "Therefore do not worry about tomorrow, for tomorrow will worry about itself. Each day has enough trouble of its own." No matter how she worried about the legal issue or Heath's feelings for her, worrying wouldn't resolve either concern.

"I'm sorry, heavenly Father," she whispered. "Shamed that I made the decisions that separated me from You. I know You've been there, looking out for Sammy and me, giving us wonderful, loving friends like the Truelove family and providing for our needs. Please forgive my sins, and help me to find my answers in You. Dear God, help me to handle this situation. Please send Your peace and comfort, and thank You for giving me this chance to come home. Amen."

A smile touched her lips as she turned the lamp off and closed her eyes. God was with her. She could feel His presence.

∽

The man delivered the papers early the following morning. When security called the house, Val and Heath walked out into the yard with her to meet him. Jane ripped open the envelope and read the document. Hurt turned her bones to mush. "The Holts have made good on their threat to file for custody."

Heath read the papers she handed him. "We need an attorney," he declared. "Val can get a referral from Mr. Henderson. They can't take Sammy from you."

"I don't have money for an attorney," Jane said, her feelings of hopelessness multiplying.

"I do."

She stared up at him. "I can't let you do that."

"You have to," Heath said. "If we don't do something, they could convince a judge to take your daughter. We have to act, and we need to do it now."

"That money is for your future."

Heath spread his hands wide, inviting her in, and said, "Don't you get it, Jane? I don't care about the money. I care about you and Sammy. I don't want to take chances."

Tears clogged her throat as she went into his arms for comfort.

∽

Heath went with her to see the attorney Mr. Henderson recommended. Val had attended high school with J. Paul Garner. After law school, he returned to Paris to set up his practice. His high success rate in the courtroom was good enough for her.

She hated feeling so emotional, so out of control. Sammy didn't know what to make of her clingy, weepy mother. The Trueloves tried to reassure her, but with all the other bad things that had happened in her life, she feared yet another nightmare. She had told Heath that on the drive to Paris.

"No judge is going to take a child away from their mother," Heath told her once again. "Tell her that, Paul."

Paul leaned back in his big chair. "Don't believe that, Heath. If Clarice Holt convinces a judge that being with Jane is not in Sammy's best interests, she could succeed."

"She will not take my child." Jane spoke with determination.

"We'll do everything possible to keep that from happening." Paul looked down at the paper on his desk. "She alleges that improper supervision resulted in your child's injury and that you left your injured daughter with a stranger while you went on dates with Heath Truelove."

Confused, Jane looked at Heath and back at Paul. "Why would she say that? When did she claim this happened?"

He checked the paper and indicated the dates and times.

"Part of my job is shopping for antiques for Val. Heath hasn't been able to work since hurting his leg and accompanied me a time or two. As for the day trip into Bardstown, we were researching garden ideas for Your Wedding Place."

"Mrs. Holt has photos of you hugging Mr. Truelove on the street in downtown Paris."

Jane couldn't believe what she was hearing. "She had me followed?"

"Why would hugging me make her a bad mother?" Heath demanded.

"Yes. That's how she got the photos," Paul told Jane. "And your relationship doesn't make her a bad mother," he said to Heath. "Evidently Clarice Holt has sufficient documentation to convince a judge to consider her case. We can't take anything for granted. Do you remember the incident?"

"Your ring," Heath said finally. "You hugged me that day."

Jane nodded. "Heath gifted me with a ring I admired in the store, and I hugged and thanked him. How could Clarice turn an innocent action into something so wrong? Sammy was with Heath's mother. Cindy Truelove cares for her while I work."

"Your mother-in-law also claims you're working all the time and not spending any time with Sammy. She says you weren't paying attention to your child the day her arm was broken."

Jane became more upset with each accusation. "My mother-in-law doesn't like me. She's made these outrageous claims ever since I married her son. Why is she making a big deal over Sammy spending time with others now? When I was the sole breadwinner for our family, Garrett didn't care for Sammy. She went to day care. I see her much more during the day with this job than when I worked at the coffee shop. I spend more quality time with her now than ever before."

"I'd advise you to let the investigators see for themselves that Clarice Holt doesn't like you. Hearing you say it makes it sound like an attempt to gain sympathy. I assume you have people who can attest to the type of mother you are?"

Heath leaned forward. "I can tell you she's wonderful with Sammy."

"We need others," the lawyer said. "The judge will feel that you're biased because of your alleged relationship with Jane."

"You mean our friendship?"

"Others may perceive it as more of a romantic relationship given the hug that was witnessed by the private investigator."

"She's grieving for Garrett. That's the reason she's doing this. She wants his child."

"We're going to do everything possible to keep Sammy with you. The judge will make his decision based on the best interests of the child and who can provide the most stable environment for her. I suggest you start making lists. The time you spend with Sammy on a daily basis. People who have witnessed you interacting with her."

When she worked long hours at the coffee shop, Jane picked Sammy up and took her home. Their quality time involved getting the child fed, bathed, and into bed. Other than the occasional visit with the staff when she picked up her check on a day off, she really had no witnesses as to the type of mother she was. The day care staff had seen her with Sammy for brief periods each day. Only the

Truelove family saw her with Sammy on a daily basis.

"Does our relationship disqualify my entire family?" Heath asked.

"No," Paul said with a shake of his head. "Of course not. Val is Jane's employer. Your mother is her day care provider. But we need others who have seen Jane interact with Sammy."

Heath looked at her and said, "People at church have seen you with her."

"They've seen me discipline her for yelling." Jane cringed at the thought. What if someone thought she was awful for doing that?

"And they know she was excited to see her mommy. I'm sure they could attest to what a good relationship the two of you have. Sammy is an active, healthy, normal three-year-old. They won't take her away from you."

"I wish I were as sure. Clarice and Ed have money. They can give her a better life than I can."

"They can't love her more than you do. Life isn't about possessions. Sammy has a good home, and you have a good support system in place. We're going to do everything possible to help you, Jane," Heath promised.

"Why does Clarice hate me so much that she'd want to take my child?"

"You saw how Sammy acted when they visited. I'm sure she wants to change that and thinks she can do so by having her closer."

"Church is good," Paul said. "Any extracurricular activities?"

"Her dance classes," Heath said. "They see the two of you together when you take her for those."

Paul nodded again. "You need to think of anything and everything you can to help prove your parental capabilities. The broken arm. . ."

"It was an accident," Jane told him.

"The judge will listen. There's no history of Sammy injuring herself in other ways, is there?"

"She's an active child and has her share of bumps and bruises when she does things she's told not to do."

Paul grinned. "I have a two-year-old myself. I know how they can be."

"I didn't realize you had a child," Heath said.

"Denise and I got married before law school. We decided we didn't want to wait to start our family. She teaches at our church's Christian academy." He turned back to Jane. "What sort of relationship have your in-laws had with Sammy?"

"They lived here when she was a baby. They left almost a year ago, after Garrett's death. It's been telephone only since then."

"How do you feel about bringing Garrett's suicide up in court?"

"I don't like talking about it, but if it's what I need to do to hold on to my daughter, I will. You should know Clarice blames me for that, too. She claims I drove Garrett to suicide."

"Why would she say that?"

Jane shrugged, shaking her head. She'd spent years trying to understand the

Holt family and was no closer than when she first started. "I worked twelve-hour shifts and took care of my child and home. He managed to get himself fired from every job he found and partied with his fraternity friends. I didn't have time to analyze Garrett's reasons for lots of things he did."

"You need to be careful with statements like that. They could reflect negatively on you."

Jane didn't understand. "Why would I look bad? I supported our family."

"Clarice Holt will come across as a grieving mother."

And she'd play the role to the hilt. Jane had no doubt that would be Clarice's first line of defense in this case. She would do everything possible to make Jane look bad. "I should tell you that I recently learned Garrett had terminal cancer. The doctor suggested the possibility that his death may have been accidental. He's willing to discuss it with an attorney, but I don't have funds to pursue the matter."

"Do the Holts know this?" Paul asked.

"No. I haven't told them. I planned to, but this situation has taken priority in my life."

"One case at a time. What can you tell me about your in-laws?"

"I can attest to how Clarice chased after Sammy when the child wanted nothing to do with her," Heath said. "And how she constantly demeans Jane." He looked at her and said, "We all saw how she treated you that week and need to make sure the judge knows as well."

The lawyer looked interested. "How do you know this?"

Heath explained the situation.

"In Sammy's defense, she hadn't seen her grandmother for a year," Jane said.

"She was very demanding," Heath added. "Seemed to think being alone with Sammy would change their relationship faster. Sammy's screams could be heard all over the house."

"Write it all down," Paul said. "I need to know what you know. I'll call as soon as I have more information."

∾

Throughout the next day Jane could think of little more than Clarice's accusations and the pending court case. She had never been the insecure type, but she had never considered having to prove herself a good mother. When had loving and providing for your child's needs stopped being enough? She didn't plan to go down without a fight. Clarice would not raise her daughter.

The Trueloves were very supportive and had prayed for her and promised to do everything possible to help. Jane felt better knowing they were there for her.

She prayed her anger would subside before she did or said something she would regret. How dare Clarice have her followed like a criminal, gathering evidence to convict her? And why couldn't she hug a man? She wasn't cheating on her husband.

Jane considered phoning Clarice but knew they would only end up arguing, which would reflect badly on her when the case came to court. Ed's sympathetic looks came to mind. Most of what she'd heard had been Clarice. Could she reach Ed? Or would he stand by his wife? The thought he could be her only hope refused to be silenced. "Val, I need to make a phone call."

"Go ahead."

Jane found her address book and looked up her father-in-law's office number. Her hands trembled, and she redialed three times before she got the numbers right. "Please God, help me," she pleaded as she waited for Ed to come on the line.

"Jane? Has something happened?"

He sounded concerned. Was it real? "Why are you doing this?"

"Doing what?"

Was it possible he didn't know? She couldn't hold back the tears. "The custody suit. Having me followed. Am I such a bad mother that you'd be cruel enough to take Sammy from me?"

"Please stop crying," Ed requested. "I can't understand you."

A snuffle escaped as she tried to regain control. "Why did Clarice file for custody of Sammy?"

"What? That's ridiculous," he roared.

"It's true."

"I have to talk to Clarice. I'll call you back."

Chapter 13

Another day passed with no word from Ed. After getting Sammy to sleep, Jane climbed into bed with paper and pen, making copious lists to share with the attorney. It was late when the phone rang.

"Jane, Ed Holt. Sorry to call now, but I wanted you to know Clarice had a massive heart attack this morning. The doctors don't know if she's going to live."

A gasp slipped out. "What happened?"

"Evidently she's been having problems for a while now. It's a miracle I got there when I did."

Sadness filled Jane. She hadn't wanted anything bad to happen to Sammy's grandmother. "What should we do?"

"I don't know. The prognosis doesn't look good."

"We can pray." Jane suggested the one thing she'd learned worked the best.

"Don't know much about that."

"Talk to God just as you'd talk to a friend," she encouraged him. "Would you like for us to come to Florida?"

"I couldn't ask you to do that."

"No matter what's happened, you're family."

"Maybe having Sammy closer would lift Clarice's spirits when she wakes."

"I'll make the arrangements and let you know. Hopefully we can get a flight out after Sammy's doctor appointment tomorrow."

"Thanks, Jane."

The next morning she and Sammy stopped by the house. Heath was in the family room. "Is Val around?"

"She's in the shower. I thought you were going into Lexington this morning."

"I am, but I needed to tell Val I need time off. Clarice had a massive heart attack yesterday. It doesn't look good."

"I'm sorry."

"Me, too," Jane said. "I didn't want it to be this way."

"When did you plan to go?"

"I booked a noon flight. We'll leave after Sammy sees her doctor. Pray for us, Heath."

"I will. Everyone will."

Because time was at a premium, Jane took the first flight she could get, which also proved to be the most expensive. She hated dipping into her savings but knew she had to do this. One of Ed's employees picked them up at the airport and took them straight to the hospital.

Jane hugged Ed and asked how Clarice was doing. He reported that nothing had changed. They were monitoring her and running tests. He became emotional when Sammy went straight into his arms. The little girl seemed to understand his need for comfort.

With her mother-in-law in the coronary intensive care unit, they spent the time between visits in the waiting area. The long hours gave them plenty of opportunity to talk.

"I'm sorry for the way you've been treated, Jane. Clarice blames you for what Garrett did because she doesn't want to accept our son was selfish. If she dies, it will be yet another wasted life."

Unsure how to respond to her father-in-law's comments, Jane said nothing. For all the years she'd known him, she believed Ed supported his son and wife completely. Now with the custody case pending, she didn't know if she could trust him. "I never meant to upset her."

Ed shook his head. "It wasn't you. I'm sorry I let this go on for so long, but I didn't know how to help Clarice through her misery. The few times I dared say something, she turned that sharp tongue on me. I got tired of fighting and started spending time at the office. I suppose leaving her alone wasn't good either.

"I didn't know what she'd done, Jane. After you called, I went home and confronted her. She told me the truth, and I told her she'd drop this immediately or I'd divorce her and see to it that she never saw Sammy again. We didn't talk again that evening. I left early the next morning, and later that afternoon I started to feel guilty and came home to try to talk some sense into her. When I walked in, I found her slumped over the kitchen island. The phone lay a few inches away. I suppose she tried to call for help."

"I'm sorry, Ed."

"It's not your fault. She had called a friend of hers in Lexington who just happens to be a judge's wife, and the woman talked to her husband. What has happened to my family, Jane?"

Fear nearly took Jane's breath as she considered his revelation. The Holts had money and connections she didn't. She could lose Sammy.

Ed passed Sammy back to her mother and rested a hand on Jane's shoulder. "I wouldn't have allowed Clarice to take Sammy from you. I talked to the judge. Explained that Clarice has been grieving herself to death and told him we don't want to pursue the custody case."

She hugged her daughter close and said, "We need to stop trying to destroy each other. Garrett is gone, but we can be a family if we try."

"Clarice thought Heath Truelove had proposed. She saw a photo of him giving you a ring."

Jane held out her hand to show him the garnet birthstone. "She should give him more credit. Someone with a name as romantic as Heathcliff would never propose in a parking lot. I admired this ring in the antique store, and he bought it for me as a gift."

He nodded. "I told her she shouldn't assume anything. She's afraid we'll never see Sammy again if you remarry."

"I wouldn't do that," Jane said. "You're her grandparents. Just as Garrett is her father. Telling her what happened to him is going to be hard, but I'll make sure she knows about her father."

"Maybe she doesn't need to know," Ed said. "Tell her he died when she was a baby and leave it at that."

An easy out, Jane thought. She shook her head. "I don't think that's the answer either. She has a right to know."

Ed's sad expression touched her heart. "I'm glad you're thinking about the future. Clarice has been so miserable since his death. She doesn't care about anything. I thought the grief would pass, but she's allowing this to destroy her. Us."

"You haven't. . ." Jane paused, afraid to hear the truth.

"No, but I'm close to calling it quits. I love her, and I loved Garrett, but I won't stop living because he chose to do so. You know how she is. It had to be someone else's fault. Her son would never do something like that."

She had to tell him what she knew. Perhaps learning the truth could help heal this unhappy existence for them all. "There's something I need to share with you."

Jane explained how she'd learned Garrett had cancer. She could see Ed was as shocked by the news as she had been.

"Why wouldn't he tell us?"

"I've asked myself that same question. He took the answer to the grave with him, but based on what the doctor said, I suspect Garrett was in shock. The terminal diagnosis was made only days before he died. The doctor said Garrett could have accidentally killed himself by mixing alcohol and painkillers."

A glimmer of hope came into the eyes that were so like Garrett's. "Do we pursue this and possibly risk renewed grief?"

"There's not much I can do," Jane told him. "The doctor said to have my lawyer contact him to discuss the matter, but I can't pay another attorney. I'm still paying off Garrett's debts. And now I owe Heath money for the custody case lawyer."

"What kind of debts?" Ed asked.

"Garrett had school loans and credit cards he used a lot."

"Why haven't you said something before? We could have helped."

Jane wanted their independence. She pleaded with Garrett to restrain his spending habits, but he didn't. "They were our obligation."

"I won't have Garrett's irresponsibility stand in the way of you caring for his daughter."

She didn't expect anything of the Holts. "I've been blessed to find a good job, and Val gives me the apartment as part of the package. That helps. I'm paying them down slowly."

Ed drew in a deep breath. "Garrett couldn't even die responsibly. If he'd told the truth and died like a man, his life insurance would have paid."

Jane frowned. "We didn't have life insurance."

"I did. Didn't help you any, though."

His overall attitude seemed so at odds from what she'd always thought about Garrett's father. "I got the impression you supported Garrett as much as Clarice."

"Sure I was proud of him, but it wasn't like he was going to make a living playing football."

"He was good."

"NFL good?"

"We'll never know."

"Clarice got that fool notion that Garrett needed to concentrate on football. One of her friends probably told her he could make a fortune when she bragged about him. I wanted him to work with me during the summers, but it was always football. I thought he'd learn the business and maybe take over when I retired."

Ed ran a successful heating and air-conditioning company in Lexington. He'd made a good profit when he sold the business to one of his employees. He'd started another company in Florida, saying he was too young to retire.

"Why didn't you offer him a job when he dropped out of college?"

"I did. He thought he'd go straight to the top. When I said laborer, he said no thanks. Thought he was too good to work his way up from the bottom like his old man. I don't know where he got the idea that I would hire him to do sales."

"He wasn't very good at it," Jane said, a wry smile touching her face.

"You don't have to tell me. I went to the dealership where he worked, thinking I would put a little business his way, and he thought I'd replace the entire fleet. The boy didn't have a clue how business works."

"He never told me you had offered him a job."

Ed shrugged. "Doesn't surprise me any. You're a good woman, Jane. A good mother, too. I promise you, things are going to change. I won't walk away the next time Clarice starts in on you."

"It's been hard on us all," Jane said, resting her hand on his arm.

He smiled back and patted her hand with his. "I'm so disappointed in Garrett. How can you forgive him?"

"With God's help. I was a believer when I met Garrett, but I allowed my love for him to tempt me into making bad decisions. Lately I've come to realize I need God in my life more than ever."

"Never had any dealings with God."

"You never went to church?"

"We did on Christmas and Easter when we visited my mom's parents."

"I went to church regularly with my parents. I accepted Christ as my Savior when I was ten. I stopped going after I married. I'm praying for Clarice, and my friends and church are praying for her, too."

"My grandmother used to pray a lot," he said thoughtfully.

Jane smiled at that. "Surely you weren't that bad."

Ed grinned for the first time since their arrival. "She believed. She prayed for me, too."

"You don't have to wait for others to pray for you. You have direct access to God. He can make things so much better if you'll just give Him a chance."

A nurse came out into the lobby where they sat. "Mrs. Holt is awake and asking to see you."

He stood and started to follow her. "Wait. This is our daughter and granddaughter. Can they come, too?"

The woman's gaze moved from one to the other. She nodded.

Jane hesitated. "It might be too much for her."

"No more running away, Jane. Knowing you're here in her time of need will do Clarice a world of good."

∽

That night Jane took Sammy to the Holt home and put her to bed. Ed gave her a key and often stayed behind in the hospital waiting room. Though Clarice was awake, the doctors weren't sure how much damage had been done to her heart. Although Jane was thankful her condition was no longer critical, Clarice hadn't had a good day, and the situation was still touch and go. The house was quiet when her cell phone rang, and she prepared herself for bad news.

"How's it going?"

"Heath." She breathed his name, relieved to hear his voice. It had been nearly a week since she'd arrived in Florida, and he had called her daily. "I thought it might be the hospital."

"Didn't mean to frighten you. Are you and Sammy okay?"

"We're good. Clarice is really scared."

"I'd think a close call with death would do that to a person."

"She apologized. Then she cried. I told her they were going to throw me out if she didn't stop. She thanked me for bringing Sammy to see her."

"We've been praying."

"I know," Jane said. "I feel God's presence so strongly. I even witnessed to Ed."

"Good for you."

"How are things there?"

"We went to visit Grandfather Truelove in prison."

Jane knew there had been talk of visiting Mathias Truelove. From what she'd been told, their grandfather had killed a man in a bar fight back when Jacob was just a young man. He blamed his father's addictions to alcohol and gambling for the problems Mathias had caused and was determined that no member of his family would follow the man's example. Val believed her father would never be happy until he forgave his father. "How did it go?"

"I've never seen Dad so upset. I could tell he didn't want to go."

"I'm sure it's difficult for him."

"Even more so when Grandfather talked down to him. When Dad introduced us, he criticized him about our names. Then he started in about us being

Christians. Val asked him not to start an argument, and I could see he wanted to say something, but he didn't. He got to her, though. She told Dad that it's sad Grandfather sits in prison day in and day out with no family who cares for him. She said we hadn't given him a reason to want to be a better person."

"How did your dad respond to that?"

"He feels Grandfather got exactly what he deserved. I looked at this old man I didn't remember and yet knew I should respect, and I resented him for what he did to my dad."

Jane understood their plight. It hurt when the people you loved let you down. "That's understandable. You never had an opportunity to bond with him."

"Val says God laid it on her heart to help heal the relationship, but I'm not sure that's possible."

"God will do the healing," Jane said with a level of confidence that surprised her. "He's started the process here between Clarice and me."

"Thanks for reminding me of that. Oh yeah, Val had a meeting at Prestige Designs today. You'll never guess who's behind these incidents with her project. Remember the guy who blamed Val for losing his job at Maddy's office? Derrick Masters. His girlfriend worked for Prestige, and she did all those things for him because Derrick lied to her about the lottery ticket. He made her believe Val cheated him and said she had to help him pay her back. The girlfriend spilled everything, including how Derrick drugged Fancy when he came for the launch party."

"You're kidding." The incidents that had plagued Val's project since the beginning made them all wonder what was going on. She had seen Val's growing frustration over it. Permitting delays, changed work orders, even cancelled supply orders popped up on a regular basis, and now they tied Jacob's accident into the sabotage. Good thing Val had hired security when she did.

"No. Val wouldn't file charges against the woman. She said she was more of a victim than accomplice."

"Will your dad file charges against Derrick Masters?"

"Dad says he won't do anything as long as Derrick stays away from Sheridan Farm."

"Surely he doesn't have the nerve to show his face after what he did."

"I don't know. Look at the mayhem he created with very little effort."

"Tell Val I'm happy things have worked out for her. I have to go," she said a few minutes later. "I need to do a load of laundry before I go to bed. I want to be at the hospital early so Ed can come home and rest."

"Give Sammy a kiss for us. We miss her."

She wondered if he missed her. "I will."

"Jane?" he called softly just before she cut him off. "Hurry home. We miss you, too."

She smiled. "I will. Pray for me."

"You know we will. Pray for us, too."

"You've got a deal, friend."

After their conversation, restlessness enveloped Heath, and he wandered out to the barn. He opened the door to Fancy's stall and smiled when she playfully thrust her nose out. He stroked her gently and fed her a peppermint. He was thankful there were no lingering problems for mother and baby. They had been upset to hear that Fancy had gone out of control and injured their father. They worried about her and the foal she carried.

The sounds of the barn comforted him. As a child, he'd spent lots of time helping his dad with the chores. Mr. Sheridan had praised him and Rom often, saying they were good boys and their father had a right to be proud. Heath always suspected the old man had an investment in their education. Probably in one of the scholarships they'd received. He'd definitely given them a good deal on the small truck they drove back and forth to Lexington.

His thoughts went back to Jane. He hoped she would come home soon. Several times a day he thought of things he wanted to share. He missed Sammy, too. They all did. He didn't want to exist this way.

Heath had prayed Jane would find peace when she told him what she planned to do. She certainly set an example by going to stand by her enemy in the woman's time of need. The women in his life seemed to understand the premise of forgiveness much better than he did.

After securing Fancy's stall, Heath wandered back to the house. He noticed his toy truck on the swing. Setting it on the ground, he settled in the swing and idly thumbed the remote, running the truck in circles.

"Having fun?"

He slid over so Val could sit. "Yeah. Gonna have to talk to the boys about leaving my toys outside though."

She laughed. "You've enjoyed that truck, haven't you?"

"I'm glad Jane insisted that I think about having fun."

"Jane sort of makes you do that, doesn't she?"

"You've noticed it, too?"

"Sure. I laugh more when she's working with us. Those daily cheers of hers are a riot."

After some teasing from them both on her cheerleading youth, Jane had taken to making up cheers to start their day. Her "Rake it to the left, rake it to the right" and the "Trim it high, trim it low" cheers were a real hoot and had them looking forward to what she'd come up with next.

"I enjoy working with her."

He missed those cheers and Jane's playful antics. "Me, too. I couldn't believe it when she insisted on buying me this thing." He hit the control, and Val laughed at the raucous noise it emitted as he ran it around in circles.

"Maybe Jane sees something missing from your life that you don't. God wants you to enjoy life, too, Heath."

"What makes us so driven, Val? Why can't we be free spirits like Jane?"

"Is she really free, Heath?"

"No, I suppose not," he said. "I'm sure there are times when she laughs to keep from crying."

"But she still laughs," Val said. "No matter how bad things get for her, she does everything in her power to lighten everyone else's spirits."

"Do you think that's why she gave me the car?"

"Maybe she thought you needed a little joy in your life. How is she?"

"Seems to be okay. From what she said, it's still touch and go with Clarice. I told her we would continue praying for them. She's proud of herself for witnessing to Ed Holt."

"Me, too. She's come a long way. We've had a few talks, and she's well versed in the Bible. She says it's like riding a bicycle. You never forget."

"That sounds like something she'd say. I miss her and Sammy."

"Did she say when they're coming home?"

"They'll be back for Mom's birthday. I told her about seeing Grandfather. She said selfish men don't mean to be that way. They just can't help themselves."

"She's got a point. We've spent our lives surrounded by generous, loving people. They taught us good life lessons, and we're better people because of them. The situation with Grandfather troubles us all. Just remember only God has the power to change people, but He expects us to forgive."

"We've lived without him all this time. I'm not sure I want him back in our lives now."

"Remember when you said Jane has to forgive Garrett if she wants to get on with her life? What about Daddy?"

"Dad seems okay to me."

"He could be better if he wasn't always struggling with his anger."

"He'll still be angry when Grandfather doesn't change."

"Forgiving someone doesn't mean they don't have the power to hurt us, but it does mean we're more understanding about the things we can't change."

"You should share that with Jane."

"She's better, Heath. I think she's come to grips with the idea that Garrett's death might not have been suicide. She told me she loved him, but he's gone and she's ready to move on."

"Move on how?"

"I know for a fact that she'd like a man in her life, a father for Sammy. More kids."

"I'd like to be that man. I suppose I should give serious consideration to my future. Find a job and prepare to support a family. Do you think I'm selfish?"

"Why would you ask that?"

He could tell his question startled her. "Because I've been thinking about myself and what I want out of life instead of my future."

"You've been an industrious student, a good son, and a great brother and friend. All commendable but what does Heath Truelove want out of life?"

"That's easy. A wife who loves me, a family, and a job I love."

"What's kept you from achieving your goals?"

"Personal doubts. You made so many sacrifices to better my life, and I've done nothing for you in return."

"That's not true. I would never have advanced as far with this project without your help."

"Sure you would. You could have hired people and gotten it done faster. Instead you're limping along with me while I recover and waste your time. I should be out there finding a job like Rom. Not living off you. That money is yours, and somehow I've managed to pocket a big chunk of it for doing nothing. It's not right."

"You don't have anything I didn't willingly give," Val reminded.

"I know, but you deserve more."

"What is this really about, Heath?"

"I've lost my sense of purpose. For years I've had one goal. Get my education and use it to help my family. Lately I'm not helping anyone but myself."

"Have I said or done anything to make you feel this way?"

He hesitated and said, "Well, Opie did say you weren't sure about me doing the garden work."

"Only because I'm afraid you feel like you owe me."

"I do."

"No. You don't. When you and Rom talk about his job, I don't see the excitement that I do when you tell him about the progress in the gardens. I know you only got your master's because you expected to help the family more that way. But guess what, it's okay to be selfish sometimes. Doing what makes you happy is important. Believe me, I've realized it more than ever before since God provided the means to fulfill my dreams.

"Do you think I didn't feel guilty about spending all that money on the farm? I knew we could have found a less expensive place, but I felt there were reasons we needed to stay at Sheridan Farm. I was selfish, too. I didn't want to give up the home I loved. I didn't want Daddy to give up the work he loved. I had my doubts, but when one of the staff tells me how blessed they feel to work for us, God soothes my soul. Did you know Daddy is holding Bible study with some of them?"

"He mentioned it."

"Those things remind me God has a plan for us all. Did you ever think that the changes in our lives were part of the plan He has for us? You feel guilty because you're not using your degree, don't you?"

He nodded.

"But you love what you're doing?"

He nodded again.

"It's okay, Heath. You worked hard for years to please others. Take time for yourself."

"But that's selfish."

"Rom and Opie aren't having problems dealing with the situation."

"Rom got a job, and Opie's using her training."

"Rom's thinking ahead to his future with Stephanie, and Opie's trying to make up her mind. I love you, Heath. I don't have the least bit of doubt that if all the money disappeared tomorrow, you would step up and do what's right. I only want the best for you."

"Just as I want it for you. I want this new venture to be everything you've dreamed of and more."

"With God's help it will be," Val told him. "It's in His hands."

Heath nodded in agreement.

Val leaned her head back against the swing cushions. "Russ should be here soon. He wants to talk."

They had all been shocked to learn who was behind all the incidents that had happened with her project. Any one of which could have put the project at a standstill.

"I'd love to get my hands on Derrick Masters."

"What would you do?" Val asked curiously.

"Though one part of me would love to pummel him into the ground, I don't imagine God or Dad would let that happen."

"How can be people be so evil?"

"More selfishness?"

Val frowned. "I feel so guilty for doubting Russ."

"You'll have to make him understand you're sorry. Any idea what he wants to discuss?"

Val shook her head. "I'm thinking he wants to talk about us, but that's probably wishful thinking on my part. Particularly since I've learned he's attending church."

"Life was so much simpler when we were kids."

"These grown-up decisions are difficult."

"Maybe that's why I'm so confused. Jane says I don't know how to be a kid, but I keep trying to figure out what I want to be when I grow up." Headlights flashed in the distance. "Looks like Russ is here."

"Want to tag along?"

"I wouldn't want to embarrass you while you eat crow."

"You should be a comedian, Heath Truelove."

"Gee thanks, yet another option for my career list."

"Don't quit your day job. I need you too much."

"That's good to know."

"Do you doubt you're needed?"

"Jane said a man should have a job and plan for the future. Made me wonder if all women feel that way?"

"I wouldn't want a man who expected me to work and support him."

"I would never expect that of my wife. In fact, I wouldn't want her to have to work at all."

"Don't tell Opie that. She'll be on your case."

He nodded. The entire family knew Opie's feelings on the matter of working women. "I'm not saying she can't work if that's what she wants. Just that I don't want her to have to work to make ends meet. I'd like to provide for my family."

"Most men would," Russ agreed as he walked up on their conversation. "My dad always told us a man's role in life is to provide."

Heath nodded.

"Enjoying this crisp fall weather?" Russ asked.

"It's nice after the summer, but winter comes much too fast," Heath said.

∾

Their stay stretched into weeks. Clarice began to improve, and Jane planned to stay until her release from the hospital. When she saw how weak the woman was, they stayed a few more days to help around the house. Jane cooked and cleaned, and Clarice rested and visited with Sammy. Her daughter's avoidance of her grandmother had lessened with the change in the woman.

The members of the Truelove family called often for progress reports. Jane missed them and longed to go home but knew she had to do this for the Holts.

After putting Sammy down for her nap, Jane asked Clarice if she wanted something to drink. Ed had gone to pick up her prescriptions. "Here you go," Jane said, placing the insulated glass on the table next to Clarice. "Water with lots of ice and a little lemon."

Clarice studied Jane closely for a few moments longer before thanking her.

"You're welcome."

"No. I mean for what you've done since my attack. You didn't have to bring Sammy to see me. Or be there for Ed when they thought I wouldn't pull through."

"Yes, I did. You're my family, Clarice. No matter what differences we've had, you became my people when I said my wedding vows."

"Some people I've been," she disparaged. "I'm surprised you put up with me as long as you have."

"I got in a few zingers of my own."

"Why did things happen as they did? I knew Garrett would grow up and marry one day. . . ."

"But you never thought it would be a sad little affair like ours?"

"I had such high hopes. I wanted him to accomplish great things. Only problem with that is I never taught him how to do that. I praised him and told him he could do anything he wanted. Then when things turned out badly, to blame him would have been to blame myself. It was easier to put it on you. Ed and I have talked a lot since I got home. I know I have to change or lose you all. I don't know how."

"Have you considered seeking God's help?"

Clarice frowned. "Why would He help me?"

"Because He loves you just as you are."

"Surely not as I am," Clarice said, her doubt-filled tone speaking volumes.

"I thought the same thing until not too long ago. Being around the Trueloves has helped me realize I needed God in my life. Sammy and I attend church, and I've renewed my commitment to God."

"What do you mean, renewed?"

"I accepted Christ as my Savior when I was ten," Jane said. "Then when I moved to Paris and got involved with Garrett, things changed. I still went to church, but I wasn't living a Christian life. I let the need to be popular convince me to make decisions I never should have made."

"You mean the baby?"

The secret she'd carried for years demanded release. Jane took a deep breath and said, "I don't want to hurt you, Clarice, but you need to know it wasn't what you thought. I loved Garrett, but I didn't willingly give him what he wanted. He cajoled and threatened to find someone else, but he never did. My mom warned me to stay clear of temptation, but I thought I could control the situation.

"One night when you and Mr. Holt were out of town, I lied and said I was spending the night with a girlfriend so I could go to an all-night party Garrett had at your house. There was alcohol. I didn't drink, but Garrett did. He got carried away, and when I said no, he didn't listen."

Clarice's face crumpled, and Jane feared she'd gone too far. "That's what Ed said," she whispered. "He was so angry when he learned about the custody case and said our family had already done you enough harm. That's when he told me Garrett all but raped you. Evidently he came to his father when he realized what he'd done. He was afraid your parents would file charges once they learned the truth."

"They don't know," Jane said.

"You let them think badly of you all this time?"

Jane patted her hand. "I blamed myself. If I hadn't gone to the party. If I hadn't lied to my parents. If I hadn't made all those wrong choices. I felt so ashamed. I cried that night. A lot. Garrett didn't know what to do. He sobered up fast, and somehow we made it through the night. I went home the next morning, but I refused to be alone with him again. Then I learned I was pregnant.

"When I told him, Garrett wanted me to get an abortion. I said no. We told my parents, and they wanted me to put the baby up for adoption. I wanted time to consider what was best."

"But that wasn't an option?"

Jane shook her head. "I married Garrett with the intention of making our marriage work."

Clarice's anguished expression tore at Jane's heart. "And I made your life miserable."

"Please don't get upset," Jane said. "It's not good for you. It was my choice. I loved Garrett."

"He loved you, too. I could tell he felt differently about you."

"Did that bother you?"

"You got in the way of my aspirations for my son."

"I had my own aspirations for him."

"Poor Garrett. There was no hope he'd ever live up to our plans for him. I suppose I always knew that, but I had my dreams. I'm sorry for the way I behaved when the baby died."

Tears welled in Jane's eyes. "I loved that baby so much."

"I lost a baby, too. After Garrett. It hurt so much that I thought I'd die, but Ed and Garrett gave me a reason to go on."

Jane knew what God wanted her to do. She had to forgive the Holt family for what they had done to her. "It's in the past, Clarice. I refuse to continue to live like that. God gave us both a wake-up call."

"He did," she agreed. "I've been so afraid. I've become so angry and bitter. Ed threatened to leave me if things don't change. I don't want to be this way. Why can't he understand?"

"You're not dead, Clarice. It's not fair to make the people who love you live with the shadow of a person you've become. You have to love Garrett enough to let go and move forward."

"It's so hard."

"Yes, but we need to go forward for Sammy's sake. She needs her family."

"Can you forgive me for what I did?"

"If you'd taken my child away, I would have hated you forever," Jane said. "I would never have forgiven you."

"I know."

"I want our relationship to be different, Clarice. Ed told me you're afraid I'll marry again and you'll lose Sammy. I promise you that won't happen. My daughter may have three sets of grandparents, but you'll always be there for her. And I will tell her about her daddy."

"What I did was wrong," Clarice said. "You are a good mother, and I had no right implying otherwise. Ed called the judge and explained. He wants to reimburse the Trueloves for the money they've expended for your legal fees."

Unable to speak, Jane nodded.

"I really appreciate the way the Truelove family has looked out for you and Sammy when we haven't. That Heath is a fine young man. He impressed me when we stayed at their home. Told me a few things I didn't want to hear, but I know he was right. Will you marry him?"

"I'd love to, but he seems to be holding back for some reason."

"Why? He obviously cares for you. He took me on about the way I treated you."

"He's a good friend. But he also has definite ideas about what he expects from a woman."

"You're worthy of him, Jane."

"You forget he knows my reputation."

"Tell him what you told me."

"I can't. Not yet. Not until I know for sure that he loves me."

They heard the door open, and Ed called out that he was home. He walked into the bedroom and handed the pharmacy bag to his wife. "You two okay?"

Clarice squeezed Jane's hand in hers and said, "We're going to be fine."

Chapter 14

When she decided to return home, Ed drove her and Sammy to the airport. On the way he asked about Heath.

"See Hef?" Sammy asked from the backseat.

"Soon, sweetie." Jane smiled and winked at Ed. "I'd marry him if he'd ask."

Ed looked interested. "Is there a reason you think he won't? I'd say the boy has feelings for you."

"His faith. Heath has very strong beliefs regarding God's intentions for him."

"Don't count yourself out. Love is a powerful motivator, and I'd say Heath loves you and Sammy. Why else would he have done some of the things he has?"

"Because he's like his family. They believe in looking out for people."

"Too bad there aren't more people like that in the world."

Jane agreed.

"Whatever happens, we're behind you all the way," Ed said. "I know you have plans for the future, and I want to help in every way possible. I hope you'll let me do that."

"I thank you for that. I want to do right by Sammy, and I think I'm in the best place for now. I'm learning a lot about myself and what I'm capable of doing."

"Starting at the bottom?" he asked with a smile.

Jane thought about what he'd said about Garrett. "Definitely."

"It's best to build a secure foundation in life. Helps you keep the other things in the right perspective."

She insisted he drop them off at the gate so he could get back to Clarice as soon as possible. "Thank you for all you've done. Knowing the custody issue is resolved takes away a major burden."

"I'm sorry it happened in the first place. Thank you for all you've done for Clarice and me. I think maybe we're on the right track now. In fact she mentioned that she'd like to attend church when she's able to get out again."

That pleased Jane a great deal. "Will you let me know how it goes?"

He nodded. "We'll be in close contact. I'll let you know how it turns out with Garrett, too."

Ed lifted their luggage out of the trunk and then unstrapped Sammy from the child seat. He hugged them both and waved good-bye before driving away.

A lot had happened in her absence. She was happy for Val when she learned she and Russ were dating with the intention of one day becoming man and wife.

She returned just in time for Cindy Truelove's birthday celebration. Jane gladly tackled her first job assignment of helping sort out plans for the two parties planned to celebrate the day for the woman who meant so much to her and Sammy. The first was a community event involving family, friends, and their church. The second was a private affair for family and friends.

As she worked with Heath, Jane considered what she must do. She couldn't be in his presence and not have his love. They discussed what had happened in Florida and how Ed planned to hire an attorney to pursue the matter of Garrett's death certificate. Jane didn't tell him her father-in-law had insisted on paying off all of Garrett's debts and she had returned to Paris with a lighter load. He had been surprised when she handed him the Holts' check reimbursing the legal fees he'd incurred with interest. She did tell him she was ready to move on with her future.

"Can you do that if you're still grieving for Garrett?"

Jane stopped filling balloons with helium and said, "Garrett is dead, Heath. I was a child when I fell in love with him. Innocent and trusting but what I didn't realize was that he was a child, too. We made decisions that changed the course of our lives, believing no one had a right to tell us what to do. Our parents, even our child, suffered from those choices. I'm a wiser woman. I understand that we can't always have everything we want in life."

"What do you mean, everything?" Heath asked.

"Sometimes the people we love don't love us back."

"Why would you say that?"

"I know you'd never consider me wife material."

Heath looked puzzled, and Jane had said far more than she intended. Maybe it would be best if she and Sammy moved on. Both of them would be hurt if they stayed around and Heath married someone else. "I have to go. Val's waiting for me in the office. She said something about running into Paris to pick up supplies. And I need to get Cindy's gift."

∾

"Jane?" Heath called after her.

What did she mean? he wondered as he watched her escape to the house. *"The people we love don't love us back."* That sounded almost as if. . . Was it possible that she was trying to tell him she loved him?

She seemed different since she'd learned that Garrett's death was possibly accidental, but that only made him fear she still loved her husband. She'd said others had disappointed her. Maybe Jane meant her parents? Even her in-laws. Heath wished he knew for sure.

"God, I love Jane and I feel like she's the one You intend for me, but I need to know she's over Garrett and ready to serve You wholeheartedly. Give us answers, and if it's Your will, grant us this happiness that love and a lifetime of commitment to You would provide."

∾

"Is that a thundercloud over your head?" Val asked when Jane stepped into the office.

"Men can be so dense."

"All men? Or one in particular?"

Disgusted, Jane said, "Heath. I know I'm not wife material in his eyes. I tried to tell him I understood. . . ."

"Why would you think that?" Val interrupted.

"Heath has shared certain expectations regarding the woman he marries. He said she will be pure of heart, and since he's saving himself for marriage, I'm sure she'll be pure in other ways as well."

"I don't believe that's Heath's reason."

"Then what is?" Frustrated, Jane paused and said, "I'm sorry. I shouldn't have asked you that."

"I know how you feel," Val told her. "I love Russ, and when I felt like there was no hope of a future together, it tore me up inside even though I knew I made the right decision. I'm happy God made it possible for us, but I had my doubts it would ever happen."

Her friend had shared her turmoil over loving a man she couldn't have. "And if it's God's will, things will work out for me."

"You can be sure that God will put the right man in your life. Pray, Jane. Ask God for what you want."

"I do, Val. It's hard when you love someone, though."

"Very hard but know that even if it doesn't happen exactly like you want, that can be an answer to a prayer, too."

∾

"Do you love Jane?"

Val's blunt question threw Heath off guard. Jane must have said something after their conversation before the party.

"Yes."

Val frowned. "Why does she think she doesn't stand a chance with you?"

"I don't have a clue."

"Have you told her how you feel?"

He shook his head. "I'm waiting for answers."

"Prayers?"

Heath nodded. "I have to be sure."

Val eyed him speculatively. "You doubt she loves you?"

"I'm not sure she's over Garrett. She's still so angry."

"Do you feel she isn't entitled?"

"I believe any hope for happiness she might have depends on her choosing to forgive. This latest revelation about his cancer has helped her. Once she got over the shock, she seemed relieved."

"What do you feel that God is telling you?"

"I'm trying to wait on His guidance. The doubts come when I remember that I wasn't enough for her in her youth. She needed excitement then. What if that happens in the future?"

"Jane experimented with popularity, and it came up lacking. If you're willing, you can provide the excitement along with the stability she craves."

"I know that she's the one, but grieving is a process. She has to be ready for the future before she moves on."

"She claims that's what she's doing."

"She's trying, but some of the things she does and says make me wonder if she's as far along as she thinks," Heath said. "What do you think she'll do?"

"I know what I'd do. I should say, did. When I realized how I felt about Russ, I offered to be his friend, and he disappeared from my life."

His forehead creased. "You think she'll offer to become my friend?"

Val shook her head. "I don't see Jane as the type to stick around when she feels she's not wanted."

Val left, and Heath thought about what she'd told him. She was right. He needed to talk to Jane. To understand what she'd been trying to tell him.

∾

"Take a walk with me?" he requested later that afternoon. He'd exchanged the cast for an orthopedic boot while she'd been gone. He moved slowly, but at least he moved without crutches.

Jane shrugged. They'd worked hard all day, but she supposed the exercise couldn't hurt. They strolled through the horse barns, checking out the new horses the farm had acquired.

"Beautiful animals," Jane said.

"Expensive but they'll pay for themselves in a very short time."

After leaving the barn, they took a circuitous route and ended up in the Oriental garden. "This is my favorite garden," Heath said, patting the bench next to him.

Jane sat down. "I like the English garden best."

"I'm surprised. It's so structured. I think of you as a free-spirited kind of girl."

"Sometimes structure can be a good thing."

He'd thought about the situation all afternoon and concluded that it was time to take action. He couldn't risk losing her because he was too afraid to step out on faith and trust God to make things work for them. "Are you thinking of leaving Sheridan Farm?"

She tensed as if shocked by his question.

"I've considered it."

"Can I ask why?"

She plucked a dying leaf from a nearby plant and shredded it with her fingers. "You really need to ask?"

"I suppose not. I care for you, Jane. A great deal. There are things I'm uncertain about, but I know that for sure. Val reminded me today how she distanced herself from Russ because she knew God wanted differently for them. Russ distanced himself from her because he couldn't bear being near her when they didn't have a future. He didn't understand why she had to make that choice. They had a very tough time."

"I know. Val told me."

"Would you do the same for me?"

Jane couldn't look him in the eye. "I care for you, too," she admitted, her head down as she spoke the words. "These past few months have opened my eyes to so much. I've made mistakes. I've confessed my sins to God, and He's forgiven me. I'm thankful for that. I truly believe that if I allow God to control my future, it will be brighter and better than anything I ever considered."

"I'm confused, too, Jane. I love you and can't tell you how happy I am that you've given your life over to God. But I'm afraid you're still grieving for Garrett."

"Why would you think that?" she demanded, sitting up and looking at him. After a brief silence, she said, "I suppose it does seem that way. I don't know if what I feel is grief or anger for what he did to us."

"You two had a lot of unresolved issues. Do you think your marriage would have survived if he were still alive?"

"I made a commitment," she said. "I would have done everything possible to keep us together, but I doubt Garrett would have done the same. Whatever his reasons for being attracted to me, Garrett knew I wasn't like the other girls. He would have left me for someone more exciting eventually."

"I doubt he'd find anyone more exciting," Heath said. How could she not see that about herself?

"I was a child. Immature and thought I was invincible."

Then Jane shared the truth of her first experience with Garrett. Emotions like he'd never known washed over him. The desire to protect her from future hurt was foremost in his heart.

"I can't believe he did that to you."

"You walked away from temptation, but if you'd stayed that night, don't you think things would have gotten out of control?"

"I know they would have."

"Every time Garrett threatened to find someone else, I believed he would. My insecurities precipitated an action that made me a woman before my time. Mistake or not, I couldn't go back. I was so ashamed. Knowing I'd disappointed God only made it worse."

"Is that why you said I don't consider you wife material?"

"Yes. And because you. . ."

"I saved myself for the woman God intended, and I'm pretty sure that woman is you. You don't have to worry about the one you love loving you back. Working so closely with you with my doubts has been difficult, but I couldn't bear not having you close either. I love you."

"Are you sure?"

He smiled and touched her cheek gently. "Very much so. I've loved you from afar for years, but I never considered there was any hope of us becoming a couple."

"Maybe not then," she admitted. "But things changed when you came back into my life. There's so much about you that I admire and love."

"So where do we go from here?"

"Where do you want to go?"

"I want to get to know Jane Kendrick Holt better. I'd like to be 100 percent sure that we're ready for our future. Once we're sure, I want to settle down and raise a family."

"What you see is what you get," she warned. "I've renewed my relationship with Christ, but I'm still human. I've been a wife and mother, and I can't go back to the innocence you once told me you wanted in your future bride. But I can promise to commit completely to you, and there's nothing in life I'd love more than to be your wife and the mother of your children."

"You agree that we need to take our time and do this right?"

She nodded. "I jumped in over my head when I was just a child and nearly drowned in all that misery I brought upon myself. I want to go into this relationship with my eyes open and my heart ready to receive all the love you have to offer. I need you to feel the same."

Chapter 15

November turned into December, and if possible, Heath felt as if every day of his life got better and better. He and Jane had their alone times, but they also spent a lot of time with Sammy. Forming a bond with her was important to their future. He loved Sammy and wanted them both to know he would never put her aside for another child.

The future seemed to be constantly on his mind. If he intended to have a family, he needed to think about finding a job. He had the money Val had given him for graduation, but how could he utilize it successfully to provide for all their needs? The most logical choice was to find a position that paid him a regular salary with benefits.

Of course that presented the probability of leaving Paris, which created yet another problem. He didn't want a long-distance relationship. He'd spent too much time apart from Jane. He knew she'd probably move to wherever he went, but she was happy living and working at the farm. Maybe they could discuss it after the New Year and come to some sort of agreement.

Hand in hand, they strolled through the antique store. "Val's already talking about how we'll decorate the house," Jane said. "She plans to have a big party. Sammy won't know what to think with so many Christmas celebrations."

The lack of space in their old house had limited the decorating. This year would be a first in many ways. "Our family has great plans for your daughter."

"Just remember our apartment is not very large."

"Then we'll have to give her a big playhouse."

She looked at him askance.

"Just kidding. No one's mentioned a playhouse," Heath said. "At least not yet."

~

Jane found herself looking forward to the holidays more than she had in years. Except for a couple of small weddings in the downstairs portion of the house, Your Wedding Place had pretty much gone on hiatus until spring. Jane didn't mind much since the focus shifted to decorating the house.

They cut tons of boxwood and holly from the gardens, and Cindy had taught them how to turn it into wreaths and garlands. The green garland combined with ribbons and miniature white lights made an impressive display both on the outside and inside of the house.

They saved the tree for last, and Val spent days coming up with the perfect decorations for the massive evergreen that would sit in the drawing room. She wanted smaller trees throughout the house and kept Jane busy coming up with ideas. The one tree that stayed the same was the family tree in the den. Those decorations were a collection of things the Truelove children had made over the years, and there was a great deal of laughter as they decorated the tree. Jane was touched when Cindy and Sammy made dough ornaments for them to include on the tree.

They found boxes of old decorations left behind by the Sheridans' son and enjoyed their beauty. "Val feels guilty over using these," Jane told Heath as they admired the glass ball ornaments.

"William obviously didn't want them."

"She says they're treasures."

"You know what they say about trash and treasure. Have you decorated your tree yet?"

"We have a little tree with nonbreakable ornaments. I've warned Sammy not to touch anything in here."

Heath grinned. "I'm sure she'll heed your warning when one of these beautiful ornaments calls her name."

"That's why these rooms are off-limits without adult supervision. I can't afford to replace them."

"They were free, remember?"

She reached for another box. "Mrs. Sheridan liked variety. I've never seen so much stuff."

"They hosted lots of parties. I'm sure she liked to vary her decorations."

"Did you see the carousel horses? Val has those on the tree in her office."

Heath shifted the boxes out of the way and sat down next to her on the sofa. "What should I get Sammy for Christmas? I tried thinking like a two-year-old, but I came up blank."

"She loves Horsie. You did good with that."

"What about a rocking horse? One of those stuffed ones that resembles the real thing."

"As long as we don't have to feed and comb it, I'm sure she'd love one."

"Is that a hint not to buy her a pony?"

Jane dropped the handful of ornament hooks she was trying to separate into the box. "I know your family really wants her to have one, but she needs to wait until she's old enough to care for a pet."

"I suppose puppies and kittens are off-limits, too?"

"Please, Heath, there are days when one little girl nearly stretches me to the limit. She can play with the animals you already have."

"Okay, I'll put the word out."

"Thanks."

"What about you? What would you like?"

"Peace and goodwill. This will be the first year Sammy really knows what's going on, and seeing her enjoy herself is really all I want. I pray her grandparents feel the same."

"Any word on Clarice?"

"She's trying. She really is," Jane said earnestly. "She wanted to buy Sammy a Christmas dress and actually called to ask my opinion."

"She's shopping?"

"From catalogs."

"Sounds like a step in the right direction."

"It's a giant leap," Jane said. "In all the years I've known her, Clarice has never been interested in my opinion on anything."

"Sounds like you might get your Christmas wish this year. So you'll be staying with them for a few days before and heading for your parents' afterward?"

"Val gave me two weeks' vacation. We'll see the Holts and come home for Christmas."

"Home?"

"Here at the farm. I want Sammy to sleep in her bed on Christmas Eve. We'll leave for Colorado the day after Christmas."

"You'll be exhausted."

"I know. I'd love to stay home, but if the family won't or can't come to us, we have to go there."

"At least Sammy will get to be in the church Christmas program."

Jane thought about her budding starlet and chuckled. "I have no idea what she'll come out with onstage. They tried her costume on her last night, and she didn't want to take it off. Maybe you should get her some dress-up outfits. Thank goodness, she's not in the live nativity. Though I'm still not sure why I let you talk me into that."

"Because you love the Lord and want to do good works in His name."

"I do," Jane agreed. Secretly she looked forward to dressing as Mary and kneeling next to Baby Jesus with Heath at her side as Joseph.

"Don't your parents want you there for Christmas?"

"Mom and I usually end up arguing. She treats me like a child and questions my judgment. I'd just as soon not hear it through the holidays."

"How do you plan to handle that?"

"With lots of prayer. I'm hoping she's seen enough of a change in our recent conversations to know that I'm trying. She has to trust me, too."

"What happens if she doesn't?"

"I've got it under control." She stuck out her tongue at him. "See the teeth marks?"

Heath grinned. "Don't bite too hard, or talking back won't be a problem."

"I always feel like I have to defend myself."

"You'll see it differently when Sammy starts telling you no," Heath said.

"She already does."

"And it's cute now, but she needs to know you mean business. Sorry. I shouldn't tell you how to parent."

Jane smiled at him. "I know I let her get away with too much, but she's so little and so cute."

"She is that. Perhaps you should consider talking openly about the past with your mother."

"You mean tell her what happened that night?" Jane couldn't help but wonder how her mother would react to that news after all this time. Jane had a feeling her mom would be even more upset because she hadn't told them the truth.

"That and what you want from the future."

"I want the same things I wanted back then. Except now my hopes center around Sammy's needs more than my own. I suppose in a way I understand Mom's feelings. When she questions my choices, she questions herself. I'm sure she thinks if she'd prepared me better I wouldn't have made mistakes."

Heath shook his head. "Mistakes aren't something we can avoid. What do you think about me going with you to visit your parents?"

Jane appeared startled. "Why would you want to?"

"I think it's time I met them, and they won't come here. I thought I'd fly up for the last day of your visit and return home with you and Sammy."

"No. Let's go together. You do need to get to know them, and they need to know you."

Chapter 16

When the remote control car bounced off her leg, Jane looked up to find Heath leaning against the door frame, grinning at her.

"Hey, I'm still learning how to drive the thing. Merry Christmas!"

Jane and Sammy had returned home from Florida in plenty of time to join the Truelove family's Christmas Eve celebration. After a delicious traditional dinner, they moved the celebration to the drawing room.

A gift rested in the body of the toy truck. The beautifully wrapped and beribboned package reeked of an elegant store's salesperson's abilities.

"You shouldn't have," she said, all the while ripping away the paper. Jane tried not to show her disappointment when the gift turned out to be a box of chocolates. "Thank you. I love them."

Heath crossed the room and sat next to her on the love seat. "Aren't you going to share?"

She held the unopened box out to him.

He pushed it back into her hands. "You have to take the first piece."

Jane noticed the way everyone in the room watched them as she pulled the outer wrapping off the box and lifted the lid. Dumbfounded, she stared down at the velvet bed stuffed where a piece of candy had previously rested. The round solitaire diamond with smaller diamonds around the band glittered against the chocolate and was the most beautiful thing she'd ever seen.

"Hope you don't mind that I already ate a piece," Heath said with a big grin. "Do you like it?"

"I love it."

He pulled the ring from the box and dropped to one knee right there in front of his entire family and asked, "Jane Kendrick Holt, will you do me the honor of becoming my wife?"

"Oh yes!" she cried, flinging her arms around his neck. "I thought you'd never ask."

He slid the ring on her finger, and laughter filled the room as the others came over to offer their congratulations.

"I can't believe you did this," Jane said later when he walked them home. Sammy slept against Heath's shoulder, and he held Jane's hand in his.

"I wanted you to understand just how serious I am."

"Does this mean you're ready to set a date?" She wanted him to say yes.

"Not right away. I still have to make provisions for supporting you and Sammy. I have to find a job and. . ."

"You have a job," she protested. "One you enjoy. I see no reason for you to give it up."

"I have to provide for my family."

"You will. We can work together with Val on her project."

"The pavilion is nearly finished."

"It needs to be landscaped. I know you have great plans for that. Then there's the other structure she plans. And all those new gardens. Why not see them through?"

"This project could go on for years."

"And I'm sure Val would be willing to tell everyone what a tremendous job you've done. You don't have to take a stodgy office job if that's not what you want. Find a way to use your degree to do something you enjoy. Life is too short to be miserable because that's what you think other people expect."

"Do you want to live in a garage apartment and not have the things you deserve because your husband is following his dream?"

Jane held up her hand. The porch light reflected off the beautiful ring. "Accepting this gives me responsibility as well. I'd rather you be happy and content than have things I don't need. Don't make the sacrifice for me, Heath. I don't want it."

He carried Sammy in and put her to bed, pausing long enough to kiss Jane good night before he left for home. The unresolved situation caused her to lose sleep that night, and she determined to track Heath down the following morning and continue the discussion. Then again, they were scheduled to fly to Colorado in two days. There would be plenty of time to discuss it on the plane.

∾

And discuss it they did. Jane remained resolute in her determination that she didn't care what he did so long as he was happy doing it.

She hadn't mentioned their engagement to her parents, and they were shocked when she called to ask if there was room for Heath.

"What's going on, Jane? You're not living with him, are you? I won't have you sharing a bedroom in my home."

Jane almost laughed at her mother's comments. "No, Mother. It's not that type of relationship. I suppose you could say we're considering a future together."

"Considering? You either are or aren't, Jane."

"Okay. He's asked me to marry him, and I said yes. I wanted to surprise you." Her mother didn't say anything.

"Mom?"

"I want to be happy for you, Jane. It's just that you've. . .well, you haven't always made the best choices."

"Just give me a chance, Mom. And you'll like Heath. I promise."

"When will you be arriving?"

Chapter 17

R eady?" Tears of joy filled her eyes as Jane nodded. In minutes she would become Mrs. Heath Truelove, and the thought filled her with extreme joy. The last few months had been better than Jane could have imagined.

She truly had witnessed the miracle of Christmas this year. The Holts, the Trueloves, even her parents had made the holiday memorable in ways she'd never forget. Next to Heath's proposal, the best gifts she'd gotten for Christmas were the pleasurable time spent with everyone and hearing her mother say she'd chosen wisely. There was no question her dad liked Heath. They had clicked immediately. Her father was very impressed with Heath's business acumen and told Jane he would go far in life.

Heath hadn't given up on his quest to convince Jane to talk with her mother. While the men helped Sammy build a snowman in the front yard, they sat in the living room and talked. After telling the story she'd kept secret for all those years, Jane explained that she accepted complete responsibility for what had happened. Tears fell as her mother apologized for pushing her into marriage and deserting her when she needed her most.

Jane told her parents that she'd found her way back to the Lord because of Heath and the Trueloves, and she hoped never to get lost again. They expressed their gratitude for all he and his family had done for her and Sammy.

When Russ proposed to Val on Valentine's Day, Jane was so happy for her friend. Every day it seemed as if Val came up with some new plan for her wedding, and Jane wished she and Heath could set the date and move forward with their lives. Val and Russ set the date for their June wedding and hired Maddy as their wedding planner. Opie finally overcame the bronchitis and bout of pneumonia that had plagued her throughout the winter and planned to cater the event from the pavilion kitchen.

They continued working with Val. Heath had plans in place for the pavilion, and they waited for a break in the weather to start work on the landscape. She knew Heath still had doubts about providing for their future. Jane wished he understood that she didn't care what he did as long as he was content.

She'd never forget the moment they chose their wedding date. The sun had finally broken through on the late March morning, and they watched from their seats on the steps as the contractors laid patio stones around the pavilion.

"You're going to have a spectacular wedding locale," Jane said.

Val nodded. "Russ and I were talking, and he suggested I throw this out there to you. We wondered if you would like to get married on the same day."

Jane looked expectantly at Heath.

He shrugged and said, "Okay with me."

Just that easily they had joined in the excitement of planning a wedding. At first Jane had been apprehensive that her simple wedding would conflict with Val's elaborate plans, but in the end it had all worked out. The rehearsal last night had gone perfectly, and Jane knew this time her wedding memories would be wonderful.

"Don't cry," her father said, using his handkerchief to dab away the tears. "Your mom will be upset if you have raccoon eyes in your wedding pictures."

She managed a misty smile as she assured him her mascara was waterproof. At times the road to forgiveness became a long journey, but Jane knew that with God's help she had arrived at her final destination.

"Where is she?"

"She wanted you to have the earrings she wore on our wedding day. She left them in our bedroom at the house. I can't get over how scatterbrained she's been this week."

Jane smiled at him, and he squeezed the hands he held in his.

"You're a beautiful bride," James Kendrick said. "This is what I wanted for you, Jane. I was so disappointed when you and Garrett were married in that civil ceremony."

"I know, Daddy. I'm sorry."

"I love you, Jane. I only want the best for you. Your mother and I know we played a role in those choices you made. We should have been less trusting and more involved in your life. We realize we depended on you to make decisions you weren't old enough to make."

"You'd only have known what I wanted you to know. I hid the truth. I knew better, but I let myself get into a situation that changed my life. I stood by my decisions, though."

"You did, and I'm proud of you and what you've accomplished. God has blessed you with a good man who loves you and Sammy. Heath will be a good provider."

Jane had no doubt about that. Heath finally got it when her dad told him the same thing after the rehearsal dinner last night. The Trueloves were very supportive and even suggested they move into the old family home. When they agreed, Val insisted on doing a few upgrades, and Jane looked forward to raising their family in the house where Heath had grown up.

When she said yes to Heath's proposal, Jane never considered a formal wedding. She thought second marriages should be low-key. Heath had other ideas. He insisted that with a sister in the wedding business they would never get away with simple. Jane knew it wasn't what he wanted anyway. As romantic as his name, Heathcliff Truelove wanted their minister to marry them in the sight of God and all their family and friends.

When she tried to get out of buying a wedding dress, the female members of the Truelove family and her mother banded together and took her shopping.

Someone had once told her that when you put on *the* dress you knew, and she certainly had. Simple but classy, the lace illusion halter followed her form in a fitted style with a swiss dot tulle overlay. The Watteau train attached to the top of the gown and trailed out behind her. A stylist had done her hair at the house that morning, and it was bigger than usual to support the tiara the Truelove women had insisted she must wear.

"Whew," Wendy Kendrick declared as she raced from stairway. "Will you wear these?"

Jane looked at the earrings her mother placed in her hand. She remembered them from childhood. They had always intrigued her, but her mother had warned her they weren't toys. The fact that she trusted Jane with them now spoke volumes. She quickly removed the earrings she wore and replaced them with her mother's diamond drop earrings. Wendy dropped the others into her clutch purse.

"Perfect." Her mother kissed her cheek. "I love you, Jane."

"I love you, too, Mom."

They rode up to the pavilion's main floor together. An usher proffered his arm, and her mother winked playfully. Jane couldn't get over the difference in her since their conversation at Christmas. Wendy Kendrick took a moment to speak to Sammy before being escorted down the aisle.

Emotion surged anew at the sight of Sammy wandering aimlessly down the aisle, tossing the occasional flower as she visited with people she knew. At the rate her daughter moved, the wedding wouldn't start for hours. After a few minutes, Cindy gestured, and Sammy ran the rest of the way and climbed into her lap.

When Wendell, Russ's brother, played the first strains of Pachelbel's Canon in D on the baby grand piano, she and her father took the first step of the rest of her life.

∿

As the woman he loved walked toward him, Heath could only smile and thank God for the miracle he had been given. Never in all his life had he ever considered that Jane would one day become his wife. Always beautiful, today she came to him wearing a white wedding gown. When she argued that she shouldn't wear white, Heath reminded her that God had washed her as white as snow. She'd cried when he told her that, admitting she had feared she could never be the pure woman he sought.

She smiled at the Holts, who sat in the pew behind her mother. Heath was glad they accepted him as a stepfather for their grandchild. Jane paused to hand roses to Clarice, her mother, and then his mother to symbolize the connection of their family before she stepped before him.

"Who gives this woman in marriage?"

Her father responded, placing her hand in his. Jane smiled her glorious smile, and Heath knew nothing else mattered as long as they had each other. In their lifetime, careers would change, children would grow up and leave home, but love would sustain them. Their future would be about choices. Some good, some bad, but every decision, just as those they'd made in the past, would make them the people God wanted them to be. Heath had no doubt God had chosen Jane to be his wife and knew that, because he had listened and allowed Him to choose, their love would prosper and bear fruit in a marriage that would last a lifetime.

OPIE'S CHALLENGE

Dedication

To God be the glory—thank You for helping me
confront the challenge of writing these stories.
To Mary and Steve with love—thanks for showing me your Kentucky.
To my family—I love you all.
And as always, a special thank you to Mary and Tammy for their help.

Chapter 1

Okay, ladies, get ready. Our final bachelor of the evening is every woman's dream man. Not only does he embody the three *H*s of Paris—horses, history, and hospitality—he's a handsome hottie looking for his number one lady." The female emcee's breathy voice filled the room, "Wendell Hunter, come on out!"

"Could she use one more *H* word?" Ophelia Truelove's sarcasm gained her a look of disbelief from her sister. She shrugged and grinned.

"Wendell owns our own Hunter Farm right here in Paris. He's looking for the woman whose focus is her family and home."

While the woman extolled his virtues, he walked out onto the runway. Opie wanted to claim he strutted like a peacock but in truth, he moved with the confidence of a man comfortable in his own skin. Wendell Hunter definitely looked as good in real life as he had in the photographs she'd seen in the article that had given Val the idea to attend the bachelor auction.

He might not be handsome by most standards but possessed a magnetism that attracted women. He wore his dark brown hair short, probably to control the curl. His heavy-lidded eyes and chiseled cheekbones belied a serious expression that didn't match the frivolity of the evening, and yet he'd smiled easily enough earlier when mingling among the women in his effort to raise more money for tonight's event.

Given their rapt expressions and the way the women leaned forward in their seats, Opie knew there would be more than one taker in this room. Too bad his viewpoints regarding women's rights were rooted years in the past. Opie admitted the comments in his interview influenced her regard for Wendell Hunter. When Val asked what she was reading a few days earlier, she'd shown her the article was on Paris's most eligible bachelors. Val laughed and asked if they really had any.

"Yeah, they're having a bachelor auction fund-raiser. Look at this guy," Opie said, pointing to the page. "Wendell Hunter. He believes a woman's sole focus should be her family and home. That's so antediluvian."

"Hunter?" Val reached for the magazine. "That's my architect's brother."

Her eyebrows shot up in surprise. "Small world."

"How would you like to go to a bachelor auction?"

Opie couldn't believe her ears. Val never wasted money on frivolous activities. "Are you nuts?"

"No. I just thought it might be fun to check out Paris's most eligible bachelors."

"You want to check out your architect's brother."

"I do," she admitted.

"I don't think seeing Wendell Hunter strut the runway is going to give you much insight."

"I don't know. It might tell us more than you know. I'll buy you a new dress," Val offered. When Opie hesitated, she said, "Shoes, too."

"Okay, I'm in," Opie agreed. "But you have to buy something for yourself, as well."

They went shopping and tonight when she dressed for this event, Opie experienced second thoughts. Though she told herself they were just going to look, Opie feared it wouldn't be that simple.

While Wendell wanted a woman whose sole focus was her husband, children, and home, Opie considered the woman's role in today's world had changed. Most women obtained their education with the intention of having a career in their chosen fields. Opie looked forward to using her bachelor's degree in culinary management to achieve her life goals.

A father who worked full-time to provide for his family's needs and a stay-at-home mother had raised Opie and her six siblings. Her dad loved his job, but she often wondered if her mother had been as fulfilled with her choice. Perhaps being a mother and wife was enough for some women but not for Opie.

Given his financial status, she doubted Wendell needed a working wife. She couldn't see any place in his plan for career women. Women had come from not being able to vote to a run for the White House, but they'd never get there if they allowed men with viewpoints like his to stand in the way of their progress.

"Hey, what do you think you're doing?" Opie demanded when Val grabbed her paddle and started the bidding war. Aware that women around them watched with interest, she discreetly tried to catch Val's hand as she outbid each woman in quick succession until the auctioneer declared number 230, Ophelia Truelove, the winner.

"Have you lost your mind?" Opie hissed.

Val smiled easily. "I bought you a date."

Opie glowered at her. "This isn't funny, Val."

"It's a good cause."

She crossed her arms and declared, "I won't go." Val shrugged. "Like I said, it's a good cause. The scholarship fund gets the money regardless of whether you take advantage of the opportunity."

"Why would you do that?" Opie couldn't say why she felt so humiliated.

"You liked what you saw in that magazine. Besides, you have something to say to Mr. Hunter and after the way you went on about his interview, I thought it might take you a couple of hours to share your opinion."

A lifetime probably wouldn't be long enough. His statements irritated her, but she did find him to be handsome. She'd never admit that to Val. "All I said was I couldn't believe how old-fashioned he was."

"I think the word was *antediluvian*. Where do you come up with those words anyway?"

She glanced around and slouched in her chair when she noted several sets of eyes watching them. Some looked curious, others positively angry. Most probably wondered who they were and where they got the money to buy a date with the prize bachelor of the evening.

"There's nothing wrong with improving your vocabulary," she muttered.

Val indicated Wendell Hunter when he stepped into the room and moved in their direction. "Here comes your opportunity."

"You know I won't say anything," Opie mumbled, wishing she could sink into the floor.

"Why? Afraid you'll embarrass yourself?"

Opie's displeasure showed in her narrowed gaze and unfriendly look. "I'm already embarrassed. This is ridiculous, Val. I've never done anything like this to you."

While she admitted to her fair share of pranks on her older sister, she didn't recall ever putting Val in such an embarrassing position. Wondering if she had time to make her getaway, Opie glanced up to find Wendell Hunter only steps away.

Lack of self-esteem was not this man's problem. Even at average height, he would tower over her five-foot-two-inch height. The expensive tuxedo and carefully styled hair made him appear very different from the men she knew. She doubted he'd ever worn a baseball cap or a cowboy hat. Of course, thus far the men in her life consisted of a couple of old boyfriends, her father and brothers, male farm employees, and the chefs she came across in the course of her work.

He stopped before them and looked at Val. "You're Ophelia?"

She shook her head. "I'm Val Truelove." She pointed to her sister. "This is Ophelia."

Recognition dawned in his gaze. "You own Sheridan Farm?"

"Yes," Val agreed with a pleased smile.

He extended his hand. "Welcome to the neighborhood."

"We've been in the neighborhood since Val was a toddler," Opie said coolly. How could he live just down the road and not know they existed? Then again, if she were fair, she hadn't really known about him either. "I'm Opie. Our father managed the farm for the Sheridans."

His dark eyebrows shot up. "Jacob Truelove is your father?"

"He is," Val said before Opie could comment.

"I've met him. Mr. Sheridan always spoke very highly of your father." He focused brilliant blue eyes on Opie and said, "It's a pleasure to meet you, Ophelia. Would you care to hear what I have planned for our date?"

His formal pronunciation of her name immediately caught her attention. The name had been the bane of her existence for as long as Opie could remember. She gladly exchanged it for a nickname even if it did sound a little tomboyish.

She wanted to say no, but yes tumbled out before she could stop herself. The mystery in his eyes beckoned to her. She purposefully turned away from Val's knowing grin and concentrated on the man before her.

"I thought we would have dinner at my home," he began, smiling when he added, "If you like French cuisine, my chef is excellent."

Of course he'd have a French chef. No doubt imported straight from France. Only the best for men like Wendell Hunter. "My father wouldn't approve of me being alone with you in your home."

He didn't miss a beat. "We wouldn't be alone. My staff would be there the entire time. Or you could invite your sister along." Again, he flashed Val a friendly smile.

Could things get any worse? she wondered, feeling her cheeks grow hot. Did he feel the need to provide her with a protector or was he interested in Val? No doubt the women who came to his home didn't require a chaperone. In fact, she knew that most women in this room wouldn't want anyone around if they had an opportunity to be alone with him. "No, that won't be necessary. Your staff will be sufficient."

Opie didn't know that she'd find the nerve to comment on his article, but she didn't need witnesses along on the date.

Wendell named a date and time, and Opie accepted his business card. "I'll check my calendar and get back to you," she said.

His smile softened his otherwise austere features. He dipped his head slightly and said, "It's truly been my pleasure, ladies. Please accept my undying gratitude for saving me from the embarrassment of being left standing on the runway."

That certainly hadn't been the case. Other women flashed those paddles as determinedly as Val in their pursuit of the date. Opie didn't doubt for one moment that he knew that.

"I'm sure the ladies are very appreciative of your contribution to their fund-raising efforts," Opie offered, sharing her own saccharine-sweet smile.

∽

At home, Wendell shed the jacket and tie on the way to his office. He'd been negotiating the purchase of a stallion prior to the event and wanted to check his progress. Tonight had proved interesting. Participating in a bachelor auction, even for a charitable cause, wasn't something he wanted to do, but his longtime friend persisted until he agreed.

The young woman who bought his date definitely caught his attention. Ophelia Truelove was his type. He had a decided leaning toward beautiful, petite blond-haired women with expressive green eyes. She'd surprised him with her sarcastic reply to his welcome and became prickly when she shared that they were the daughters of the former manager of Sheridan Farm. The Trueloves now owned the farm and if what he'd seen on the news and read was fact, their wealth equaled or exceeded that of a number of people in Bourbon County.

At least Val Truelove's did.

When introducing himself, Wendell noted the two women seemed at odds. At first, he feared he'd become embroiled in some sort of feud. Both women held paddles and yet Catherine pointed out Val as the winning bidder. Had they competed for his date? He didn't think so. Val Truelove quickly declared her sister as the winner.

He found Ophelia Truelove to be a bit of a contradiction. Outspoken but sheltered if what she'd said about her father objecting to her coming to his home alone was true. Still, she'd rejected his suggestion that she bring her sister. Evidently, it would be okay so long as they weren't alone in the house.

He'd have to instruct his staff to remain that evening. Everyone but Jean-Pierre. The chef would leave as soon as he completed service. He prepared incredible food, but Wendell found his temperament less than desirable. Then, what else did one expect of a French chef? Jean-Pierre impressed his business associates and that pleased Wendell. He'd put up with artistic temperament for that.

As for the date, Catherine reminded him before the auction that it was only one night out of his life for a good cause. Wendell considered that spending a few hours in a beautiful woman's company couldn't be all bad. Pushing the evening from his thoughts, he sat down at his desk and pulled up his e-mail on the laptop. A pleased smile changed his expression when he read that he now owned a new stallion.

∾

Still fuming over Val's prank, Opie said little after they left the event.

"What calendar is it you need to check?" Val teased as they got into the car.

"I didn't care to appear overly eager," Opie offered stiffly as she fastened her seat belt.

"That was fun."

"When did watching men flaunt themselves become fun for you?"

A jangle of keys and the click of her seat belt preceded Val's response, "I appreciate that they're willing to donate their time and efforts for charity. Besides, it was a new experience for us both."

They rode in silence. Opie wanted to be angry but knew her sister intended no harm. Besides, if she hadn't made such a big deal over the article, Val would never have realized he was Russ's brother and this would never have happened.

When Val suggested they attend and threw in the offer of a new dress and shoes, Opie believed she'd gotten the better end of the deal. Instead, she now suffered the consequences of giving in to temptation.

Inviting Russ Hunter to join them for lunch last week started this. Opie knew Val didn't care to spend more time in the young architect's presence, particularly after he'd produced and presented a disappointing set of plans for Val's new business venture that same day.

But Opie needed to know more about Russ Hunter. Even though he did business with Val, she needed to form her own opinion about the man whose plans would bring changes to their longtime home.

She'd also wondered at Val's strong reaction to Russ and thought perhaps there was more to the situation than met the eye. The twins liked Russ and she did, too. She found both Hunter men to be attractive.

"Just tell me why you did it," she said, not yet willing to let the subject drop.

Val sighed. "Because you said you wanted to tell him how you felt."

"Did it occur to you that I didn't actually mean I wanted to give him a piece of my mind?"

"Then why didn't you just say no?"

Because she didn't want to refuse. Thankful for the darkness inside the car, Opie said, "You paid a lot for that date. I didn't want to appear any more stupid than I already felt."

"Why would you feel stupid?"

"Did you really look at him, Val?"

"He seemed a nice enough man."

"Exactly. A very handsome, wealthy man who probably thinks I'm the most immature child he's ever met. I can't believe I told him I couldn't be alone with him in his house."

"You can't. Daddy wouldn't allow it. But why do you care what he thinks?"

Opie wished she had the answer to that one. Maybe she didn't want to care, but she did. From the first time she saw him in the magazine and even after she'd met him in person, Wendell Hunter captured her attention in a way no other man had ever done. "Because I should be able to do whatever I want."

"Who says you can't?"

"Men like Wendell Hunter."

"There are plenty of men who don't mind working wives, Opie."

"I know, but I feel challenged to help him understand one person shouldn't limit another's possibilities."

"The future Mrs. Hunter will decide whether she wants to fulfill the role he's set forth for her."

"Will she?" Opie demanded. "What about love? What happens when a woman is attracted to a man with this kind of thought process?"

"They decide what they're willing to give up for love."

"Like Mom did?"

"I don't think Mom feels she gave up anything."

Opie believed her mother could do anything, but Cindy Truelove's focus was her husband and children. "Look at her talents, Val. She could do anything she wanted," she argued.

"Or she could do what she did and use those talents in her home to benefit her husband and children and still feel fulfilled."

Opie saw nothing wrong with being career-minded. "How is that possible? What does she have to show for all her effort?"

"A husband and seven children who love her very much."

"Do you honestly believe that's enough?"

"It is for most women. Working outside the home changed our worlds. We spend our days occupied with other responsibilities and then put them aside when we come home. Mom works 24/7. She's every bit as determined to excel as we are in our chosen fields.

"Opie, why are you struggling with this? It's not as if you're in love with Wendell Hunter. He's nearly ten years older than you."

She didn't know why she cared, but she did. "The years don't matter when you meet the right person."

Val braked, slowing down to turn into their driveway. The loud click of the signal indicator filled the sudden silence. "Are you saying you're interested in him?"

"No," Opie declared, stumbling over her hasty denial. "I just meant that an age difference wouldn't hold me back if I met the right man."

"You're a rebel, Opie Truelove. You have problems with people saying you can't do things."

"Daddy says we're determined."

"Stubborn. Determined. Tenacious," Val recited. "Call it what you want. They're all the same."

Opie's defiant nature came to life. "There's nothing wrong with being determined."

"Not as long as you seek God's plan for you. You can't decide your own fate. You can't even steer the ship."

❧

The following afternoon, Opie rifled through the top drawer of her nightstand and removed the magazine she hadn't been able to toss. It opened voluntarily to the exact page. Opie studied Wendell's photo. What did she really know about him? She couldn't say whether he possessed the qualities touted at the auction. She didn't know anything beyond what she'd read and heard and Val's comments regarding Russ's negativity toward his brother. What made him feel as he did about a woman's role in his life?

Had his mother been the ultimate homemaker? Not likely, Opie thought. Considering their wealth, if anything, he'd lived with options she'd never imagined as a child of working-class parents. His mother could have been a socialite. Opie remembered the parties at the Sheridans' mansion. Surely as neighbors with common interests, the Hunters were regulars on their guest list.

Not that she'd ever been there to see who attended. Opie remembered asking her dad why they were never invited. The question generated her first lesson on social status. Despite her father's efforts to make her understand that workers and employers didn't move in the same circles, Opie hadn't understood. Too smart for her own good, she'd reminded him they went to the annual Christmas party.

"Because that party is for the staff," her dad said. "There are places for everyone in this world, Opie. The rich don't rub elbows with the poor." She'd kept on with the questions until he grew tired. He sent her off to ask her mother, who gave her the same answers.

Maybe guaranteed entrée into any party of her choice motivated her to become a chef. She intended to do great things in the culinary world. One day, people would be happy to have Opie Truelove's name on their guest lists.

She considered the pros and cons of accepting the invitation. No reasons to refuse came to mind. He'd even chosen a Tuesday night, which meant she couldn't claim church conflict. Opie glanced at the photo again. She wanted to go out with Wendell Hunter.

When he answered the cell number on his business card, she said, "Hi, it's Opie Truelove. I'm calling about our date."

Chapter 2

"You eat like this every day?"

Wendell shook his head and chuckled. "This special dinner is in your honor. My way of showing my appreciation for your contribution. Too many of these meals, and my clothes wouldn't fit."

Earlier, when she walked into the drawing room, Wendell couldn't take his eyes off her. She carried herself confidently, wearing a fitted white shirt with a black skirt and high heels that suited her slender, willowy body. He took a few steps forward to accept her hand, noting the short nails nicely buffed to a shine. She smiled, and he stared at her delicate facial features and full lips. Her shiny shoulder-length blond hair framed her face. Definitely his type.

When he signed up for the date, Wendell enlisted Jean-Pierre's help in creating a menu worthy of his charitable contribution. His chef had not let him down. Over canapés of *tapanade* and crab with lemon, Ophelia and Wendell conversed comfortably on a variety of subjects. When offered an aperitif, Ophelia requested tap water.

After moving into the dining room, Wendell watched her eat his favorite, an entrée of *terrine de filets de sole*. Most of his guests ate and enjoyed the food, but she savored every bite. He'd never dined with anyone as expressive as Ophelia. Her auditory sighs and frequent exclamations of praise would make anyone consider her an extreme foodie.

When the server placed the *coq au vin* second course before her, she used her hand to waft the odor and inhaled. Pleasure filled her delicate expression. She tore a piece of french bread from the loaf on her bread plate. "Oh, I'd enjoy this excuse for outgrowing my clothes." She took a bite. "This is wonderful."

Wendell supposed her career choice would be reason enough for her love of food. She'd spoken of her recent graduation from culinary school and plans for the future. "What made you become a chef?" he asked.

"Food is my passion," she offered.

Wendell considered it a trite reason for choosing such a complex career. "Wouldn't most chefs make that claim?"

Ophelia shrugged, tilting her head to the side as she spoke. She pushed the bangs of her silky blond hair from her eyes. "I suppose, but in my case it's true. For as long as I can remember, I've wanted nothing more than to cook. When we were little and Mama ordered us outside so she could prepare a meal, I pleaded with her to let me stay. I pored over cookbooks as if they were great literature, planning the meals that I would one day prepare."

"No toys?" he asked.

"My best-ever Christmas present was a toy oven. Everyone loved my little cakes. Of course, they checked first to make sure they were the real thing and not those dirt cakes I sometimes made when I didn't have ingredients for the others."

He chuckled. "Surely you never got anyone to eat those."

She laughed, shaking her head. "No. They usually threw them at me when they realized what I'd done. Mom taught me to bake when she realized I'd bankrupt them with my supply requests."

Wendell had never known a woman who admitted to making mud pies. Despite his love for the farm, he couldn't claim any special affinity with the soil. "So you've cooked since childhood?"

"Not as often as I would have liked," Ophelia admitted, her focus shifting from the food to him. "I knew early on that I wanted to work with food but had no idea how to get started. When I was fourteen, I cornered one of the Sheridans' caterers. She was up to her eyeballs in hors d'oeuvres and short one of her wait staff. She didn't have time for an inquisitive kid.

"When she asked if I wanted to make a few dollars, I told her I'd rather learn how to prepare the food. She agreed and gave me three or four lessons in exchange for working that night. I picked up quickly, and we worked together for a couple of years."

He nodded, impressed by her willingness to go after what she desired.

"When I got my driver's license, I took a summer job in Paris," she continued. "I convinced the diner owner that I'd rather cook on the grill than serve, and he agreed to let me try. It wasn't easy, but I did it well."

Wendell noted her self-confidence. He'd witnessed that very same characteristic in Jean-Pierre. Wendell appreciated that the chef did his job well even when his bad language and erratic behaviors left something to be desired. "Are you an obnoxious chef?"

She smiled her thanks to the server who replaced her plate with the *salade d'endives, noix et roquefort*, endive salad with walnuts and roquefort cheese. "I suppose I could be if the situation demanded. I don't shout and curse if that's what you mean."

"It's a stressful occupation," he allowed.

"There are ways to overcome the stress."

She ate every bite of the endive salad and dipped her finger into the remaining dressing a couple of times.

Curious about her behavior, he asked, "Would you like more?"

Pushing the plate away, she colored slightly. "Sorry. My mom would tell you my atrocious table manners are an occupational hazard. I was trying to determine what's in the dressing."

He found it intriguing that anyone could identify all the flavors on their plate. "Did you?"

A tiny frown touched her expressive face. "There's a little something extra I can't place."

"Impressive." He sipped his drink. Next Jean-Pierre sent out a cheese plate of Chevretine, Camembert, and Roquefort with baguette slices. "So tell me why they pointed your sister out to me as Ophelia Truelove."

"Val used my paddle to bid on you."

Confused, he asked, "So the date was with her?"

"No, she bought the date for me."

"You mean as a favor?"

She paused and then admitted, "More of a prank."

Aha, he had noticed something between the two of them. In a way, Wendell found their juvenile behavior humorous, but he didn't appreciate feeling used either. "Why would she do that?"

She leaned forward, confiding the truth. "When I first read about you in the magazine, I voiced my opinion about your comments to Val. She had met your brother and said we should attend the auction. Do you truly believe what you said?"

Her reference to Russ caught Wendell by surprise. He had not seen his half brother since their parents' death and found it interesting that he now worked for the Trueloves. "I shared what I'm seeking in a wife so, yes, I do believe that."

"To clean your house and nurture your children?"

Finding her appraisal somewhat insulting, Wendell emphasized, "She would manage our home. The staff would carry out her instructions."

"The staff," Ophelia repeated, almost mocking him. "They have names, you know."

"Yes, I do know. Some have been with me since my childhood."

"What does nurture your children mean?" she persisted. "Give birth and get them walking and talking before shipping them off to heaven only knows where?"

Ophelia's gaze fixed on him. He noted her eyes matched the tiny emerald earrings she wore. Not understanding her determination to dissect him, Wendell answered anyway. "It's loving our children and providing for their needs. And while boarding school is a tradition in my family, that will be a decision we make together."

She nodded. "I thought so. I never saw any reference to you at public school." Before he could comment, Ophelia continued to question him about his personal viewpoints. "What if your wife wants her own career? How would that fit into your plan?"

Exasperated, Wendell said stiffly, "There is no plan. We all have ideas of what we desire in a life partner. I intend to choose carefully."

"How do you find such an ideal partner? It's not as if you can go to the store and pick up the ingredients for the perfect wife. She'll be some woman to meet your stringent requirements."

Her comment angered Wendell. She didn't know him well enough to make that call. He considered his initial assessment of Ophelia. The confidence of youth allowed her to make brash judgments. Though some were right on target, other generalities bothered him.

"So let me get this straight. You're taking this stand against my beliefs for all women?"

She looked perturbed. "No." Before she ducked her head, he caught a glimpse of tightened lips and narrowed gaze. "I can only speak for myself. But I do believe no one should limit another's dreams."

"Surely I'm not the first man you know who made such statements?"

"Well, no."

"Then why do you feel the need for this personal attack?"

Her head dropped. "I don't know." She focused on removing bread crumbs from the tablecloth. "Maybe your interview pushed me over the edge."

"Again, why me?"

"I don't know," she repeated, a distinctive edge to her voice.

"Do you always speak first and apologize later?"

Her head jerked up. "I didn't apologize."

"But you will once you realize how wrong you are."

Her head tilted to the side. "How do you know that?"

"Because your parents taught you right from wrong."

"Is it your turn to analyze me?"

He idly moved his glass as he responded.

"Is that what we've been doing?"

Ophelia sighed heavily. "I only want to understand why you feel as you do."

Wendell wasn't used to explaining himself. "May I ask why?"

"Because I believe women should have the same opportunities as men. No woman should be required to play house and rock babies if she wants more out of life."

She threw down the words like a gauntlet, as if expecting him to battle for his rights. "That's your prerogative Ophelia. Just as believing as I do is my right."

"Surely you knew your date would ask questions based on that article."

Wendell smiled. "Most women aren't so curious." She flushed, and he regretted that he'd embarrassed her. "You obviously came here tonight with your own agenda. I'm thinking that might have been to tell me how outdated you consider me to be."

She grimaced. "That obvious, huh?"

"Let's just say you aren't as practiced in womanly wiles as some of your female counterparts."

Another blush, this time with a rise of spirit. "Nor am I likely to be. I told Val this would be embarrassing. I told you it was a prank, but honestly she saw how irritated I got when I read your article and took me at my word when I said I'd like to give you a piece of my mind. I wondered if you even thought about how you could limit some woman's dreams."

"I would hope her love for me would be the most important factor."

Her icy stare reproved him. "It doesn't bother you that love could stand in the way of your wife's fulfillment?"

"I plan to choose carefully. The woman I marry will want the same things I want in life."

Ophelia shook her head. "Maybe, or it could be her love for you will force her to give up the things that make her happy."

Wendell was attracted to educated, well-spoken women. He'd never ruled out a woman focused on her career. "When you meet the man of your dreams, what happens when your desires clash? Do you say no thanks or try to make the relationship work?"

He could see from Ophelia's expression that he'd made his point.

"I'd try to make it work. I'm sorry, Wendell. My parents would be horrified if they knew how I'd behaved tonight."

The dawning realization in her eyes revealed her distress. "Don't be. I admire your willingness to take on things you don't agree with even if I don't feel my thinking is flawed. My future wife will fulfill a much greater role in my life. She'll be my support, my friend, my confidant, the reason I live. I'll fulfill those same roles for her."

A sad smile touched her expressive face. "And I've wasted your evening by coming here when you could have met that woman instead."

"It's not likely I'd look for the woman of my dreams at a bachelor auction," Wendell said. "I've enjoyed our evening, Ophelia." Her youthful, spirited beauty touched him. Perhaps if she were older or he younger. . . "It is important to consider a woman's expectations of life. You've reminded me not to be selfish."

"I enjoyed this evening, too." Her admission made her smile. "There's so much I want for women, and I wanted you to understand. I've enjoyed seeing your home, too. I remember coming here and thinking how grand it was from the outside. Your mother was leaving and didn't invite me in."

Wendell knew she'd never met his mother. "My mom died before you were born." He could almost see her mind working. "Nicole was Russ's mother. My father's second wife," he explained. "My mother, Meredith, lived at Hunter Farm a brief time."

"Was she sick?"

Wendell didn't like remembering the senseless loss of his mother. Maybe if his father had been around to take care of her, she'd be alive today. "The diagnosis was complications from pneumonia."

"Losing her must have been difficult."

He nodded. "I was three. I don't remember a lot about her."

They concentrated on the meal until Wendell asked, "What were you looking for when you came here tonight, Ophelia?"

"Please stop calling me that. I prefer Opie."

Wendell refused to use the unsuitable tomboyish nickname. He shook his head. "It doesn't fit."

She sighed deeply before answering his earlier question. "I don't know. My future husband will need to understand how important my career is to me. We'll share roles in our home. Whether it's doing chores or raising our children. If we have children. I'm not even sure I want to be a mother."

"No children?" Wendell asked, appalled that she'd consider a career more important than motherhood. "That's a woman's most fulfilling role."

Once more, she rose to the challenge. "How do you know what fulfills a woman? Did whoever raised you with those archaic viewpoints tell you that?"

He didn't much care for her insisting his point of view was ancient. "Why wouldn't you want children?"

"I'm fourth out of seven childern. Right smack in the middle."

He frowned and shrugged. "What does that have to do with becoming a mother? Loving and caring for your siblings is nothing like loving a child you've created with the man you love. A child you've nurtured inside your body." Even as he spoke, Wendell couldn't help but question what qualified him as an expert on the matter. He didn't have children.

"I haven't totally ruled it out. I have a lot to accomplish before I do. I'm only twenty-three."

Wendell thought she sounded a bit defensive. "Ah, I'm thirty-two."

"Men don't have the same problem with biological clocks," she reminded.

"Still, I'd prefer to look like my children's father rather than their grandfather."

She laughed at his droll response, and Wendell enjoyed the pleasant sound. "Why have you waited so long?"

"Sometimes things don't happen when we want. No matter how differently we plan. So what do you plan for your career?"

"There's a world of possibilities. I've considered opening a restaurant at the farm."

"Why not Paris?" Wendell had heard rumors of plans underway at Sheridan Farm and hated to think what the Trueloves might be planning to do to their peaceful community.

"I think coming to a horse farm would give it a unique flavor. Patrons would be drawn to the glorious scenery."

"It's too much," Wendell declared with a shake of his head. "All those people filling our roads would destroy the ambiance of the area."

Before she could respond, the server entered and asked, "Is there anything else, sir?"

Wendell smiled at the woman and said, "We'll take our dessert and coffee in the drawing room."

"Would you relay my compliments to the chef?" Opie requested when the woman started to leave.

"Please ask Jean-Pierre to join us," Wendell instructed.

Ophelia appeared pleased by his request. When the chef entered the room, she said, "My compliments on the meal. The food was some of the best I've ever eaten. That vinaigrette dressing was out of control. There was a little something I couldn't identify."

"Miss Truelove shares your love of fine cuisine, Jean-Pierre," Wendell said. "She's also a chef."

Something stirred inside when Opie looked at him and smiled, showing he'd pleased her with his acknowledgment. Jean-Pierre bowed slightly and greeted her, "I'm honored, chef. As for the recipe, my dear *grand-mère* made me promise to keep the secret in the family. But alas, I have no heir."

"It would be mankind's loss that such a fabulous dressing would cease to be served," she countered.

Jean-Pierre's eyes twinkled with merriment. "Ah, not only a beautiful woman but one with a discerning palate. I can see I need to watch my step or you'll charm the recipe right from my lips."

"I can only hope you continue your line," she offered with laughter in her voice. "Otherwise, it will be a terrible loss to the culinary world."

"Perhaps if I do not, I might be tempted to leave my secret to one so lovely as you."

"I would be most honored," she said, flashing him another huge smile.

"We should discuss our mutual love of food at a future time," he suggested.

Ophelia's pleased smile spoke volumes. "I would love to talk food with a fellow chef."

Wendell watched their exchange with interest and experienced a jolt of dissatisfaction at the thought of the two chefs coming together for any reason.

Jean-Pierre bowed slightly. "Again, I thank you, mademoiselle."

"The pleasure was mine. A truly memorable dining experience."

After the pleased chef disappeared back into the kitchen, Wendell pulled back her chair and gestured toward the drawing room across the hall. "I've never heard Jean-Pierre talk that much. Perhaps I should ask for his recipe file. Though I doubt I'd be nearly as successful with my request. He loves his Parisian grandmother a great deal."

She placed her napkin on the table and stood, looking up at Wendell. "Paris, Kentucky to Paris, France. A world away."

"Yes, but we are connected. They renamed our beautiful area to reflect appreciation to the French for their assistance during the Revolutionary War. Would you care to see more of the house?" he asked. "I'm very proud of my home."

"Val said Russ seems particularly fond of the farm as well."

Wendell knew curiosity prompted her to make the comment. "I haven't seen Russ since our parents died. How is he?"

"He seems fine. Family is important, you know."

"Interesting you would say that. It doesn't conform to your plan not to have children."

"I didn't say I wouldn't have a child or two, but they will have a working mother if I do."

Something caught in his chest when an almost flirtatious smile touched her face. He'd have to be careful around this one, Wendell thought, cupping her elbow with his hand. Their conversation over dinner challenged him, and he didn't doubt she could hold her own in any discussion. "Isn't every mother a working mother?"

"You know what I mean."

"I do and I apologize for teasing you. Exactly what is your sister planning?"

She paused to study the portrait hanging in the entry hallway and glanced at him.

"My father," Wendell said.

"You resemble him a great deal. Val's plans are still in early stages, and she's asked us not to discuss them until things are finalized."

"I see."

Wendell led her through the lower floors of the house he'd called home all his years. From the moment he'd welcomed her, Wendell had been aware of her seeking gaze. She'd been outspoken about the home's beauty.

The elegantly decorated drawing room had changed little over the years. Comfortable sofas replaced the antique settees, but most of the home's original features remained. From all accounts, his mother loved those details. Wendell took great comfort in knowing Nicole had not managed to remove Meredith Hunter from the house.

Wendell showed her the library and the sitting room office his mother claimed as her own. While he didn't doubt she'd like to see the upper floor, Wendell knew Ophelia would never ask.

She touched the artfully carved banister as they walked by and said, "These old homes are beautiful."

He nodded agreement and asked, "Do you plan to live in the Sheridan house? It's quite palatial."

"We haven't decided."

Why would they buy such a grand home and not live there? "I always appreciated coming home to this house."

"It's magnificent."

Wendell agreed. "Shall we take our coffee on the porch?"

The porch wrapped around the grand old manor house, overlooking a beautiful garden area. A number of trees hid the working areas of the farm in the distance. The rockers moved easily on the bricked floor as they enjoyed the evening much as previous generations of families had done.

"You'd like the kitchen," he said. "I upgraded to a commercial kitchen when Jean-Pierre agreed to work for me."

"Where did you find him?"

"He worked for an elderly relative. When she died, I talked him into moving to the States."

"I'm sure he appreciates the modernized kitchen. I can hardly wait to have my own. Our kitchen is my mother's domain."

"You mean a restaurant kitchen?"

"Maybe." She shrugged. "I'm not exactly sure what I want to do. I have a million ideas and the list grows daily."

"I thought you wanted a restaurant on the farm?"

She twisted the silver ring on her finger as she spoke. "I want to cook."

"Don't you do that at home?"

"Not like I want. Mom prepares very basic meals. I have to work hard to convince her to allow me to try something new."

Why would a mother send her daughter to culinary school and not allow her to cook at home? "But you're trained. Why wouldn't she want you to prepare the dishes you've learned?"

She laughed at the thought. "I think she's afraid I'll serve them something weird."

"So you're not a horse person like your father?"

"I love horses. They're beautiful animals, but there's a difference between having horses for business and enjoyment. A few of our friends couldn't imagine having access to horses you never rode."

"You don't ride?" Wendell found her comment curious. He'd ridden since he was a young boy. He accepted the cup of coffee and the *profiteroles au chocolat*, pastry with vanilla ice cream and hot chocolate sauce, from the server.

"We rode in our limited spare time. We had chores around the home and the farm. Organized activities our parents planned to keep us out of trouble."

"Did you ever go to the races?" She shook her head and he asked, "Never?" His world revolved around the industry.

"My dad has very strong feelings about gambling."

"Didn't your sister win the lottery?"

"Yes, but she didn't buy the ticket."

"So how does one come by a winning lottery ticket without making a purchase?"

"One's boss gives it to them as a gift."

Wendell admired Ophelia's boldness as she mocked him. "Now that's an incredible gift."

"Actually Val considers it the answer to a prayer. She asked God to keep us at Sheridan Farm if it was His will."

He noted her reference to God. "You're a religious family?"

She nodded. "Very much so. I noticed the grand piano in the drawing room. Do you play?"

He inclined his head. "I do. My father said my mother said I would play the piano."

"How did she know?"

"Like you, my favorite toys were tiny pianos. Evidently, I banged on them enough to make her believe I had talent. I started lessons when I was very young. I surprised them by learning quickly."

"Would you play for me?"

He stood, offered his hand, and escorted her into the drawing room. "What would you like to hear?"

"You decide."

Wendell opted for Beethoven's "Moonlight Sonata." When he noted her rapt expression, he played through all three movements.

"That was beautiful," she said. Ophelia discreetly wiped away the tears. She brushed her hands up and down her arms. "You gave me chills. See."

He smiled and inclined his head.

"Have you ever played professionally?"

Wendell left the bench and took the chair across from her. "A time or two. Now I play for my friends and guests."

"You have an incredible gift."

He tilted his head again. "I'm honored."

"No. You're much too talented to play just for fun," she persisted. "You should use that talent to accomplish great things."

"Great things?" he repeated. After their earlier conversation, Wendell knew she would share her opinion soon enough.

"Yes. The world deserves to hear more of Wendell Hunter."

"You can tell that from one piece of music?"

"I appreciate beautiful music and those who make it happen. Yours is the type of talent that steals one's breath away."

"I wouldn't go that far."

"I would."

Wendell smiled. "You flatter me."

"You could play on any stage in the world. Why are you here in Kentucky?"

"It's where I belong."

All the time he'd worked toward a degree in music and trained with the best, Wendell's longing to know his father far exceeded his drive and ambition when it came to becoming a concert pianist. "In music, you perform or teach. I didn't care to do either on a professional level.

"So I returned home after college. Dad was spending more time on the farm, and the opportunity to get to know him warred with my music. I chose home."

"You could have done concerts and spent time with him."

"Not quality time. I learned more about my father in the last few years of his life than I did in all the years past. I wouldn't exchange that time for any amount of fame."

The grandfather clock in the entry hall gonged the hour. "It's getting late," she said. "I should go. I'm sure your staff would like to call it a night."

Wendell stood and took her hand in his. Their gazes met and held. "I meant what I said, Ophelia. I don't regret tonight. It's been my pleasure."

"Mine, too."

"Even though you don't understand me?"

"I have a better idea of who you are," she said softly. "I suspect you share qualities with my dad. He's a man who values family above all else. You're searching for a woman who feels the same as you."

Her conclusion was right on target. "Do you value family, Ophelia?"

She nodded. "Every member of my family is precious to me. I depend on them to be there for me, and I do the same for them. There's nothing they could ask that I wouldn't do for them."

"What if they asked you to do something you considered to be wrong?"

"They'd never do that."

"How do you know?"

She winked at him. "Remember the parents who taught me right from wrong? That included not getting your brothers and sisters into trouble."

"They ruled with a firm hand?"

"Most definitely. With seven kids, they had to. Good night, Wendell. Thank you for a wonderful evening."

He walked her out to her car and opened the door for her. "Thank you for a very pleasurable experience, Ophelia. Drive safely."

Chapter 3

Two nights later, Opie found herself dining in the presence of the other Hunter brother. She did comparisons between the two and found them to be very different.

That day, she'd considered her options while spending time with Jane's daughter, Sammy. When Jane took the job as Val's assistant, their mother suggested she bring her two-year-old to the farm every day. The little girl held a special place in the entire family's heart. When the child went down for her afternoon nap, Opie helped her mother prepare their evening meal. As usual, she lost the debate over trying something different with the ham.

A confrontation with a visitor brought her father in early. While Opie watched over dinner, her mother and Val calmed him down.

Later she learned Val's former coworker caused the uproar that upset their dad, blaming Val for losing his job and making threats. Opie hadn't been overly excited to hear they were thinking of hiring security but supposed it made sense to protect the family. As long as it didn't limit her freedom.

Thrilled over his new plans for her project, Val invited Russ to dinner to show the family what he'd done. She seated him next to their dad. Opie took her regular chair next to Val, and the noise died down when their father blessed the food.

As they passed bowls, Val introduced the family to Russ. When the conversation turned to the plans, Opie decided to speak up. "What do you think about me converting one of the outbuildings into a restaurant? I'd need to get financing, but I think it could work."

Val exchanged looks with their parents. "Are you sure? I thought you wanted to expand your horizons."

She'd considered where her degree could take her but found she enjoyed being home with her family. "I want to cook," she said. "And I've pretty much decided that I can be happier here than off somewhere missing all of you."

Val smiled. "We could find a restaurant in Lexington or Paris for that matter. Financing won't be as difficult as you fear. I've set aside monetary gifts for all three graduates."

"No, Val," Opie said without hesitation. "You've done enough."

Her sister grimaced playfully. "I have to give you something, and you can use the money to get what you want."

"It's a loan, Val. I intend to repay every dime," Opie declared. How would she prove herself if she leaned on her sister?

"Not your graduation gift."

"You're so stubborn."

"Wonder where I get it from," Val countered with a grin.

"All of you get it from your father," their mother teased, smiling at her husband.

"Hey now," their father exclaimed in mock affront. "In my family, it's called determination."

After the laughter died down, Opie said, "I could offer catering services to Your Wedding Place clientele."

"Won't that be too much?"

"Not if I hire sufficient staff. They should be able to work out of my restaurant kitchens."

Val said they'd discuss the catering later but expressed her concern that Opie would be much too busy once she opened a restaurant.

Russ caught her attention when he volunteered that there would be a commercial kitchen area in the structure's lower floor that could be used for catering. She definitely liked the idea of having access to a commercial kitchen.

The brainstorming session ended late. While Opie finished up in the kitchen, Val walked Russ out to his car. Opie noted a change in their attitudes toward each other tonight. Obviously, Russ redeemed himself with the new plans. When she checked the dining room one last time, she heard Val and her dad talking in the living room and paused when she heard her name.

"What about Opie's idea?" Val asked. "You think she could make it work?"

"I don't doubt any of my children can do anything they put their minds to. Opie's been a little flighty over the years, but cooking is the one thing she's stuck with. And she's good."

"I can see the benefit of having her here. In fact, I'd be willing to finance her restaurant."

"I don't think she wants you to do that," Jacob said.

She didn't. Opie went to their bedroom, grabbed her robe, and stomped into the bathroom. This family made it difficult to shine in a sky of stars. While the others knew what they wanted and worked hard to achieve it, she'd searched for herself. Now that her direction for the future was fixed, they doubted she could carry through. Opie knew exactly when she'd acquired the reputation for flightiness.

She couldn't blame anyone else for her father's opinion of her. Back when she'd been sixteen and working at the restaurant, she'd considered dropping out of high school. Her dad said she'd go if he had to sit in the chair next to hers all day. Eventually she lost her fascination with the dead-end job. Opie knew the only way she'd ever be able to do what she wanted was to have her own kitchen. She changed her focus and got her degree from culinary school.

Wrapped in her robe with a towel about her head, Opie sat on the bed polishing her toenails. Their younger sister, Jules, talked to a friend on the phone.

Opie glanced up when Val entered the shared bedroom and asked, "Russ get off okay?"

"Why wouldn't he?" Val asked.

"I thought maybe his head had exploded from all those questions Jules asked," Opie remarked, dodging the stuffed animal their younger sister threw at her. "He had a distinct deer-in-the-headlights look a few times there when all of us got started."

Jules grabbed her robe and headed for the shower, leaving them alone.

"I think it came closer to bursting when I told him you went out with Wendell." Val dropped down on her bed. "He accused me of trying to interfere in their relationship."

Why had Val bought the date? She wouldn't mind knowing the answer to that one herself. Personally, Opie thought there was more to it than providing her an opportunity to get on her soapbox. She finished her toes and placed the polish on the nightstand. "What did you say to that?"

"That it had nothing to do with him."

Opie removed the towel and fluffed the damp tendrils. "Russ gets along well with the family, don't you think?"

Val refused to bite. "If you're so determined to play matchmaker, why don't you work on Heath and Jane?"

"Is that why you made her your assistant?"

"She needed the job, and I know she'll be an asset. She has a lot of managerial experience. Just wait. You'll see how good she is."

Opie shoved a pillow behind her back and propped against the headboard. "Have you seen how Heath looks at her?"

"I think he's always had a crush on Jane but decided she was out of his league."

"And now she's going to be working here all day while he's landscaping your project."

"I don't know about that, Opie," Val said, expressing her concern. "I can't reconcile him spending years in college to come home and landscape."

"You heard what Mom said. It's Heath's choice."

"But is he doing it for the right reason?"

"You told Rom he had time when he went for the interview. Why not offer Heath the same option?"

"I'll talk to him," Val said. "Is this restaurant what you want to do?"

Opie shrugged. "Ideas are bouncing around in my head faster than I can process. Even more since Russ mentioned expanding the kitchen in the structure. I could run a catering business from there."

"You just like the idea of having a commercial kitchen at your disposal," Val teased.

"Every chef's dream," Opie agreed.

"Nothing has to be decided right away."

Opie pumped lotion into her hand and smoothed it over her arms and legs. "Russ really redeemed himself with that plan today, didn't he?"

"Yes," Val said. "I couldn't believe you said what you did."

She made a major faux pas when she commented that the plans had come a long way. Opie grinned and said, "Sorry. It slipped out. I tried to backpedal."

Val giggled. "We noticed." She hesitated. "Opie, what do you think about moving into the Sheridans' house?"

Definitely an idea she could appreciate. "Having my own bedroom? Sign me up."

"Daddy and I are praying over the situation. Will you pray, too?" Opie nodded and Val continued. "There's something else. I feel God is directing me to visit Grandfather Truelove."

"I doubt Daddy would jump on board with that."

"Daddy has to forgive Grandfather. I think God wants us to help him find peace."

"I'll add that to my prayer list," she promised.

ॐ

Thoughts of Ophelia's ambush stayed with Wendell. Though he hadn't told her, he found it interesting that her career choice reflected largely in a traditional homemaker's role. He knew she'd come to that realization as she matured.

He considered the points she'd made and wondered if she was right. Did the woman he sought exist? Or had he made choices that would keep him searching forever? Still, he did plan to choose carefully and fully commit when he found her. With the obligation of the date behind him, Wendell returned to business as usual. He scheduled a meeting to discuss Dell Air's future with his trainer that afternoon.

The horse's name always made him chuckle. Two years before, his romantic interest at the time wanted to name the new foal. They were in the office, and she'd been looking over the sheet of stud fees for the various stallions on the farm. "You should name this one Dell Air. You know, like Bel Air. He's pretty exclusive, too."

He submitted the name to the Jockey Club for approval, and it was accepted. The colt did well in his maiden race, and Wendell hadn't minded having his name associated with a winner. He felt optimistic that the progeny of his father's Triple Crown stallion might help him break free of the losing streak he'd been on since his father's death.

Mrs. Carroll tapped on his office door. "Sorry to disturb you, Mr. Hunter, but we have a situation."

His executive housekeeper immediately captured his attention. They rarely had situations. His home ran so smoothly that he'd come to expect things with very little regard as to how they happened. He supposed that attitude did sound a bit feudal. Ophelia's admonishment about taking his employees for granted came to mind.

"Jean-Pierre has been called home due to family sickness. He would like to fly out tonight if possible."

"His grandmother?" Wendell knew the elderly woman wasn't in the best of health.

She nodded, her solemn expression telling him the news wasn't good.

"What does the schedule look like?" Wendell didn't mind fending for himself, but he'd hired a chef to provide his guests with the best.

"Your next guests come closer to the end of June."

"Will he be back by then?"

"He doesn't know. He did say his grandmother is very ill."

Wendell knew how he'd felt about his own grandmother. Nothing would have kept him from her in her time of need. "Tell him to make his plans. We'll find a temporary replacement."

"I'll inform Jean-Pierre."

"Mrs. Carroll," he called when she started from the room. "Please tell Jean-Pierre I'm thinking of them both."

After she'd gone, Wendell thumbed through the Rolodex, looking for the number of the Lexington employment agency.

∾

No matter how she tried, Opie found it impossible to get Wendell Hunter off her mind. One evening had given her a better understanding, but Opie knew unraveling the man's complexity would take a lifetime. She'd only seen the glimpses that he'd allowed her to see. She would have liked to see more.

He and Russ were very different. She wondered what could have caused the incident that tore them apart.

Losing his mother so young must have been very difficult for a small boy. Opie could see how that would make it even more imperative that he proceed cautiously in his search for his soul mate. And even if she didn't care for his requirements for a wife, she liked that he was committed to finding a woman and making a home for his family. So many men seemed not to care about settling down.

She heard the phone ring and her mother's voice. "Opie, phone."

Pushing aside her second cup of coffee, she rose and picked up the cordless from the counter. "Hi, Opie. It's Sarah Beth." They caught up for a few minutes before the young woman asked, "Are you looking for work?"

Opie supposed she was looking in a roundabout way. Or at least she would be once she made up her mind about the future. "I should be."

"Someone there in Paris needs a chef for a limited time."

She stood straighter.

"They want extensive training in various cuisines and cooking skills," Sarah Beth said. "Team environment, respect for other's property, discretion, good work ethics," she read as by rote. "Duties include preparing up to three meals per day along with organizing food orders. They want references and plan to do a background check." She chuckled and said, "Of course that's not an issue for you."

This job sounded custom-made for her, Opie thought. "Where do I apply?"

"They said to fax résumés to Hunter Farm." She recited the number.

What had happened to Wendell's chef? Limited time meant he hadn't resigned. Whatever the case, this was the perfect opportunity to tell Wendell about her personal chef services.

"So are you interested? Mom says it's okay if the two of you work out a mutually beneficial deal."

Opie was confused. Elizabeth King ran a staffing agency. "But what about the placement fee?"

"She's not worried about that. Your parents have helped us more than once over the years. She says we can repay the favor and not disappoint Mr. Hunter at the same time. She gets a lot of business from him and his friends. So can I tell her you'll follow up with him?"

"Yes, I'll get in touch with Wendell Hunter right away. Thanks, Sarah Beth. And thank your mom for thinking of me."

For Opie, *right away* meant now. She didn't intend to let this possibility slip between her fingers. She opted for a surprise attack.

After changing into a soft plum summer suit, Opie applied a bit of lipstick. She then placed her current résumé into a presentation folder and slipped it into the briefcase she'd received from her parents for graduation.

Taking keys from the rack by the door, Opie told her mother where she was going. She formulated what she would say to Wendell during the drive to Hunter Farm.

After giving her name, Opie waited in the entry hall until the woman returned to escort her to his office. Wendell rose from behind his desk when she entered. Today he wore jeans as easily as he'd worn the tuxedo. "Ophelia, come in," he greeted. "What a pleasant surprise. What can I do for you?"

"I'm your woman."

Wendell looked taken aback.

"For the job," she tacked on hurriedly. "The agency gave me a call. I know you said to fax a résumé, but I had an idea I wanted to propose."

He came around the desk and indicated she should have a seat on the sofa. He chose a leather wingback chair for himself and asked, "What did you have in mind?"

She immediately jumped into the speech she'd rehearsed. "I thought you might consider the services of a personal chef. You wouldn't have to pay a full-time person. I could come into your kitchen and prepare food on a per meal basis. Think of it as on-site catering."

"Did you bring the résumé?"

Hoping to wow him with her qualifications and accomplishments, Opie pulled the folder from her case and handed it over.

He reviewed the information and glanced at her. "May I consider your proposal and get back to you?"

Opie nodded. "Certainly. I'd love the opportunity to demonstrate my skills. I don't think you'd be disappointed."

"What is your specialty?"

"American regional cuisine. Though I am capable of a wide variety of dishes."

"I'll let you know," Wendell said. "Would you care to join me for a cool drink before you go?"

She agreed, and he called the kitchen to request lemonade.

∾

Wendell noted that she'd made herself completely at home. She'd kicked off her shoes and sat with her legs curled underneath her just as his mother had done in the portrait over the sofa. Meredith Steele Hunter had also been a petite blond. Probably close to Ophelia's age when she married his father.

His dad said his mother loved to curl up on the sofa while he worked. Maybe that was why his father hadn't allowed Nicole to replace the black leather couch. He'd claimed to like the room as it was.

Wendell did, too. After their deaths, he'd been tempted to rid the house of Nicole's decorating choices, but he'd only done a judicious editing for Russ's sake. When he considered Russ hadn't set foot in the house since his furtive weekend departure, he wondered why he bothered.

Russ removed items listed as his in the will and left a childish I-hate-you letter. Wendell attempted to contact him, but Russ refused to take his calls and changed his numbers. The attorney contacted Russ to no avail. Wendell tired of the games and decided Russ would be the one to initiate any future communication.

Wendell found his gaze shifting from Ophelia to the painting, searching for similarities. There were few beyond hair and eye color. And the way she sat.

He'd found the portrait in the attic along with boxes of photos from his childhood. Other items that Nicole must have decided were better out of sight reposed there as well. Wendell returned the painting to its rightful place in this room. Then he placed the other items where he could enjoy them.

Over the years, Nicole made a point of focusing on her husband and son and pushing anything to do with Wendell and his mother deep into the recesses of her husband's mind. Wendell didn't know whom he resented more—his dad for allowing it or Nicole for treating him that way.

Throughout his childhood, the only photos downstairs were of his dad and Nicole with a tiny photo of him with Russ on their father's desk. Portraits of mother and son, namely Nicole and Russ, had been prominent in the master suite.

Wendell personally removed those items to the bedroom that had been Russ's since birth. Maybe one day he'd pass them on to his half brother. Or follow Nicole's example and banish them to the attic when he married and started his own family. Whatever the case, her efforts to push him out of his father's life to benefit her son had been wasted when the will indicated Russ was not entitled to one inch of Hunter Farm. Wendell derived more enjoyment from Nicole's failure than his fractured relationship with his brother.

"Wendell? Did you hear me?"

He looked up. "Sorry. What were you saying?"

"You were a million miles away. I asked what happened to Jean-Pierre."

"He had a family emergency in Paris."

"Oh, I'm sorry. I hope everything is okay."

He nodded. "He called Mrs. Carroll to say his grandmother is improving."

"Good. Russ came to dinner at our place Thursday night."

How could she possibly know he'd been thinking of Russ? "How is he?"

Wendell knew exactly how his half brother was doing. They might not get along, but, out of respect to their father, he did what he could to help his younger brother.

"Val wasn't impressed by his first efforts, but he did a complete three-sixty on the new idea."

Her slip of the tongue caught Wendell's attention. Back when Russ graduated and went looking for a job, Wendell phoned Randall King and requested a favor. Russ didn't know, and Wendell did not intend to tell him what he'd done. He'd spoken to Randall a couple of times since and learned he was satisfied with Russ's work.

Ophelia gasped, covering her mouth with her hands as she said, "I shouldn't have told you that."

In his brother's defense, Wendell knew creating plans was no easy task. He recalled the work they put in with their architect when they added the new barn a few years back. They sent the man back to the drawing table several times.

"I promise not to tell him." Wendell didn't add that it would be impossible since he never saw Russ. "I take it these plans are close to completion. Can you tell me anything more?"

"I suppose I could say she plans to operate a wedding venue business at Sheridan Farm."

Wendell didn't understand. "Wedding venue? On a horse farm?"

"Why not? It's a beautiful area."

He frowned and said, "I'm not disputing that, but it's a working horse farm."

"You're sounding like your brother."

Perhaps they still shared similar feelings on the things that truly mattered. "Russ didn't agree with the project?"

"He put aside his reservations for the sake of his job."

"Do you mean she's not going to operate the farm any longer?"

"I never said any such thing," she exclaimed in irritation. "Why would you think that?"

"You said a wedding business," Wendell said, thinking he'd never heard anything so stupid in his life.

"Only on a minimal portion of the acreage. Daddy will run the farm while Val runs Your Wedding Place."

"Your Wedding Place?"

"That's the name of her business."

"And what is it you say she's providing? Venues?"

"I've already said more than I should." Ophelia shut up tighter than a clam.

"I'm sorry," he offered, hoping to appease her. "I'm curious about what's going on in the neighborhood."

"I'll tell Val you have concerns."

"I'm sure she's aware that others will take issue with changes affecting our lifestyles," Wendell offered, trying not to antagonize her even more.

"She's as entitled to her business as you are."

"She is," he agreed, "but there are considerations to this type of business. That's why I asked about your plans for a restaurant at the farm. Increasing the traffic in this area will destroy the easy lifestyle we all enjoy."

"Everything will be handled properly. Val is sensitive to the needs of others and won't do anything to harm the community. She loves it as much as you do."

She might not plan to change things, but Wendell knew the best-laid plans often went awry. "How does your father feel about her plans?"

"He supports Val." Her gaze shifted to the far wall and the small portrait hanging there. "That horse reminds me of Fancy. Daddy says she has the potential to produce a winner. He claims she's got a bit of gazelle in her when she runs."

"She's that fast?"

She nodded. "Daddy says she runs like the wind."

The horse in the portrait was Merri's Girl. She'd been his father's wedding gift to his mother when they married thirty-three years before. Could this Fancy somehow be related to his mother's mare? "How did your dad acquire his horse?"

"She's a four-year-old filly. Daddy attended a sale with Mr. Sheridan. From the moment he laid eyes on her, he insisted she showed great potential. Mom always said she'd be jealous if Fancy wasn't a horse," Ophelia offered with a little laugh. "Anyway, Mr. Sheridan bought her and named her Jacob's Fancy. He left her to Daddy."

"You say she looks like the horse in the picture?"

Ophelia nodded. A wave of nostalgia washed over him. Merri's Girl died when Wendell was eighteen years old. Both he and his dad stood by when they laid her heart, hooves, and head to rest on the farm. Her death severed yet another link with his mother.

"So what do you think?"

Her question confused him. "About the horse?"

"No," she said. "Do you think we could work together? I'm an excellent chef. I think you'd find having a personal chef easier than hiring a stranger to fill a temporary position." She leaned forward and asked, "What's your favorite meal? I'd love to cook for you and show you how good I am."

Wendell remained noncommittal. He wasn't about to agree to anything before giving it a great deal of thought. His experience with Ophelia Truelove guaranteed she'd shake up his home and probably his life if he said yes. "There's no need for that. I'm sure your references will speak for themselves. I'll look over your résumé and let you know."

She finished her lemonade and set the glass on the tray. "I should let you get back to work. Thanks for your time."

∾

Wendell decided to visit Jacob Truelove with a proposition of his own. It took one look at the filly they called Jacob's Fancy to know she came from Hunter Farm. The beautiful bay stood sixteen hands high and was a chestnut color with three white socks.

Wendell remembered the filly. She'd been the produce of Stryker Heart, Merri's Girl's daughter. His dad insisted on selling the foal. Wendell hadn't known who bought her, hadn't wanted to know for fear he might try to buy her back. For as long as he could remember, his father insisted he not become attached to the horses. "Ophelia's right. She does look like Merri's Girl. Your Fancy came from Hunter Farm."

"She did." Jacob named her dam.

"Ophelia says that you think she has potential."

Jacob nodded. "I worked with her and the trainer. Watching her run gave me this gut feeling that she has potential for greatness."

"I don't suppose Dad saw her in the same way. He always said you couldn't keep every animal that comes across your farm."

"I knew Mr. Sheridan could sell her at any time, but I think he realized how attached I'd become and decided to give her to me."

Wendell wondered if his father would have made a winner of the filly if she'd stayed at Hunter Farm. "So Mr. Sheridan raced her?"

"He did. She managed a fair number of first, second, and third place finishes until she injured her leg."

"What makes you feel as you do?"

"I've seen enough champion horseflesh to know. Fancy has an incredible spirit."

"How will the leg affect her as a brood mare?"

"She'll be okay," Jacob said confidently. "She's tough, my Fancy."

Wendell remembered what Ophelia said about her father's relationship with the horse. "I have Thrill Hunter at the farm. What if we cover her and see what happens?"

Jacob Truelove hesitated. "That stallion has a steep stud fee."

"I could waive the fee if you're willing to make a deal. If the foal is a colt, I get it and we cover your Fancy a second time. If it's a filly, you keep it and pay stud fees for future dealings."

"You make it hard to say no."

"Then don't." Wendell reached out his hand. After a slight hesitation, Jacob Truelove shook on the deal. "Ophelia mentioned her sister's plans to run a business from the farm." From his closed expression, Wendell could see Jacob wasn't going to tell him anything either.

"She shouldn't have said anything."

"She didn't say a lot. Just enough to give me concerns about the influence on the neighborhood. What's your thought?"

"There will be spurts of activity, but I don't think it will be unmanageable. Val has your brother working up plans, and I'm sure they're taking everything into consideration."

"So you're okay with her converting the farm for her business?"

"Don't see how I can complain. It's hers to do as she pleases."

"Why wouldn't she want to keep Sheridan Farm as is?"

"The farm won't change. Val gave it to her mother and me. This other business is her dream. I can understand that she'd want to carry through now that she has means to do so."

Wendell doubted things would go as smoothly as they thought. "I hope it doesn't cause problems."

"Val will do everything possible to make it work for everyone. That's the kind of person she is."

"That's what Ophelia said. I'll be in touch with you to finalize the arrangements."

Jacob nodded. "I'll look forward to hearing from you."

∾

"Did he come to see me?" Opie asked over lunch when her father mentioned Wendell Hunter's visit.

"No. He came to see me about a horse. And to express his concern about your business," he told Val.

She stopped eating and asked, "What does he know about my business?"

"You'll have to ask your sister."

Opie swallowed hard. "I'm sorry, Val. I thought it would be okay to say you planned to open a wedding venue business. I didn't say any more after it became obvious he didn't like the idea. When he started asking questions, I told him I'd tell you he's concerned about the increased traffic flow."

"And when did you plan to tell me?"

"When the time was right?" She grimaced. "I'm really sorry. Guess I was nervous or something. We were talking, and it slipped out."

Val's spluttered laughter burst forth with abandon. "Nervous? You? I'd think he would be the nervous one once you got started. Mom said you went to talk to him about a job. How did it go?"

"He's thinking it over. Probably thinks I'm too young. It's just as well. Lulu called this morning. She offered to pay my airfare to New York if I'd come up to help her. Said we'd go to the food show."

"So now you understand why I asked everyone to keep the business information quiet?"

"Yes. I should have realized he'd go overboard." Opie glanced at her dad. "You say he came to see you about a horse?" She couldn't imagine they had anything Wendell considered worthy of his stables. Val negotiated the sale to retain a few of the Sheridan's more expensive stallions, and her dad planned to buy more, but it would take time for them to reach Hunter Farm's standards.

"He's offered to cover Fancy free of charge." Their dad went on to outline the plan.

"Sounds like he's getting the better end of the deal," Opie offered.

"Equal possibility the foal will be female," her dad said. "And if not, there's always the second time. Any way you look at it, I get a quality horse out of the deal."

"Yeah, but that's two years away if it's a colt."

"Doesn't matter. Fancy came from Hunter Farm. She holds a special place in Wendell's heart."

Opie supposed that with his love of the farm he would share equal regard for the animals that supported his livelihood. Still she found the idea that he felt a sentimental attachment to a horse surprising. "Why would you think that?"

"I could see it in his expression when he looked at her. Her dam came from his mother's horse."

"He sure didn't lose any time getting over here to check her out. I saw a portrait at his home and mentioned the horse reminded me of Fancy."

Her dad shook his head in amazement. "Free stud fees to a Derby winner. I can't reject that kind of deal."

Chapter 4

"May I speak to Ophelia?"

After giving the matter a great deal of consideration, Wendell concluded he had nothing to lose by accepting Ophelia's proposal. Her references were very complimentary and assured him she was an excellent cook. He looked forward to learning what comprised American Regional Cuisine.

"Opie's not here."

"Do you know when she'll be home?" he asked, thinking she was out running errands.

"Next week. She's in New York."

That surprised him. "I just returned from Belmont and wanted to talk to her about the job I have."

"Did she give you her cell number?"

He rifled through the papers on his desktop and pulled out her résumé folder. "Yes. It's here on the business card."

"You should call her. I'm sure she wouldn't mind."

"I will. Thanks."

"Wendell?"

He paused as Val Truelove called his name just before he disconnected. "Yes?"

"Did you have a horse running in the Stakes?"

Wendell wondered why she'd asked. "Not this year. Thanks for your help. Have a good day."

There were similar inquiries from his father's friends. His gaze shifted to the glass case. The numerous trophies were a testament to his father's ability to choose winning horses. Wendell knew people expected him to assume his father's role. At present, his breeding program prospered because of his father's winning stallions, but that would only last so long. His own Triple Crown hope for this year died the week before the Preakness.

He dialed Ophelia's cell number. She called hello among the cacophony of kitchen sounds.

"Hi. It's Wendell Hunter."

"Wendell?" She sounded far away.

"Hope you don't mind me calling you there. Your sister told me you were in New York."

"No. Not at all."

"I wanted to talk about your proposal."

The clatter was almost deafening.

"Let me get out of this kitchen so I can hear you." The noise volume lessened. "There that's better," she said shortly. "Kitchens are always controlled chaos. Now what did you want to discuss?"

"Your proposal. I have important guests arriving in two weeks. Jean-Pierre is not going to be back, and I wanted to engage you as my personal chef while they're in-house. I'll need three meals a day for the majority of the time though there are a few days they will only be around for dinner. Are you willing to work around their schedules?"

"Of course. When would you like to discuss menus?"

Other than special requests now and then, Wendell left the menu planning to his staff. "Why don't you prepare those?"

"Do your guests have food preferences? Any allergies?"

"I have no idea." He wined and dined buyers and breeders on a regular basis, hoping to make a favorable impression with his horses and hospitality. And he depended on his staff to keep him apprised of who was expected and when.

"Where are they from?"

Wendell didn't have the answers. "I pay Jean-Pierre to handle those details."

"I can prepare the food, but I'll need to know what to prepare," she insisted.

He hired people to deal with the minutiae, leaving him free to deal with the more important things demanding his attention. "Check with Mrs. Carroll. Give her your lists, and she'll see to it that your orders are placed."

"I prefer doing some of my shopping," Opie said. "The farmer's market has such wonderful fresh produce this time of year."

"That's fine. Once we come to an agreement, I'll expect you to handle everything. I'll draw up the contract for your signature. When will you be back?"

"When do you need me?"

"Next week."

"I'll be there."

Wendell hoped Ophelia wouldn't let him down. Her decision to go to New York after the interview bothered him. But as promised, she arrived home at the first of the week and contacted Mrs. Carroll right away. She came to see him to sign the agreement he'd drawn up.

"Mrs. Carroll says your guests are Americans. That makes my job easier."

"Sorry I couldn't answer that for you." He'd just received the list that morning in an e-mail. "Did you enjoy your trip to New York?"

"I stayed busy. A friend asked me to help at her restaurant, and I attended a food show. Val said you were in New York. Did you have a horse running in the Belmont Stakes?"

Why were the Truelove women so interested in his horses? "No. I haven't had a run of good luck with my horses since my father's death. He always had horses in the Triple Crown races."

"Don't you own the same horses?"

"I've retired some recently. They're standing stud. A couple more were euthanized after severe injuries. I'm always on the lookout for that next winner. I know they're out there."

"They are. Daddy raises beautiful horses."

"But he doesn't race them?"

"No. He breeds quality stock and works with the trainers. He loves to watch them on the track at the farm."

"Why bother?"

"There's nothing more beautiful than a Thoroughbred stretched out in a full run, his shiny coat and muscles flexing in the joy of the moment. Their pleasure in running far exceeds the thrill of money wins."

Wendell agreed but found it difficult to reconcile one with the other. "I'd ask how he plans to support the farm if he's not planning to race, but I already know." No doubt, his daughter would pay out a substantial portion of her winnings to keep the farm afloat.

"Daddy plans to make the farm self-supporting. He will breed and sell horses. He can claim a champion just as easily from the breeding standpoint as the racing. He'll also board animals."

"William Sheridan raced his horses."

"Daddy managed the farm, but he never dealt with that side of the business. Mr. Sheridan was satisfied to leave the farm in his hands and let the trainers and jockeys handle the races."

"Why does your father object to racing?"

"It's not the racing," Opie said. "It's the gambling."

"Does he have a problem?" Wendell had never heard any gossip about Jacob Truelove in the horse circles but supposed it could be the case.

"Daddy?" Opie asked, sounding incredulous. "The man who questioned his daughter accepting the proceeds of a lottery ticket her boss gifted her? You think he has a problem?"

"Well no, but generally people who are that antigambling either have a problem or have family members. . ."

Wendell trailed off. He never understood how his conversations with Ophelia kept going until he got himself in too deep to get out.

"My grandfather Truelove has a problem. Gambling is not something we do in the Truelove home."

Wendell paid a great deal of attention to stacking the papers she handed him. "I'm sorry. I didn't know." He ran the pages through the copier and handed her a set. He had to ask the next question. "What happened to your grandfather?"

"Daddy's entire family suffered because he refused to change his behavior. My grandmother nearly died of a heart attack. Daddy had a difficult life but taught us that God would take care of us if we trusted in Him."

A red flag went up in Wendell's head. She hadn't been as open to the conversation as usual. Perhaps he'd been too personal on a topic she didn't care to discuss.

"That doesn't work for me, Ophelia. If there is a God, He took my mother and then my father when I finally had a chance to know him. And my brother."

"You still have Russ," she protested.

"He wants nothing to do with me. We haven't spoken to each other since I inherited the farm. It's all about luck, Ophelia. I'll find the horse that makes it happen for me and when I do, you'll see God has nothing to do with it."

"That's not true! God has everything to do with our lives. Whether you believe that or not, God is in control."

∽

Opie met her dad in the yard when coming out of the house. "Will you give this to Wendell?" he asked. "It's Fancy's daybook. I thought he might like to take a look."

She tucked it into her big purse and climbed into the waiting SUV. Upon her arrival, Opie checked in with Mrs. Carroll and mentioned that she needed to drop off something to Wendell. After their last conversation, she expected the situation between them to be tense.

"Daddy thought you might like to see this."

She noted his interest as he thumbed through the pages. "Tell him thanks. I'll get it back to him soon."

"I'm finalizing the plans today," Opie said. "Anything special you'd care to see included?"

"I'm a big fan of desserts."

She smiled. "I'll see what I can do."

"Ophelia," he called when she started from the room. She paused, wondering if he would bring up the exchange. "Did something happen over at your place? I noticed the security vehicles by the gate."

"You mean our own little secret service?" Opie didn't care for the restrictions placed on them by the new security firm. Used to going where she wanted when she wanted, she didn't like having to ask someone to drive her. "The women in our family are no longer allowed to travel without escort. Security brought me over and will pick me up when I call to say I'm ready. I'm surprised they don't stand guard outside."

"What happened?"

"A disgruntled former coworker of Val's showed up at the farm. I never imagined her winning the money would make us prisoners in our own home. Daddy wants Val to hire a bodyguard. Can you imagine? And he said she needs to get a better car."

"She doesn't like the idea?"

"She did say it would look silly to have a driver with the old car she has now." Opie giggled at the thought. "Mom thinks it's a small price to pay for the blessings we've been given."

"There are a lot of bad things going on in the world, Ophelia. It makes sense to watch your back until you see how things go. I can't say people will ever forget anyone winning that kind of money."

"It does give people ideas. Val's convinced that anyone who wanted to get to her would go through us to do so. I know she has a point. Doesn't mean I have to like it, though. Gotta run. Mrs. Carroll is waiting on me."

∾

Wendell didn't understand the need for overkill. He'd lived in their peaceful community for years and never considered a need for security. Of course, he wasn't a woman. Perhaps Jacob had a point. Fear for a wife or child could change his mind.

As a single man with no one they could use to get to him, Wendell didn't present a similar problem. He couldn't even name a person who would pay his ransom. Certainly not Russ.

Growing up, his dad warned him to be cautious. He stayed out of the places where he could get into trouble. Even in college, when his friends visited bars in the worst sections of town, he refused to go. He'd witnessed the battered faces his friends sported after a night of drinking with a rough crowd.

When they kept going back for more, Wendell decided they liked to fight.

He'd hate to see anything happen to Ophelia or any of her family. While it didn't seem fair to curtail her travel, it was prudent of them to think ahead.

Chapter 5

How could two weeks pass so quickly? Opie wondered as she prepared for her final service. Tonight Wendell invited several of his Paris friends to join him and his guests for dinner. She'd reworked the menu after Mrs. Carroll phoned to tell her.

"Is there anyone who could help in the kitchen?" Opie knew she'd need another set of hands with more people to feed.

"I'll ask Mr. Wendell."

"If not, I can ask my family."

Mrs. Carroll called back to say that one of the staff would help. Opie liked the young woman who introduced herself as April. She gave her a list of tasks and started work on her own list.

"Is this what you want?" April asked, showing Opie the pile of red bell peppers.

"Chop them a bit finer," Opie said, taking the knife and demonstrating what she wanted. "And curl your fingers under. I don't need you chopping off anything important."

The young woman chuckled and went back to work.

"That's perfect," Opie said after looking on for a minute.

"I help Jean-Pierre at times. He calls me his *sous*-chef. Whatever that is."

"That means he's made you his second in command. Do you like to cook?"

"I like to eat Jean-Pierre's food."

"It is good," Opie agreed.

"That looks really good," April commented when Opie dipped soup into demitasse cups. "What is it?"

"Cucumber gazpacho."

When April's stomach growled, she grinned and said, "I missed lunch today."

"You shouldn't do that."

"Yes I should," April said. "I'm not blessed to be a tiny little thing like you."

Opie filled an extra cup and handed it to her. "Try this, and tell me what you think."

She put the others on a serving tray and sent the *amuse-bouche*, flavorful little bite, out to the guests.

"That was yummy," April exclaimed. "What's for dessert?"

"Didn't I hear something about not being blessed?"

"You wouldn't make a grown woman cry, would you?"

Opie chuckled. "I made three desserts for tonight. I'm sure we can find something to appeal to you."

"My mouth is watering already."

The menu consisted of a fresh mixed greens salad with Dijon vinaigrette, homemade yeast rolls, an entrée of beef tenderloin with blue cheese and herb crust, sautéed green beans, and roasted garlic mashed potatoes. Opie set aside samples of each for an appreciative April.

After plating the dessert choices of cheesecake with strawberries, tiny chocolate cakes, and lemon squares, she breathed a sigh of relief and sat down. "I think we're okay. No one sent anything back."

"Only empty plates. I'd say it was a successful party."

Opie smiled and said, "That's the only kind I like."

April yawned widely and apologized. "My baby woke me at five this morning. He's teething."

"Where is he now?"

"My mom keeps him while I work. My husband picks him up when he gets off."

Opie sent April home and attacked the cleanup on her own. Sometime later, she heard car doors slamming and knew the party was over.

She finished packing her knives and looked around the kitchen one last time to assure herself everything was in order. She'd enjoyed working for Wendell. The buyers, longtime acquaintances of the Sheridan family, were very appreciative of her efforts. Opie felt encouraged that more people in the area would welcome the services of a private chef. She just needed to promote herself.

"Good. You're still here," Wendell said as he hurried into the room. "I wanted to give you this."

She accepted the envelope. "I would have billed you."

"I wanted to tell you personally how much I've appreciated everything you've done. Mrs. Carroll says you've been a pleasure to work with."

Opie smiled. "I enjoyed working with her, too. You're fortunate to have such caring staff."

"They make my life easier. What will you do now?"

Her mind whirled with the possibilities. "I was just thinking about that. I've enjoyed working as a private chef, so I'll probably look for more work and maybe some catering on the side if I can find a kitchen. I'm in charge of the church's annual food drive, and then I'm cooking for Daddy's birthday party in August."

"Feel free to use me as a reference."

Pleasure filled her. Just maybe Wendell understood how important this was to her. "Thank you. Would you care for café mocha before I go?"

Each night after dinner, she'd prepared pots of the coffee-hot chocolate combination for the dinner guests. When Wendell said yes, she took down a pot from the overhead rack, removed milk from the fridge, and reached for the canister she'd left on the counter. She planned to leave the mixture as a thank-you gift for Wendell.

Opie turned on the stove, and there was a hesitation before the fire leaped up in the air. Surprised, she fell back, and Wendell grabbed her, swiftly turning off the stove before using his hands to beat out the flames that engulfed the sleeve of her white chef's jacket.

"Are you okay? Remove the jacket and let me check your arm," he demanded.

Dazed, Opie didn't protest when he reached for her buttons. She wore a white tee underneath. Together they examined her arm. There were one or two red spots. "What happened?"

"I have no idea," he said, pulling her over to place her arm under cold water from the faucet. "Has the stove given you any problems this week?"

"Not at all. It's been one of the better stoves I've used."

"I'll get a serviceman out here tomorrow. Are you okay?"

"A little surprised." Opie trembled beneath the hand resting on her shoulder.

"You need to calm down before you leave. I'll fix you a cold drink."

"I can. . ."

"No," Wendell said, his voice sounding strange. He handed her a towel. "Sit down. I can put ice and soda in a glass."

"It's not the first time I've been on fire, you know," Opie said as she watched him mop milk from the floor with a paper towel.

Wendell paused and stared at her. "Does this type of thing happen often in the kitchen?"

"There's always a safety consideration. Hot pots, handles, spoons, grease flare-ups, splashes. All part of the job."

"You could have been badly burned."

"But I wasn't," she countered. "I'm just a bit unnerved by the unexpectedness of the incident."

He filled two glasses with ice and took a bottle from the fridge. "Let's sit on the porch."

Opie followed and chose the swing looking out onto the Hunters' garden. Her gaze shifted from place to place with the nightscape lighting, and the sound of water caught her ear. "It's beautiful. Heath would love this area."

"Who is Heath?"

She recalled Wendell didn't know the rest of her family. "My brother. He and Rom, they're twins, graduated from Harvard last month. Rom took a job in Lexington. Heath is helping Val with the gardens while he considers his options."

"You all have nicknames?"

Opie explained that her mother loved the classics and gave them her favorite name at the time. "Val is Valentine, Heath is Heathcliff, Rom is Romeo, Jules is Juliet, Roc is Rochester, and Cy is Darcy. Jules, Roc, and Cy are still in school. Jules plans to become an architect, and Cy wants to be a vet. Roc will probably do something in science."

"Impressive. Your parents must be proud."

"My dad's determined that none of his children will follow in his father's footsteps. He helped my uncle Zeb get his degree. He's a Harvard professor. Uncle Zeb helped my aunt Karen become a doctor. She lives near my grandmother in Florida and does cancer research. I stayed with her when I attended culinary school."

"How's your arm?"

Opie fingered the places that were only slightly sensitive. "I'm fine. Like I said, burns and cuts are everyday occurrences in the kitchen."

"Not in my kitchen."

"You should warn Jean-Pierre the stove is acting up." The chef planned to report back to work at the first of the week.

"I'll see to it that the situation is corrected first thing tomorrow."

Opie didn't doubt someone would be out immediately.

"I can't thank you enough, Ophelia. You've certainly impressed me. You're a wonderful chef."

She bloomed with the compliment. Hearing Wendell say it meant so much more.

"One of the men threatened to steal you away."

"You didn't tell him I'm the substitute?"

"A smart man never plays all his cards. I think they were most impressed when you managed to learn their favorites and prepare them. They said they don't generally get such a treat."

"I appreciate the opportunity. Mom is such a stickler for basic food that I don't experiment as often as I'd like."

"Why did you come back to Paris?"

"I missed my family."

Opie wondered if he considered that a silly reason not to strike out into new frontiers for the career she wanted so badly.

"Val won the money and started making plans for her business. She gifted me with money to help finance my dream."

"And your dream is a restaurant at the farm?"

"I don't know," she admitted. "Restaurants entail a level of responsibility I don't know that I want to take on. I want to cook. Catering and private chef work appeals to me. Thanks to Val I can consider options I didn't have before."

"I'd like to help. Though I'm not fully convinced I'm doing you a favor. That fire incident tonight showed me how dangerous your work could be. But if you're determined to do this, I'll certainly refer you to my friends."

Opie barely noticed the sting of the burn. She'd done more damage in her student days. "You have a passion for horses. I have that same zeal for food. We take the risks associated with our respective careers as routine occurrences." She paused for a moment and added, "I'm thankful the stove didn't malfunction when I had meals to prepare and that I wasn't hurt any worse." A clock chimed the midnight hour in distant parts of the house. "It's getting late. I should get home."

When she stood, he did the same. She stretched out her hand to him. "Thanks again for the opportunity. Please keep me in mind for the future."

Wendell grimaced slightly when he took her hand.

"Are you okay?" she demanded, turning his hand over in hers. His reddened palm answered the question. "Why didn't you say something? You were hurt worse than me. Are they uncomfortable?"

"I'm fine."

"That's such a man answer," she disparaged, quickly taking control. "There's burn cream in the first-aid kit."

She held his hand and pulled him along into the kitchen. Mrs. Carroll had shown her the location of the kit and the fire extinguisher on her first day. Opie quickly found what she needed. Taking his hand in hers, she carefully massaged the cream into his palm. Aware of him, she paused and looked into his eyes. "I don't want to hurt you."

Wendell took over the task. "I suppose the ice in the glass masked the sting."

"I'm sorry."

"It was my stove that malfunctioned. My hands will be fine by the morning." She hesitated and Wendell said, "I should drive you home."

"I'll call for someone to pick me up. Your hands are too uncomfortable to hold a steering wheel."

He nodded. "Thanks again for all your help."

⁀

Later, after she'd gone, Wendell sat in his office mulling over their conversation. He couldn't help but be impressed by Ophelia's revelation about her brothers. He wanted to ask how they had afforded the expensive education. He knew what he paid his manager, and there was no way he could support a family of nine and send three children to college.

The Trueloves struck him as a resourceful family. Hadn't Ophelia mentioned living with her aunt while attending culinary school? No doubt there were scholarships and student loans as well.

Idly, Wendell massaged his tingling hands with more of the cream she applied earlier. He smiled as he considered her disparaging comment over his tough guy reply. He'd seen her concern, and his heartbeat quickened. He'd wanted to kiss her when he suggested she go home instead.

She'd spoken of her passion for her profession. He understood that passion, the same one he felt for his horses and farm. He needed to steer clear of young Ophelia Truelove. She was getting too close for comfort.

Chapter 6

What a day. Opie shifted a bag of food to the cart and reached for the next one. Their plan to restock the church's food pantry and aid the food bank had been a huge success. Every family bought more than the five cans per person required for admission to the concert. Opie could hear the roar of the crowd in the background. They sounded as though they enjoyed themselves. Maybe they should make this a regular event.

The planning committee spent a lot of time thinking of ways to increase their pantry supply. One member mentioned the sports events where admission was a toy or cans of food, and they came up with the concert. Another had a friend who sang in a well-known group that was willing to perform. They donated their time in exchange for selling merchandise and gave another 10 percent of their proceeds to the food bank. The committee promoted their generosity and asked those in attendance to support the group that gave so much.

July had been a busy month. Opie placed an advertisement in the paper that resulted in a few personal chef jobs and catered a couple of small events from the kitchen at the big house.

Now that weddings were booked for August, work in the gardens continued at a hectic pace. Val hadn't refused anyone's help, and many days were spent working together to accomplish the goal.

As problems arose with the plans for Val's project, her sister expressed concern over Russ's involvement. Opie thought Val cared more for Russ than she wanted to say. She shared a similar attraction for Wendell, but he obviously didn't feel the same. Lately, she'd seen him when he came to the farm to see her dad and at parties she'd done for people he referred.

"Miss, can I speak with you?"

Opie turned to find a young woman in the doorway. She held a small baby, and two smaller children held on to her legs.

"I saw the sign and I..."

She suspected from the woman's demeanor that she needed help and didn't know how to ask. "Please tell me you came to eat some of the sandwiches." Opie prepared a number of cold cut subs to feed the volunteers. More than enough remained to feed this family. "You will help me out, won't you? I hate to see good food go to waste."

A grateful smile touched the woman's face. "My children would love a sandwich."

She took the family over to a table and provided them with plates and napkins. She set the platter in the center. "I wish you'd come earlier when there were more choices."

"These are fine."

Opie stooped down to child level and said, "I have cookies, too, but only if you eat your sandwiches. Would you like chocolate milk?"

Their eyes brightened in the way of kids unused to treats, and her heart hurt for the beautiful children. She pushed the tray toward their mother. "Help yourselves. I'll get the milk." In the church kitchen, she took two cartons each for the children and their mother and returned to find them eating a half sandwich.

"Oh, you have to eat more than that," Opie said as she passed the cartons around. "I'll never get rid of the sandwiches if you don't."

The children looked to their mother with big hopeful eyes, and she placed another sandwich on their plates.

Opie busied herself opening the milk cartons and giving the children straws. "My name is Opie Truelove."

The woman swallowed hurriedly and wiped her hands on her napkin before accepting Opie's hand. "I'm Brenda Clarke. This is Ronnie and Bonnie, and the baby is Shelley."

The boy and girl looked to be the same age. "Are you twins?" When they nodded, Opie said, "My brothers are twins, too. They're identical."

"We can't be," the boy said. " 'Cause she's a girl."

"No, 'cause you're a boy," his sister countered.

Their mother called their names and they settled down.

She pulled out one of the small chairs and sat down. "It's a pleasure meeting you all. Where do you attend church?"

"My husband works on Sunday. He drives our truck."

"Do you live nearby? We have a church bus if you'd like to attend."

"We live at Hunter Farm. My husband works there."

"Oh, we're neighbors. I live at Sheridan Farm. I know Wendell Hunter."

The woman looked panicked as she stood and stepped away from the table. She beckoned and Opie followed. Her voice dropped low as she said, "Please, miss, don't tell him I came here. Ronald would be so embarrassed. He doesn't mean to take from our children. He just wants to make things better. I tell him it's better if the children eat.

"I can't thank you enough. The children. . ." she began, pausing when she choked up. "They were hungry and I didn't know how I was going to feed them." Tears sprang to her eyes.

Opie pushed a clean paper napkin into her hand. "Don't worry, Brenda. We all have times when we need help. The most important thing is making sure these precious little ones are fed. Do you have formula for the baby?"

"No. I feed her."

"So we need to feed you," Opie said. A nursing mother needed nutrients as well. "There are programs that provide milk and other items for families that

291

qualify. Would you like the information?"

A sad expression covered the young mother's face as she nodded. "Yes, please."

Opie smiled encouragement. "Take your time and eat all you want. Then the children can play while we shop in the pantry. We just stocked it today, and there's plenty of good food for your family. How did you get here?"

"My friend dropped me off. She's going to come back after she runs her errands."

"We'll be ready when she arrives."

Seeing that the children had cleaned their plates, Opie walked over to the counter and picked up the container of chocolate chip cookies she'd baked last night. They eagerly accepted the cookie she handed them, and Opie placed a couple more on their plates.

Later they departed with the remaining sandwiches, groceries, and even cash from Opie's own pocket to use for meats. She'd also given Brenda the number for assistance and urged her to return if she found herself in need again.

Opie repeated her invitation to church and gave the young mother the church's number in case they wanted to ride the bus. She didn't know if she'd ever see the family again, but it pleased Opie to know they would sleep well that night with full stomachs.

A bit of anger toward Wendell welled up in her. How could he live in that big house, eat meals prepared by a chef, and not be aware people were hungry on his farm? Based on what the woman said, Opie suspected the husband might have a problem. Didn't Wendell have any type of personal relationship with the workers on his farm?

God must have sent this young mother her way today. Maybe it was her personal connection with food, but the idea of anyone going hungry bothered Opie a great deal. That's why she volunteered for the food drive and cooked at the shelters.

She said a prayer for the family and completed her tasks, eager to get home. The desire to do more for the family was strong, but Opie knew they needed their pride. She'd provided them with a start tonight.

Her parents told her she couldn't outdo God. Opie knew that, but it would have been hard for her to sit at the table and stuff her face with thoughts of them in need. How many other families suffered in the same way? For a country with so much, there were a number of people with so little.

∽

As he dressed for the party, Wendell found himself uncertain. When Ophelia invited him to her father's birthday party, he considered whether he should be a good neighbor or refuse. He liked Jacob. In fact, he'd yet to meet a member of this family he didn't like, but his doubts over becoming further involved with them gave him pause.

When the release of information regarding Val's venue business became public, Wendell adopted a wait-and-see attitude. He'd seen a vast improvement in the gardens when he'd visited, and it occurred to him that it might not be what he originally thought. Maybe he should go and see if he could learn more.

The wedding this past weekend hadn't seemed to make a difference in traffic. Wendell supposed that would depend on the size of the wedding. He liked his privacy. When someone suggested he should offer farm tours like others in the community, he rejected the idea for that same reason.

When they talked, Ophelia told him she planned to prepare an English tea for Val's launch party and her father's favorites for his birthday on the same day. He'd cautioned her about taking on too much.

Wendell wondered if Russ would be present. If so, tonight could provide an opportunity to interact with his brother.

He asked about her father's likes, and she told him a gift wasn't expected. Wendell disagreed. He'd considered some of the things he liked and settled on a gift card from the local farm supply store.

Ophelia welcomed Wendell and took him over to speak to her dad. When called to the kitchen, she left him with her dad. Jacob sat with his leg propped up and an ice bag resting gingerly against his scalp.

Shocked to find the man battered and bruised, he asked, "What happened?"

"I wish I knew," Jacob said. "Fancy went crazy and kicked me up against the fence."

"Have you been checked out?"

"Don't get them started again," Jacob said quietly. "My head hurts from where I got knocked unconscious and my leg is sore, but I'll survive."

The news troubled Wendell. "And you have no idea what happened?"

"I told them to call in the vet to check Fancy out. I'll let you know what I find out."

"I appreciate that," he said, noting the number of people waiting to speak to Jacob. "We should let your guests offer their birthday wishes."

"I'm glad you came, Wendell."

Russ was present and his evasion skills had improved. Other than the initial cool nod when they first saw each other, his brother gave no indication that Wendell existed. He caught glimpses of him about the room and if Russ was there when Wendell showed up, he quickly moved on. He could only assume Russ's anger increased with the passage of time. Wendell felt no need to be the bigger man.

While Ophelia rushed around finishing her preparations for the meal, Val came over to speak to him. She introduced him to Rom and Heath, and they talked for a while before Heath went off with an attractive young woman named Jane Holt.

"Val tells me you're concerned about how her business will affect the neighborhood," Rom said.

"Traffic is a major concern," Wendell admitted.

Dinner was announced, and Rom accompanied him to the buffet tables. He gestured for him to go first. Wendell picked up a plate and studied the array of foods on the tables. All too soon he'd placed far more than he needed on the plate.

"We can sit over here," Rom said, leading the way. "You don't need to worry. Val plans to bring traffic in off the main road which enables her to give the guests a scenic view and doesn't affect our road at all."

Wendell hadn't considered the possibility of doing that. "Sounds as if it could work."

"It will. You should discuss your concerns with Val. She wants to do what's best for everyone involved."

He'd seen enough effort on Val Truelove's part to believe this to be the case. "I like knowing what's going on in my community."

Rom nodded. "I can understand that."

As he ate, it occurred to Wendell just how different the party atmosphere was from his usual experience. Casual, comfortable, with lots of laughter best described what he witnessed in this room. Most of the guests wore comfortable clothes without designer labels. Respect for all availed. Inexpensive gifts were as appreciated as the more expensive ones. Wendell found it ironic that he and Russ gave the same thing.

"You two must have known I have my eye on a few things down at Joe's," Jacob said, waving the gift cards in the air.

"As every horseman should," he replied.

When the twins showed their father their gift, Wendell admired the horse blankets. The royal blue and gold color combination was impressive with the Truelove Inc. logo. "Nice," he commented to Ophelia when she came to stand by his side.

"They are, aren't they? Val designed that logo."

"I didn't realize she was an artist."

"She calls herself a doodler. She created the design for her business, and we agreed it made a perfect logo for the farm."

"How's your dad doing?"

Wendell broached the subject that controlled his thoughts ever since he learned about the incident. Secretly he had hopes for the foal and Jacob's gut instinct that Fancy could produce a winner. When he learned Jacob owned the filly, his first instinct was to make him an offer. He knew his dad's belief that every horse was for sale would not prove true with this family. Fancy held a special place in her owner's heart. He wanted answers. What caused the incident? Was the horse unstable? Had she ever done this before?

He admired Jacob's horse sense. Back in July, he'd asked Jacob's opinion on a colt he'd found. Where Wendell saw potential with training and time, Jacob wasn't as certain of the animal's abilities. He'd pointed out a couple of things right away that Wendell hadn't seen for himself, and he could only question why.

His dad would have noticed those things. Jacob noticed them. Why didn't he? Would he ever develop his horse sense?

"Daddy's tough," she responded. "I'm sure he'll be okay. Did you get enough to eat?"

Wendell laughed. "Are you kidding? You prepared enough to feed a small country."

"There's never enough for that."

Her sad expression made him ask, "What's on your mind?"

"I met someone at the church recently who was having problems feeding her kids. I can't give you a name, but they were associated with your farm. It bothered me that you didn't see their needs."

"Why should I?" Wendell asked, going on to defend himself. "I pay my staff well. Other than rules for those who live on the property, I don't get involved in their personal lives."

"You have to care about what happens to others, Wendell."

Her insistence irritated him. "Why do you think I don't? I provide the job that feeds this person's family. Why is what he does with his money my concern?"

"Because it's the right thing to do," she said, her voice rising. "We have to love our brother."

Wendell looked around to see if anyone had overheard. As far as he was concerned, the only brother he knew didn't want his love. "They're adults, Ophelia. It's their responsibility to manage their funds. If they need a raise, they can discuss it with the manager. I provide them with living accommodations. That's more than most workers get from their employers."

"I think this man might have other issues."

"What sort of issues?" Wendell demanded.

"I don't know, but she said something about him wanting to make things better for his family."

"He could be saving for the future."

"To the extent that his wife and children are hungry?" she asked with disbelief. "That's ridiculous."

"Perhaps she's not good with finances," he suggested.

"I saw them, Wendell. This woman isn't spending money on herself. They were hungry but not greedy when I offered them food. She was desperate enough to take the number of an agency to help her provide for her children."

Seeing she wasn't going to let up, he asked, "What do you want me to do, Ophelia?"

"I want you to care that someone you know might be in trouble."

She wanted too much. If Hunter Farm went under tomorrow, where would those people be? Certainly not worrying about whether he would survive.

"You and your brother avoided each other all evening," she threw out. "If you're like that with him, why would I expect you to be any different with someone else?"

"In case you didn't notice, Russ avoided me." Wendell glanced about and demanded, "Where is he? Maybe you can get your brothers to hold him down while I ask what his problem is."

She touched his arm, her expression one of appeal. "Please don't do anything in anger, Wendell."

He shook her hand off. "I should go. Please extend my wishes to your father."

"Wendell, please don't leave angry."

He refused to look into her pleading gaze, to hear the voice that made him want to do things he never did. "Good night, Ophelia. Thanks for inviting me."

Regardless of what she thought, her news did bother him, and Wendell was determined to find out what was going on with his employee. As for Russ, Wendell couldn't think of a single way to remedy that situation.

❧

After their guests left, the family busied themselves with the cleanup. The twins helped their dad to bed and went out to check that the farm had been secured for the night. Jules and the younger boys picked up the living and dining rooms while Opie and Val helped their mom with the dishes. They could see Mom was distracted and sent her to be with their dad.

"Too bad we don't have a dishwasher," Opie said as she slid another stack of plates into the sink.

"We'll have one when we move. Did you plan to paint your room?"

Opie found the idea of moving into the Sheridans' house exciting, particularly the idea of having her own space without leaving home. "No. I like the wallpaper."

Val dried the dish and added it to the stack. "We can start moving our things anytime. After the wedding this weekend, we'll work on the rest of the house." She polished a plate with the drying cloth for a minute or two before she spoke. "I need to talk to you about Wendell."

Had Val heard them arguing earlier? Opie regretted what she'd said. Her timing stunk. "What about him?"

"I told Russ we can never be more than friends tonight. He didn't take it well."

She shared a sympathetic smile and wondered where Wendell fitted into the discussion.

"He was angry when he said it, but Russ said I should warn you about Wendell. He said Wendell has less use for religion than he does."

Opie concentrated on rinsing the plate and stood it in the drain. "Wendell has issues, but I know God can change him."

"Yes, God can. You can't," Val warned.

"I care for him," Opie said.

"You're attracted to him. I knew you were interested the first time you showed me his photo."

She sighed. "I didn't think I'd feel this way."

"We have to be strong. Trying to take matters into our own hands will only make us more miserable in the end."

Opie refused to stop trying. Wendell needed someone who cared in a major way. "I'm not giving up. If anyone needs to hear God's message, it's Wendell. If I walk away, he won't."

"You don't know that. Please don't look at him as a challenge, Opie."

"I'm not," she protested. She planned to follow God's leading in the matter.

"You show no fear in confronting Wendell. Did it occur to you that you could be making matters worse?"

"Like saying 'we can only be friends' to a man who indicates his interest in you is going to improve your situation?"

"I was honest with Russ."

Opie wiped down the countertops. "How is this going to impact your project?"

"I can only hope he's professional enough to separate his personal life from his business. Just be careful, Opie."

"I know what I'm doing, Val."

Chapter 7

Those words were still on her mind the following morning. She owed Wendell an apology. After breakfast, she took the cordless and slipped outside to make the call. "Hi. It's Opie. I'm sorry about last night," she said when he answered. "I shouldn't have said anything."

She expected him to tear into her. In fact, she couldn't blame him if he did. She knew better than to antagonize a guest in their home.

"It's different for us, Ophelia," Wendell said with quiet emphasis. "We weren't raised in the same nurturing environment you have."

"What happened?" She sat in the swing and nudged it into motion. When he didn't say anything, Opie thought she'd overstepped her boundaries again.

"Russ didn't take well to learning he didn't inherit a portion of the farm. Our father died without making us aware of the true situation."

That caught her attention. She leaned forward, bringing the movement to a sudden halt. "What situation?"

"My dad and I didn't have the best relationship. He didn't know what to do with me. Then Nicole came along, and she was more interested in having fun than in mothering a child who wasn't hers. Dad hired a succession of nannies and left me behind while they traveled to races and took vacations. Between nannies, Dad sent me to stay with my mom's parents."

"Did they like your father?" Opie wished she had gone to his house for this conversation.

"No. They never wanted her to marry him. My parents eloped."

It sounded as if his mom had a mind of her own.

"They didn't disown her?"

"No. She was their only child. My grandparents gave Stryker-Steele Farm to my mother as a wedding gift. She changed the name, but they stipulated the farm would go to her firstborn son in the event of her death."

Opie didn't understand. "Why would they do that?"

"She struggled with breathing issues as a child. I suppose the doctors might have given them some warning."

"Does Russ know about their stipulation?"

"No. He never gave me an opportunity to explain. Dad met Nicole at the tracks. He brought her here, and they lived together until my grandparents threatened to take me away. Nicole became pregnant around the same time, and they married. Russ's birth impeded her travels. Dad wasn't about to drag a newborn along. When he left for the races, she concentrated on removing every trace of my mother from the house. She even tried to get him to sell the place, but he refused. She took her frustrations out on me."

His situation tore at her heart. How lonely he must have been. Not only had he lost his mother but his father as well. "Why did she dislike you so?"

"It was what I represented," he said. Opie noted the faint tremor in his voice. "My father loved my mother, and Nicole felt threatened. Maybe she would have been nicer if she'd known the farm was mine. Then again, there's no telling what she would have done if she had."

Opie gasped at his sarcastic laugh. "Didn't anyone see how she treated you?"

"Nicole was careful. She staged incidents so that I came off as the brat. After a while, I decided to play her game. I was crying out for attention, but my dad was too blind to see.

"They sent me off to boarding school. I was a behavioral problem until one of the counselors listened and became like a big brother to me. After that, I didn't want to come back. Dad would show up and make me come home. I think my grandparents must have insisted he be a better father, and he was afraid they would put him off the farm if he didn't."

"Did you tell them what was going on?"

"No. They were getting older and not in the best of health, and I knew they weren't up to a fight against my dad. After he died, I understood why he kept me around."

"I'm sure he loved you, Wendell."

His snort indicated he lacked her certainty. "After I finished college, he proposed we get to know each other. In my ignorance, I thought he wanted to spend time together. Now I believe they told him he needed to train me. He did, but he didn't plan to give up the reins any time soon."

"How could he keep it a secret? Why didn't your grandparents do something?"

"What choice did they have? I was his trump card. If they sent him away, they lost their only grandchild. Then after my grandfather died, my grandmother went to live with her sister in France."

"I'm sorry, Wendell."

"Makes you appreciate your parents, doesn't it?"

"Oh, I'm very thankful for them both. We've always been wealthy in the things that truly mattered."

"I'd choose loving parents any day," Wendell agreed.

"You say Russ won't let you explain?"

"Russ took his things and left a note one weekend when I was away. That's the last I've seen or heard of him until the party last night. He doesn't want to hear the truth. It's his choice."

"Does that mean you don't care?"

"He's my brother, Ophelia. We're not close, but I prefer he not hate me for something outside my control. I'd like for him to understand, but if he's determined not to listen, it's not likely I'll ever tell him the truth."

"He'll listen one day, Wendell."

"Maybe. What are you doing today?"

"As little as possible." Tired from the previous day's events, she planned to relax.

"Would you like to visit the Horse Park?"

Opie could only wonder why he invited her. Her first thought would be that he'd keep his distance after her last attack. "Are you playing tourist?"

"I have to conduct a bit of business, but I wouldn't mind touring the site."

"I haven't been there in years. What time?"

"I'm meeting with my manager in a few minutes. Let's say ten thirty?"

"I'll be ready."

∾

Wendell hung up. Why had he shared all that with Opie? Maybe because he wanted her to understand he wasn't a bad person.

"Hey boss, you wanted to see me?"

Wendell gestured his farm manager in. He sat down at his desk and reached for a pen. "How many young families do we have on the farm?"

"Maybe three or four."

"Any of them exhibiting financial problems?"

"Not that I've heard, but then it's not likely they would share that kind of information."

"Anyone asked for a raise lately?"

Jack Pitt shrugged. "Hints but no outright requests."

"I want to know if you hear anything. And I want this kept between us." Wendell resolved to do his own detective work. He didn't care for looking bad in situations outside his control. He paid his men, and what they did with the money was their concern so long as they weren't into anything that could affect his farm. "What about gambling? Anyone you think might have a problem?"

"Most place bets at the tracks."

"Does anyone regularly borrow money to get them through to their next check?"

The man's brow furrowed. "Now that you mention it, someone mentioned young Clarke borrowing money before his last check. You think he's in financial trouble?"

"I don't know. We need to keep our eyes and ears open." Wendell knew that employees with financial problems were more likely to cave in to temptations.

"Clarke has a wife and three small kids," Jack said. "I attributed it to him having the family, but it could be something else. He's young. Midtwenties. Hard worker. Eager to get ahead in life."

"Does he bet?"

Another shrug. "I could ask around."

Wendell didn't need convincing. He knew this was his man. "No. Keep it between us. Report back if anything comes to your attention. If he has a problem,

I'll see to it that he gets help before it gets out of control. His family should come first."

"I agree. Taking a wife and having children is a responsibility only a man should assume."

He agreed with the manager. "Does he drink? Go out at night?"

"He strikes me as a family man. If anything, he's probably trying to win the big one and get ahead in life."

"Difficult to do when one income supports five people."

You'd think we'd learn, Wendell thought, realizing the same applied to him. He kept trying for the big one, hoping to prove himself worthy of being his father's son. He'd been more fortunate financially than the young man, but at least young Clarke had a wife and family. More than he could say for himself.

When had he put his hunt for Mrs. Right on hold? He hadn't given up totally, but there were things that needed doing first. Was he really too busy, or did it have more to do with wanting something or someone he couldn't have?

Spending time with a loving family with hearts big enough to encompass each other and their friends was nice. He regretted arguing with Ophelia. She couldn't help caring about people. It was her nature.

∽

The hot August day made Opie wonder if she'd made the wisest choice. After their earlier conversation, the idea of spending more time with Wendell appealed to her. She needed him to see she cared for him as a friend. She truly regretted arguing with him. Val had a point. She had to stop confronting him over her beliefs or she'd push him away forever.

Located half an hour outside Paris, the Kentucky Horse Park promoted itself as the only park dedicated to man's relationship with the horse. She'd taken a few minutes to tour their Web site while she waited for Wendell.

They parked and strolled toward the building, their eyes going immediately to the huge painting of horses running through water with the slogan, THOU SHALT FLY WITHOUT WINGS, above the doors. They went inside and made plans to meet later.

Wendell left to conduct his business, and Opie went back outside to enjoy the area. She snapped photos of the impressive statues with her digital camera. After awhile, she used the admission ticket Wendell bought to visit the International Museum of the Horse. She read histories; viewed tack and hardware, wagons, displays; and concluded with the history of some of the most popular horses ever to race. After finishing, she went back out to the visitor information center and found him waiting.

"How was the museum?"

"Informative."

"I can't think of a better place for the park. There have been horses here for more than two hundred years. What did you plan to do next?" he asked.

She unfolded her visitor map, and they viewed the schedule of activities.

"Let's take the Horse Drawn Trolley Ride and go see the Parade of Breeds."

They also visited the Hall of Champions and American Saddlebred Museum and managed to fit the *Thou Shalt Fly without Wings* film into the schedule. As she listened to Wendell, she realized she'd heard that same excitement when her dad talked horses.

"Had enough?" he asked when they exited the film.

Opie nodded, and they strolled toward the main gate. "I need to remind Heath about this place. Sammy loves horses."

"She could ride the ponies."

"You should see how excited she gets when we take her to the barn." She paused to admire two foal statues. "The statuary is great."

"It is. I've thought about commissioning a piece for the farm but never have."

"You should. It's beautiful work. Maybe a couple of smaller pieces at the entrance."

He nodded. "Before I forget, are you available to prepare a dinner next Tuesday night? I'm having a birthday dinner party for Catherine and Jean-Pierre has the flu."

"He's having a difficult time lately," Opie commented. She wondered about the woman Wendell cared enough for to throw a party.

"He is," Wendell agreed. "It's Catherine's thirtieth birthday. She wasn't going to do anything, but we insisted on marking the occasion."

"We?" she asked.

"Her husband Leo and myself. We attended private school together. They're in real estate. Cat's the one who talked me into the bachelor auction."

Relief surged through Opie. "Any ideas on the menu? A cake?"

"Actually she'd prefer those desserts you prepared last time. She still talks about how good they were. I know it's not much notice."

"I'll come over Tuesday morning and get everything together."

They arrived at the car, and Wendell unlocked the door for her. "Thanks, Ophelia. By the way, I think I figured out who came to the church."

Her head jerked about. "You didn't say anything, did you?"

"No, but I plan to keep my eyes and ears open. Employees with financial troubles can be a liability in my business. My source says this particular young man is eager to get ahead, and I hope he's not going about it the wrong way."

She'd never considered that aspect. "Wendell, please don't embarrass his wife. She's doing the best she can."

He looked at her for several seconds. "That's never been my intention, Ophelia."

Opie smiled. She believed him. "Thanks, Wendell."

Chapter 8

After dinner that night, Opie and Val started moving boxes to the truck. Opie would miss the home where she'd grown up. She'd been the first child born after they moved to the manager's house, and she remained there until she went off to culinary school.

After her first trip to her new bedroom, Opie veered off to the kitchen. The Sheridans renovated the old kitchen, turning it into a huge commercial-type kitchen with granite countertops and quality appliances. A few things were a little outdated, but Opie knew it was going to be one of her favorite rooms in the house.

"There you are," Val said when she walked into the room. "I should have known."

"You think there's enough room in this kitchen for two cooks?"

She glanced around. "Should be, but you and Mom will have to come to an agreement."

"I know."

"So you went to the Horse Park with Wendell today," Val said.

Opie nodded. She'd mentioned it over dinner, telling Heath he needed to take Sammy. The mention of horses set the little girl off, and she'd talked nonstop until Heath promised to take her to the barn after dinner.

"I called this morning to apologize, and he really opened up about his past. Said Russ wouldn't listen when he tried to tell him his mother's will stipulated the farm go to her firstborn son. Their dad never told them about the will. I wish I could help them work out their relationship."

"Pray. God could make you their mediator. Come on. We need to unload those boxes. I have a busy day tomorrow."

"Need help with the wedding?"

"An extra set of hands is always appreciated."

"Wendell asked me to prepare a dinner party for his friend's birthday Tuesday night, but that shouldn't be too hard."

"Opie, about what Wendell told you... You're not..."

"I told you, Val. I just want to be his friend."

Even as she spoke the words, Opie knew she wanted to be far more to Wendell.

Heath and Jane took Monday off and went into Paris. Opie and Val worked on sorting their belongings and deciding what to take with them. With two successful weddings and the launch party under her belt, Val was thrilled with her progress.

Tuesday morning, Opie prepared for Wendell's event while the others started to move the family. She was leaving when her father called to say Heath and Sammy fell down the stairs. She hurried over to find them both badly injured and in a great deal of pain. Heath told the emergency personnel to take Sammy and Jane in the ambulance. He would ride in the SUV with their security. The attendants immobilized his leg and helped get him inside. He was white by the time they finished.

"I have to be over at Wendell's all day," Opie told Val before they left. "His party is tonight."

"Take your phone. I'll keep you updated. I'll leave a message if you don't answer."

Opie trailed her to the vehicle, torn between family and commitment. "I'd cancel, but Jean-Pierre is sick."

"Do the job, Opie. He won't be alone. We have to go."

She leaned inside the vehicle and touched his arm. "I love you, Heath. I'm praying."

He nodded and closed his eyes.

Wendell was coming out of the house when she arrived. "Sorry I'm late. Heath tripped over Sammy on the stairs this morning."

"Are they okay?" Wendell asked.

"They think she broke her arm. Heath broke his leg. He was moving a big box and didn't see her."

"Do you need to go? I can take my guests out to dinner."

Opie shook her head. "The family is with him, and Val said she'd keep me informed. I'd rather be busy here than worried at the hospital."

"Let me know if anything changes," he said. "Do you need anything?"

"Is April around today? I could use an extra set of hands."

"Ask Mrs. Carroll to call her."

"I will." She smiled her thanks to Glenn, the security staff member who brought her bag of produce from the vehicle.

"The farmers market must love you," Wendell commented doing a quick save when a couple of zucchini fell from the bag. He tucked them back inside.

"Actually this came from a friend's garden. She shared with Mom, and she told me to take the excess."

"Thank them both for me."

"Just wait until you taste the great things I do with them."

"I look forward to it," he said.

"You'll be planting your own garden next year."

Opie stayed busy. Val called a couple of times to say they were waiting on X-rays and doctors and promised to let her know as soon as they knew something definite. Since she hadn't heard from her again, she could only assume they were still waiting.

Though curious about Wendell's friends, Opie blocked out the party and concentrated on getting the food out. After serving the dessert course, she took a moment to call and check on Heath.

"He's spending the night at the hospital," Val said. "They casted Sammy's arm and sent her home with Jane. She's not a happy baby, but she's okay."

"Thank God for that."

"Are you almost finished?"

"I just sent out the last of it," Opie said. "I need to clean up before heading for the hospital."

"You might as well go home. Heath is pretty much out of it. I think we're all going to head that way shortly."

"Okay, I'll see you soon." Wendell and a woman stepped into the room. "Gotta go. Wendell's just come in."

"That was Val," she explained as she slipped the phone into her pocket.

"How are Heath and Sammy?"

"He's staying at the hospital tonight. They casted Sammy's arm and sent her home."

He grimaced. "Sorry. Ophelia, this is Susan Boone. She wanted to meet you."

Susan Boone smiled up at him, never releasing her hold on Wendell's arm. Opie recognized her from the social pages. Her family came from old Kentucky money and supported a number of charities and foundations. She was closer to the twins' age and from the looks of her, a perfect match for Wendell's wish list.

"I just loved your food," she enthused. "I'd like to engage your services to cater an event next month. We're between chefs, and I think this could be the perfect solution."

Opie pulled a business card from her pocket. "Give me a call, and we'll discuss the particulars."

Wendell smiled at Susan and patted her hand. "Go back to the party. I'll be there after I speak with Ophelia."

"Nice meeting you. Hurry back," she told Wendell, pausing to kiss his cheek.

Opie watched her leave the room and asked, "Miss Right?"

"I've known Susan and her family for years. You should go ahead and leave. I can get Mrs. Carroll to handle this."

"I'll finish up here and head home."

Wendell glanced toward the door. "I have to get back to my guests. Take off whenever you need to. Thanks for doing this at the last minute."

"It's my job."

"Don't you mean career?"

"Yes, my career."

After he'd gone, Opie concentrated on finishing service. All too soon, the tears trailed down her cheeks. Why had she allowed this to happen? Wendell hadn't lied to her about what he wanted in life. She knew she didn't stand a chance. Why did it hurt so much?

Opie called security, finished packing up her knives, and walked out to the waiting SUV. After catching up on Heath, she went to prepare for bed.

"What's wrong?" Val asked when she came out of the bathroom. "Why are you moping around?"

"I'm not."

Val's doubt-filled expression disputed her response. Her sister's ability to read her so well was definitely a negative of close families.

"It's Wendell."

"What about him? I thought you were pleased that he gave you another job."

"I was. I thought maybe he'd reconsidered about working women."

"What happened?" Val asked.

"He had a date. Susan Boone."

"What are you going to do, Opie?"

"Nothing. He's out of my league. He has money. Social standing."

"You have money."

"Not like those women he dates. They're blue-blooded down to their expensive pointy-toed heels. He brought her into the kitchen to meet me. She raved about the food and said he'd told her I was a personal chef. They're between chefs, and she wants to book an event next month."

"That's good news, isn't it?"

"I suppose," Opie said, wishing she could tell the woman no.

"Take care, little sister," Val warned. "Wendell Hunter appeals to you, and you're blinding yourself to reality."

"I know it can't be, Val. That doesn't mean I can't appreciate his finer qualities."

"That second and third look is often what gets you in over your head. You start thinking you can change the things you can't. Please don't make me wish I'd never bought you that date."

Opie didn't tell Val she wished she'd never read the magazine article that started all this. Life was so much simpler before Wendell Hunter came into her life.

Chapter 9

Where did you say your mother is?" Jacob Truelove requested when Opie set the plate of food on the table before him.

"At church. Her woman's group is having a luncheon. I promised I'd feed you."

When she planned chow mein for lunch, Opie hadn't realized her father would invite Wendell to join them. At least he'd given her a bit of warning when he called up to the house to tell her to set another place at the table.

After grace, Jacob took a bite and asked, "What did you say this is?"

Opie glanced at Wendell, wondering what he thought. In today's world, most people ate Chinese cuisine on a regular basis. "It's chicken chow mein. Do you want me to fix you something else?"

"No," Jacob said with a shake of his head. "This is tasty. What's this?" he asked, lifting a sprout with his fork. "Looks like grass."

She felt her skin growing warm. "It's a bean sprout. They're good for you."

"Did you think Opie was feeding you horse food, Dad?"

Opie would have thumped Heath if he hadn't already been in pain. He had come home from the hospital the day before. Because of his limited mobility, she offered to take his food into the family room, but he insisted on coming to the table. He sat with his casted leg propped up on an extra chair.

"Heath," Jane admonished as she paused in feeding Sammy. "Opie worked hard to make this food for us."

"Not really," she admitted. "But Heath obviously prefers horse food to hospital food."

Val laughed and high-fived her. Heath grinned.

"You kids behave," Jacob ordered. "Wendell will think we didn't teach you any manners." He glanced at their guest. "They pick on Opie's cooking all the time, but I've never seen anyone leave the table yet."

Wendell smiled. "You're lucky to have her. She's been a big hit with my guests."

"This family has been blessed with good cooks." Jacob glanced at Opie and said, "If your mom's schedule gets any fuller, I might have to hire you to cook for us."

"You can't afford me."

He pretended shock. "You'd charge your old dad?"

Everyone chuckled when she promised to give him a good rate.

"Believe me, she's worth every penny she charges," Wendell said.

His statement rated up there with the highest praise she'd ever received. Opie shut everyone out as she focused on Wendell. "So you understand why I have to cook?"

He met and held her gaze. "I respect that you do what you love."

"That should be the same for every woman," she said.

Heath groaned. "Don't get her started on equality for women."

Opie shot him a warning look. "You're awfully brave for a man with a cast on his leg."

"We've had this discussion before, and we're not going to have it again now, are we, Ophelia? Your father invited me to share your lunch, but I won't disrupt the meal with a disagreement."

"I'm not trying to start an argument," she protested. "I just want everyone to understand my work is important to me."

"We know that, Opie," Val said. "In fact, we feel blessed to enjoy the results of your work."

"You're doing what God intended for you," her dad added. "And you'll use that talent in the way He intends whether you're a homemaker like your mother or the next famous chef."

She played with the food on her plate as the others changed the topic. Her growing feelings for Wendell made her consider the prospect of becoming a homemaker. Could she be happy preparing meals for him and their family and guests? For that matter, would he allow her to do that? Or insist on a chef?

"Opie, did you hear Daddy?"

Val's question made her look up. "I'm sorry. What?"

"He asked if there's any dessert left from last night."

She pushed her chair back and stood. "I made a cake. I'll get it."

"I'll help," Val said.

Opie picked up their plates and carried them into the kitchen.

"Are you okay?" Val asked.

"Yeah, I'm fine." She stacked dessert plates, cups, and saucers on a tray. One of the cups toppled and shattered on the tile floor. She started to sob as she knelt on the floor.

Val knelt by her side, one hand resting on her shoulder. "Opie?"

"No, I'm not okay," she declared. "I've done something really stupid."

"What? Stop before you cut yourself," Val ordered when Opie fumbled the pieces. "I'll get the broom."

She left them on the floor and stood. "I let myself fall in love with a man who doesn't want me."

"Oh, Opie." Val pulled her into a hug.

"Everything okay in there?" her dad called out.

"Yes," Val responded. "We dropped a cup." She turned and reached for the cake stand. "Take your time. I'll serve this."

Opie wiped her eyes and said, "I can do it." She balanced the tray on one arm, grabbed the coffee carafe from the counter, and led the way. Val followed with the cake.

"It's pecan fudge delight." Wendell's favorite. She hadn't realized he'd be there when she made the dessert that morning.

He grinned. "It must be my lucky day."

"You keep cooking like this and some man is going to steal you away." Her father winked at her.

"I plan to get better," Opie assured as she sliced the cake with deft, precise cuts. "Cooking is my life."

She served them, leaving Heath until last. "I shouldn't give you any after that grass comment."

"Please. 'Cause you love me."

His pitiful plea made her laugh, and she cut an extra large piece. She hugged him as she set the plate down on the table. "I do love you, and I'm glad you're home."

After the others left the table, Opie collected the dishes and carried them into the kitchen.

Wendell returned to place a check on the counter. "I didn't get a chance to give you that before you left the other night."

"I wanted to check on Heath."

"I know. Everyone raved about your food. Don't be surprised if some of those business cards you displayed so discreetly result in more work."

She'd placed a basket of hand-dipped chocolates on the table by his front door with a holder of business cards. "Too obvious?" she asked.

"I'd say nice touch. The candy was delicious by the way. I forgot your basket and holder."

She laughed. "Thanks. I'll pick it up soon."

Wendell propped against the island. "Susan said you weren't able to cater her event."

She called Opie the morning after the party. After hearing Susan Boone's plans, she told her it wasn't possible. "I don't have a kitchen large enough to prepare for a group that size."

"What do you need?"

"A commercial kitchen. She's planning on between two and three hundred people. And I'd have to hire staff."

"You don't want the event?"

"I won't take on a job I can't complete."

"Susan was disappointed."

She shrugged. "In a few months, I'll have the kitchen at the pavilion and will be able to take on bigger jobs. Maybe she'll give me another chance."

Wendell accepted her excuse. "Ophelia, what was your objective with that confrontation at lunch?"

She fiddled with the cloth she picked up from the countertop. "I let myself hope."

"Hope?" he repeated.

Her need to make him understand shocked her. "That maybe you'd wake up and see that what you think you want isn't how it has to be."

"You mean us? It wouldn't work, Ophelia." His head moved in a slow back-and-forth sideways. "I'm all wrong for you. I'm too old."

"You're not that old," she protested. Opie meant what she'd told Val about age. She didn't care that Wendell was older than her.

"We're too different in all the ways that count."

"How can you know that? Do you really know me?" she asked, staring at him.

"I know your values. I know what you want out of life. It wouldn't work."

"You think you know me so well, but you don't," she argued, turning away from him.

"I know you better than you realize. I know you'd never do anything to hurt your family, which would happen if you became involved with an old sinner like me."

Opie tossed the dishcloth into the sink and whirled back to face him. "You don't have to be that way, Wendell. God loves you. Accepting Him as your Savior would make you happier than you've ever been."

"I don't feel unhappy."

Frustrated, she cried, "Because you're blind to your misery. You hate a loving God for what happened to your mom. Did it ever occur to you that He didn't want her to die? That He gave her freedom of choice and she chose not to go to the doctor?

"You said yourself that you never had a good relationship with your father, and you're heading down that same path with Russ. If you don't stop and take a long look at yourself, you'll probably marry a woman who can't make you happy and produce children who won't love and respect their father either."

He pushed himself upright, standing stiffly. "You don't know that."

"I know that people who are always searching for personal happiness don't care who they hurt in the process."

"Don't judge me, Ophelia."

She couldn't begin to imagine his life, but Opie wanted so much for him. "I care for you, Wendell. I want to see you happier than you've ever been. Life has its ups and downs, but when you claim God as your Father, you have someone to turn to in the tough times."

Heath swung into the kitchen on his crutches. "Opie, can you help me. . ." He paused. "Sorry. I didn't realize you were still here."

"That's okay. I was on my way out." He glanced at her and said, "Thanks for lunch. It was delicious as usual."

Heath noted Wendell's hasty departure before turning to her. "What was that about?"

She wasn't ready to discuss this. "He wanted to give me a check. What did you need?"

After she helped Heath locate the acetaminophen, Opie returned to the kitchen and started preparations for dinner. She was fixing the roast when her mom returned and asked how things had gone.

"Daddy seemed to like the stir fry. He invited Wendell Hunter to join us."

"Oh," her mother voiced her surprise. "I didn't realize he planned to invite anyone to lunch."

"He didn't. Wendell stopped by and Daddy asked him to stay."

"I'm sure everything was fine. Thank you, Opie."

"You're welcome, Mom. How was your luncheon?"

They discussed the event, and Opie could see her mother enjoyed her outing. "You should do things more often. I don't mind helping out."

"You're a big help, and I probably don't tell you thanks often enough."

"You don't need to thank me. I love doing things for you. Always have."

Her mother touched her cheek with the gentleness that only a mother could share. "Your father and I have been tremendously blessed with our children. I listen to others request prayer for their wayward children, and I feel I should fall to my knees and thank the Lord for all He's given me."

Her words reminded Opie that she needed to turn to God for her answers. Sometimes she forgot to practice what she preached.

Chapter 10

September moved on and Opie's life got even busier. She hadn't seen Wendell since the day he came to lunch. Realizing she didn't have the answers, she placed the situation in God's hands and did her best not to force the issue. Even though her belief she could help never wavered, there were times when Opie doubted she could get beyond her feelings for him.

"Any word from Prestige?" Opie asked Val over breakfast. They were all struggling with a recent incident concerning the pavilion project that had thrown Russ into a very bad light. He denied sending the contractor the e-mail changing the concrete pour and Opie believed him.

"Russ called to say Randall King is looking into the situation."

Opie frowned. She knew Val didn't have good feelings about the owner of the architectural firm that employed Russ. "What does that mean?"

"I'm sure he's looking at things from a liability aspect."

"Any more problems?" She spread a thin layer of jelly on her slice of toast and took a bite.

"No. Todd says Russ is watching things like a hawk. I think he's afraid someone's out to hurt me and determined they won't."

Fear rose up in Opie's throat, the toast nearly choking her as she considered Val's words. "Why haven't you told me this before? That's crazy. What have you done to anyone to cause this?"

"I won the lottery."

"Right. You won," she agreed, shoving the plate away. "What you do with the money is your concern. You aren't hurting anyone with your plans."

"But whoever is behind this feels entitled to share in my wealth. I just hope Russ can prove his innocence. It doesn't look good."

"Why did you give him another chance?"

"Because he asked and gave me a reason to believe I should."

Opie knew Val cared for Russ a lot and hoped they could work things out. She hadn't given a lot of thought to work until Susan Boone called again.

"Wendell says you refused because you don't have a large enough kitchen?"

"That's right."

"I have an idea. My friend owns a restaurant downtown. He's willing to rent the space to you from midnight until around five a.m. Would that work?"

Her suggestion puzzled Opie. "Why are you going out of your way like this? Surely you know other caterers."

"Wendell says I won't be disappointed, and I believe him."

Opie appreciated his support, but she didn't understand why he had gone back to Susan with what she'd told him. Why was it so important that she cater this event? She weighed the pros and cons and said, "Give me your friend's number. If we can work things out, I'll be happy to cater your event." She scribbled the name and number on a scrap of paper.

"Wendell said you did an English tea party for your sister. Would you be willing to do a themed party for me?"

"Name your theme, and I'll plan the menu."

Opie promised to get back to her as soon as possible. She was able to work a deal with Ken Brown and called to let Susan know.

"I'm so glad," Susan said. "Wendell will be happy that you're catering the engagement party."

Opie's heart plummeted. No wonder Wendell claimed he wasn't right for her. He'd already found his Mrs. Right. A wealthy, perfect woman who befitted his social status. Never a rebellious upstart who didn't know when to shut up.

Her heart took another hit when Susan said she wanted a costume ball. The theme would be romance, and their guests would come dressed as famous lovers throughout the ages.

Opie didn't want to see Wendell in the role of another woman's lover, famous or not. She wanted him for herself. She forced herself to listen as Susan named a few specific menu items she wanted.

"I'm giving you free rein with the rest of the food."

"I'll get the menu and cost projections to you by the end of the week."

"Thanks, Ophelia. I want this to be the party everyone remembers."

"It will be." Opie knew she'd never forget the event.

She threw herself into her work, determined to make Wendell's engagement party unforgettable. Though she wanted to dislike the woman he'd chosen, Opie found Susan to be very likeable and easy to work with. No doubt they would call on her for future work. The idea gnawed at Opie. How could she cater events for the man she loved and another woman? She pushed the idea away. She'd cross that bridge in the future. Maybe this was God's way of directing her path elsewhere.

The strong temptation to confront Wendell ate at Opie. He'd said he'd known Susan for years, but why had she never been present at the events when she'd cooked for him and his guests? What kind of relationship did he have with his future wife? She wanted answers.

Yet, Opie knew she had no rights where Wendell was concerned. He'd made no promises to her. He hadn't led her on. It wasn't fair to him or to her to pursue the matter. Wendell had made his decision. A realist, she allowed herself to cry for what she couldn't have but refused to embarrass him or herself with further declarations of love. Opie held firm and as the week for preparation arrived, she only grew more despondent. While she worked, she fantasized about ways to convince him to change his mind.

Opie planned to take a week to prepare for the event. She hired sufficient staff, and her lists grew by the day. Her assistants worked the same long night hours. Opie was thankful when Susan's friend offered her the use of an empty walk-in fridge to store the items until the night of the party. At times, she feared she'd never complete service, but as always everything fell into place. On the night of the party, she took a moment to step out into the Boones' drawing room to see the happy couple. Maybe seeing Wendell in love would help her accept the situation. She really did want his happiness.

The room sparkled with understated elegance, taking Susan's theme of romance far from the Valentine-red heart variety. Candles and ambient lighting, fine china, heirloom silver, crystal stemware, and masses of red roses filled the long buffet tables. Servers stood ready to fill the guests' plates.

This was every woman's dream—the perfect event and the perfect man.

Opie spotted Wendell talking with a couple of people over by the french doors. His lack of costume surprised her. Surely, he wouldn't break Susan's heart by refusing to participate in her party theme. She looked around and spotted Susan dressed as Cinderella. Another man dressed as Prince Charming stood with his arm about her waist. How could Wendell stand by while another man took his place on the most important night of his life? Opie walked to where Wendell now stood alone.

"Why aren't you wearing your Prince Charming costume?"

"I can't see me in that getup. I opted to come as myself."

She sniffed. "You hardly qualify as a world's greatest lover. Why aren't you with Susan?"

"I doubt she'd care for my intrusion on her romantic moment." He took a sip from his glass.

"But it's your engagement party."

Liquid sprayed from his lips as Wendell's brows arched. "What are you talking about? I'm not marrying Susan."

"You let me believe you cared for her." Opie sucked in a deep breath as it occurred to her that she'd made the wrong assumption. Grabbing a napkin, she patted at the wet spots on her coat. She handed him a napkin. "You knew I'd think it was you when she said engagement party."

She heard his quick intake of breath.

"I never indicated any relationship with Susan beyond our friendship. You came to that conclusion on your own."

"But you knew I thought. . ."

"It's not me, Ophelia. What does it matter, anyway?" he asked as if bored with the conversation.

"You know why. She loves you."

"She does. As a friend. We dated a few times before I introduced her to Tony."

She frowned, unsure about what she was hearing. "She dumped you for your friend?"

"No. She didn't dump me." He sounded exasperated by her assumptions. "We never had that kind of relationship."

"So you're okay with her marrying your friend?"

He shrugged. "They make a great couple."

Embarrassed, Opie said, "I need to get back to the kitchen. Enjoy the party."

"You've done an excellent job, Ophelia. I can see your career taking off after tonight."

Opie mumbled thanks and pushed through her confused emotions to complete service.

∽

Her bookings did increase. Susan asked her to do a charity event, and over the next couple of weeks Opie received a number of calls from people who wanted a private chef to prepare a special dinner. Ken agreed to continue their working arrangement for the charity event, but Opie knew she needed her own place if she wanted to carry out her other plan as well. She'd catered the dinner events from her customers' kitchens and then gone on to the restaurant after closing hours to prepare for the bigger party.

"How did it go?" Val asked when they passed each other in the yard.

She'd worked all night and felt comfortable with her accomplishments. "I'm ready for tonight's party."

"What did you find out about the storefront you looked at?"

"We're negotiating. The owner wants more than I'm willing to invest. I'd have to renovate the kitchen. I wish the pavilion were ready. That would be perfect."

"Renting the restaurant kitchen has worked out okay, hasn't it?"

"Yeah, but hauling supplies in and rushing to clean up before they open for breakfast is difficult. I need a place that opens for lunch."

"How can you work all night and still be together for the event?"

Her back ached between her shoulders, and her eyes burned from exhaustion. "I'll be fine. Lots of kids my age burn the candle at both ends."

"Have you decided if you're going with us next week?"

Now that the plan to visit their grandfather was definite, Opie struggled with doubts about meeting him. She felt no bond or respect, nor had she ever seen any indication her dad cared about a relationship with his father. "Part of me thinks we should let it go. Daddy's lived with it this long."

"That doesn't sound like you," Val protested. "You always want to right the wrongs of the world."

"When I see a wrong," she agreed. "I prayed over your request, but I think we're making more problems for ourselves."

Val appeared disappointed by her decision. "We don't know him well enough to think anything, Opie. I haven't seen him since I was a child, and I certainly don't remember him."

"Tell me again why you feel the need to do this."

"For Daddy. You don't have to go. The twins plan to come."

"I didn't say I wouldn't go," she protested. She was part of this family, and if the visit benefited their dad, she'd support him 100 percent. "I just want to know what you hope to accomplish. You're forcing Daddy to do something he doesn't want to do."

"I didn't force him," Val protested. "I told him I planned to visit and gave him the option to come if he wanted."

"You knew he wouldn't say no." They both knew their protective father.

"Aren't you curious? He's our grandfather."

"Not really. He's not like Grammy, Uncle Zeb, and Aunt Karen. They're Daddy's family who we know and love."

"And your heart isn't big enough to love a stranger?"

Val's comment hit home. This stranger's blood flowed through their veins. "You know it is."

"I feel God wants me to do something. You didn't see how upset Daddy was."

Opie had witnessed her dad's controlled anger a few times, but she'd never seen him out of control. Evidently learning his father knew about the lottery winnings pushed him over the edge. "Haven't you ever noticed how Daddy acts after they talk on the phone?" Val asked.

"He doesn't have much to say."

"Because he's so angry with Grandfather he can hardly bear to speak to him. Daddy's asked me not to do things, but he's never forbidden me before. I didn't plan to give Grandfather money, but Daddy spoke to me as if I were a small child. Said he couldn't stop Grammy, but he could stop me. Does that sound like Daddy to you?"

"No," Opie agreed.

"I need to see why Daddy is afraid of him."

"Are you nuts? If a big strong man like our father has fears, you don't think you should, too?"

"It's not physical, Opie. It's emotional. I think Daddy wanted to look up to his father. We can't begin to understand disappointment on that level. He's never let any of us down. I only want to help them have a future relationship."

Opie massaged the sudden pain in her forehead. "I suppose we need to give Daddy the emotional support he needs to confront his demon."

"Don't call him a demon," Val said.

She sighed. "You know what I mean."

"This is important. I have this feeling Daddy's happiness hinges on forgiving Grandfather."

Hadn't she recently told Wendell he needed to forgive, as well? Opie yawned. "Don't be disappointed if things don't turn out as you expect."

"Wouldn't it be wonderful if they connected?"

"That only happens in movies and books," Opie said.

"I know, but whatever happens, we have God by our side."

"Amen to that. See you later. I need sleep."

A few minutes later, Opie lay on her bed, her mind spinning as she tried to sort out the wild tangle of emotions. She wasn't convinced their visit would serve a positive purpose but would go for her father's sake. The idea that they were about to awake a furor that might never be silenced wouldn't go away.

Eventually she slept and rose when the alarm went off to dress for her event. Her mother worked in the kitchen. Sammy came running, holding up a paper plate mask to her face. "Oh, you frightened me." Opie gasped and the child giggled in delight. After admiring Sammy's coloring, she took a bottle of water from the fridge. "Mom, what do you think about us visiting grandfather?"

Mom rinsed the potatoes and turned off the water. She reached for the potato peeler. "I think Val could be right. Your dad hasn't visited Mathias in years."

"Did you ever meet him?"

"Once. Your dad took Val and the twins to meet his father. It didn't go well, and after that Jacob insisted we keep that part of his life separate."

Opie couldn't believe what she was hearing. "Is that really possible?"

"I respected his feelings and tried not to interfere."

She drank from the bottle and twisted the cap back on. "You never felt God wanted you to do anything?"

Her mother rinsed the potatoes again and dumped them into a pot. "I'm sensitive to what this does to your dad. I listen and we talk. When he's upset, I pray with him. I've prayed for Mathias as well."

"Has Dad said how he feels about this trip?"

Mom chuckled. "You mean other than he'd rather be hit in the head with a sledgehammer?"

Her dad always said that about things he didn't like doing. Opie hugged her mom. "Gotta run. I'll be late tonight."

She paused to say bye to Sammy and rushed off, her thoughts turning to the job she was about to do.

Chapter 11

By the end of the night, Opie felt as if someone had taken a snuffer to her double-ended candle. She welcomed the break in her schedule and looked forward to time for herself. Later that morning, she took a walk out into the gardens and decided to call Wendell. She hadn't seen him at the parties she'd done for his friends and wanted to thank him for recommending her. Unsure whether he was home or away on business, she dialed his cell phone.

They talked for a few minutes before he said, "Have lunch with me on Saturday."

Opie knew her schedule was clear. "What did you have in mind?"

"A surprise."

She found that curious. Wendell Hunter didn't strike her as a man who cared for surprises.

"Okay. What time?"

"I'll pick you up around ten."

"What should I wear?"

"Dressy casual."

The conversation ended, and Opie shut off her cell phone and puzzled over the invitation. After all this time, why would he invite her to lunch? They hadn't spoken since the engagement party. She was no closer to an answer when he arrived Saturday morning.

"You look really nice," Wendell said when she greeted him at the door.

Opie thought him very handsome in his navy blazer and khaki slacks. "Thanks." She opted for a black pantsuit with a lacy purple top underneath, hoping it would be okay for their destination. She'd added a pair of wedge heels.

"I was surprised that you called," Wendell said.

His words seemed tentative. Opie didn't tell him she'd been equally surprised when he invited her to lunch. "I wanted to thank you. I've been so busy I haven't had the opportunity until now. You haven't been at the parties," she offered, almost an accusation.

"I've been traveling for business."

Opie knew the farm wasn't his only business interest. She felt hopeful they'd get past that last uncomfortable session.

Even if they could never be more than friends, she needed to be part of his life.

When they approached Keeneland, Opie instinctively knew this was Wendell's surprise. She'd never set foot inside the gates of the national historic landmark Thoroughbred horseracing and sales facility. She'd seen photos of the limestone buildings and the well designed, meticulous landscaping and read articles extolling the traditions of the track founded by Jack Keene in 1935 on 147 acres of farmland west of Lexington. From its onset, Keeneland used proceeds from the spring and fall live races and auctions to further the Thoroughbred industry and contribute back to the community.

"Hunter Farm has a couple of horses running today, and I hoped you might help me cheer them on to victory," Wendell said.

He made it difficult to say no. Opie told herself it was only lunch, but her desire to witness his world warred against her dad's displeasure. Wendell won. "I've never been here before."

People filled the area. As with other sports, tailgaters had set up beneath the glorious red and gold trees in the parking lot.

"Jacob was probably here last month for the yearling sales," Wendell commented as they entered.

Opie didn't know. He never mentioned the tracks. "It's possible."

Wendell slowed his stride to match hers. "You'd probably like to visit the kitchens. We should have come for breakfast at the Track Kitchen and watched the horses work out this morning." He stopped walking and asked, "Is something wrong? You're awfully quiet."

Sensory overload from trying to take in too much too fast, Opie thought. "No, I'm fine." She'd worry about how to explain this to her dad later.

Even she knew this wasn't a typical sightseeing experience. Wendell gave her a complete tour of the area before he said, "Let's eat, and then we can check out the horses prior to post time. We're having lunch in the clubhouse."

Opie admired the beautifully set up buffet luncheon in the clubhouse but could barely recall what she'd eaten. She saw a different side of Wendell as he talked horses with the other owners and trainers. He confidently advised them he was there to win today and spirited disputes rose up over the race outcome. In the end, they wished each other the best of luck.

Eventually they made it down to the paddock. The area swarmed with people. Owners, trainers, and jockeys viewed the competition and received last-minute advice while fans admired the beautiful horses and made their picks for the winner. The beautiful hats drew Opie's attention. She'd never been able to keep them on her head and often wished she could wear them as well as these women did.

Wendell introduced her to his trainer, Terrence Malone. Opie stood by while they discussed the upcoming races.

"I have a good feeling about today, Mr. Hunter."

Wendell nodded and glanced at the jockey who wore the Hunter Farm silks. "What about you, Dan?"

"Dell Air's the one to beat today, sir. There he is."

Opie's gaze turned to the impressive gray Thoroughbred. It was the first time she'd seen Wendell's colt. Standing at almost seventeen hands, Dell Air's sleek muscles rippled beneath his well-groomed coat. Opie experienced the eeriest feeling that Dell Air knew he was on display. She would almost say he posed for those who watched.

A few minutes later, the trainer gave Dan a leg up.

They arrived back at their seats just before the call-to-post bugle. Opie felt the crowd's excitement when the horses came out onto the track to parade before the grandstand before they moved toward the gate. Wendell pointed to Dell Air, and breathless anticipation filled her as the horses rocketed from the gates and down the track. Soon the jockeys rode so low all she could see was the color of their caps. The gray hugged the inside, moving through the ranks and to the front and was soon neck and neck with the leader. In the last few seconds, he pulled ahead and won the race.

Opie hadn't realized she'd been yelling encouragement until Wendell chuckled. She couldn't take her eyes off his smiling face when they declared his colt the winner. Wendell swung her up and around, and then he kissed her. "I should bring you along for good luck every time," he declared.

She touched her lips, struggling to understand what had just happened.

"Come on," Wendell said, grabbing her hand.

"No. You go ahead. I need to visit the ladies room."

Wendell looked confused. "Are you sure?"

Opie nodded. Not only did she need time alone, but also there was no place for her in the winner's circle among the photographers and media. "I'll meet you back here."

She stood before the bathroom mirror for some time, reliving the touch of his lips against hers. *It was the excitement*, she thought. The gesture hadn't meant anything to him. Unfortunately, it meant too much to her.

Jubilant upon his return, Wendell placed the ticket in her hand, "Here's a little gift for you."

Opie saw it was for the race Dell Air had just won. "No. I couldn't," she said, pushing it back at him.

Wendell frowned. "I bought it for you."

"I can't."

His mouth thinned with his displeasure. "Your sister took her winnings."

"Val worked hard on her project. The gift was her bonus. I haven't done anything."

"Sure you have. You've done a stellar job this summer. Here, take it."

She shook her head and stepped back. "I can't, Wendell. I'm sorry."

Tension stretched between them. "What's going on, Ophelia? You wouldn't go to the winner's circle, and now you're refusing my gift."

Would he understand if she told him she'd been overcome by her emotions after the kiss or that she hadn't wanted to risk her family seeing her on television? The furtiveness of this outing weighed heavy on her heart.

He seemed disappointed at her hesitation. "You want to leave?"

Opie considered his question and nodded. "I'll call someone to pick me up. I don't want to take you away from the races."

"I brought you here. I'll take you home."

A less talkative Wendell escorted her to the car. Silence stretched as he drove toward home. Finally he spoke. "What's going on in your head, Ophelia?"

"I shouldn't have gone." She sensed his immediate withdrawal. "You don't need to feel guilty. It was my decision. I could have refused, but I wanted to see for myself."

"It's business, Ophelia. I can't keep horses for pleasure. They have to pay for themselves."

"I know."

"Why is your family so against racing?"

"I told you before Wendell. It's the temptation. Daddy will be upset when I tell him."

"You're a grown woman, Ophelia. Your father doesn't control your actions."

"No, but my love and respect for him does," she said.

"I don't get it," Wendell said. "He supports his family breeding Thoroughbreds. And you said he doesn't have a problem."

Opie knew Wendell needed to hear the whole story. "My grandfather did." Her voice lowered as she said, "He killed a man over a petty bet in a drunken brawl. He's serving a life sentence and has been in prison since my dad was seventeen years old."

He took in a sharp, quick breath. "I'm sorry, Ophelia. I thought we could have a fun outing. It never occurred to me that your family was dealing with something of that magnitude."

∾

Opie knew she needed to tell her family what she'd done but was glad no one asked where she'd been. She could still see Wendell's expression when she'd told him about her grandfather. Had she imagined his reaction? She didn't think so.

A few days later, the trip to Eddyville was history and as Opie suspected, neither father nor son greeted each other with open arms.

She could definitely see her dad in Mathias Truelove's outer self, but they were nothing alike. Her dad hadn't been happy. In fact, he'd been almost disrespectful to his father. That surprised Opie. If anything, she expected him to treat his dad with respect.

Opie appreciated the way Val controlled the visit, asking their father and grandfather not to argue and even defending her when Mathias commented that she was goofing off and could easily find a job if she was any good. When he brought up the lottery win, Val maintained that it was a gift from God. He'd been critical of their beliefs, but they assured him there was nothing wrong with serving the Lord. He asked his son if he still ran that farm, and no one mentioned the change of ownership. Their dad insisted they keep their personal business to themselves.

One point stuck in Opie's head. Even after thirty years in prison, her grandfather's fondest memories weren't of his family but of racing. "Going to the tracks always got my heart pumping," he'd said with a laugh. "There were days when I got so close to a big win that I thought I'd die right there of a heart attack."

After witnessing his exhilaration, Opie compared her reaction. She'd experienced the excitement in terms of seeing the horses run. Like any sports fan, she'd rooted for her horse and found satisfaction in Dell Air's victory. But when it came to memories, her first kiss from Wendell scored much higher.

Opie definitely understood Val's concerns when she witnessed her dad's strong reaction after they left the prison. Jacob admitted he'd tried to forgive his father but couldn't. His harsh comment that every man in the prison deserved to be there made Val ask if he'd love them any less if they made wrong decisions. Even though he'd said he wouldn't, Opie couldn't help but think how disappointed he would be when she told him what she'd done. She knew that only God could heal the father-son relationship.

After a restless night, Opie felt she wouldn't find peace until she told her dad the truth. Wendell might not understand why they avoided temptation, but she learned a valuable lesson. After hearing her grandfather yesterday, she knew why her dad felt as he did.

Opie went to find Jacob. She found him watching the exercise boys breeze the yearling they'd recently acquired. She remembered innocently asking what that meant once. Her father had gone into detail about the training method where the horses ran at more than a fast gallop over varying track lengths. There had been more, but she'd zoned out and missed that part. *Had this colt come from the Keeneland sales?* Opie wondered.

Jacob spoke to the trainer before he turned to her. "Is something wrong?"

Opie understood why he'd think that. She rarely searched him up on his turf. She should come back when he wasn't busy. "I can wait."

"Not if it's important enough to bring you out here now."

She couldn't look him in the eye as she said, "I went to the track with Wendell last Saturday." He didn't say anything, and she hurriedly explained, "He invited me to lunch. I didn't know we were going to Keeneland. Dell Air won."

Jacob started walking back to the farm office. Opie walked beside him. "Wendell has high hopes for that horse. Did you place a bet?"

"No," Opie said with an emphatic shake of her head. "Wendell tried to give me a winning ticket after the race and got upset when I turned him down. He brought up Val's winnings. I tried to explain the difference. While they were both gifts, this seemed more like ill-gotten gains."

"Conscience?" her dad asked.

"Exactly," Opie agree with a barely perceptible dip of her head. "I told myself it would be okay so long as I didn't gamble."

"People don't always understand others' values. What did you hope to find out by going?"

Her father's calm handling of the situation made things harder. She almost wished he would yell or shout. "I should have said no, but I wanted to see for myself. I guess I wanted it to not be what you've always told us."

His eyebrows slanted in a frown. "Why?"

"Because of Wendell." Her voice broke miserably with the admission.

"You care for him?"

She nodded. "He calls himself an old sinner and says he's not good for me. I know I'll never have more than his friendship."

"He's given your business a leg up," Jacob said. "You know, Opie, I can only ask you kids not to do things and give you what I hope are good reasons as to why it's a bad idea, but ultimately God gave you freedom of choice. Each of you has to decide what's right and wrong.

"What you witnessed Saturday is Bluegrass tradition. The Sport of Kings," he emphasized. "Millions of dollars change hands at the tracks. The majority of people there hope to put a substantial portion in their bank account. Some will go home content with a fun outing, but others will suffer major disappointment."

He stopped and looked at her. "Your mom and I have been blessed not to see our children in trouble over the years, and I believe it's because God has been a shining light in your decision-making process. I know each of you asks what Jesus would do."

Opie couldn't say she'd done that this time. The urge to see Wendell in his environment pushed the thought right out of her head. "I felt guilty because I knew you'd be disappointed."

"Conscience will get you every time," Jacob agreed with a crooked smile. "All my father cared about was a good time, and in the end it became his downfall. He wasted his life and money.

"We were in the courtroom the day they found him guilty. He refused to accept the blame for his actions. If he got drunk, it was the bartender's fault. If he lost his money, it was the horse's fault. He claimed the man picked a fight and yet rather than walk away, he made a choice that cost a man his life and him his freedom.

"That's why I've always talked about accepting the consequences of your decisions. I will say he was role model enough to show me that I never wanted that kind of life for my children. I've been a tough taskmaster, but I do what I do out of love. I may not tell you enough, but I love you. I'd willingly give up everything, including my life, for you."

Choked with emotion, Opie nodded.

"Wendell feels the need to prove himself worthy of being his father's son."

"You should have seen him in the clubhouse. He was in his element."

"He's spent the last ten years of his life doing that."

"He says the horses have to pay for themselves," Opie said. "How will we survive without that income?"

"God will show us the way."

323

"Will buying and selling horses be enough?"

"We're looking at other ways of raising capital."

"Yet another reason I should make a decision about my future and be less of a drain on the family budget," Opie said as they walked on. "I'll let you get back to work. I needed to get this off my chest. I'm sorry, Daddy."

"Don't be sorry, Opie. I appreciate your honesty. Learning the truth from another source would have hurt more."

"I know. I never meant to hurt you, Daddy. I just wanted to see for myself. Did you know they feed thousands of people there every day?"

He nodded. "I've eaten breakfast at the Track Kitchen when I go for the sales."

"Wendell mentioned that place."

Her dad chuckled. "Leave it to you to go to Keeneland and come home thinking about food."

Opie smiled at his teasing remark. "Do I need to tell the others?"

"Only if you want to. As far as I'm concerned, it's between you and God."

She hugged him. "Forgive me?"

"There's nothing to forgive, Opie. I won't promise not to try to convince you not to follow your heart, but I do promise to be there for you whatever the outcome."

Chapter 12

The sun shone brightly on a crisp early November day as the Truelove family prepared for the arrival of their guests. Opie and her siblings enjoyed surprising their parents with breakfast in bed.

"I have horses to attend to," Jacob argued when they settled the tray across his lap.

"Not today." Opie tucked a cloth napkin into the neck of his pajama top. "It's an official holiday on the property. No horses on Cindy Day."

Her mother laughed. "I take it you couldn't get the mayor to make it official in Paris?"

"We tried, but he couldn't see his way clear to grant our request. Something about others wanting their own official day," Val declared with a frown. "Sorry, Mom, no key to the city."

"Here at home will do just fine," Mom assured with a chuckle.

Opie removed the domed cover to reveal all her mother's breakfast favorites. "We want you to take it easy today. The guest rooms are ready for your sisters, Grammy, Uncle Zeb, and Jen. Aunt Karen couldn't make it." Opie looked forward to seeing her cousin, Jennifer. They became close when she lived with them while attending culinary school.

"When do their flights get in?"

"Everything's handled," Heath said. "A limo will transport them to the farm in style."

"They will think we've gone crazy," Mom said.

"Not until later," Val said, sharing a grin with her siblings.

"Valentine," her mother asked, "what are you planning?"

"It's a surprise, Mom. Don't worry. You're going to have the time of your life."

"I suppose as long as you didn't bring the circus to town," she muttered uneasily.

"Oh, you don't like the circus?" Val asked with mock concern.

Opie giggled at her startled expression.

"She's pulling your leg, Mom," Rom said.

"Spoilsport," Val called, nudging him with her shoulder.

After a few minutes, Opie left them to enjoy their breakfast. Her role for the day was a busy one. There were plans for breakfast, a barbecue luncheon for two hundred guests, and a sit-down dinner. Any one event would have been enough for their mother, but they wanted to ensure that everyone who mattered to her had the opportunity to celebrate her birthday. Breakfast was for their parents;

lunch for church, community friends, and family; and dinner for family and close friends.

Opie took a few minutes around two to fix herself a plate. She enjoyed the succulent barbecue as she watched the this-is-your-life large screen presentation Jules put together with photos of her mom from birth to present including interviews with their dad, her children, siblings, and friends. When Cindy Truelove smiled at the newborn in her arms—probably Cy given the more current hairstyle—Opie accepted her mother had exactly what she'd always wanted.

All this time, she'd thought her mother needed more to be fulfilled when in reality her children were the woman's finest creations. She might spend hours putting a delectable meal on the table, but what did she have after it was eaten? A few compliments and maybe more work. Food couldn't love her back like a family. Couldn't be there for her in the future when she was elderly and retired from a career that would probably give her ulcers and turn her hair gray.

Opie continued to mull this over as she visited with their guests for a while and then went back to the kitchen to prepare the rack of lamb for their sit-down dinner. A second birthday cake layered three levels high and covered with the delicate pastel sugar flowers she'd spent hours making by hand sat on the sideboard in the dining room.

Her catering assistants' familiarity with her work methods made things go smoothly. The servers ensured their guests had everything they needed. At six, Opie checked one last time to be sure the rooms were set up properly. Tables from the tent would seat the guests who did not fit around the dining table.

The fantasy took her breath away. Candles flickered in their antique holders, beautiful linens draped the tables, and their mother's favorite roses filled the crystal vases throughout the room. A small gift commemorating the event sat at each place. Never in all her wildest imagining would Opie have thought they would host such a party.

She exchanged her chef whites for the lavender silk maxi-dress she'd chosen for the event. She could hardly wait to see the others in their formal wear. No doubt her parents had been surprised to find the new formal dress and tux laid out on the bed in their room.

After appetizers in the drawing room, Val said, "Everyone find your place cards and have a seat."

Opie hadn't noticed the cards earlier. When she stepped into the room, Wendell tipped his head to indicate the chair next to him. He stood and watched her approach. "You're looking particularly beautiful tonight."

The open admiration in his expression nearly left Opie speechless. "Thank you," she managed after getting herself seated.

"I hope you don't mind that I'm here."

Memories of their times together filled her head. "How have you been?"

"Busy. I owe you an apology."

"No," she said sharply. "Let's don't talk about that."

"But. . ."

"Wendell, please don't," she said softly, smiling at her aunts and cousin Jennifer when they joined them. She introduced him as their friend and neighbor. Mostly thanks to her aunts, the conversation flowed throughout the meal. Opie contributed, but her attention focused on the servers.

"Relax. They have everything under control," Wendell whispered in her ear.

"I know. I just want it to be perfect."

His gaze lingered on her face. "It is."

Tears came to her eyes when her tuxedo-clad father presented his wife with a diamond cross necklace. The love in their expressions spoke volumes as he brushed aside her hair and fastened the necklace before kissing her. Wendell caught her hand underneath the table and squeezed comfortingly.

"It's all too much," her teary-eyed mom protested.

"It can never be enough," her dad countered.

The dinner concluded with her mother blowing out her candles and everyone singing "Happy Birthday." Her aunts went off to visit with their sister.

"Opie, the food was spectacular," her grandmother Truelove enthused when her son escorted her from the dining room. "You children did your mother proud."

"Thanks, Grammy." Opie stood and hugged her.

"When are you coming to see me again? I've missed those special dishes you prepared."

She'd often prepared meals for her aunt's family and took food over to her grandmother when she lived in Florida. "I've missed you, too."

"She tells me I should go to culinary school," Jen told her. "I tell her I can barely boil water."

Opie chuckled. She knew that to be a fact. Her attempts to interest her cousin in cooking had been a major flop.

"I'm so happy you came," she said, squeezing Jen's shoulder and sliding her arm about her grandmother's waist. "You're staying through tomorrow, I hope."

"We don't fly out until late Monday afternoon," Jen said. "Uncle Jacob said he'd give me a tour of the farm after church tomorrow."

"Val suggested I spend more time here at the farm with your family," Lena Truelove said. "I told her perhaps when the weather is warmer."

"Put us on your schedule for next August for sure. We're already planning Dad's birthday event for next year."

"No way," Jacob declared. "I want to celebrate my birthday just like we did this year."

"Horse kick and all?"

"Now that part we can skip. My family, friends, and favorite foods are all I ever want."

"This has been fun, Jacob," his mother said. "I'm looking forward to seeing what you plan for Cindy next year to top this."

Opie laughed at her father's helpless look. "Don't worry, Daddy. We plan to come up with lots of reasons for you to wear that tux."

They chuckled when he tugged at the collar of his shirt and said, "I was afraid of that."

After they moved on, she dropped back into her chair.

"How are you doing?" Wendell asked. "From all accounts, you've done a marathon food service today."

"Tired but happy," Opie told him. "I wasn't sure I could pull it off."

Wendell smiled. "But you did."

The photographer they'd hired to capture the memories of the day came by and asked Wendell to move closer. He placed his arm about the back of her chair. His warmth radiated through her.

She'd steered clear of him lately, not wanting to embarrass him or herself further. Wendell seemed to have the same intention.

"I saw you and Russ talking earlier," she commented after the photographer left. "Everything okay?"

Wendell looked briefly over his shoulder in his brother's direction. "He wants to talk."

"I told Val what you told me," Opie admitted. "She told him this afternoon."

Wendell didn't say how he felt about what she'd done, but Opie thought Russ needed to know the truth.

"We'll see what happens. What else have you been doing?"

"Mostly working. Your friends have kept me busy with the parties. And we visited my grandfather in prison."

Wendell's brows rose. "How did that go?"

"Pretty much as expected. Daddy didn't want to be there. Val feels sorry for Grandfather. She says he doesn't have any reason to change if his family doesn't care for him."

"She's got a point. But people can't always be what other people expect."

Opie knew he referred to the times she'd challenged his choices. "I owe you an apology, Wendell."

"No, you don't. Even if we don't always agree, I like that you care about your friends, Ophelia."

∽

When Russ indicated his desire to talk, Wendell suggested he come to the house the next day. He'd had no idea what was on his mind until Ophelia told him what she'd done. He wondered if they'd be able to communicate without blowing up at each other. Only time would tell. The hurt surely wouldn't go away overnight. His brother arrived right on time.

"Come into the drawing room," Wendell invited.

Russ chose the sofa and Wendell the armchair. "Why didn't you tell me about the farm?"

"I would have if you hadn't run off before I could."

When Russ would have protested, he shrugged and said, "You're right. I never gave you an opportunity." After a brief pause, he added, "I always felt you didn't like me."

Wendell decided not to sugarcoat the situation. "It wasn't you. I didn't like what you meant to Dad. I was three when my mother died. At a time when he could have taken a more active role in my life, he met your mother. He didn't have time for me after that."

"I'm sure he didn't mean. . ."

"I felt abandoned. First by my mother and then my father."

"Mom tried to love you," Russ defended.

Wendell supposed Russ would see it that way. He'd been a surly withdrawn kid for most of his brother's childhood. He could tell him the truth, but he wouldn't do that to Russ. "I suppose she did in her own way, but she loved my father and you more. She was more than happy to agree with Dad when he suggested boarding school. I needed a home with real parents. Not some institution that cared more about education than the child they were teaching."

"I'm sorry, Wendell. I didn't understand."

"You were a child. You got a bad deal, too," he admitted grudgingly. "Your mom didn't object when Dad shipped you off later."

"I don't suppose he would have listened if she had. He had only one thing on his mind—horses."

"Hunter Farm and horses," Wendell corrected.

A crease formed between Russ's brows. "How do you suppose he felt knowing the farm would never be his?"

Wendell sat with his elbow propped on the chair arm, his head resting against his hand. "He made his mark on the racing world. There's more than one trophy with him as owner/breeder. I suppose he thought that if he had to keep the farm for me, he might as well prosper, too. You know, as far as the outside world knew, it was his farm. My mother changed the name after they were married. I guess she wanted to prove she was dedicated to their future."

"And yet she left it to you?"

He shrugged. "She didn't have a choice. This land has been in her family for years. My grandfather wasn't about to risk losing it to our dad. I don't think the two of them got along very well. He opposed my mother marrying him. And even though he legally tied her hands against giving the farm to Dad, she could call it whatever she wanted."

"So she salvaged Dad's pride, and he told us it was a man's job to provide for his family."

Wendell's brow rose at Russ's comment. "He did say that often, didn't he?"

Russ nodded. "I wonder what else he hid from us."

"He was what he was, Russ. Maybe he wasn't the greatest, most understanding father, but he provided well for us. I worked with him in those last years, and I'd be the first to tell you the man knew his business when it came to horses."

"But it was always business for him. I think the Trueloves have the best attitude about their farm. They don't put it ahead of everything else."

"Like Dad did with family?" Wendell asked.

Russ nodded.

"So you plan to marry Val Truelove?"

"In time. If she'll have me."

That surprised Wendell. "Why wouldn't she?"

"Surely you know they're a very religious family."

Wendell rose to his feet and walked over to pour himself a glass of water. He held the pitcher up and Russ nodded. After handing his brother the glass, he sat back down. "Yes. Ophelia made sure I'm aware of that."

Russ chuckled. "Opie hates being called by her full name."

"She's a beautiful young woman. Not at all suited to a tomboy name like Opie."

"Do you know why they all have nicknames?"

Wendell nodded. "Ophelia told me." He took another sip of water. "So when's the wedding?"

"I haven't proposed. We only agreed last night to pursue a future together."

"That's not a proposal?" Wendell asked, puzzled by the reference.

"It's a courtship. I need to develop my relationship with God before we take any further steps."

Wendell laughed. "She's got you in church?"

"It was my decision," Russ defended. "I've been miserable for a very long time. Lonely, depressed, and determined to show you I didn't need you, either. A rash of problems with Val's project made her doubt me. I didn't like it. Rom's been living at my condo and helped me understand the real reason for my unhappiness."

"You think religion is the answer?"

"I know it is," Russ answered confidently. "I'm tired of going it alone. God has filled the void left by the loss of my parents and sent someone for me to love. He's even enabled me to seek your forgiveness."

"Does she love you?"

Russ nodded. "She's the reason I'm here. She asked me to make peace with you. They're big believers in family. I owe you an apology, Wendell. I hope you'll forgive me. When I have children, I'd like them to know their uncle. It's not as if we have a great deal of family."

"You won't be able to say that if you marry into the Truelove family."

Russ grinned and said, "That's the best part. They're a great group."

"They are," Wendell agreed. Each time he'd been in their presence, he'd come away with a feeling he couldn't quite describe—a warmth that reached deep inside and made him crave more. "Quite accomplished. How are you going to handle your wife's wealth?"

"I won't let the money come between us like it did you and me."

Wendell eyed him speculatively. "Do you think it was only the money, Russ?"

"No. It was my attitude," he admitted, adding with a grin, "and your stubbornness. I made a wrong assumption. I regret that most of all. Dad and Mom looked out for me. They left me sufficient funds to finish school and establish myself. If I'd been more mature when I lost them, I might have realized how blessed I was not to have inherited the farm." He pointed to the piano. "Do you still play?"

Wendell nodded. "Occasionally."

"I'm sure you've only gotten better over the years. Do you regret not becoming a concert pianist?"

"No. I didn't want to travel and wasn't one to enjoy the acclaim."

"I'd love to hear you play again."

"Perhaps we can get together for dinner soon."

Russ nodded. "I'm serious about us, Wendell. I'm sorry for the selfish way I shoved you from my life."

"You were a kid, Russ."

"Old enough to try to understand. I'm sorry for being such a pain as a brother."

"I resented you far too much for us to have been closer," Wendell admitted. "Perhaps we can put the past behind us and look forward to a future as friends."

"Closer than friends, I hope. I want what Val has with her siblings."

"You have high hopes for us, brother."

"Very high. I'd better get back to Val. I know she's waiting to hear the outcome."

"You think she thought I'd kick you out?"

Russ stood and shrugged. "I might have considered it if I'd been you."

"If you can be man enough to apologize, I can be man enough to accept," Wendell said, holding out his hand. Russ pulled him into a hug, and Wendell silently thanked Ophelia for her interference.

Chapter 13

Opie could never remember a bad holiday, and this year had been no exception. She'd accepted a number of catering jobs and private chef services for dinner parties straight through the New Year. She also found time to help prepare special meals at the homeless shelter and collect gifts for the people who attended.

She ran into Wendell occasionally. The first time, he thanked her for what she'd done for him and Russ. She'd felt a little envious when Val attended a dinner party at Wendell's home. No doubt he was interested in getting to know the woman who could become his future sister-in-law.

Wendell wasn't the only one getting a new sister-in-law. Heath surprised Jane with his Christmas Eve proposal. Opie would never have guessed Heath had that much romance in him.

The Hunters and Trueloves spent the holidays together. After Christmas dinner, Opie watched Wendell across the room and wished things could be different. He caught her watching him and concluded his conversation, rising from the chair and pausing to pick up a gift from underneath the tree.

"I bought you something."

"You shouldn't have. I didn't get you anything," Opie said. Actually, she'd sent him the same homemade cookies she'd made to thank her clients and promote her business.

"Didn't expect you to. Open it."

The gift surprised her. He'd gone to the trouble of having her name embroidered on a chef's jacket. "Oh, thank you. You shouldn't have."

"It's to replace the one you ruined at my house. And I thought it would be good advertising to have your name right there on your coat where everyone can see it."

He rambled on, explaining the gift. Opie fingered the material, finding it nicer than anything she'd buy for herself. "I'll save this one for special occasions. Thank you."

"You're welcome. Russ and I appreciate the invitation to dinner."

Opie busied herself with folding the tissue back and putting the lid back on the box. "Get used to it. Now that Val and Russ are together, you'll be treated as family."

"I can handle that," Wendell said with a wide grin.

∾

Opie made it through all the Christmas and New Year bookings and looked forward to a short break before their church choir started preparing for the Easter cantata. The cold symptoms started right after New Year's. She visited the drugstore, but the over-the-counter medicines didn't help. As she sniffled and sneezed her way through multiple boxes of tissues, she felt thankful that it hadn't affected her holiday business. Her bank account showed a tidy sum.

She kept her distance at the Sunday afternoon choir practice, not wanting to share her bounty of cold germs.

"I'm sorry, but I can't commit to playing the piano for this year's cantata," Sue Kelly announced after they listened to the Easter program. "Our tax business is picking up, and it looks as though I'm going to have to work overtime."

Sighs followed her announcement. With the downturn in the economy, no one could blame the couple for going after all the business they could get. Unfortunately, their regular pianist fell and broke her hip before Christmas. Their director Dean had carpal tunnel surgery a couple of weeks before. Things weren't looking so good for their Easter program.

"I have an idea." Everyone's attention turned to Opie. "I know this guy who is tremendously talented. He could be a concert pianist. But he's not a believer."

"I'm okay with that," Dean said. "The music and narrative in this program is so awesome that I feel it's going to touch a number of hearts, perhaps even this man."

She coughed, blew her nose, and muttered a sorry. "So it's okay if I ask?"

"Definitely. I'll get a book and CD for you to share with him."

"I don't know that he'll agree," Opie warned. "It can't hurt to ask."

After they prayed, the group called their good nights and headed for the parking lot. The twins ran on ahead and unlocked the car. Val and Opie climbed into the backseat, and Val reached for her seat belt before she said, "You're going to ask Wendell, aren't you?"

"He's fantastic, Val," she enthused. "You've heard him play. His talent is incredible, truly God-given."

Heath started the vehicle and waited for the defroster to clear the ice from the windows. He looked at her in the rearview mirror and said, "I'd like to know how you think you're going to convince a non-Christian to play for a church cantata."

"You know Opie," Rom said to his brother. "She'd take on the devil for one of her causes."

"I would not." She'd be the first to admit she didn't know how she'd get Wendell to agree, but it wouldn't happen if she didn't try. "I'll ask. If he says yes, we'll have the best cantata ever."

"I can't believe Mrs. Keaton, Sue, and Dean are all out of commission at the same time," Val said.

"Could be God at work. If I can get Wendell to the church, God can do the rest."

"It's not just a way to spend more time with him?" Val inquired softly as the twins carried on a conversation up front.

While Opie couldn't deny the fact with certainty, she'd given the matter over to God. Her feelings for Wendell were strong, and the initial challenge of convincing him to accept her as she was gave way to helping him find the Lord.

Opie didn't agree with Wendell's belief he was too old and cynical for her. She found much to admire about him, but there were times when she wished she'd never met him. If she'd known how quickly her attraction would grow out of control, she'd have steered clear of the bachelor auction that had put him in her life.

"I know it seems very unlikely that he will say yes, but if he does agree, it's a way of salvaging our cantata. You know the orchestra wants to perform, and they can't without a pianist."

"Don't get your hopes up, Opie," Val said. "Wendell's piano skills go far beyond a simple Easter program."

Opie agreed. "He's so blasé about his talent."

"Would you like for me to see if Russ will ask him?"

She considered the merits of the idea. Would Russ and Wendell's renewed relationship make him more willing to say yes? Opie doubted it. Besides, it wasn't fair to Russ. "No, but thanks."

"Have you decided how you're going to do this?"

Opie laughed and ticked off the three-point plan on her fingers. "I pray, ask, and when he says no, I beg."

∽

Wendell wondered what was on Ophelia's mind. He'd given her his cell number the night of the bachelor auction, and Ophelia didn't hesitate to contact him. So far she'd called to ask about his hands, Jean-Pierre's grandmother, thank him for the job referrals, and a couple of times just to say hello.

He liked Ophelia. A lot. If he let her, she'd get under his skin. Wendell was a realist. He knew he wasn't the man for Ophelia Truelove. He cared about her enough to stay away from her idealistic beliefs. They clashed badly enough on their fundamental beliefs of what a wife and home entailed. But he did admit to missing her since the surprise trip to the track. He'd wanted to see how she responded to his world, and she'd done fine up until he'd kissed her and tried to foist the ticket on her.

Wendell glanced at the offending object. He hadn't even cashed it in, just brought the ticket home and tucked it into the picture frame on his desk to serve as a reminder of their differences.

The doorbell rang, and he glanced at his watch. She must have been standing by the door when she called. Knowing Opie, maybe even sitting in the car, Wendell considered with a grin.

"Hi. I brought you a present," she announced, laying the package of cookies on his desk.

His mouth watered. He'd downed the first sleeve in one sitting. His intention of eating one cookie soon become another and another until all that remained were a few crumbs in the bottom of the cellophane wrapper. "What's this? A bribe?"

She shrugged and said, "I do have a favor to ask." Ophelia rummaged through her huge purse and removed a book and CD. "Our pianists at church are out of commission, and we really need help with our Easter cantata. I hoped you might consider playing for us."

"I don't do church, Ophelia." How many times would he have to tell her he wasn't interested before she got the message?

"I know, but you do music. What if I promise no one will try to change your mind? We can create a contract. Pay you for your services. Please. We really need you."

"It wouldn't work."

She paused for a coughing spasm, the sound deep and abrasive. Opie pulled a tissue from her pocket and dabbed at her eyes. "You're the most talented pianist I've ever heard," she said, flashing him a winsome smile. "All you'd have to do is play the songs along with our orchestra. You could make our Easter program the best we've ever had."

Wendell poured her a cup of water from the pitcher on his desk. She thanked him and took a sip.

"It's a busy time of year."

"We only practice once a week."

He knew from experience that it took hours to become comfortable with the music.

"I don't think. . ."

"Please," she said, laying the book and CD before him. "At least listen. After that, if you say no, we'll try to find someone else."

"You can't find another pianist?"

"Not like you. Just think about it," she pleaded, noting his unyielding expression.

"I'm not making any promises."

"We'd only ask you to commit to playing for us until the Easter performance," she assured. "After the rave reviews, you can go your way knowing you have the undying gratitude of the choir and musicians."

"I'll let you know."

"It's a beautiful program, Wendell. Just listen and maybe play a couple of the songs."

She didn't know when to quit. "Okay," he relented. Maybe it was the eagerness of her expression or the desire to give her what she asked when it was so little. Perhaps he could carve out a few hours in his schedule. He couldn't imagine how she'd keep her promise but knowing Ophelia, she'd do everything possible to make it happen.

"I'm only saying I'll listen. Not that I'll agree to play."

"Thanks so much, Wendell."

Another wave of coughing hit her, so deep and rough that he thought it would tear her apart. "Have you seen the doctor yet?"

She sipped the water, her voice hoarse when she spoke. "I'm better. Rest, fluids, and ten days," Opie said. "That's all he'll tell me."

"Let's make a deal. You see the doctor, and I'll listen to your program and get back to you."

"Deal." The brilliance of her smile increased by megawatts. "I'd shake hands, but you don't want my germs. Our next practice is Sunday afternoon at 4:30. If you could let me know before then. Enjoy your cookies and don't worry, I didn't cough on them." All of a sudden, she seemed eager to escape.

The rest of Wendell's day didn't go as planned. The hopes he'd held for his meeting dissipated when the other party didn't see the benefits of his proposal. They agreed to a later discussion and went their separate ways. Terrence called to say he'd entered Dell Air in a number of upcoming races. At least the colt was earning his keep.

After dinner, he opted for a book and early night. On Thursday, while digging through the papers on his desk searching for car keys, he spotted the CD and remembered his promise to Ophelia. He'd listen to it on the drive to Louisville. At least then he'd be able to say he'd done as she asked when he refused her offer. He hoped she'd kept her end of the bargain and seen a doctor.

∾

Three days with no word from Wendell convinced Opie he wasn't going to agree. The thought saddened her.

Opie knew she shouldn't expect miracles when it came to Wendell Hunter. She also knew the promise that no one would try to proselytize him was unrealistic. Members of her church would share their faith despite her promise. Like an ostrich tucking its head in the sand, she'd hoped he would say yes and not ignore their message.

She'd give Wendell another day or so before calling Dean. Meanwhile, she needed to get to the doctor's office for her appointment.

∾

Wendell was hooked. He'd listened to the cantata and found himself captivated. The music and words touched him. Oh, he'd done his best to block out the feelings, but God refused to be silenced. Even now, the music and a few lines of dialogue played in his head. He hadn't looked at the book, but could all but see his fingers moving over the piano keys. Hands that played the masters itched to play this program.

A wry smile tilted his mouth. No doubt Ophelia hoped this would happen. How would she react if he agreed? Maybe he should put some outrageous spin on his acceptance. He could demand a grand piano. At least then, he could bow out gracefully when she said it wasn't possible. Or would Ophelia rush out to rent or buy one? She'd mentioned a church orchestra. He'd played with orchestras but never a church group. How good were they?

Wendell couldn't help but feel flattered by her praise. He'd written a few songs. Even once recorded a CD as a gift for his father. He doubted the old man cared about his son's piano playing, but Nicole often asked him to play for their party guests. Wendell suspected that was the only thing he did that impressed her.

That night he sat and listened again, this time uninterrupted. The surround sound from his expensive system magnified the music, and it resonated throughout the room.

He took the book to the piano and played through the one song that made the greatest impact on him. When the music seemed to flow from his fingers, Wendell continued, playing through song after song until he completed the program.

He checked the time and dialed Ophelia's cell number. "I'll do it. When do we start?"

The silence stretched on for several seconds before she spoke. "Oh, Wendell, thank you."

"What kind of piano do you have at church?" he asked, expecting to hear they had a traditional upright. He didn't really care. He'd rent his own piano if need be.

"It's a big one like yours. Only it's white."

That surprised him. Small churches rarely had grand pianos. "How big is your church, Ophelia?"

"We have about five thousand members."

The numbers didn't bother him. He'd played for many more. Still, five thousand members and only two pianists? Something didn't sound right. "When can I see the piano?"

"I'll ask Dean, our director, to give you a call and set up a time." She grew silent and he could hear her coughing. "Sorry. We do appreciate this, Wendell."

"Did you see the doctor?"

"Yes. He gave me an antibiotic."

"Good. I suppose I need to audition?"

"Oh no," she exclaimed. "Everyone's very excited about the possibility. I'm so thankful I don't have to disappoint them."

"See you Sunday."

∽

Opie turned off the phone and let out a scream of joy as she raced downstairs to the drawing room. "He said yes."

Taken aback by her excitement, Val glanced at Russ and back at Opie. "Who?"

"Wendell. He just called to say he'll play for our cantata."

"Congratulations, Opie," Val said. "I didn't think you'd be able to convince him."

"I didn't. God did. I left the program music and asked him to listen. I'd pretty much given up hope until he called tonight. Only thing is I promised no one would talk to him about God."

"How will you manage that?" Val asked.

"I'll play it by ear."

"I think we should pray," Russ said. "Wendell needs to know God. Let's send up a specific prayer that he hears a message he can't reject, whether it be in the program or someone's words."

They bowed their heads and joined hands, sending up the request. Opie closed with a fervent amen.

❦

Wendell met with the choir director Friday afternoon. The piano was the same model he had at home.

"It was donated by a member who decided she'd rather have a black piano. The church was happy to take it off her hands."

Did people really do that? He'd never considered changing his piano to suit a decorating style. Of course, his piano was for use and not display.

"You're very talented," Dean said after Wendell played through one of the songs. "Opie said you were."

"Did you really need a pianist?" Wendell asked.

Dean held up his bandaged hand. "Carpal tunnel surgery. We've also got a broken hip and a pianist with financial needs. That's everyone in our group that plays the piano."

"You don't think anyone will be offended if you don't ask the church?" Wendell's brow lifted with the question. He knew people often felt territorial in certain environments, and he wouldn't want his presence to cause dissension.

"Based on Opie's comments, I feel we can promote you as a special gift from above. A guest musician. Of course, learning a long musical program isn't an easy task. Are you okay with that?"

"Ophelia seems to think I can handle it with one practice a week," Wendell said with a smile.

"She doesn't understand. Do you have the time?"

Wendell nodded. "I'll make time. The music hooked me the first time I heard the CD. I've already played it through."

"The whole book?" Dean asked. When Wendell nodded, he said, "We have the orchestra accompaniment here at church."

"Ophelia mentioned an orchestra. What instruments?"

"There's a good variety. Trumpet, clarinet, french horn, harp, drums, and violin."

"How good are they?"

"One or two actively pursue their music. Most have played since they were children and use their talent for the Lord."

Wendell considered his own reasons for not doing the same. The Lord didn't care for him or his talent. "When do we start?"

"Practice is on Sunday at 4:30. You're welcome to play anytime you like to get a feel for the sound. We could have used the split track, but everyone agrees its better when we have live musicians."

Wendell grinned. "You won't find a musician who would argue that point."

~

Ophelia called to invite Wendell to ride to the church with them. "I appreciate the offer, but I'll drive myself." He didn't want to be stranded if things didn't work out. No matter what Ophelia promised, he figured someone would bring up religion, and he needed to be prepared.

Later, when he parked next to the Trueloves' SUV, Opie climbed out and waited for him to exit his vehicle.

"I waited to walk in with you."

"Always a pleasure to be accompanied by a lovely lady."

"The others are inside."

"Others?"

"Russ, Val, and Heath. Rom couldn't make it this afternoon."

"They're all in the choir?"

Opie nodded.

As indicated, the choir assembled at the front of the church. Dean introduced him to the group. "This is Wendell Hunter. Opie told us he's very talented, and I must admit she did not exaggerate."

She wrinkled her nose playfully at the director.

"We'll miss Mrs. Keaton and Sue, but Mr. Hunter's ability will enable us to give our best to God."

"Please, call me Wendell."

"Okay everyone, you heard the man. Let's get started." After a brief prayer, they got serious about their music.

Wendell found the orchestration version on the piano and played through the introduction. Applause filled the sanctuary. "Keep that up and my head will be too big to get through the doors," he said with a laugh.

"Maybe Val should let us sing at the pavilion," Opie said. "Plenty of room for a big head out there."

"I'd love to have a summer performance, but for Easter I prefer the church," Dean said.

The others agreed as they took their places and opened their choral books.

There were a few mix-ups before the musicians settled into the program, but Wendell found them to be talented. The practice flew by and soon the director brought it to a close.

"You did really well tonight," Opie told Wendell. She coughed a time or two.

"You have a beautiful voice," he complimented, speaking of her solo in the program.

"You mean compared to a walrus?" she asked with a grin.

He shook his head at her teasing, and she called good night before going out to the vehicle where the others waited.

Chapter 14

T hat cold isn't going to get any better if you don't take care of yourself," Mom said after Opie suffered through another bout of coughing. She'd finished the antibiotics, but the cold hung on.

Her mother insisted she rest, but Opie found it difficult to be idle. "I haven't worked since I got sick."

"You've spent a lot of time at the pavilion. It's cold out there."

Opie glanced around. "Where's Val?"

"She and Heath went into Lexington. He's found some stone he wanted her to see."

"He can't lay stone in the snow."

"That's what I told him, but he says he can have everything ready for when the weather changes."

"Another couple of months at least," Opie said, pulling her feet up into the chair and wrapping her arms about her legs. "It's going to be difficult to get people out to the pavilion."

"Your dad says he'll haul them out in a horse-drawn sleigh if need be. Heath says the ground is solid. He mentioned some sort of rock base that's helping keep the area from being too wet."

"That's good to know. I'm trying to come up with a special menu. Of course, it's impossible to top what Russ has in mind."

When Russ revealed his plan to propose to Val on Valentine's Day, which also happened to be her birthday, he enlisted the help of her entire family. Opie promised to get her sister out to the pavilion.

Opie planned to cater the event from the pavilion's lower floor kitchen. She cleared her schedule for the week. Nothing would stand in the way of doing this for Val.

"If you don't get better, you'll spend Valentine's Day in bed."

"Okay, Mom. I get the message. It's just that there are so many details to be worked out."

Her cell rang, and Opie fished it out of her robe pocket.

"Russ tells me your cold's worse."

"Hello, Wendell," Opie managed just before she went off into a paroxysm of coughing. "I'm doing my best to shake this thing."

"I'm sure that's what my mother thought."

Opie recalled that his mother died of pneumonia. Her heart went out to the little boy who had been deprived of his mother. "Wendell, I'll be fine," she said, smiling her thanks to her mom when she handed her the orange juice. "Did Russ fill you in on his plan?"

"He came by this morning for breakfast. Said you're cooking. Are you up to that?"

"I'll be 100 percent by then. I'm so happy for them. God is in control."

"Why would you think that?"

"Not think. Know. These things don't just happen. Heath and Jane. Val and Russ. Even you and Russ. Did you ever think that you would reconcile as you have?"

"I hoped that one day we might. I don't necessarily see that God played a role in what happened."

Opie wished she could reach through the phone and shake him. "God used two women you didn't even know existed a few months ago to relay your message to Russ. Believe what you will, but there are too many signs to deny the obvious." Her talking brought on another fit of coughing that exhausted her with its violence. "You shouldn't get me so worked up."

"You should rest and drink plenty of fluids."

Opie sipped her juice and said, "Yes, doctor. I even made chicken soup."

"Does it work?"

"Who cares? It tastes good."

"Chicken soup isn't enough if you're run-down or have an infection."

"I'll be okay," she stressed.

"Get better soon. I need you at church. You got me into this."

"Don't worry. I plan to be there."

But Opie found it difficult to keep that promise. Her cold worsened and she returned to the doctor who diagnosed walking pneumonia. He sent her home with strict orders to follow his instructions and threatened to put her in the hospital if she didn't.

She'd missed two practices when Wendell came by. He set the vase of flowers on the coffee table and dragged a chair over next to the sofa. Opie knew she looked as haggard as she felt. She hadn't washed her hair and wasn't wearing makeup. The old sweats belonged to one of the twins and had seen better days, but she was too sick to care.

"Why did you do this to yourself?" Wendell demanded.

She rested her head against the pillow. "Do what?"

"Work yourself to exhaustion. Look where your career crusade got you. You don't have anything to prove to anyone."

"You and I have a lot in common," Opie said with a derisive laugh. "Our drive to prove ourselves keeps us from backing down from the challenge. You're determined to be the winner your dad was, but from what you've told me he was better with horses than kids. I'm determined to prove I can carry through with my career choice."

"Who needs that proof?"

"My family. I've never been known for my ability to carry through. I want everyone to see I can do this. I can't dabble my way through life."

"We've already seen that. Look at the events you've handled in the past few months."

"All thanks to referrals from you."

"Only a few. Once people taste your food, they can't wait to get you into their kitchen."

She turned onto her side and pulled the throw up about her arms. "I compare myself to my siblings just as you compare yourself to your father. Why do you want to be like him?"

"Why do you want to be like them?" he asked, tilting his head and stretching out his hands, palms up. "I have an obligation to the people at the farm, Ophelia."

"Is it the people or the trophies, Wendell?"

"Winning races is how I make my living. My father's horses aren't going to be around forever. No one is going to come for stud animals with mediocre showings at best."

"I'd tell you to hand it over to God, but you don't believe He can help you."

"You don't understand. I need to win."

"I do understand. I feel driven to do something worthwhile, too."

"Not if you make yourself sick in the process."

"People get sick." She began to cough. Opie grabbed a tissue and dabbed at her moist eyes. "You'll have to forgive me, but I'm not up to fighting speed right now. I'm doing what the doctor ordered—getting plenty of rest, and Mom has me drinking fluids by the gallon."

"Please take care of yourself, Ophelia."

"Can we talk about something else? Tell me how the cantata is going."

"Dean seems pleased."

"I knew he would be. Are you enjoying the music?"

"Very much."

"I'm glad you stopped by." She drew a finger along the flowers—a beautiful arrangement of red, pink, and white roses. Opie wondered at the mixed symbolism of the bouquet. Had Wendell bought them because he thought she'd like them, or was he trying to tell her something? "These are beautiful. Thank you."

"They reminded me of your gardens. I hoped they might lift your spirits."

They had. More than he realized. "I'm determined to beat this thing. You'll see. I have to get well soon. Russ is depending on me."

∽

Wendell knew he'd come on too strong, and he knew why. He was afraid for her. Afraid he would lose Ophelia as he'd lost his mother. Her violent coughing frightened him. His grandmother told him about his mother's weak lungs and problems from childhood. He suspected that had been why they hadn't wanted her to marry his father. They knew her life wouldn't be easy. She'd caught the cold from his father. He'd gone off to a horse race, leaving her home to recover.

Within days, she'd been in critical condition. Another week later, she died.

His fear of losing Ophelia had more to do with his feelings for her. He could tell himself she was too young and he was all wrong for her, but lately that hadn't kept him from missing her and wondering what his life would be like with her by his side.

Opie had told him to turn it over to God. She'd been talking about his feeling inadequate in terms of the farm, but Wendell couldn't help but consider the possibility of doing the same with his feelings for Ophelia.

What would it be like to depend on God for the answers? He'd never considered that option. His father told him where he'd go to school and chose not to tell him about the farm, but Wendell made the decisions that really mattered. He'd worked through all the pain and doubt to find the man he had become. Though at times, like now, it felt as if he were still looking.

Maybe even more so because of Ophelia's expectations of him. She wanted him to care about others. She wanted him to know God's love. In his heart, all Wendell knew was that he wanted her in his life, and it was very unlikely that she'd ever be there.

∾

To his trained ear, the group improved with every week. Wendell honored his commitment but didn't tell his friends. But when he started refusing all Sunday afternoon invitations, they demanded to know what he was doing. Wendell only smiled and said it was personal.

His social circle wasn't religious either. Like him, his friends' interests revolved around the Paris social scene and horses. Derby season would soon be upon them, and they couldn't imagine what he was doing that he considered more important than that. Leo and Catherine were totally bewildered when his acceptance of their lunch invitations resulted in an early departure.

How did he explain that the Easter music revived feelings that drew him to music years before? He'd stopped writing after his father's death, but now he picked out notes on the piano as he scribbled on sheet music.

Ophelia's return to practice the week before the engagement party gave Wendell's heart a lift. She'd lost weight and looked pale, but to him she'd never been more beautiful. She sat on the front row, claiming it would be better if she experienced a coughing jag and had to leave the room. Even with the remnants of her cold, she had a wonderful alto voice that he could hear so much better with her sitting nearby.

"Opie, do you want to try your solo?" Dean asked.

"I suppose I should."

"You can sing from there."

She took the microphone Dean handed her and smiled at Wendell when he played the introduction. Wendell knew the exact moment that she lost herself in the music. Her eyes drifted closed, and her love for the Lord became even more evident in that moment.

Chapter 15

Hello, Opie." She immediately recognized the caller as Sally from church. "A Brenda Clarke called here today looking for you. She sounded upset."

She remembered the young woman. "I'll give her a call," she said after Sally recited the number.

Before she could dial, security called from the gate. "There's a woman here to see you, Ms. Truelove."

"Send her to the house."

"She's on foot. Has little kids with her."

With the birthday-engagement party tomorrow night, this was the last thing she needed, but Opie could hardly turn them away. "Put them in a cart and bring them to the house."

"I'm sorry, Ms. Truelove," Brenda said minutes later when she met them outside. "I didn't know what else to do. It's Ronald. He's in jail."

"Oh," Opie gasped. "What happened?"

"He got into a fight."

"Was he drinking?" she asked softly, not wanting the children to overhear.

"Oh no, ma'am. He doesn't drink. Ronald's coworker introduced him to this man who guaranteed he could treble our investment. Now he's disappeared with our money. I told Ronald we couldn't afford this, but he wouldn't listen. He insisted we had to find a way to come up with the money. I don't know what to do," she worried. "We don't have money for bail."

Opie wished her dad were there. He'd know how to handle this, but he'd gone into Lexington, and she didn't know when he'd be home. Wendell immediately came to mind. "We need to talk to Wendell Hunter." Brenda's horrified expression showed fear. "I called Ronald in sick today. He'll lose his job if they find out where he really is."

"No, he won't," Opie declared. And if he did, she'd personally ask her dad to help the young family. She reached for the twins' hands and took them inside. "Mom, this is Brenda Clarke and her children, Ronnie, Bonnie, and Shelley. Will you watch the kids until we get back?"

Her mother smiled at them and said, "I just took a batch of cookies from the oven. May I?" She held out her arms.

Brenda cautiously surrendered the infant. "I forgot to bring diapers."

Her years of experience showed as Opie's mother cuddled the little girl to her chest. "We'll be fine."

Opie called security for a driver, and Glenn arrived within minutes. The young mother was frightened and glanced back as Opie shepherded her into the truck. "They'll be fine. My mom is great with children."

Brenda twisted the handle of her purse nervously. "Ronald will be so angry with me."

Opie couldn't see that the man was doing such a great job on his own. "Could be Ronald needs to trust you more. He hasn't left you a lot of options."

Brenda didn't respond, and they arrived at Wendell's a couple of minutes later. Opie asked Glenn to wait for them. She reached for the doorbell, holding Brenda's arm for fear she would bolt. When she opened the door, Mrs. Carroll smiled at Opie and invited them to come in. She came inside with Brenda in tow and asked to see Wendell.

"He's changing to go out."

"We really need to see him," she pleaded, and the woman asked her to wait.

"Ophelia, what's happened?" Wendell asked as he came down the stairs at a brisk pace.

"We need your help." She glanced at Brenda and back at him. "This is Brenda Clarke. Her husband works for you." After he acknowledged her with a nod, Opie said, "He's been arrested. He got into a fight last night, and she doesn't have money to bail him out."

Wendell frowned. "What do you want me to do?"

"Help them," Opie declared without hesitation. She looked at Brenda and said, "Tell him what you told me."

The woman swiped at her watery eyes and revealed the truth. "His friend said they could make a lot of money fast."

"Have you talked to him?"

Brenda nodded her head. "Yes, sir. He said he lost his temper when his friend told him the guy took off with their money. Ronald lost over two thousand dollars. I told him it sounded too good to be true, but he's stubborn."

"She can't afford the bail, Wendell."

"I'll see what I can do."

"You have to help them," Opie insisted. "They have three small children who need their father at home."

He looked at Brenda. "Does Jack Pitt have your home number?"

"Yes, sir." Brenda looked down at the floor.

"Go home and wait to hear from me."

"But I need to go back to Ms. Opie's to pick up my children."

"I'll take you home and bring them back," Opie said. "Thank you, Wendell. I knew you'd know what to do."

∾

Her faith in him made him feel like a bigger man. "It's not over yet, Ophelia. Depending on what the friend decides to do, Ronald could go back to jail." He glanced at Brenda and asked, "Who is the other man?"

She obviously didn't want to tell him.

"You might as well share his name. Everyone will know once they see the effects of their fight."

She named Seth Canon, one of his stallion handlers.

"We'll get to the bottom of this. Go on home. Ophelia will bring your children," he said, looking to her for confirmation before he continued, "I'll let you know something as soon as possible."

After they left, he dialed the office and spoke to the manager.

"She called him in sick this morning."

He detected censure in Jack's tone. "The woman's scared out of her mind. Clarke probably told her to do that hoping to give them time to figure out what to do."

"Guess you were right about him."

Wendell didn't want to be right. He'd never struggled with money but he understood anger, particularly when someone cheated a man of his hard-earned money. He intended to look into this further. Just to be sure Seth Canon hadn't played a part in defrauding Ronald Clarke. "Get Clarke out and take him home. I'll stand his bond."

He called Ophelia's cell. "Let Mrs. Clarke know that Jack will bring her husband home."

∾

"Will these do for where you're taking me tonight?" Val asked as she entered Opie's room carrying a pair of boots. She wore the long-sleeved, purple jewel-toned wool dress Opie said would look nice and help ward off the winter chill.

"They're fine," Opie said. "You might as well give up, birthday girl. It's a surprise, and you're not going to get it out of me. And would you please stop moping around like you've lost your best friend?"

Val looked meaningfully at the vase of roses sitting on Opie's nightstand. "At least the man in your life remembered Valentine's Day. You should have gone out with him. You would have had more fun."

Opie walked closer and rubbed two fingers together in Val's face. "Know what this is? The world's smallest violin player. The poor-little-me act isn't working."

Val laughed. "Okay. I'll try to have fun."

"That's all I'm asking." Opie walked away and paused at the window. "Looks like someone left the pavilion lights on again."

Dropping onto the side of the bed, Val tugged on her boots. "I'll run out and turn them off while you finish dressing."

"I'll be ready by the time you get back," Opie promised before she disappeared into the bathroom.

After Val left, Opie flung off her robe and pulled on the dress she planned to wear. As she came out of the bathroom, her gaze drifted to the vase on her nightstand. Val must really be depressed if she envied her these dried-up roses.

She really should toss them but held off, hoping for one more day. If only there had been a romantic reason for the flowers. But maybe Wendell had bought them out of love. For a friend. She couldn't imagine anything better than spending Valentine's Day with the man she loved. Opie pushed the emotion away. Her day would come. Just like Val and Heath.

Opie wished she could see Val's face when she saw Russ at the pavilion. She thanked God that she'd started feeling like her old self. She'd enjoyed her part in the birthday-engagement party. Heath and Jane kept Val away from home all day while she organized the food. The rest of the family decorated the pavilion's lower floor while Russ and his friends worked on the main floor, clearing away the snow and ice and setting up for his proposal. When he came down for a coffee break, Opie said, "You're going to freeze up there tonight."

"We'll have our love to keep us warm."

She groaned. "Hate to tell you, but it's not enough. You'd better find some extra heavy-duty blankets. One of those fire pits wouldn't hurt. I'll make sure she's got her coat and gloves when she leaves the house."

"What about a couple of faux fur blankets? Think those would work?"

"I imagine you could get away with horse blankets if your proposal's romantic enough."

Russ chuckled, lifting his hand in good-bye as he went off to complete his task. "Thanks for the idea."

It pleased her dad that they managed to hide their guests' vehicles about the farm and transport them to the pavilion. Her parents, family members, and other guests waited in the lower-floor room.

Opie pulled on her coat as the doorbell rang. *Probably a last-minute guest*, she thought as she opened the door. "Wendell? Why aren't you at the pavilion?"

"I waited for you. I saw Val leave a few minutes ago."

"We'd better hurry. I don't think they'll be able to stand this cold for long."

He pulled her scarf tighter and insisted she put on her gloves, taking her arm as they navigated the snowy pathway.

Later, when Val stepped into the room, Opie knew she'd never forget the glow on her sister's face. She pushed her way through the crowd, Wendell in her wake. "Did you say yes?"

Val held up her hand to reveal her heart-shaped diamond ring. "You know I did."

"Beautiful. Good job," Opie commented, clapping her future brother-in-law on the back.

"Thanks for sending her out," Russ said.

"We weren't sure how to get you out here," Opie explained. "The lights did the trick."

"Congratulations," Wendell said, hugging Val and then his brother.

When Val asked where their parents were, Opie pointed to the far side of the room.

"Do they know?" she asked.

"Everyone knew but you," Opie teased. "They're pleased with your choice."

∾

On Easter Sunday, Wendell rose early and dressed in a dark suit. He didn't want to call attention to himself any more than necessary today. They would perform at the eleven o'clock morning service. Afterward the pastor would speak, and everyone would go home to enjoy their families and holiday meal. He and Russ would dine with the Trueloves.

He'd spread himself thin over the past month and a half with business, travel, practices, rehearsal, and preparing for the spring meet. As Ophelia said, he saw the Trueloves regularly now that Russ and Val were engaged. They'd already involved him in their planning sessions, asking him to play for their wedding. He was curious as to how Val planned to get a piano out to the pavilion, but she promised to do it if he agreed.

Ophelia had been busy as well. After getting over her cold, she'd jumped right back into her hectic schedule. Some nights when he saw her at practice, she looked so weary that he feared she would get sick again. She stubbornly insisted she could handle the work.

He rarely experienced performance jitters, but today Wendell found himself with butterflies. Everything about this experience seemed strange to him. He waited in the choir room. When the others arrived, obviously filled with the joy of worship, Wendell felt he'd missed out on something important. He couldn't blame them. The church was open to all. He was the one who decided not to come.

Soon everyone was in place. The rustlings and stirrings of the audience gave way to silence when the lights went down on the crowd. Dean gestured toward him and Wendell began to play. The orchestra joined in and the choir followed suit.

A strange emotion welled up in him—extreme happiness for their group's success. He'd spent most of his life solo, and for the first time he felt like part of the group. He caught Ophelia's gaze on him, her smile wide with pleasure. She winked and turned the page, though he noticed that she rarely looked at the book.

When she stepped forward for her solo, he accompanied her, playing softly as her pure, sweet voice sang of her love for the Lord. So many sensations hit him at once—Ophelia's glowing beauty. Her joy in serving the Lord. His love for her.

He almost stopped playing with the realization, but the professional musician in him rushed to fill the gap. A few minutes later, the program concluded to thunderous applause.

From his vantage point on the stage, Wendell could see the pastor walking up the steps. An image of Jesus rising up into the clouds flashed onto the screen.

Pastor John David Skipper stepped onto the stage and shouted, "Alleluia! He has risen!" A chorus of amens erupted from the congregation. "Today we celebrate the most joyous of occasions," he said. "Ah, I see that confusion on your faces. You're wondering how this can be when our Lord was crucified?

"If you have your Bibles, turn with me to 1 John 4:9. 'In this was manifested the love of God toward us, because that God sent his only begotten Son into the world, that we might live through him.'

"Because of that love for His lambs, the Good Shepherd became the ultimate sacrifice. He suffered the vilest possible death out of love for us. He deemed us worthy of becoming joint heirs of His Father's Kingdom. Thank you, Jesus!" he cried out, again accompanied by the chorus of amens.

He turned and raised his hand toward the choir. "This group honored God and us today with this wonderful program. I know they worked many long and difficult hours to give Jesus their all. They didn't have to do it. They wanted to."

Wendell didn't understand why, but he'd never wanted to play a program of music as much as this one. The sacrifice of time in practice and rehearsal had been worth his effort. The pastor's next words took him by surprise.

"But their works won't get them into heaven," the pastor said. "Ephesians 2:8 says, "For by grace are ye saved through faith; and that not of yourselves: it is the gift of God.' Faith. Their belief that they serve a risen Lord who died for their sins, who washed them white as snow, will take them there."

FAITH in big bold print appeared on the screen. Where was his faith? Wendell wondered. Why had he rejected Jesus' gift? The image changed to two hands reaching out to each other.

"Have you made that choice?" Pastor Skipper asked. "If not, it's not too late. I'm going to ask the choir to lead us in 'Just as I Am.' Jesus wants you," he declared, pointing at the audience, "just as you are. He doesn't care what you've done in the past. He will forgive you if you just ask. It's a simple prayer that can lead you to a lifetime of joy. Repent and accept this enduring gift of love." With that, John David Skipper bowed his head.

Wendell didn't know the tune, so the choir sang a cappella. The congregation sat with their heads bowed, but he was aware of the people who approached the altar.

"It's time, Wendell. Accept My love."

He couldn't be sure who spoke the words in his ear. He rose and took the first step, and soon he knelt at the altar. *Forgive me*, he pleaded silently. *Show me how to be the man You desire me to be. A man worthy of Your love.* The thoughts came faster and faster. He started slightly when a hand touched his shoulder. He looked at Jacob Truelove through tears of emotion and smiled.

"Do you understand the decision you're making?" Jacob asked.

Wendell shook his head. "No, sir. Not completely."

"Do you believe Jesus Christ died for your sins and was resurrected from the dead?" He paused. "Have you sinned against God and want to seek His forgiveness?" Another pause. "And do you plan to turn away from the past and invite Jesus to become Lord of your life?"

Wendell hesitated. The magnitude of the decision seemed overwhelming, and yet he knew he couldn't walk away. "I can only try to do my best."

"That's all He asks of us. Tell Him, Wendell, in your own words, what you plan to do."

He did, and freedom greater than he'd ever known filled him. Afterward Jacob patted his shoulder again and smiled widely.

"You've made a wise decision, son."

When Wendell looked up at Ophelia, she smiled and swiped away tears.

Every remaining doubt drifted away. He loved her. Whether he deserved her or not, she loved him.

After the service, people wanting to thank him for the music but more importantly, believers who wanted to extend the right hand of fellowship and welcome Wendell to the fold, delayed his departure. When her turn came, Ophelia threw her arms about his neck.

"I'm so happy for you."

He held her loosely, all the while wanting to pull her close and never let go. "Me, too. I'm not sure what happened, but I had to do this."

"The Holy Ghost guided you to make the right decision."

Wendell knew she spoke of the Trinity. "Looks like I'm going to be here for a while," he said, indicating the line that stretched down the aisle.

"Me, too," she said happily.

"I don't want to keep you from your lunch."

"You won't. This is more important than food."

He felt his jaw drop. He'd never thought he'd hear those words from her lips. "Ophelia Truelove considers standing next to me more important than food?"

She blushed. "Don't look at me like that. You're extremely important to me, Wendell."

He squeezed her hand, and she stepped aside so he could greet the next person. She remained by his side, thanking people for their compliments on her solo. "It wouldn't have happened without Wendell. Isn't he a wonderful pianist?"

People smiled and nodded, and her words lifted him higher than any self-pride.

❧

Their late lunch at the Trueloves' turned into a celebration of his decision.

"We had an honorary lunch for Russ when he made his decision," Val said, smiling at her fiancé.

"I'm glad to have my brother as my new brother in Christ," Russ agreed.

"It's all so new," Wendell commented. "I haven't even begun to understand this decision I've made."

"All in good time," Jacob said. "The most important thing is that you took that first step."

Later, Wendell went out to the barn with Jacob to check on Fancy. As her time approached, Wendell found himself growing more hopeful she would produce a winner. When she thrust her inquisitive head out of the stall, he ran his hand along the horse's neck. "Sir, I've wanted to ask how you can work in an industry and consider a major part of it a sin."

"It's not so cut-and-dried," Jacob said.

"When I step into this world, my thoughts turn to racing. How will I reconcile what I do with the choice I made this morning?" Wendell asked.

"God created these beautiful animals to run, and then He gave us this love of horses and put us right here in the midst of some of His most beautiful work."

Wendell couldn't dispute that.

"My problem with gambling relates to how it affected me personally," Jacob explained, tapping his chest as he emphasized the words. "I believe God put me here on this farm for a purpose. I pray and seek His guidance daily to understand what He'd have me do. Fear keeps me away from the tracks. I have my father's genes. Except for grace, I could be right where he is. Matthew 26:41 directs us to watch and pray that we don't enter into temptation.

"Just remember that you're a baby in Christ. You need to read your Bible, attend church, pray, and grow in Christ. As you grow, just as you did as a child, you learn to make judgment calls on what's right and wrong for you."

Wendell considered the choices of his childhood. They hadn't always been right choices. "What if I never make those calls?"

Jacob pulled an apple from his pocket and used his knife to cut it in half before feeding it to the mare. "God nudges you along. If He sees something standing in the way of you serving Him to your fullest, He prompts you to change. Back in November, He used a conversation between Val and Russ to show me I sinned against my father."

He didn't know Jacob that well, but he'd never seen anything that warranted the man calling himself a sinner. "Why would you think that?"

"I've been angry with him since I was a little boy. I didn't understand why he couldn't be like other dads. Then when he went to prison, I hated him for embarrassing us. He attached a stigma to our name that took years for us to overcome. We had to prove we weren't like him to regain people's respect. That's why my good name is important to me. I felt I earned it."

"Your anger was justified."

Jacob shook his head. "It's never justified, Wendell. My mother was the Sheridans' housekeeper. When she asked, Mr. Sheridan took me on. He taught me everything I know about horses and when he was satisfied I could do the job, he gave me the manager position. William Sheridan was a fine Christian man. I have him to thank for my salvation. He understood why I didn't want anything to do with the tracks and made it possible for me to stay away.

"I was determined my mother and siblings wouldn't suffer because of my father. I worked to help pay my brother's tuition. At times, the money was so tight I didn't know how I'd manage, but God made a way."

Jacob patted Fancy's head one last time and secured the door. They walked out to the golf cart. "That day Val told Russ he needed to seek your forgiveness," he said as they drove back toward the house, "he didn't think you'd listen, but she said he had to try. That got my attention. I'd decided my father didn't care and I shouldn't either. I appointed myself judge and jury. My father wasn't worthy of my love. Me," he declared, pointing to himself, "a simple man, for whom Christ hung on the cross and died, dared to consider he was better than his father.

"I won't say it's going to be easy. We went to visit him again and when I asked his forgiveness, he said he should be the one doing the asking. I felt so humbled."

Wendell understood the feeling. He hadn't given Russ much reason to love him, and yet his brother felt he'd wronged him. Even when he wanted nothing to do with religion, God had been at work. He'd salvaged another broken family and given them hope for the future.

They approached the house in silence, and Jacob parked the cart. He hopped out and paused to look Wendell in the eye. "Trust God with your life, son. He'll help you make the right decisions."

As he listened to Jacob tell his family's story, Wendell understood what motivated this group. He believed Ophelia's desire to become a successful chef stemmed from this same need to help her family. No doubt she'd heard this story often, even achieved her goal with the intention of helping her younger siblings. He'd never experienced anything like this family's dedication. No doubt even now they grappled with how they could use the sudden influx of money to God's glory.

He came around the front of the cart and asked, "How would you feel about my asking Ophelia to marry me?"

Jacob stopped walking and turned to look at him. "You love her?"

With all his heart and soul. Wendell thought about that perfect-wife list. Had he given those items any thought since Ophelia came into his life? "Yes, sir, I do. I finally realized how much when I looked up at her today and knew my life would never be right without her."

Jacob clapped him on the back. "Son, you obviously made two life decisions today. And while I'm not against you asking for her hand, I advise you to pray before you act."

"I do have a lot to think about before I talk to her. I don't intend to push Ophelia," he allowed. "The decision will be hers. I'm concerned I'm too old for her."

"Opie could probably use someone to help settle her down. I love that girl, but she can be all over the place at times."

"I've never seen that side of Ophelia," Wendell defended. "In the time I've known her, she's done everything she set out to do. And that includes helping me find my way to God."

Jacob grinned. "I think you'll be good for my little girl, Wendell Hunter. Mighty good."

∾

Wendell and Opie walked out to the pavilion with the rest of the family trailing behind.

"Isn't it a glorious day?"

Opie twirled playfully, and Wendell found himself entranced by this side of her. He knew she didn't speak of the early spring weather with the newly budding trees and singing birds. Today's happiness was about successes and worthwhile decisions and just being together.

"Wonderful," he agreed, catching her hand and pulling her close.

"The kids," she murmured softly when he would have kissed her.

He groaned. He definitely had his work cut out for him in romancing this woman. He took her hand and said, "Let's go." The day before, Rom and Heath hid candy-filled Easter eggs for the farm children's egg hunt that afternoon. Opie had extended the invitation to the Clarke children and any others from Hunter Farm who wanted to attend the event. She smiled as she looked upon the children sitting on the pavilion steps, waiting for the official announcement that they could find the eggs. They swung their Easter baskets restlessly, eager eyes looking around for the goodies.

"They're excited," she whispered.

"I can see."

"Did you ever have an egg hunt?"

"Daddy would hide the eggs. The real thing. We decorated boiled eggs with food coloring, wax pens, and decals. We had one specially marked lucky egg that generally got the finder a dollar."

"Wow, a whole dollar," he teased.

She tapped his arm. "There will be better prizes today," Opie said. "Heath and Rom hid eggs in all sorts of places. Some more obvious ones for the little kids and the not-so-obvious for the older ones."

Ronnie and Bonnie Clarke came running and grabbed her hands. "Ms. Truelove, we're going to hunt Easter eggs."

She smiled at their enthusiasm. "Yes, we are."

"Will you help us?"

Every adult present would be helping the children. "I will. Mr. Hunter will help, too. Won't you?" she asked, looking at Wendell.

"Definitely," he agreed with a twinkle in his eye as he declared, "My team is going to find the most eggs today."

Ronnie broke away from her and went over to take Wendell's hand. "Can I be on your team?"

"What's your name, son?" he asked.

"Ronnie."

"Well, Ronnie, I think we should get over there, so we can be the first ones to start looking." He winked at her before they took off running across the pavilion yard.

"Come on, Bonnie," Opie said with a laugh. "We can't let them beat us."

Minutes later, all the children carried baskets piled high with their bounty.

"Look, Daddy," Ronnie said to the young man who came to retrieve his children. "Mr. Hunter helped me find all these."

Ronald Clarke's skin turned ruddy with embarrassment as his gaze shifted to his employer. "Thank you, Mr. Hunter. And thanks for helping me out of my predicament."

Wendell reached out to shake Ronald's hand. "It was my pleasure. You have two fine children. Take care of them."

"Yes, sir, I will."

"Ronald," he called when father and son started to walk away. The man looked back. "Next time you need investment advice, come see me. I know a thing or two about making money."

Opie slipped her arm about Wendell's, smiling up at him as she whispered, "Thank you."

Chapter 16

Before he left that night, Wendell invited Ophelia to join him for lunch the following day. She agreed. He'd given his staff the day off for the holiday and decided to pick up items for a picnic and take her out to the farm. When he arrived to pick her up, she wore pink capri pants with a white sleeveless blouse. "You might want to take a jacket." The spring days could get a little chilly at times.

"Got it," she said, taking a knit coat from the coatrack in the entry hall. "Where are we going?"

Wendell didn't plan to use the word *surprise.* "I thought we'd have a picnic at my favorite place on the farm. Sound good?"

"Perfect."

He walked her out to a Jeep and waited as she climbed inside. "I thought about riding out there, but the Jeep is just as good."

A few minutes later, he parked at the perfect vantage point to look out over Hunter Farm. Rolling hills of bluegrass spread before them, mature trees providing shade. Trails of black fences surrounded the area, some containing horses. They could see the house in the distance. Wendell took a blanket from the backseat. Ophelia indicated an area, and he shook out the blanket and let it settle on the ground. She helped pull out the corners.

"I have no idea what's in here," he said as he set the basket in the corner.

"You should have asked me to put something together."

"You deserved a holiday, too." He stood and held out his hand, "Let's take a walk."

Ophelia took his hand, and he boosted her to her feet. He pulled her closer.

"Still reeling from yesterday?" she asked as they strolled along.

"Some. I'm handling it with prayer. Your dad calls them life-changing decisions. I'm sure it will take time to sort out the particulars. But I plan to attend your church, and the pastor mentioned a new Christians' class."

"Call me if you feel the need to talk," she told him.

"That's why I asked you over today."

Her brows lifted. "What did you have on your mind?"

Wendell noticed her struggle to be as casual as possible with the question. "You."

She stopped and looked up at him. "Me? What do you mean?"

"There were tears in your eyes yesterday. Was that because you were joyous over my decision to follow Christ, or do you feel something more for me?"

355

"You know I care about you, Wendell. I've never made any secret of that. And yes, I am happy for you."

"Friend happy?"

A suggestion of annoyance touched her face. "What are you asking, Wendell?"

"Do you love me?"

"Yes, I do. Despite your insistence that you're not right for me," she said with a defiant smile. "I care for you a great deal."

"I came to the same realization yesterday. I love you and hoped you felt the same for me."

Her eyes brightened with pleasure. "So what are we going to do about it?"

"Get to know each other. I think I already know a few things about you. Like how you love your family and your career. About your work. . ."

"Okay, Wendell," she interrupted. "I wasn't about to tell you this when you said there could be no us, but I decided awhile back that you were more important than my work," she admitted in a rush of words. "That doesn't mean I'll ever stop cooking. I will prepare meals for my family, but I'd give up my career for you."

Her admission knocked the breath out of him. "Why?"

"I think you need to be your wife's focus. Being a middle child wasn't easy. I always felt like I needed to compete with my siblings for my parents' love. I know that wasn't the case, but I wouldn't want you to feel anything is more important to me than you, and I'm afraid you might feel that way about my career."

He doubted he could love her more than he did in that moment. "I might have felt that way before I understood your work is a part of you. You like the compliments and you deserve them. I think you do what you do because a completed job shows you can take a project to completion. I won't ask you to give that up."

"What are you saying?"

"We support each other in the things that make us happy. We make time in our busy schedules for each other. And when things go as I hope they will, you'll be at my side forever."

She threw her arms about his waist and hugged him. Wendell looped his arms about her back. He leaned to kiss her, savoring the sweetness that was Ophelia Truelove. "Will it be uncomfortable for you to socialize with the people you've cooked for?"

"I feel your friends respect me for who I am, and I doubt any of them would ever say no to a meal at our house," she said, flashing him a cheeky grin.

He laughed. "Now that I understand about the races, I won't ask you to do anything that might make you uncomfortable."

"I enjoyed the races, Wendell. It's exciting to witness those horses doing what they were born to do." She giggled and said, "When I was admiring Dell

Air before the race, I felt he was thinking 'Yeah, I know I look good.'"

"It's the stallion in him."

"I felt I let Daddy down by doing something he asked us not to do."

"I'm surprised he didn't say something to me about taking you."

"Daddy understands you, Wendell."

Wendell hoped so. He wanted the respect of the man he admired so much. "Jacob says I'm a babe in Christ. He says that as I grow in my faith, I'll learn what God wants me to do."

"You will. Let's go check out that basket. All this fresh air and sunshine has given me an appetite."

∾

Wendell embraced the idea of courtship, and the more time he spent with Ophelia, the more he realized a woman with the qualities he'd thought he wanted would have bored him to death in no time. He recalled her insistence that God was at work in their lives and accepted it was true.

He took her to his social engagements, and Ophelia provided him with the family he'd always wanted. He spent nearly as many evenings in the Truelove home as he did in his own. They explored the things they had in common and enjoyed being together. They even went horseback riding frequently.

Three weeks later, Wendell invited Val and Russ over for dinner and they accepted. Ophelia worked that night and he'd thought about waiting until she could attend, but he wanted their opinion on his plan.

"I have some things I thought you might like for your place," Wendell told Russ after dinner.

He indicated the portrait of Russ's mother and another of their father and Russ's mother. A similar portrait hung in the hallway. There were boxes of photos. "I copied the ones that meant something to me, but they're part of your childhood and I think you should have them."

Russ looked somewhat overwhelmed. "Please don't think it's my intention to remove you from Hunter Farm," Wendell said. "I hope you'll always think of it as your home."

"I will. I have fond memories of my childhood home, but it's only right that it belong to you and your children. Besides, I've come to think of home in a different way lately."

"Certain things do lose their significance in the greater scheme of things," Wendell agreed. As he spent time reading his Bible, Wendell accepted that worldly possessions weren't as important as he'd once believed. "I hope our kids will play here together in a way we never did."

Val smiled at him and asked, "The thought pleases you, doesn't it?"

"A great deal. I haven't been much of a brother, but I intend to change."

They moved into the drawing room. "Val, I plan to propose to your sister, and I'd like to surprise her. Will you help?"

"What did you have in mind?"

"I thought we'd have a dinner party for your family, and I'd ask Ophelia to prepare the meal. Give her free rein to try some of the things your mother won't let her cook at home."

"You plan to make us guinea pigs?" Val teased.

"Ophelia knows how far she can go. I'm asking her to be my hostess."

"I'm sure she'll love playing lady of the manor, but she'll probably think it's a weird request."

He chuckled. "It's a twofold plan. She gets to do what she loves and then after dinner, I perform a piece I wrote for her. The first music I've written since Dad died. It's entitled 'Ophelia's Song.'"

"Oh wow," Val said. "She'll love that."

"After the music, I'll ask her to marry me."

"Have you talked to Daddy?"

Wendell nodded. "We discussed the age difference, and he feels it's not an issue."

"Is the age thing the only problem you have?" Russ asked.

"You know my background, Russ. I feel life with Ophelia will make a difference. I appreciate the way she's always so happy and desires to see others happy as well. She makes me laugh and deals well with my sarcasm. We both like to do things spur of the moment. That's why I think she'll like my proposal."

"Sounds almost as romantic as mine," Val said. "The pavilion is available, and the weather is really beautiful if you'd like to do this outside."

"No," Wendell said with a shake of his head. "That was your fantasy. It's better if we come here. I need my piano, and Ophelia needs my kitchen."

"I think she knew from the moment she laid eyes on you in that magazine that you would play a major role in her life. There were times I regretted taking her to that bachelor auction."

"She let me know how she felt, but I fought her," Wendell admitted.

"Believe me, I know. She was miserable. When she suggested we ask you to play for the cantata, I thought she'd lost her mind. I thought it might be her way of staying in your life. She didn't deny it."

"I was hooked from the time I listened to the CD. I had no idea how I'd find the time, but that music filled me heart and soul. I'm thankful she asked."

"She thought she could change you with God's help."

"She did."

"You challenge her. She wouldn't give up even though she had no idea how to reach you."

Wendell smiled. "I couldn't fight her. She may be tiny, but she's huge when it comes to love. If you have time, I'd like to show you what I'm planning for her engagement gift. We'll need to ride into Paris."

Val looked at Russ and he shrugged. "Sure."

∽

Wendell parked in front of one of the old storefronts and pulled a key from his pocket. He opened the door, turned on the lights, and gestured for Val to go first.

"She's going to love this," she exclaimed after they examined the building.

"I know she's wanted her own kitchen for a long time." Opie had told him she wanted to teach women to prepare tasty nutritious meals for their families. "I think she can renovate this building to serve her purpose."

"She has the pavilion kitchen now," Russ offered.

"But she'll need to be in Paris for the cooking school."

"What happens if she refuses?"

"If she does, I'll rent her this place at a ridiculously low price. I want to see her achieve her dreams, too. You won't tell her, will you?"

"I don't think so," Val said with a little laugh. "She sent me out into the freezing cold to turn out the lights knowing Russ planned to propose. I'm going to enjoy seeing her surprise when it happens to her."

Wendell shook his head. "You two and your pranks."

"All in good fun. You and Russ might do the same one day."

Wendell grinned. "I hope so."

"I'll keep that in mind," Russ said.

After they locked up and returned to the vehicle, Val asked, "Do you think you'd have met if I hadn't talked her into the bachelor auction?"

"As Opie tells me all the time, God is in control."

Val smiled at Russ. "God does work in wonderful ways. I never dreamed He'd answer my prayer and then send Russ to help me achieve my goal."

Russ pointed at her and said, "He sent you to help me find Him."

"And He used Ophelia to bring me home," Wendell said.

❧

The next day Wendell drove over to the pavilion where he knew Ophelia was preparing for a party that night. She whipped off the net that covered her hair when he walked in and brushed her hands over her apron. "Wendell, hi."

"Do you have a minute?"

"If you don't mind talking while I work."

"I want you to help me host a party for your family at my house. I've enjoyed their hospitality many times, and I'd like to return the favor. I want you to prepare the meal, too. I'll give Jean-Pierre the night off."

She looked puzzled by his request. "Let me get this straight. You want me to come to your house and prepare a meal my family might or might not like and then cohost the dinner?"

Wendell nodded. "That's what I'm suggesting. The two of us entertaining your family at a dinner party." He noted a spark of interest in the green gaze.

"And I get to serve whatever I want?"

"Whatever you want," Wendell agreed.

"When do you want to do this?"

"What about Friday night two weeks?"

"Sounds wacky but I'm on board."

"It wouldn't be any different if Jean-Pierre prepared the meal. The food could still be outside their comfort zone."

She grinned. "I'll make sure it's food they'll eat, but I'm going to put a new spin on the menu just because I can."

~

On the night before the dinner party, Wendell pushed back the overwhelming emotion as he practiced the piece he'd written. He thanked God for bringing Ophelia into his life and making it possible for them to be together.

She arrived with her supplies early the next morning. He stopped in to find her consumed with her lists, systematically working her way through the menu, while her assistants worked on the lists she'd given them. Just before their guests arrived, he went into the kitchen again. "Everything okay in here?"

"Time isn't a luxury in the kitchen, Wendell. If service is in minutes, the food must be ready. It's not like I can ask everyone to wait."

"In other words, you're telling me to get lost?"

"Only with the greatest of love," she agreed with a sweet smile.

Val and Russ were the first to arrive. "Ready for tonight?" she asked softly.

Wendell nodded. "I'm not as sure about Ophelia. I'm afraid she'll be too tired to enjoy herself."

"Cooking energizes Opie."

"Why don't you see if she has time to change before dinner?" Wendell suggested.

"She'd rather wear her chef's jacket than anything else."

"For her proposal?"

Val shrugged. "With Opie, you never know. A photo of you proposing to her in chef whites and a toque would probably make it into the paper as your engagement photo."

"You think she'll choose those for our wedding?"

"Oh no way. I've seen her favorite bridal gown and it's fantastic."

"That's good to know," Wendell said with a pleased smile. He looked forward to seeing Ophelia in her wedding dress. Of course, he needed to propose first.

She did change and dinner was extraordinary.

"What have you done?" Wendell asked when they served the appetizer of fried Louisiana shrimp balls.

She only winked and shrugged.

The dinner menu consisted of game hens with cornbread stuffing, green beans, and hot yeast rolls and butter. Chocolate mousse with raspberry sauce finished it off to perfection.

"What do you call these?" Cy asked as he held up a green bean with his fork.

"Beans?" Opie said, her tongue-in-cheek response gaining his childish reaction. "They're not. You call them 'hairy covers.' "

Opie grinned and pronounced the term properly. "*Haricots vert.*"

"Man, you chefs take something easy and make it hard."

"Actually we take something simple and make it delectable," she corrected.

"My little girl knows how to cook," Jacob said. "I'm proud of you, Opie."

"To Ophelia," Wendell said, raising his glass in a toast.

After dinner, they moved into the drawing room.

"You really did a wonderful job with the Easter program," Cindy said, running a hand over the piano as she passed. "You're incredibly talented."

"Thank you," Wendell said. "I thought I might play a little something I wrote. I dabbled at writing music but lost the desire after my dad died. Recently I've been inspired by a young woman who turned my life upside down."

Ophelia was intrigued. He could see it in her eyes. "This woman challenged me in ways I couldn't imagine. She told me life could be better. Then she helped me find my way to that new life."

He stood and held out his hand to Ophelia. She took it, and Wendell led her over to the armchair by the piano. He seated himself at the bench. "I call this 'Ophelia's Song.'"

His gaze never left hers as he played the song from his heart. Tears streamed down her cheeks. When he finished, Wendell pulled a box from his pocket and went down on bended knee before her. "I love you, Ophelia. More than I can say. This may not be the most spectacular way of sharing that. . ."

"You wrote a song for me," she interrupted.

He grinned at her exuberance.

"I wanted you to know how I felt." He popped open the box to show her the ring. His mother's ring. He'd found it among her jewelry in the attic and thought that one day his bride might want to wear the three-carat pear-shaped diamond. "Ophelia, will you marry me?"

"Only if you stop calling me Ophelia."

Startled by her response, Wendell broke into laughter. Soon the others joined in.

"We've got a dilemma, my love. I don't see an Opie when I look at you."

"I suppose I could get used to *my love*," she said. "Yes, Wendell, I'll marry you." She held his face in her hands and declared, "I love you, and there's nothing I want more than to be your wife."

He kissed her, not caring that their family looked on as they sealed their commitment to a future together.

Chapter 17

R eady?" Jacob Truelove asked.

Opie could only nod. Last night when Wendell kissed her good night, he'd requested that she remember how much he loved her when he played "Ophelia's Song" today just for her. As if she could ever forget. He'd even gone to the extreme of giving her a storefront for her business. She'd willingly give up her career for him, but his action spoke of his faith that she would be everything he needed in a wife.

"Three of you married in one day," Jacob said. "It's almost more than a man can take in."

Opie shared her father's amazement. "I told you we had plans for you and that tux."

"Yeah, you did. I suppose Rom and Stephanie will make me wear it to their wedding."

Stephanie had flown in over the weekend and though he hadn't wanted to take away from their happiness, Rom announced at lunch that she agreed to become his wife. They reveled in his joy and teased him about being too late to join them.

"Admit it, Daddy, you'll be glad to have us out of your hair."

"Sweet, sweet Opie, when you have babies of your own you'll realize that's impossible."

Babies. Hard to imagine, but she looked forward to having a family with Wendell. She'd realized that a career and following your dreams meant nothing compared to love.

"You're grown and very shortly you'll be married, but I'd never be glad to be without any of you. I praised God the day your mother told me you were on the way, and I praise Him today for your happiness and well-being. But I am not losing three children," Jacob said. "I'm gaining three. With your vows, Jane, Russ, and Wendell become my daughter and sons as well. They're as much a part of our family as my own blood."

"Wendell said he loves my family almost as much as he loves me," Opie said.

"Don't feel threatened by that, sweetheart. No one knows more than you do how tough his life has been. He needs a family to love and care for him. We'll be there to back you up."

"Thanks, Daddy. I wouldn't have it any other way."

∾

When Wendell proposed, Cy said they might as well get married on the same day and have the Truelove Triple Crown of weddings. Val had asked Heath and Jane to share her day and immediately said she'd love it if Opie and Wendell did the same. Wendell joked that planning a parachute jump in a windstorm would be easier than one event for three couples but admitted the Trueloves did weddings in style.

The weddings would follow the order of their engagements. Each bride would have one attendant to help with her dress and flowers. Each groom would have a best man. Their minister would marry each couple and then they would remain on their pedestal, which would slide to the side and rotate the next couple to the altar. He didn't want to guess what Val paid for that piece of equipment. Val, Jane, and Ophelia pleaded with him to play for the weddings. After he played "Ophelia's Song," he would turn the piano over to someone else for Ophelia's wedding march.

Last night, after the rehearsal and dinner, they left the group to stroll along the lighted pathway about the pavilion.

"Fancy's baby came last night," she told him. "It was a girl. I'm sorry."

Wendell lifted her hand to his lips. "I'm not. Your dad got his girl. I got mine." Ophelia smiled at him. "And I'm sure ours won't be the only Hunter/Truelove union. Your dad and I have plans to make our own place in Thoroughbred horse history."

"With God's help, I know we'll accomplish wonderful things."

Later after he'd said his good nights and gone home, Ophelia's promise stayed with him. The very idea that she would make him the happiest man alive in a few hours kept him awake. Wendell went into the kitchen and found a small basket on the island. He smiled at the coffee-hot cocoa mix in the heart mug and a sleeve of her delicious cookies. As he waited for the milk to heat, Wendell looked at the tag on the package, finding that she'd written him a love note. He grinned, sending up a special prayer of thanks for Ophelia.

As Wendell enjoyed the comfort of the hot drink and cookies, he went over the schedule for the next day. He'd invited the grooms, their best men, Jacob, and the younger Truelove boys to join him for breakfast the next morning. After that, they'd dress and head over to the pavilion.

The morning passed in a flash. The three men prayed together before they took their places.

Not a tremble, Wendell thought as his hands moved over the keyboard. But then he played "Ophelia's Song" and a fine nervousness touched him. "Please, God," he whispered, "make me the man she deserves."

Wendell left the piano and grinned when Russ gave him the thumbs-up. He felt honored to share this wonderful family with his brother. He took his place with his friend Leo at his side. When Ophelia stepped into view, every thought in his head went away.

"Breathe, man."

Following Leo's instruction, he sucked in a deep breath and managed a smile.

All those years he'd mistakenly thought that winning a Triple Crown would be the ultimate. It couldn't compare to this. To say she looked stunning would be an understatement. Though it was his first time seeing the dress, Ophelia teased him with words like beaded lace and mermaid. All he could think was that she'd packaged the beauty of her love and was about to present him with the gift. Wendell hugged Jacob and took Ophelia's hand in his. They stepped up onto the pedestal, and her cousin Jennifer adjusted her dress. As Ophelia held on to his arm, the feeling of rightness overwhelmed him. Ophelia told him she'd planned for her future and career, but not for love. She'd said she now understood how senseless her life would have been without him. Wendell understood precisely what she meant.

She admitted the true challenge she'd confronted hadn't been changing him. It had been changing herself, understanding that she couldn't do anything because the only plans that triumphed were those of God. She'd learned that the hard way when she'd become convinced she could change Wendell with God's help. As it turned out, God used her to accomplish His plan.

Wendell had never imagined he would overcome the anger and hurt that had filled him for so long. Now as he stood beside her, he experienced a second great joy—that of becoming one with the woman he loved.

"Do you, Wendell, take Ophelia to be your lawfully wedded wife?" Pastor Skipper asked.

Ophelia grinned and whispered, "Are you up to the challenge?"

"God is," Wendell said softly before adding his own loud, emphatic, "I do."

A Letter to Our Readers

Dear Readers:

In order that we might better contribute to your reading enjoyment, we would appreciate you taking a few minutes to respond to the following questions. When completed, please return to the following: Fiction Editor, Barbour Publishing, Inc., P.O. Box 719, Uhrichsville, OH 44683.

1. Did you enjoy reading *Kentucky Weddings* by Terry Fowler?
   ❑ Very much. I would like to see more books like this.
   ❑ Moderately—I would have enjoyed it more if _____
   _____
   _____

2. What influenced your decision to purchase this book?
   (Check those that apply.)
   ❑ Cover   ❑ Back cover copy   ❑ Title   ❑ Price
   ❑ Friends   ❑ Publicity   ❑ Other

3. Which story was your favorite?
   ❑ *Val's Prayer*   ❑ *Opie's Challenge*
   ❑ *Heath's Choice*

4. Please check your age range:
   ❑ Under 18   ❑ 18–24   ❑ 25–34
   ❑ 35–45   ❑ 46–55   ❑ Over 55

5. How many hours per week do you read? _____

Name _____

Occupation _____

Address _____

City_____ State_____ Zip_____

E-mail _____

Epilogue

A little more than two weeks later, the entire family gathered to watch a news feature that ran while the three couples were on their honeymoons. The well-known face of the reporter who interviewed Val all those months before flashed on the screen. She stood just outside the pavilion.

"Today this reporter had the privilege of attending an event such as I've never before witnessed. The wedding venue site resonated with love as three couples shared their joy with family and friends. When asked, Valentine Truelove Hunter said that she'd never imagined how wonderful it would be to marry the man of her dreams in the beauty of the Kentucky countryside.

"Darcy, the youngest Truelove child, referred to the event as the Triple Crown of weddings and this reporter would agree. I found it to be among the unique experiences of my life. A beautiful venue, three beautiful brides, three handsome grooms, a bevy of equally gorgeous attendants along with the sweetest flower girl I've ever seen, delicious food, and count 'em, three beautiful wedding cakes." The camera went to the three individually designed cakes. "Every bride's dream.

"The remaining single twin, Romeo, which rumor has he is newly engaged this week, summed it up best in his toast." The scene flipped to a shot of Rom standing atop the pavilion stage.

"Today I have the honor of toasting three very precious people in my life— my sisters, Val and Opie, and my twin Heath. Each of you have found your soul mate and committed to love and honor each other. May you always have joy in your lives and may you always dream Bluegrass Dreams."

A chorus of "hear, hear!" rose up in the Paris countryside.

The camera went back to the reporter. "Your Wedding Place has quite a future here in our community, and after this experience I expect we'll see many more perfect weddings at this spectacular venue."